Praise for *Restitution*

"Rich, immersive, and intelligent, *Restitution* interrogates childhood memories with adult wisdom. It asks whether what's broken—in us, our families, our nations—can ever be put back together again. It is gorgeous."

—Julia Phillips, bestselling author of *Bear* and *Disappearing Earth*

"A mesmerizing, haunting story about the ruptures caused by family secrets and forced departures. A novel steeped in the complex history of German reunification, *Restitution* is a deeply moving examination of separation—across borders, generations, memories, and the Berlin Wall. Tamar Shapiro asks us to consider: What makes a family? How do we honor and atone for our lineage and legacy? What would we risk to hold onto our homelands? An intricate, piercing novel written by an astounding talent."

—Crystal Hana Kim, author of *The Stone Home* and *If You Leave Me*

"A deeply felt, beautifully crafted exploration of the ways a family can lose and find each other. *Restitution*'s events are as vast in scope as the division and reunification of Germany, and as particular and human as the struggles and misunderstandings between husband and wife, brother and sister, parent and child; Shapiro is at home in all registers. Deft, wildly intelligent, and moving—a marvelous debut from a writer at the start of what's sure to be a thrilling career."

—Clare Beams, author of *The Garden* and *The Illness Lesson*

"With lush, evocative, and assured prose, Tamar Shapiro delivers an unforgettable generational saga about foundations—both literal and figurative—and the ways they can hold us up and hold us down. Shapiro does not shy away from the 'yes and' nature of family, immersing readers in a narrative of love and anger, home and groundlessness, betrayal and ever-so-complicated redemption. You'll never believe this is a debut."

—John Vercher, author of *Devil is Fine*

"I have rarely encountered a debut novel as potent, moving, and assured as *Restitution.* Tamar Shapiro twines the past and present, the political and the personal, into a story of tantalizing secrets. How much do we know about the people who raised us? To what extent are we defined by the legacies of family, culture, and country? Is it necessary—or even possible—to atone for the sins of our ancestors? *Restitution* is a book that lingers in the mind, asking important questions and resisting easy answers. Shapiro is a marvel."

—Abby Geni, author of *The Body Farm*, *The Wildlands*, and *The Lightkeepers*

"*Restitution* is a stunning book that moves gracefully through both time and place. Tamar Shapiro's debut novel, which focuses on an American family and their ancestral home in Germany in the wake of the fall of the Berlin Wall, considers how the past is always connected to the present and how understanding that relationship is often the key to moving forward. Shapiro's beautiful prose and her exquisite development of both character and place brings this unique and fascinating story to life."

—Laura Spence-Ash, author of *Beyond That, the Sea*

"Tender and deeply-wrought, *Restitution* is about all the ways war and political division splinter countries and families, but also how they can fracture a person's spirit. Shapiro takes us into the years immediately following WWII in Germany, through division and reunification, and the ways these shattering events are carried through the lives of ordinary citizens and their descendents. In her nimble hands the story she weaves is hauntingly personal and universal."

—Elizabeth Gonzalez James, author of *The Bullet Swallower*

"The year is 1989. The Wall has fallen, and Germany is in the throes of reunification. Kate and Martin, American siblings whose grandparents fled East Germany in the 1950s, now face a dilemma—ought they attempt to reclaim the family home they never knew? And what does that mean for the other family that has lived there for decades? Powerfully intertwining the personal and the political, Tamar Shapiro's debut tracks a family that begins to fracture under the weight of secrets, betrayals and resentments. *Restitution* is an elegiac reminder of how our lives play out against the backdrop of the past and are shaped by forces larger than our own."

—Susan Coll, author of *Real Life and Other Fictions* and former president of the PEN/Faulkner Foundation

Restitution

Tamar Shapiro

Regal House Publishing

Published by
Regal House Publishing, LLC
Raleigh, NC 27605

ISBN -13 (paperback): 9781646036196
ISBN -13 (epub): 9781646036202
Library of Congress Control Number: 2024951663

Cover images and design by © studiochi.art

Printed in the United States of America

Regal House Publishing, LLC
https://regalhousepublishing.com

For Mama and Papa
who gave me so many worlds

And for John, Clara, and Leo
who are my world

Prologue

2005

Sometimes people mention my brother Martin, and I say, "We're not in touch." Concise as possible, no further explanation. When Mom comes to visit, she always asks, and I say, "Still no." Then we sit in silence by the kitchen window, watching crows loop low over cornfields.

What I remember most about Martin is not the angry grimace on his face the last time I saw him nearly fifteen years ago. No, what I can't get out of my mind are the younger versions of my brother. Martin under poplars by the German lake where we spent our childhood summers, his tanned legs shimmering in the water's angled light. Martin digging for worms in our Illinois garden, hands black from the earthy roots of tomato plants. Martin after Dad left us, a camera pressed so tightly to his face that it traced lines on his cheeks, eyes obscured by the viewfinder, lips taut below the lens. And of course, Martin on the day our grandfather died, trembling next to me in that dim room, curtains drawn against the reckless sun.

Opa died in 1973. West Germany. A summer day turned dark. I see him all covered up, carried past the living room door by his hands and feet, the draped sheet dragging on the ground, the points of his toes stretching the fabric, his body sagging like a shallow *u*. The voices of the men carrying him were low and urgent. They moved as one, a formless, buzzing beast, the sheet its bright white heart. Oma and Mom followed with quick steps, chins high, faces blank. Not even a glance toward the sofa, where Martin and I—only fourteen and eleven—had been told to sit, aware that something had gone terribly wrong. As if there were a right kind of death, a proper death. The kind of death our Opa should have had.

I'm forty-three years old now. All this a distant memory. Opa, Oma, our childhood summers in Germany, the worn cushions of that sofa, the feel of Martin's shaking shoulder against mine. We haven't spoken since 1991, since the moment I slammed the door to that lawyer's office in Leipzig, carrying my rage along with me, leaving Martin behind. A decade and a half of transitions—a new millennium, a marriage, a daughter—all without exchanging a single word with my brother, my only news of him arriving in careful snippets from Mom.

Yet here I am, walking toward his house, Hannah and Darren on either side of me. My sparkling daughter who asked to meet the uncle she's never known, and my forthright husband, who simply said, "It's time." I focus on the sound of gravel under our feet, three pairs of shoes moving forward together until, before I'm ready, there's no farther to go.

When Martin opens the door, I take a step back toward our car, as if that one step could carry me from his front porch to my yard, from the salty freshness of this New England summer to the humid lull of Illinois. But before I can escape, Darren puts his arm around my shoulder. I hear Hannah say, "Uncle Martin." Then she turns back toward me, uncertain, her round face framed by gray wooden slats and peeling paint. She crosses her arms awkwardly, like the brand-new teenager she is, tucks one leg behind the other, squints at the sun. Martin laughs and follows her gaze. In that moment, their two faces raised to the sky, I see how much they both take after Opa. The same wild curls, the same lopsided grin. Martin puts his hand on her shoulder. "Hannah, it's so nice to finally meet you." Then he looks at me, eyes wide under thick brows, shoulders broad like the rest of him.

"Kate. *Da bist du endlich.*" There you finally are.

And something inside me crumbles. Because there *he* is. My brother. Older now. Settled, heavy and earthbound. I know it won't be easy. I feel the weight of my doubts, of our many mistakes. But when he looks at me and smiles, the right corner of his mouth drawn wide, I see him. The boy who's been there all along.

PART I

After the Wall

1989–1990

1

Endings and Beginnings

Illinois, November 9, 1989

We were sitting on our front porch, Darren and I, when the Berlin Wall fell. One of the defining moments of our generation, and there we were huddled in parkas, watching thick November clouds descend over the barren fields of Central Illinois.

Our car stood in the driveway, parked crookedly like an afterthought, the front passenger seat pushed all the way back, headlights still on, forgotten. In the dimming afternoon gloom, the beams shone wobbly streaks onto cracked concrete. Less than half an hour had passed since we'd returned from the hospital empty-handed, Darren lifting me carefully out of the front seat, his touch as tender as my insides. Yet everything had changed.

Yesterday we'd rushed the contractor along, excited to renovate our house for the baby. A new room on the side, casement windows looking over the fields, a cushioned seat designed for curling up, tiny nose fogging winter glass. Today, construction dust hung in the house, heavy as a shroud, and we sat on the porch with wind-chapped cheeks, watching a lifeless horizon that had felt like home until we returned from the hospital to a loneliness I had not known was possible. We hadn't yet shared our good news with anyone, not even Mom, so there was no one with whom to share our grief. No calls to make. Just the two of us bound by the weight of lips held tight and shoulders high, our jagged breaths casting white clouds toward the gray ones that fell from above.

When my bleeding began that morning, our house stood open to the outside, a tarp keeping out the chill, edges flapping. The foundation of the new room had been poured days earlier in heavy, irreversible concrete. The outlines of a growth I now feared would forever remind me of the child we did not have. I started bleeding after breakfast. Not a spot here or there, but a river that pulled and clawed and turned me inside out. When the intake nurse asked how much blood there was, I told her exactly that. "It's a river." Within minutes, I was lying on a hospital bed, Darren next to me, holding my hand like a lifeline—his and mine.

"You'll be fine," he said, tightening his grip. What he left unsaid pinned me to the bed.

"What about the baby?"

I was three months pregnant, had known about the baby for just over two. Nine weeks of learning about infant sleep patterns, eating habits, development stages, language acquisition. A fleeting moment. An eternity.

We'd hoped to be young parents, and after years of trying, we certainly weren't yet old, but also no longer so very young. Both of us in our late twenties and eager to start the family we'd been waiting for. We'd agreed that we would teach the baby German—my mother's language and Darren's passion. We'd spent hours naming the baby after fruits—*Ananas, Aprikose, Birnchen*—and joking which of those names we'd keep after birth. We sometimes woke in the middle of the night, worried we weren't ready. After all, I was a landscape architect, good at growing plants, not people. Darren was a history professor, forever looking back. And yet this futuristic, hairless, pudgy creature we imagined ever more clearly with each passing week was our common project, our common joy.

"The baby will be fine too," Darren said into the echoing hospital room, but I knew from the deepening shadows on the doctor's face that he was wrong. I heard the words "hemorrhage," "emergency," and "D&C." Darren's fingers massaged a nervous rhythm up and down my arm. Someone gave me sedatives, laid me down under bright lights, told me everything would be all right. And while I slept, they scraped our dreams away from deep inside me.

Then we were home again, pulling into the driveway as if nothing had happened, as if we were returning from work or from the library or from a movie. A couple's outing. Two of us had left, two of us came back. Darren went into the house and emerged with blankets, tucking one around my legs as I settled into the rocking chair. He wrapped the second around his shoulders and sat on the bench. Not touching but close enough to reach me if he needed to.

When the sky had grown purple, the air too cold even for our parkas and blankets, Darren said, "I'll make dinner now." Through the door, I heard him turn on the TV. Habit, I guess. Or a need to fill our empty house with sound. I pulled my hood tighter around my face, disappearing, until I heard Darren shout, "Kate, come here! You need to see this."

He was flipping back and forth between channels, all synchronized, all showing the same scenes. Dancing and jubilation. Gawking crowds from East Germany swarming West Berlin department stores, hammers and chisels taking down bits of the Wall. Darren grabbed my hand, and said, "Jesus!"

I was holding the blanket, clenching it. Darren loosened my grip, and we watched the white fade from my knuckles.

"Imagine your mom, Kate," Darren said, his voice low and hesitant, seeking approval to talk about something other than the baby. "She can finally go back to the place she grew up."

There was something about his tone that made me want to push back, to prod and argue. So I said, "She only lived in the East till she was twelve. She always says she basically grew up in West Germany. Besides, she could have gone back before if she'd wanted to. Other people visited the East. She just never chose to."

"But now everything's changed, hasn't it?"

In my mind, I could hear Mom. *You can only live forward.* That's what she'd always taught me. I pulled my hand away from Darren. "But why would she want to go to a place she fled from as a child? Why would she want to relive all that?"

My voice bounced off the walls, tinny and sharp. We both knew those weren't my real questions. What I actually wanted to ask was how Darren could expect me to let go of my sorrow, how he could let go of his own, even for a moment, even for a reason this big. Darren took a quick step toward the TV, as if he wanted to flee our house, join the joyous crowd on screen instead.

"Either way, we have to call her," he said. "And Martin. We have to call them both."

"Because of the news or because of the baby they don't even know about yet?" My tone was even sharper than before, sharper than I had intended.

"So you can share this moment with them," Darren said carefully. "You can tell them as much or as little as you want about the baby. But sharing this history…" He waved toward the TV. "It might make you feel less alone."

His face was tight, torn between grief and joy, and I wanted to say yes, assure him that I too could feel that joy, would share it with others when I was ready, and above all, with him.

But I didn't have the energy to talk to Mom or Martin. Not right then. Especially not Martin. He and I spoke by phone most weeks. We swapped lighthearted gripes about Mom, shared funny client stories—the frosted-hair ladies who made me plant Callery pear trees no matter how often I said they'd regret the smell, and the cocky men in double-breasted suits who strutted into his lawyer's office, feet tapping as though the whole world were playing a melody just for them. "They sound like you," I once told him. "No, the whole *universe* plays my melody," he quipped back. I laughed more with my brother than with anyone else, but I rolled my eyes more too. Now I could hear his voice in my mind, announcing the fall of the Wall, triumphant as if this grand sweep of history were his doing, his soaring words overshadowing my aching body.

"Tomorrow," I said. "I'll talk to them tomorrow."

Darren wrapped his arms around me, rested his chin on my shoulder. Behind him on the screen, a young man with long hair took off his shirt and swung it around his head, his chest concave, ribs drawing lines across his torso, straight hips gyrating awkwardly to music I could not hear. He held his hands high above his head, fingers spread, swaying, and his lips were pulled back, revealing large, uneven teeth. I reached up to touch my own unsmiling mouth, its corners newly weighted, and as I did so, I saw the man on the screen lower one of his hands and run it briefly over his beaming face, wiping away sweat and spittle. I wanted to hate him.

"Look at that," I said, pulling away from Darren. "All that sweating and dripping. All those bodies." I shuddered and dropped my hands to cup my belly where yesterday there'd been something to celebrate. On screen, the man finished wiping his mouth. Then he lifted his arms high again and tilted his chin back, his face illuminated by the fireworks of many flashing cameras. In that moment, he was transformed, radiant. A prophet surrounded by followers. His fingers moved with nimble elegance, weaving through the cameras' strobe lights. His jubilant arms framed his cheeks, his deep-set eyes glimmered to the beat of the flashes, and his jumbled teeth danced and jostled with the joy of the entire dancing, jostling crowd.

I sat down on the rug, pulled Darren with me, and began to cry. Big quaking jolts, belly to limbs, sharp shards of air in my throat. Next to me I felt Darren shake too. Together we breathed in the dust, our hands resting on plaster and debris, our eyes fixed on the pictures of Berlin, on that primal roar of joy and release that surrounded us, taunted us, touched us. I put my palm on the TV screen, feeling the slight fuzz of the static, holding on to the scene as if it could save me. A young woman in jeans and a crop top danced out from under my hand. Her long hair swung side to side with her hips. Her smile was magnetic.

"It is amazing," I whispered. "I know it is."

The camera panned away from the crowd toward a reporter in a thin winter coat. He clutched his microphone, wide-eyed and wordless even as the whole world waited for his words. Darren put his hand next to mine, both of us touching the screen now, touching each other.

"We're going to have a baby someday, Kate," he said. "It's going to be okay."

2

MY MAYBE-CHILD

VERMONT, DECEMBER 1989

I decided I would tell Mom about the miscarriage a month and a half later in Vermont. My first chance to speak with her in person. I hadn't intended to tell Martin yet, but in the end, he found out too. We were all at Mom's house for Christmas. Martin, Darren, and I. Most years, Darren celebrated with his own family in Iowa, but this year we weren't quite ready to be apart. Mom gave us her master bedroom with the picture window overlooking the lake, and when Martin started to complain, she cut him off. "For god's sake, Martin, there are two of them." Then she placed her hand on my elbow for a moment, a touch so light it felt unintentional.

Darren and I weren't married yet, but this wasn't the kind of thing that bothered Mom. I was certain she wouldn't hold it against me, my desire for a child before marriage. After all, Mom knew marriage wasn't what made a family. She had all the proof she needed in my long-estranged dad. They'd met while he was visiting a friend stationed near her home in West Germany, and she'd followed him back to the Midwest, married and pregnant at nineteen, only to be consigned to a landscape and a people whose openness she couldn't grasp. None of it lasted. Not the marriage, not the new home. She moved to Vermont the summer after I graduated from college, shortly after helping Darren and me buy our house on the edge of the cornfields, just a mile from where she'd raised me and Martin. "You and your beloved corn," she'd joked the first time I visited her in Vermont that same summer. "I'll take my view over yours any day."

Now, as Darren and I unpacked, I looked out her window toward the lake and the mountains beyond, their shadows punctuating the bright shimmer of the not-quite-frozen lake. You had to hand it to Mom.

After decades of not belonging, she'd found a spectacular place to call her own, leaving me behind in the place she'd never accepted.

Our second day in Vermont, Mom organized a holiday cocktail party. "Just a few neighbors," she said, placing her hand on mine. Darren and I got the living room ready, while Martin helped Mom with appetizers in the kitchen.

"No pressure, but have you told her yet?" Darren asked as soon as we were alone.

"I haven't found the right time. But I feel like she knows something's off. She's being so affectionate."

"You call that affectionate?" Darren laughed, glasses tinkling as he pulled them off the top shelf two at a time and handed them to me.

"Well, you know what she's normally like."

But the truth is, he only knew half of her. Mom was a different person in English than in German, more reserved. So I had two different mothers growing up. A real mother and a summer mother. In Illinois, she spoke in short English phrases. "It's cold outside. Wear a coat. Be home by six." But during the summer months we spent in Germany each year, I heard her laughter through windows thrown wide on slow afternoons, the smell of baked fish and potatoes lingering. And I heard it late at night, matched with the clink of glasses, with Oma's low chuckle and Tante Lara's giggle. My grandmother, my aunt, and my mother. A string trio. Mom was the viola.

Darren handed me two more glasses to put on the sideboard. "Yes," he said. "She's being downright solicitous, giving us the room and all. But who knows why? She's always been a mystery to me."

When the guests began to arrive, Mom announced them all by name. The Crofts, the Setworths, Frank Helling, Marjorie Tall. That's where I lost count. They gathered around the fireplace, a cluster of baggy wool sweaters and rough red cheeks. Martin came to stand by the window with Darren and me, balancing a bottle of scotch and three glasses. He set the glasses down on the windowsill and poured, one for each of us.

"A prize for the favored second-born," he said, as he handed me my glass. So, he had noticed Mom's warmth too.

In the window, Darren's reflection raised its eyebrows, but I just gave Martin an exaggerated nod. "And a bow for the beloved first-born."

Martin grinned. Then he took a sip of scotch and wrinkled his nose. "Wow, this is some strong stuff Mom's got, but that's exactly what I need. You wouldn't believe the month I've had."

Darren put his arm around my shoulder and squeezed. "We've had a hard couple months too."

Martin tilted his head at me, a brief gesture of concern. But he was in high spirits, already two drinks in, and he kept talking. Something about meetings in New York that week, business with both French and German companies, deals that needed lawyers like beaches need sand. Halfway through a story about his favorite Parisian tailor, we heard Mom clink her fork on the side of her glass.

"Winter in Vermont can be cold, as we all know," she said. "Damned cold!" She paused for the chuckles. Then she waved her hand at her guests around the fireplace and the three of us by the window. "But with neighbors like this…and family like that, winter seems an awful lot warmer. Thanks for coming."

One of the husbands by the fireplace raised his glass, and the rest of the guests followed suit. Then the older man (was it Frank?) said, "But here we are with a German hostess, and we haven't even talked about the Wall!"

Mom put her drink down. "I was never much good at history. I like simpler stories," she said. "Why else would I have chosen to teach German to sullen teens?" Again, more chuckles. My mother could perform when she wanted to. Then she pointed at Darren. "But we've got a German history professor right here."

Before Darren could even begin speaking, Martin jumped in. He was on his third or fourth glass of scotch by now, his motions slow and exaggerated. Like me, he didn't usually drink much. We'd both seen what it had done to our father, what it had done to our family.

"Mom, you're too modest. You know a lot," he said. Then he looked at the guests. "We've been getting first-hand stories from my aunt."

"That's true." Mom nodded. "The West German news seems a bit more detailed than here, so my sister Lara in Bonn keeps us up to speed."

Martin interrupted again, his right hand holding his scotch high, his left hand emphasizing each word. "She told us about the weekly protests in Leipzig. Apparently, they'd been happening every Monday for months before they opened the borders. That's only about an hour from Grimma, the town where she grew up before they left for the West!" He pointed at Mom.

None of this was new to me, of course. I'd been on those same calls with Tante Lara. And I'd also talked to Mom about Grimma many times in the month and a half since November 9th, about the first twelve years of her life. Darren always lurked in the background on those calls, half-hoping to catch tidbits about Mom's childhood in the East, half-hoping the topic of children wouldn't come up. I could see it in the way he cocked his head whenever he heard the name *Grimma*, and I could feel it in the way he put his hand gently on my arm whenever he heard the word *Kind*. And yet in all those calls, I never found the courage to talk to her about our child, about our *Kind*.

Now Darren leaned back against the windowsill. Together we watched Martin walk to the middle of the room and take a big sip. He paused for a moment with the scotch in his mouth before swallowing. Then he told Mom's neighbors what Tante Lara had told us on the phone, his voice as agitated as hers had been, his hands swaying back and forth as he painted the picture. The barely visible silhouettes of people braving everything on dark autumn nights. The fear and tension in the streets. The pressure building week after week, marchers flowing through Leipzig. Each time with more courage, more determination. Until the turning point came on October 9th, exactly one month before the borders were opened. Nearly a hundred thousand candles held high, the threat of violence, the surprising decision of the authorities to let the marchers pass, the way the footage was smuggled out for West German TV, the way the regime began to crumble.

Martin's audience was rapt, captured by his story and by the warmth in the room, the crackles and shifting orange-yellows of the fire. I understood his excitement, his need to be in the middle. For once our broken family was connected to something good. For once we had something to offer.

"But no one thought it would happen quite so fast," Martin said, eyes glistening. "In the end, all the pressure forced the government's hand. They *had* to announce that the borders would be opened." Now he lifted his arms and raised his voice, as if he were making a closing argument in a courtroom. "But who could have imagined they would be so unprepared for the obvious question: When? Who could have imagined that the Wall would finally come down because one confused official would say: Immediately."

Martin looked around at Mom's guests, all nodding and murmuring. Next to me, Darren whispered, "Remarkable courage and bureaucratic indecision giving history a helping hand." I could tell it was a line he'd prepared for one of his upcoming lectures. A bit awkward, a bit too perfect. A line he would have loved to try out on this group, no matter how small.

Martin glanced toward us. "What?"

Darren's lanky frame melted farther into the window. He waved the question away with a gesture meant to show deference. But Martin swallowed hard, and I knew right away he'd taken it differently. My brother, always full of bravado yet so ready to feel dismissed.

"No, no. Be my guest, Darren," he said with a sweep of his own hand. "You're the expert, after all. I mean, you don't have any personal connection to it, of course, but you've studied it for so long. And that's almost as good. Like secondhand smoke, am I right?" Martin laughed and surveyed the room again.

"Martin!" Mom said. "We've got company!" Definitely our winter mother. A warning condensed into three words.

But Martin was on a roll. He picked up his glass, took another gulp, and raised it in my direction. "I mean, you've been totally out of it on our calls with Tante Lara, not even excited about what's happening, Kate. And *now* you have something to say?"

Mom's guests shifted uncomfortably. The older man murmured, "Now, now," and two of the couples moved slowly toward the doorway. The party had taken a turn. We seemed headed for disaster, and I knew I should walk away. But Martin's face, so alive with sudden fury, was mesmeric. I didn't budge.

"That's enough, Martin," Mom said. "It's time to move on."

"That's what you always say." Martin's voice was sharp and penetrating, his shoulders twitching up and down. "But now this thing has happened, this amazing thing that we have a connection to, and you want to move on, and from what I can tell, Kate isn't even interested!"

Something in me snapped. That morning, I'd awakened to find blood in my pajamas. My first period since the miscarriage, each drop a reminder of what could have been. "This is a good thing, Kate!" Darren had told me. "It's the first step back!" But I couldn't help sobbing, pressing my face into the pillow so no one would hear me through the thin walls.

I watched as Mom walked over and took the glass out of Martin's hand with a flick of the wrist I'd seen so often as a child, the way she always disarmed Dad, pulled the glass away from him before he knew what was happening. But this was Martin, not Dad. And even flush with liquor, Martin looked nothing like Dad. No, Martin's red cheeks and glassy eyes were those of a stranger. I took one step toward him, liberated from family ties.

"Go to hell, Martin," I said. Out of the corner of my eye, I saw one of the wives gasp and take another step toward the door, but I couldn't stop myself.

"Mom?" my brother-stranger said, his voice plaintive now. Mom was as frozen as everyone else.

"You think November 9th is the day the Wall fell," I said. "But for me, November 9th is the day I lost the baby Darren and I were going to have. So yeah, I've been too busy crying and healing and dealing with the house expansion we don't even need or want anymore. And you? You can go to hell."

Mom stared at me, mouth pulled tight, eyes questioning. I moved to the center of the room where Martin had been giving his history lesson moments earlier and waved my arm as he had. "I was going to tell you, Mom. I was saving it for a quiet moment. But now look, I've told all of you. Even him." I pointed my finger at Martin and laughed. The sound echoed around me, thin and desperate. I'd had too much to drink too. The room wobbled, and Darren grabbed my arm just in time. Together we walked past the couple near the door, almost free and yet so trapped. I didn't breathe until we were in our room, the door closed behind us.

The next morning was bright. Too bright. When Darren opened the curtains, I rolled over toward the wall, away from all that light, the snow and the ice-edged lake. Away from the glistening world.

"Too much scotch, huh?" Darren said. "You and Martin both."

"Way too much." I curled into a ball, pulled the covers over my head, and tried not to think of the stony faces of Mom's neighbors.

"You'll have to deal with it sooner or later," Darren said. "You go down first. I'll give you space."

Mom and Martin were both in the kitchen. Without saying a word,

Mom handed me a cup of coffee. I sat down in the nook by the window, put my face close to the cup, and let the warm steam soak my skin. Martin was resting on one of the stools near the sink. He was in worse shape than me, elbows on the counter, head in his hands. Mom put a cup in front of him too and gave him a little nudge. When he didn't move, she shrugged and sat across from me. We both took a sip together, then I said, "I'm sorry."

"Now why would you be sorry?" Mom asked. "No reason for you to be sorry at all. I'm the one who should have noticed something was wrong. I'm the one who's sorry this happened."

"And me," Martin said without lifting his head. "Also, that wasn't actually me yesterday. Not sure who that was."

Mom laughed her summer laugh despite the snow outside. Then she held my wrist. "I did think you seemed sad, but I wasn't sure why, and I didn't want to pry. Are you okay? Is Darren okay?"

"I guess. Some days I feel almost normal again, like nothing's wrong. Other days, I can't believe this whole life we envisioned won't happen."

Martin finally raised his head. "Don't say that. I'm sure it will happen. Just not exactly when you thought it would."

"That's what Darren tells me."

"Smart man, that Darren. Should have let him talk at the party yesterday." Martin shrugged dramatically, hands raised, palms up, like the night before, except that he looked like my brother again. More rumpled, but definitely my brother. I smiled and stuck my tongue out, accepting his apology, giving him mine.

"Too much drink," I said. "We should know better."

When we were done with our coffees, Mom gathered the cups and put them in the sink. Her back toward us, she said, "What if we took a trip to Grimma?"

Martin opened his mouth in mock shock. "Wow, Mom! When I suggested that weeks ago, you said no way."

"I know," she said. "But I'm serious. There's so much you don't know. I mean, my god, there's so much even I don't know. And, Kate, I've been thinking. Our family stories—the ones we don't know—you can gather them for the child I'm sure you'll have. You can tell my grandchild about my home, the place I came from. The people you come from."

Martin's mouth hung open even wider, but now there was nothing fake about his surprise. I didn't know what to say either. This was a third mother, completely unlike our other mothers. Sentimental, nostalgic. Something had come loose inside her. She turned from the sink, hands wet from washing the cups, and said, "Well?"

Martin smacked the counter with his right hand. "That's what I'm talking about. That's what I've wanted all along. To see *my* Opa and Oma's house. But sure, if it helps you to think of it as a family lesson for *your* future grandkid…" Then he pointed at me and grinned. "To be clear: that's the kid *you're* going to have, not me."

"Maybe going to have," I corrected him. "My Maybe-Child."

I stared at them. My mom, her face expectant, hands dripping soapy water all over her pants. And my brother, his hair uncombed, curls reaching toward the ceiling, eyes wide. I'd do it for them, I decided. For the two of them, staring questions at me. For Darren waiting so patiently upstairs. And for the Maybe-Child of our dreams. For all of them.

"Yes," I said. "Let's take that trip together."

And Mom, who always had the final word in our family, nodded. "*Na dann.*"

Well then.

We were going to Grimma. We were going east.

3

Return to Grimma

Grimma, July 1990

Opa and Oma's old house stood near the edge of town in Grimma, two unremarkable stories under a steep roof. Through the small double windows, we could see white crocheted curtains. A flowerpot with red geraniums colored one of the first-floor windows. The outside walls, set close to the street, were stucco. It was hard to tell if they had, at some point, been painted. Like all the houses nearby, years of neglect and pollution had left only smudges of brownish gray. Long grasses grew up the fence, not quite hiding the bright, clashing begonias in the small flower bed beyond. A trellis ran the length of the house with vines growing over it and onto the walls. Near the trellis, a rusty white metal table sat on the gravel, eight chairs scattered around it, as if a party had recently broken up. There was nothing to set the house apart from the others on the street. Nothing notable about any of it, really. Yet I remember that first glimpse so vividly.

All of us were there. Mom, Martin, Tante Lara, and I. Even Darren, who'd never met Oma or Opa. This was, he said with a wink at Martin, our small connection to the grand arc of history. Who would waste a rare chance like that?

We'd flown to Bonn to meet Tante Lara before driving east to Grimma. We figured it would be less complicated that way, easier to cross the border by car. Back then Grimma was still in East Germany, the two Germanies separate, negotiating their way toward unification throughout much of 1990. But by the time we landed in July, all border controls had been removed. Less than three months later, in October 1990, there'd be just one country again. That's how quickly things were changing.

Grimma itself had no hotels, or at least none we would have chosen to book. So we planned to stay in Leipzig instead. Before we left Bonn, we had the usual squabbling over what to pack, who would make the sandwiches, and the best route. We climbed into Tante Lara's Volkswagen three hours later than we had hoped. Late afternoon on a gray, rainy July day.

It was almost nighttime as we approached the border. By then, we had finished all our snacks. The radio reception was no longer working well, and we drove mostly in silence. Finally, the border towers emerged from the wet mist, looming against the dusky gray sky—tall gangly creatures, their empty windows like blind eyes. Giants frozen in time. Barbed-wire fence still cut through the landscape below, small and defeated, a miniature version of what I had imagined the border to be. And yet, even empty and powerless, the crossing held menace. Tante Lara drove a little faster. The car in front of us, its rear lights a reddish shimmer in the drizzle, did the same.

What we noticed most on the rest of the trip was the darkness. When I pointed this out, Tante Lara said, "Obviously it's dark, it's night. *Ist ja logisch!*" But there was a different intensity, a different texture to this darkness. It was deep and uninterrupted. It had a power to it, inexorably pulling us farther into the unknown. Every once in a while, a dim light from a barely visible cluster of buildings somewhere off to the side of the road cut into the purple-black fabric. A village? A farm? There was never enough light to tell.

That night I slept deeply, tired from the drive. We hadn't stayed up, hadn't even grabbed dinner in Leipzig. The streets around the hotel were empty anyway, no lights beckoning us, no chattering voices to suggest a destination. Only our rooms were a refuge. But when Darren and I turned off the lamps next to our bed, the darkness reached us even there.

Morning in Leipzig took us by surprise. We met in the hotel lobby bright and early despite our jet lag. As we walked outside, we found ourselves across from the main train station. Dark gray stone stretched for several city blocks, entrances on either end, doors wedged beneath vertical lines of dirty paned glass. Above them, a row of stone figures black with soot. It was as if the building had absorbed all the darkness from the night before. But then, as we gazed at this behemoth, the sun came out, and the sudden light performed a miracle on the stone.

Where there had been gloomy gray, there was now earth-toned brown, the color of a paper bag backlit by sun. Still unfinished and raw, but warm, inviting. A glimpse of the transformation awaiting this city. "Well, Grimma sure doesn't have anything as big and grand as this," Tante Lara said.

It turned out she was both right and wrong about Grimma. The buildings along the narrow main street were small and tight, two stories, sometimes three. Gray soot everywhere here too, but there was an echo of something else. Delicate carvings around the windows, heavy timber doors with ornate knockers, steep rooflines that lent even the smallest houses ambition and grace. When I squinted, the long, straight cobblestoned street grew grainy, like a black-and-white photo from a long-lost time of grandeur.

Tante Lara drove one loop around the tight core of the town, then parked by the Mulde. It was a glorious spot on the grassy riverbank, to the right of us a suspension bridge, behind us a steep hill. On the top of the hill, we saw a villa, romantic with a tower and vines. Tante Lara told us it was the Gattersburg, a name that made me think of a gray castle, half-ruined, perched on a cliff over a raging river. But the Mulde was mostly placid that day. And though there were, in fact, ruins in the park next door, Tante Lara told us those ruins were imitations, already ruined the day they were built. The distressed jeans of architecture.

"I had a boyfriend back then. Konrad. We called him Konni," she said. "He was Krista's son. Did Oma ever tell you about her best friend Krista?"

Martin and I shook our heads.

"That's strange. They were so close. Anyway, Konni and I used to meet here to watch the sun set. In summer, we'd stay even later."

Mom laughed. "I always wondered where you disappeared off to."

It was, in fact, a perfect place for a teenage tryst. Grassy, shaded. Set apart from the main road. Now Tante Lara led us away from where we'd parked and out onto the bridge. Then she began talking again, as if she'd never stopped.

"Konni was special to me. There was something about that time, about that feeling of opposition that was budding in us. This is where I last saw him." She pointed back at the riverbank, then dropped her hand.

"When you left for the West?" I asked.

"Yes," she said. "*Republikflucht* the East German government called it. Flight from the Republic. The Berlin Wall hadn't been built yet, back when we left, but they'd already tightened the border elsewhere. Barbed wire, restricted zones and all. Even in Berlin, they'd upped their controls because too many people were leaving. It was all risky. If you succeeded, you left your whole life behind. But if you failed, you paid an even heavier price. You'd be investigated for sure. And they'd find something if they wanted to. There was always something that could land you in prison. Either way, it tainted your family, those you left behind. It made everyone you knew a target. It was a big deal, so your Oma didn't give us the chance to ruin it. She only told us late at night that we were leaving the very next morning. I guess she really didn't trust us. And she was right because what's the first thing I did?" Tante Lara laughed. "I climbed out my window and ran over to Konni's house, brought him here to the river one last time."

"What did you tell him?" I asked.

"Well, what do you say at a moment like that? I told him we were leaving. We swore we'd love each other forever. He said he'd come for me. Six months later, I had my first boyfriend in the West." She smiled wryly.

I closed my eyes and concentrated until I saw Oma and Opa's other house, the one I knew from my childhood summers in West Germany, so real I could almost touch it. Sunny and welcoming with a mossy roof like in a picture book. The house was just a stone's throw from the Bodensee, that magical lake where Oma and Opa settled after they left Grimma, its gnarled fingers stretching between hills and vineyards, linking Austria, Switzerland, and West Germany. I imagined Tante Lara and Mom at sixteen and twelve years old, starting over, suitcases in hand, exchanging one small town for another. A new life built on those suitcases, memories of war, and the loss of home and country. When I opened my eyes, I saw that Tante Lara had put an arm around Mom's shoulder, drawing her close. Two sisters surveying what they'd lost so long ago.

Then Tante Lara rubbed her temples. "Headache," she said apologetically. "Too much excitement, I guess." She braced her hand on the railing of the bridge and straightened up. "Anyway, let's go see our old home."

It's hard to believe, but I'd never seen a photo of Oma and Opa's house in Grimma. I'd asked Mom about this once, and she said, "You don't pack a lot of photos when no one can know you're leaving for good." But I did have one favorite photo from their life in the East: a faded picture of Oma and Opa's wedding. They got married in the town hall on the main square in Grimma. A small ceremony, barely even that. Oma was wearing a light sweater and a skirt, flared at the bottom, swinging just below the knees. Opa was in a simple dark suit. The photo showed them alone, arms around each other, grinning. Oma was holding her left leg out in front of her right leg, as if she were about to start line dancing. Opa was glancing down at that stray leg, laughing. They looked giddy, silly, full of joy. In the background, the swooping, swerving roofline of the town hall danced along with them.

Oma was the one who showed me that photo years ago. She told me that they'd gotten married in 1925. Long before the Second World War. Long before the bridges over the Mulde were blown up by the retreating German army. Long before the Americans occupied the town west of the now bridgeless river. And long before they pulled out of Grimma again, turning it over to the Soviets in keeping with faraway negotiations and agreements. A grim twist in my family's history. Back then, Oma told me, there was no East and West, just hope and uncertainty mixing dreadfully, paving the way for what was to come. As a kid, I wasn't sure what she meant. I saw only hope in their faces on the photo, nothing dreadful at all.

Now we drove right past the town hall I still remembered from that shot. Tante Lara needed no directions, had no trouble recalling each turn. And then, there we were, in front of Oma and Opa's unremarkable house. "Is it the way you remember?" Martin asked. Tante Lara took it all in. "A bit more run down, but yes. Right, Lena?" And Mom said, "God, it all comes back, doesn't it?"

A door slammed, and a woman came around the corner of the house. She stopped when she saw us. Clearly outsiders. We had not prepared for this moment, had not discussed whether we'd knock, whether we even wanted to see the inside of the house. I figured it was up to Mom and Tante Lara, but now I saw they too were unprepared. We were standing at the edge of a different world.

It was Tante Lara who took charge and walked up to the gate. "*Guten Tag. Tut mir leid daß wir so stehen und gucken. Wir sind hier aufgewachsen.*" Sorry for standing and staring. We grew up here.

"Greta Schultz," the woman said, shaking Tante Lara's hand, and that everyday gesture transformed the moment, made it reassuringly banal. "*Na dann, kommen Sie doch rein.*" Come on in.

We sat around the kitchen table drinking tea. Greta, Tante Lara, and Mom were quickly deep in conversation, discovering mutual acquaintances—the neighbors and another family down the street. They were good together, chatty and open.

"So, are you from Grimma?" Mom asked.

"Yes, we're from here. Never left, never lived anywhere else." Greta took a sip of her tea. "There was no reason to leave. Right out of school, I got a job down at the paper-goods factory. It's hard work, but we make things that make people happy. Christmas crackers, paper garlands, carnival hats, wrapping paper."

She stood and walked over to a cupboard in the corner. From behind the heavy oak doors, she pulled out an armful of colorful knickknacks. Spiral notebooks with bright covers, Christmas ornaments, bundles of paper flowers. She spread it all out on the table, hodgepodge, and surveyed her wares.

"*Da*," she said. There. As if she had proven something we had doubted. Then she plucked what looked like a dunce's cap out of the pile.

"*Zuckertüten,*" she said, holding it with the point facing down. "These are my favorites."

I'd never had one, but I knew all about *Zuckertüten,* the oversized, brightly decorated cardboard cones full of candy that parents all over Germany—East and West—gave to first graders to celebrate the start of school. We'd always called them *Schultüten.* Not sugar cone, but school cone. Still, that didn't change anything about the envy I always felt toward the end of our summer vacations when the German school year started. I wanted to be one of those kids, balancing the treasure that stretched from their waists all the way to their foreheads, peering around the sides of the cone, trying not to trip.

Greta tapped the cone she was holding. "Each year we had new patterns. Some were based on TV shows. Or sometimes the news. The summer after Sputnik, we had satellite designs. And spaceships, cosmonauts, even aliens."

"From sweets to the space race," Martin said. "Never too soon to start kids on politics."

"Yes," Greta said with an emphatic nod. She'd missed his sarcasm or had chosen to overlook it. "But my favorites were the ones that never went out of style. Stars and moons, horses, butterflies, flowers. Or balloons like this one."

She put the *Zuckertüte* she was holding back into the pile. Carefully, reverently. "I always wanted to be a teacher. But that didn't work out. Like so many things in life. *Nicht wahr*?" She looked around the table for confirmation, and we nodded. My own loss was still fresh enough that her words took my breath away for a moment. I pressed my stomach against the edge of the table. But then Greta chuckled.

"Still, I love making the *Zuckertüten* each year. My own small contribution to the next generation. Now I don't know what's going to happen. They say everything's going to shut down. I'm one of the lucky ones. So far. My Klaus might lose his job any day now. His factory's been laying people off for months."

"Yes, we've heard about what's happening." Darren leaned forward, brow furrowed. The history professor collecting information. I rolled my eyes, hoping he'd see, but he kept his gaze on Greta. We had argued about this when he said he wanted to come along on the trip. "Fine," I'd said, "but only if you don't turn every single personal story into a historical moment." He'd just laughed. "In a way that's what we're all doing, isn't it?"

I too had been reading the papers. The *Währungsunion*, the adoption of the Western Deutschmark in the East, had taken place weeks earlier on July 1. We'd seen the stories of factories in the East shutting down overnight, out-of-date to begin with and no longer able to compete with cheaper labor even farther east. The first cracks in the euphoric narrative, coming far too soon. One currency, even before there was one country. A symbolic success, but the impacts were so immediate, so devastating, it made you wonder why they hadn't been foreseen.

Years later, in an essay he wrote about the *Wende*—the word many Germans used for this time of change—Darren described reunification as a headlong rush to fulfill someone's dream. There was back-and-forth about whose dream. That was the real point of the essay: a lack of clarity about the dreamer. "Dreams themselves are also not clear," I told him after I read it. "Dreams are full of things that make no sense: boats sailing on land, balconies floating in the air, places that look like home but are full of tropical birds." Darren raised his hand. "Stop, you're making light of the situation." I wasn't though. I've had all those dreams, and they were disconcerting, even terrifying.

But back then, sitting at Greta's kitchen table, I wanted to steer clear of the political, stick to the personal. So I asked what I thought was an easy question, a chatty one. "How long have you lived in this house?"

"A long time," Greta said more cheerfully. "Klaus was already living here, and I moved in when we got married. It was our first home together. Our only home together."

Greta looked around the kitchen. "Of course, it needed so much work over the years. A new roof, new kitchen cabinets, new wallpaper. Klaus did it all on the weekends with some friends. No one had money for that kind of thing, but everyone pitched in. That's the way it was. *Damals*." Back then.

Martin's eyes followed Greta's fingers as she pointed out the many things they'd done to the house. He looked at the ceiling, at the kitchen cabinets. His eyes scanned the wallpaper.

Then Greta pointed out the window. "Klaus and I built the trellis together. In the summers, we spent every weekend outside with friends. No one had much, but we had each other. Now, so many people are leaving. Two families on this street left this month. Two more are thinking about it. Our community just isn't the same."

Tante Lara reached out to pat her hand. "We were just talking about that," she said. "That sense of community, of belonging. I was young when we left, but I know what you mean."

A phone rang in the hallway. An old-fashioned ring that matched the house. I imagined a wall phone, probably green. Greta said, "Excuse me a minute," and left the kitchen, closing the door gently behind her.

Martin turned toward Tante Lara. "Well, belonging's all fine and good, but sounds to me like you belonged on opposite sides, right?" Then, without waiting for an answer, he added: "It's like she's talking about a time she can barely remember. Like it was all decades ago, not less than a year."

"Well, I bet it feels that way to her," Tante Lara said.

"It makes no sense. It's like inverse dog years or something. It's absurd."

I half-smiled, half-frowned at his joke, not sure when Greta might walk back in. And Mom said, "Shhh, Martin," though we were all speaking English, even Tante Lara. It was our language for moments like this.

Then Tante Lara said, "You know, a few weeks after we got to the Bodensee, I felt like I'd never really lived in Grimma. It felt like that had been someone else's life. That's how far away and long ago it seemed. But there were times I missed it more than you can imagine. There were times I thought there'd never been anything better even though I knew that wasn't true."

Greta came back into the kitchen right as Tante Lara turned to Martin and snapped, "You shouldn't make jokes when you have no idea what you're talking about." Tante Lara was rarely harsh, had little of the reserve that could make Mom seem cold. But now her tone was angry, cutting. Greta heard it and stood inside the doorway, smiling awkwardly. When Tante Lara stopped speaking, she came back to the table.

"Oh," said Tante Lara, switching into German. "I'm sorry."

Greta smiled. "Don't worry. I don't speak English. It's not something we learned. *Damals.*"

That's when Martin stood up. "Do you mind if I use the bathroom?" he asked, and Greta pointed toward the hallway. As he walked out of the kitchen, his shoulders were pulled high, his neck bent forward. A posture I recognized from his teenage years. The years after Dad left. But why now?

Greta walked back over to the corner cupboard. This time she pulled out a photo album and sat down between Mom and me. Together we flipped through pages of black-and-white photos. Young children playing naked by a marshy pond, tents in the background. Kids and adults clustered around a picnic table near a mustached man grilling over a wood fire. Greta, about ten years younger, at the same kitchen table where we were gathered, opening a present surrounded by kids. Her hands were paused over the ribbon, her face sheepish. And then, suddenly, a photo in color. It showed Greta and a man (her husband?) standing in front of the house. She was holding a piece of paper up in the air, he was raising a glass beer tankard with an ornate metal top and thick handle. The man's thumb was depressing the handle, and the lid was halfway up, its strange, pointy top perfectly aligned with the slope of the house's roof. The glass caught the sun, and the glare created an unexpected halo around the man's raised hand—a holy offering.

Mom gasped and pointed at the photo. "Look, Lara! Do you remember that? That was our father's. He served me my first beer out of that glass!"

"Your first beer?" I asked. "How old were you then?"

Mom winked at me and said, "In the privacy of our home…"

Greta pulled the photo out of the album and put it on the table between us. "That one's recent. Just a few weeks ago. That's the day we finally bought this house. You know, it wasn't possible for us before, but now it is." She pushed the photo across the table toward Mom. "You take it. Your first beer! It's so important to have memories like that."

Mom shook her head. "I couldn't."

But Greta pushed the photo even closer to Mom. "We can print another. And anyway, we have the house now. That's what really matters. Not the photo." She closed the album with a snap, a show of finality, and put it back in the cupboard. Mom still hesitated, so I took the photo and put it in my bag, wedged between the pages of the book Darren had bought me for this trip—Peter Schneider's *The Wall Jumper* ("The perfect intro," he'd told me). Then I excused myself to go find Martin.

He was standing in the narrow hallway, its walls decorated with more photos in elaborate bronze frames. Plump birds with outspread wings cradling some photos. Bronze vines encircling others, Sleeping Beauty style. There were even more pictures of kids out here. So very many photos, so very many kids. I put my hands on my hips and massaged inwards over my belly, pressure relieving emptiness, a gesture that had brought me comfort more times than I could count since that grim November day. I glanced at Martin, but he was unfazed by all the children, and I felt torn between relief that my brother did not feel the need to tiptoe around my loss and resentment that it wouldn't even occur to him. I turned back to the wall and finally spotted a photo without any kids. Greta working in the garden, planting flowers around a small stone marker, a memorial of some sort. She was facing away from the camera, hands deep in the dirt. I moved closer to try to read the words carved on the front of the stone. The shape and length of the carving suggested a name (maybe Hanna or Anna?) and two dates, like a gravestone, but the photo was too grainy to tell for sure.

"What do you think this stone is?" I asked. Martin made an odd grunting sound. His head was bent toward another photo as if he were examining it, but his eyes were closed. It was an old photo of the house. Winter or late fall. No leaves on the trees, the trellis not yet built. A forlorn ladder up against the wall next to paint cans. The house was dingy yet somehow expectant, waiting for someone to pick up a brush and brighten it. It was an unattractive view of the house, the way it must have looked decades earlier. I could see what Greta meant about the amount of work they'd put into it.

"What do you think that's all about?" I asked.

Martin opened his eyes, surprised, as if he hadn't noticed I was there. "Well," he said, "it's the house. Just the way Opa described it in his story."

"What story?"

Over the years, Opa had told us countless stories. Tall tales about running to Poland and back all in a day to buy a rare sausage, or about the weightlifting competition he won after raising not one, but two pieces of timber as tall as trees. Boasts I wanted to believe as a kid, though I knew they couldn't be true. Martin and I had spent so many hours sitting on the sofa at the Bodensee watching our usually withdrawn Opa puff himself up until he became a different person. I can still see the way he sat in the nubby beige chair across from us, arms flung wide to encompass his grand words. "Have I told you how I vanquished the wild boar?" he would start, and Martin and I would scramble into position, curled up against either arm of the sofa. Sometimes, if I wasn't in the mood, I'd roll my eyes. "Yes, Opa, you've already told us." But he was moved not by our desire to hear but by his need to tell. And so he would simply say, "I'll tell you again. It's a bit different each time anyway. Just like all the best stories."

Yet I didn't remember a single story about this house.

"Just like Opa described," Martin repeated. Then he raised his hand as if to say, *Enough, no more questions.* And that's when Darren came looking for us.

"You've been out here so long they're starting to wonder," he said. "Anyway, Greta's husband is here."

When we returned to the kitchen, the man from the photo was standing by the sink. Greta turned to Martin and me. "This is my husband, Klaus Schultz." I leaned in for the usual handshake, but Klaus grumbled a greeting instead. He was holding the edge of the counter behind him, propped back against his hands, feet out in front, his weight resting on the counter and on his heels. A deliberate show of not moving.

"I'm Kate Porter," I said. "My grandparents lived here."

"I know who you are," Klaus said. "We already did introductions."

The tea was still on the table, everyone in the same place. My chair stood at an angle, the way I'd pushed it back when I'd left the table. Now I straightened it but did not sit down.

"I knew your grandfather, actually," Klaus said. "He was still living here when I moved into the back room." He gestured toward the hallway where the photos were. "We drank beers together sometimes, here or there." A quick gesture toward the window, the garden. "But mostly he kept to himself. I had no idea he was planning to leave." Again, a pause. "Then he was gone."

Martin's arms were crossed tightly across his chest. Klaus walked to the table, picked up two of the teacups, and took them to the sink. With his back to us, he rinsed them out, humming. I wanted to ask about Opa, but everything about Klaus discouraged it. His posture, his humming, even the story he'd told, the ending so definite, so final. "Then he was gone." What more was there to say?

Tante Lara stood up. "Well, I think it's time for us to go."

Greta gathered our rain jackets from the front hallway and handed them to us one by one. In her rush, she gave me Mom's and Mom mine, but we took them anyway, draped them over our arms. We'd switch them outside.

"If you come again, I'll make cake. We didn't expect you this time. And you know, it's all a little much for us these days. For him. With all the changes," Greta said, her voice apologetic, quiet enough so Klaus wouldn't hear. She stretched her hand out. More a plea than a proposed handshake.

Tante Lara took her hand anyway and held it briefly. "It's been so kind of you to talk with us. So nice to meet you," she said.

"And thank you for the tea," Mom added, as we all backed out the door.

"What a piece of work," Martin said once we were in the car. Darren, Martin, and I were squeezed into the back seat, knees pushing against knees, elbows against elbows. A tight tangle. Tante Lara drove.

"Who? Klaus?" Mom asked.

"No. Greta. I mean, here we are, half a year after one of the most successful peaceful revolutions ever, and she can't stop thinking about the past."

"But she's right in a way," Tante Lara said without turning around. "There was a sense of belonging. That's how I remember it."

"Oh, come on," Martin said. "You belonged because you were opposed. She belonged because she accepted. That's two different worlds. You didn't belong at all, actually. It's completely the wrong word."

"Maybe so, yet the feeling could still be right."

But Martin wasn't listening. "It's probably because of the claims," he said. "That's probably why Klaus was so cagey. Because he knows we could claim the property."

"We could what?" I asked.

"There's a process to reclaim properties in East Germany. For people like us. Descendants of the people who used to own them. People like you." He waved his hand toward Mom and Tante Lara.

"Why would we want the house?" Mom asked.

Martin put his hands on his knees and braced himself, pausing for a second before answering. "Well, why not? It was Opa's house."

"Yes. And Oma's and ours. But now it's Klaus and Greta's. Has been for decades," Tante Lara said, her voice loud and sharp in the small car. "Besides," she added, "weren't you the one just saying I never belonged here?"

Martin started to speak, but I put my hand on his arm. "Don't," I said. I wanted to avoid an argument.

He looked at me for a second, then crossed his arms, shoulders high. Again, that tense posture I remembered from the years after Dad left. Back then I learned to avoid his moods, to walk away when I saw the signs. But sometimes, on generous days, I'd try something else. I'd move toward him, rather than away. Grab his arm or poke him with my finger. Lightly. Make a joke. Waking up the old Martin, the brother I'd had before Dad left. That's how I thought about it then. Now it was the new Martin I was trying to reach, the one he'd grown into. But I figured the method could be the same. So I poked him and said, "Tante Lara belonged in Grimma like Che Guevara belonged in a capitalist world."

Martin glanced over. He couldn't help himself. "Don't you have the roles reversed there?"

"So then, Tante Lara belonged the way Madame Defarge belonged in the French aristocracy. Better?"

"Still not right," he said, smiling. But he got into the game anyway. "Tante Lara belonged the way Ivan Denisovich belonged in—"

"That's totally inappropriate. And not funny. She was never imprisoned," I interrupted.

"Fair enough." He laughed. "So Tante Lara belonged the way—"

"For Christ's sake," Tante Lara said. "Will you two shut up? You really don't know what you're talking about." Then, softening, she nodded at Mom. "Definitely your brats. You read to them too much."

And just like that, we left the house behind. "Opa's house." That's what Martin had called it, but I didn't give that much thought. No, what I noticed back then, what I still remember years later, is the comfort of our sibling sparring, the warmth of being wedged between him and Darren, all of us lost in our own thoughts. Snug. Close. Quiet.

PART II

When Dad Left

1969–1970

4

The Rainbow Trap

Illinois, 1969–1970

When Dad left, Martin fell apart. But that makes it sound like Dad walked out on us, and that's not how it was. Mom made him go.

Mom and Dad's first big fight, at least the first one we witnessed, happened in early May 1969, six months before he left us. I was seven, still in Miss Edmonds's first-grade class, a month and a half to go before summer break. Dad came home from work that day in a great mood. Cheerful, charming, a tad too brash, his face moist and shining, his movements expansive. Mom was in the kitchen making pork chops for dinner. Our favorite. The living room was filled with the smell of meat, or maybe it was the smell of the onions and paprika she cooked with the chops. Dad nodded when he came into the living room. "Pork chops," he said, licking his lips theatrically, his head bobbing up and down. He called Martin and me over. I hesitated. This outsized version of my dad made me wary. I preferred the low-key dad who gardened with us every spring weekend, who stood in the yard in dirty jeans, trowel in hand, and said, "Ready for Dad-kiddo time?" But Martin wasn't so picky. He ran over to Dad, and Dad pulled him into a huge hug.

"So, you're the one I can count on," he said. Then he grinned at me over Martin's head, keeping me on his side too.

Martin had celebrated his tenth birthday earlier that week, and he'd been building a village on the living-room floor with the Lego blocks he'd gotten. Now he held up one of the houses he'd built, a multicolored hut with a jagged roof and holes on either side. "Look," he said. "It's got special windows for cannons."

Dad took it from his hands and turned it over appraisingly. "You got quite some house here, Marty," he said. "Who you planning to shoot?"

"Whoever attacks. I want to be ready."

"Are you one of the good guys? Or a bad guy?" Dad asked.

Martin ignored the question. "Want to build something with me? You can build the garage. What colors do you want to use?"

"Well, Marty, let's see. Does a house with cannon holes really need a garage? Maybe we can build a great fence instead? Make sure it's protected on all sides." Dad took a handful of Legos and started piecing them together, but Martin said, "That's not what a fence looks like, Dad. You've got to pick one color. It's got to be red or white. Five rows at least."

That was Martin back then, before Dad left. Sure of what he wanted, always with that shining smile of his. Dad loved Martin's confidence yet still found a way to push back. Gently. And Martin always accepted it.

"It's a rainbow fence, kid. That way the enemy won't be expecting us to be serious. They'll walk right into our rainbow trap. See what I mean?" He added another row of yellow, blue, and red squares.

Martin nodded, grinning up at Dad. He'd forgotten I was there, but Dad had not.

"Katie, how about you run and pour me a glass of wine," he said, turning in my direction.

Mom and Dad never owned a wine-rack; we were not that kind of family. Not the kind of family that bought storage boxes or labeled shelves. Things just found a place in our house, naturally, over time, even if it meant that the recent mail ended up in the same bowl as the painted wooden napkin rings. Or that the extra keys were in a pile on the shelf behind the sugar bowl. For as long as I could remember, Mom and Dad had stored the wine bottles on the kitchen counter by the toaster, a row of dark shapes that glimmered when Mom turned on the lights. Sometimes, when she was cooking, I'd sit on the counter. She'd help me jump up, her hands around my waist, "One-two-three," until we were face-to-face, and then I'd watch. The way she stirred the onions with the wooden spoon, swirling her wrists loosely. Or the way she tossed pans into the sink when she was done with them, so they clattered on top of each other, a record of her work with just a hint of resentment. I loved all the different shapes. The jumble of curves and straight lines in the dish rack, the folds of the kitchen towel hanging off the dishwasher handle, and those bottles, their swooping sides holding such a deep red.

But that year, Mom started hiding the bottles deep on the bottom shelf of the sideboard. So that's where I went to get one of them now, handing it to Dad along with a glass I'd pulled from the top shelf. I felt very adult. He uncorked the already open bottle, poured himself a glass, and handed the bottle back to me with a complicit nod. Then he said, "Tell me, Marty, now that your birthday's over, your next chance for a haul is Christmas. Do you have any big dreams for Christmas this year?"

"Desmond got his own record player last year."

"So, that's what you want, is it? And what makes you think you deserve that, Sergeant Pepper?" Dad winked at me.

Martin was just starting to get hooked on music. A couple months earlier Dad had bought him his first album on tape. *Sergeant Pepper's Lonely Hearts Club Band.* That evening and on the evenings that followed, Dad and Martin danced around the kitchen with the opening chords, spun in dizzy circles to the tune of "Lucy in the Sky with Diamonds," crooned the chorus of "When I'm Sixty-Four."

Dad was more of an Elvis guy himself, but he liked The Beatles too. Who didn't? Now he pulled Martin onto his lap and howled the opening line of "Getting Better." Then he paused, waiting for Martin to chime in with the next line, the one about hating school. That was usually Martin's favorite. But Martin slid off Dad's lap. "No, not The Beatles, Dad." Desmond—a few houses down the block, a couple years older—had introduced him to The Who, and together they'd watched on TV as the band smashed their guitars after a show. They'd also heard about (though not seen) the drum loaded with explosives, sending shrapnel across the stage. Dad was an engineer. He built things, disapproved of breaking them. But he was in a good mood now, so he teased Martin: "Oh, so you want to use *my* record player, the one I'm going to give you, to listen to those lunatics? How do you even sing that stuff?" Head nodding to the beat, he launched into a strange snarling version of the opening bars of "My Generation," a song Martin had introduced to us a few weeks earlier. Dad could carry a tune, any tune, but even his voice could not capture the wild guttural sounds of the electric guitar. He sounded like a frog, hoarse and throaty, repeating the five syllables of the song's title again and again, head nodding ever more wildly to his own grunting beat. Then as he growled louder and louder, he tore open his shirt and leapt around the living room like a bare-chested rock star, gripping the incomplete rainbow fence in one hand and his nearly empty wine glass in the other. Just as Mom came in from the kitchen to see what all the noise was, he lifted his hands high in the air, yelled, "Here goes my guitar!" and smashed both Legos and wine glass down on the ground. They splintered at Martin's feet.

Mom took in the scene. Martin surrounded by a pile of glass and Lego pieces, his mouth stretched wide with the remnants of laughter, the last splashes of wine staining the carpet around his feet, and me, still holding the bottle. Dad stopped leaping.

"Kate and Martin, go to your rooms!" Mom said.

Martin protested. He was basking in Dad's supercharged glow, didn't want it to end. Mom grabbed him by the shoulders and pushed him up the stairs. I followed, trying to stay close to her. From downstairs, I heard Dad yell, "Oh, come on, Lena, it was only a bit of fun." On the top landing, she let Martin go and headed back down. She knew she didn't have to take us all the way to our rooms. By then, even Martin must have realized we couldn't go back down those stairs, that this sparkly evening had gone irreversibly wrong. From my room I could still hear them fighting.

"It's one thing for you to come home drunk," Mom yelled. "Even though I've asked you not to. But to expose the kids to it? Throwing wine glasses? God damn it, it's got to stop!"

"I'm sorry, Lena." Dad's voice was quieter, soothing. "I got carried away. Marty said he wanted a record player for Christmas, so we were singing. Just for fun."

"And what, you're going to get him that record player? How's that going to work? Give it another couple of months and you won't even have a job anymore. I'll be the one buying him his presents."

"Don't you worry about me and my work, Lena. I'll be fine. I promise."

"How can you promise? They've sent you home twice this week alone! Don't make promises you can't keep. Not to the kids and not to me!"

Dad's voice grew sharper. "Damn it, Lena, what do you want me to do?"

"Keep your voice down, that's what," Mom said, though she was the one screaming. "They can hear every damn word, you know."

The door slammed as they moved from the living room into the kitchen. Now I could only hear muffled voices. I snuck into Martin's room. He too was sitting by the door listening.

"Does Dad not have a job anymore?" I asked.

"Of course he does." Martin turned away. "Mom and I dropped him off at work yesterday. Mom's being mean."

I sat in Martin's room a while longer, but he clearly didn't want to talk. So I tiptoed back down the hallway. They'd stopped yelling, but they also hadn't come upstairs. I crawled into bed and listened for any sound. Conversation, footsteps. Anything. But no one came to get us for dinner. Eventually I fell asleep to that eerie silence, the tense hush of disappointment and anger. Hungry.

The next morning, there was no sign of Dad in the house, even though we always had breakfast together as a family. Mom insisted on it.

I was too nervous to ask, but Martin said, "Mom, where's Dad?"

"He's going to be gone for a couple days," she said, her back to us, making our bag lunches at the counter.

"But where?" Martin persisted.

"I don't know, Martin. Staying with friends, I guess."

"Dad doesn't have any friends."

This wasn't quite true. Dad had a few colleagues who came over to dinner occasionally. Still, Martin had a point. I couldn't imagine Dad staying with any of them.

"Well, I guess he should have thought of that first." Mom's voice cut through us. "Stop moping around, Martin, and eat your cereal."

"Will he come back?"

"We'll see, I guess," Mom snapped, and Martin began to cry. She finally turned to face us, came to the table, and put her arms around him. "Yes, of course he will."

Then she said, more to herself than to us, "You know, he's got demons to fight, but I can't do that for him. He's got to choose to move forward." And, though I had no idea what she meant, I could see them clearly in my mind. Then and for years afterwards. Spiky little monsters trailing my father, ready to pounce if he ever looked back. Ready to follow me too if I let them.

At school that morning, I must have been unusually quiet. Miss Edmonds pulled me aside at recess to ask if I was okay. "Yes, I'm fine," I said. She held on to my arm, trying to stare the truth out of me, but when the bell rang, she had to let me go. Out to the blacktop, where I stood in a tide of children, watching the tetherball fly, first one way, then the other, in tightening circles. Miss Edmonds took me aside several more times that spring to ask what was wrong. But Dad was back home by then, and despite all her good intentions, I never told her a thing. It would have felt like a betrayal.

That summer, when we left for the Bodensee, Dad drove us to the airport. Back then, in 1969, the new airport had not yet been built, and the old one was the airport equivalent of a one-room schoolhouse. Tiny, low-ceilinged, a cozy jumble of check-in, departures, and baggage claim all side by side. As we pulled up to the entrance, Mom said to Dad, "No need to park. You can drop us off."

He pulled our suitcases out of the trunk, gave Martin and me a long hug, squeezed Mom on the arm. Then he got back into the car and pulled onto the road, his arm stretched out of the window, waving until we couldn't see him anymore. There we stood, staring across the empty parking lot, down the road where Dad's car, our car, had disappeared. "Time to go," Mom said, and we followed her into the building, the three of us heading to our summer paradise. The next time we were at the airport, just over two months later in August, on our return from Germany, Dad was not there to pick us up. We took a taxi home.

So, when Dad finally did leave for good on a cold, sunny day in November, it had been a long time coming. They sat us down at the breakfast table in front of bowls of cereal, like a regular morning before school.

"Martin, Kate," Dad said. "Your mother and I…" He paused, not sure how to go on. Then he said, "I've been drinking too much. You two know that, and I'm so sorry. I didn't mean to hurt you." He looked at his bowl and winced. "It makes me different, the drinking. It might seem like it makes me happy, but it doesn't." Looking straight at Martin, he repeated, "It really doesn't. It's called an addiction. It's a kind of sickness, and I've been struggling with it for years. I've tried, but I can't get better here. Your mother and I have decided that it's best for me to try to get well elsewhere. Lena?" He looked at Mom like he hoped she'd step in. But Mom sat still, eyes fixed on her coffee mug.

So Dad kept talking. "I love both of you more than anything. Every day when I wake up, all I want to do is make you proud. And you make me so proud."

He turned to Martin. "You are so full of life, kid. So bright. Keep bouncing. Don't ever lose your joy."

Mom tensed her shoulders and raised her chin, a small act of aggression. Dad saw it too. Turning his head toward me, he continued: "And, Katie, you are so full of thoughts. Always thinking new things. Keep sharing those thoughts with me, okay?"

Mom leaned against the wall in her chair, pulling herself ever farther out of the circle around the table.

"And none of this is your fault at all," Dad said to Martin and me.

Martin's face was wet with tears. I pushed my chair toward the wall and put my cheek up against it, trying to see if I could be like Mom, far away, not involved. For my cheek to touch the wall, I had to tip my chair sideways, its right legs raised off the ground. Rocking on our chairs like this was forbidden in our house, but no one said anything, so I tilted farther until the chair wobbled, the whole side of my face flattened against the soothing cool plaster.

It was Martin who pulled me back into the moment. "Of course it's not our fault," he yelled. "It's all your fault, Mom! This is what you wanted. You're a bitch! A fucking bitch!" His face shook with shock as he said these words, testing insults he had never before used. I froze, my cheek glued to the wall. But Martin stood up, and his chair fell backward, wood echoing against tile. He kicked at it and would have kept kicking if Dad had not grabbed him. Mom stared at both of them in horror as Dad pinned Martin's flailing arms to his sides and said, "It's not her fault, it's not her fault. It's no one's fault."

That's when Mom left the room, and Dad held Martin tight until he calmed down, stopped shaking.

Dad drove us to school that morning and kissed us goodbye as he had done on so many other mornings. I think it was this kiss that misled me more than anything, made me believe I'd see my dad again. It was a see-you-soon kiss, not a goodbye-forever kiss. Maybe we all believed that.

And we did see our dad again, of course. We visited him in the first rehab center. When he walked out of that one, Mom found him and brought him to a second rehab center. And then to another and another. After the fourth rehab center, three years after he'd left home, Mom stopped trying to find him, and we stopped visiting him. Just like that.

Martin didn't get a record player that first Christmas after Dad left. He stopped listening to music anyway. Every day after school, he retreated into his room, and when Mom asked him what he was doing, he said, "Nothing." She got him a camera along with a photo album and a series of science-fiction books. He never liked the books, but he used the camera so much that he wore out the wrist strap. He documented every detail of our house as if it might all disappear—a close-up of the brown shag carpeting in the upstairs hallway, the flowery patterns on the wallpaper in the guest bedroom, the crack on the bottom of the sink in the downstairs bathroom. And a whole series of photos documenting everything Dad had left behind. Dad's favorite books still sitting on the bookshelf, the mug Dad used to drink coffee out of, the old shirt and shoes Dad used for gardening on weekends. Mom got all the photos developed, never complained about the cost.

She caught me in Martin's room once while he was out, sitting with my closest friend, giggling over the album, making fun of this record of mundane items. Even then I knew I shouldn't have been laughing. And yet I giggled, because for one short moment, I wanted to forget what it was like to have a shrunken family, wanted to feel instead what it was like to have a friend. After Mom sent my friend home, she sat me down, her voice cold, and told me how disappointed she was. "Your brother needs your support, not your mockery," she said. I've never forgotten that word. Mockery. I'm pretty sure I'd never heard it before, but I knew instantly what it meant. She spat out the sharp *k* sound in the middle and looked straight at me, eye to eye. Then she walked out and left me alone at the kitchen table, listening to the wall clock tick its relentless rhythm.

5

Peace at the Lake

The Bodensee and Illinois, 1970

I can still feel the cool air of our German childhood summer mornings on my skin. Never the hot, hazy sun of Illinois, but a gentler sun that lit Oma's garden without warming it. And I remember Martin and me outside, just the two of us. An early image, yet so vivid.

"Let's play train," he said.

When we first came out that morning, barefoot as always, we ran into the garden, but the grass was cold and damp. Now we were standing on the patio next to the front door. I wiggled my toes on the ever-so-slightly warm, yellow-brown stones. Without waiting for me to answer, Martin began pulling chairs from the patio table, arranging them in a line. "You be the travelers, I'll be the conductor."

And so I moved between the chairs quickly, needing to stay ahead of Martin, sitting down as a new person each time. Once a grumpy old lady like the ones we often met in the village, once a tourist not sure where she was headed. Martin pranced behind me, carrying an imaginary bag and an imaginary hole-punch with which he punched each imaginary ticket. All our conversations started the same way. "*Guten Morgen*," he'd say. "*Die Fahrkarte, bitte*." Ticket please. We had only six chairs, so I had to start over and over at the front of the row, working my way back, Martin following right behind me. "Your role is easier," I complained. "You say the same thing each time." But he bounced on the balls of his feet, his hand opening and closing the imaginary bag with a flourish, and said, "Well, I react differently each time, don't I?" Then he threw his head back with that broad, glowing smile that made me laugh but also made me envious every time Dad said, "Martin and his million-dollar smile."

Later, when our relationship became complicated—when Martin became complicated—I missed the easy Martin. The one who held out his hand, waved an imaginary ticket at me, grinned, and said, "*Gute Reise.*" Have a good trip.

The inn Oma ran at the Bodensee was painted yellow with green shutters. A deep, sunny yellow, nothing light or lemony about it. Vines grew along the side, framing the windows that looked over the garden. Behind the inn itself, Oma and Opa's small white house glittered, soft moss blurring the tiles on its roof. Tall bushes shielded both houses from the street. The inn's front entrance was on the left side, the garden side, a large wooden door with curved panes of glass, the inn's name painted in dark green letters. Seefrieden. Peace at the Lake.

I always envied Mom for growing up in a house with a name. Especially a name like that. But when I mentioned this to Tante Lara one time, she said, "Your mom and I only half grew up there, you know. We did a lot of growing up before we got there. In a house with no name. Back in Grimma." Then, seeing my disappointment, she added, "But you're right. It is a lovely thought, isn't it?"

Peace at the lake was all I wanted the summer of 1970, the summer after Dad left, taking with him most of the bottles of wine. Seven in all. I didn't see him pack them, but I'd counted carefully. Just the way I'd seen Mom counting them many times before. Seven missing bottles. Seven months since he'd moved out the previous November. Seven months of Mom closing doors with extra sharp clicks, then putting her hand on our foreheads at bedtime saying: "It will be all right." Seven months of Martin leaving his curtains closed all day. Seven months during which I couldn't decide what I wanted more: to remember Dad or to forget him.

We finally flew to Germany in June of that year, a few days after school ended. Mom, Martin, and me. Dad had never spent summers with us in Germany. Unlike Mom, he never had enough vacation. And so in that one way, nothing had changed. I was eight years old, had just finished second grade. The week before our flight, Mom pulled our suitcases out of the hallway closet and laid them on the floor in our rooms. The red suitcase in mine, the blue one in Martin's. She always let us do the packing, didn't object the time I took the strappy silver sandals she hated, didn't complain when Martin filled his suitcase with puzzles, not sweaters. "You make the choice, you bear the consequences," she said firmly. But we knew our summer mother would emerge once we arrived in Germany, and our packing mistakes would be forgiven. "What a great excuse to go shopping in Konstanz," Mom would say with a laugh and a shake of the head, her voice softened by summer and by family.

But that year, the summer after Dad left, Martin's suitcase stayed empty all week before our flight. Mom walked in and out of his room each evening, not commenting. Finally, the night before our departure, she did the unthinkable. While Martin watched from his bed and I watched from the hallway, she packed his suitcase herself, zipped it closed, and put it by the front door. Then she walked back to Martin's room, pulled the covers over his shoulders, and kissed him on the head.

The next day was departure day, always a blur. Before the taxi showed up, Mom did one last check of the house, made sure all the appliances were unplugged. I was waiting by the front door, ready to go, but Martin was nowhere.

"Where's your brother?" Mom asked. I shrugged, so she opened the door and gave me a push. "Kate, you wait outside."

When the taxi pulled up, I waved at the driver, as if to say: *We're all good here.* He waved back and turned on his radio. From the stoop, I could only hear the bass, so I tried to piece together the songs. What melody went with which beat? But I didn't recognize most of the rhythms, and I found myself wishing Martin were there to help. Finally, eight or nine songs later, Mom came out carrying Martin. He was too tall to be carried, already eleven years old, and he slipped through her arms as she walked, her legs kicking into his dangling feet with each step. She made it down the stoop, but once she reached the front walkway, Martin slipped further from her grasp, feet dragging on the ground. Finally, she put him down and said under her breath, "Martin, for god's sake."

Martin looked at her then, as if the sound of his name had awakened him. His arms were down by his sides, his hands balled into tight fists.

"No," he said. "I'm not leaving until Dad comes to say goodbye."

"He's not here, Martin, he's not coming." She held on to his shoulders and shook him. "We're going to miss our flight."

"You can go then," Martin said. "I'll stay here and wait for Dad. I choose him anyway."

I'd never seen Mom slap Martin before. I didn't even recognize the sound, didn't know what had happened until I saw him cover his cheek, twisting his whole body away from us.

That's when he finally started walking toward the taxi, his steps uneven, his back hunched under tense shoulders. Mom followed him with one hand over her mouth, the other clasping her forehead, leaving me to struggle with the suitcases. I tried not to look at the taxi driver, tried not to imagine what we must have looked like to him.

When Martin reached the taxi, he stopped. "I'm still not going, you know."

Mom just nodded. "You'll be happy when we get there. I promise." She lifted her hand and wiped Martin's cheek, as if she could undo what she had done. He didn't move until she dropped her hand again. Then he slowly got into the cab.

Martin didn't say a word after we drove away from the house. I'd grown used to his silence in the months since Dad left. But this was an active, exhausting silence, a soundless crescendo searching for an end. On the short turboprop flight to Chicago, Martin had the window seat on the other side of Mom. I bent forward to keep an eye on him, to see what would happen. As we began our descent, Mom rested her hand on his arm. "Okay?" she asked him. He looked out the window, but his head moved. The tiniest of nods. That's when I finally leaned back and closed my eyes.

At O'Hare, we settled into a corner at the gate. It was already dark outside, as it usually was before we boarded the late-night flight to Germany, so I stood by the windows and made faces at my reflection.

"Look," I said to Martin. "I bet you can't do this." I stuck out my tongue and rolled it into a perfect cylinder.

"Let him be, Kate," Mom said.

But I knew my brother, knew that he couldn't say no to a challenge. Maybe it was that need to win that finally broke the spell. Or maybe it was the distance from home, those miles separating us from Dad, from his absence. Either way, Martin joined me at the window. When I glanced over, his tongue was twisted like a three-leaf clover, pink petals against his dark throat. It was a new trick, one I'd seen him practicing for weeks. I had tried too but had never managed more than the cylinder.

"Ha," he said, breaking his long silence with a big breath. "One for me." And then he stuck out his tongue again in its full twisted glory. I only had one simple trick I could fall back on. So I winked. Right, then left, back and forth, always quicker, my nose twitching. Martin could only wink with his right eye. I knew this, so I said, "Do the other one now." His face scrunched up with the effort of bringing his left eyelids, top and bottom, together. Just when they were so close I thought it would finally work, his right eye snapped shut. Like always. Still, he stood there, both eyes squeezed tightly, sure he'd succeeded. Until I told him, "You're still not doing it."

Years later, long after our summers at Seefrieden had come to an end, when Martin and I weren't speaking anymore, I sometimes remembered this scene, Martin reflected in the dark window, squinting as if his life depended on it. Still claiming success when it was already out of reach. He was never good at conceding defeat. I knew it then, I should have remembered it later.

Martin and I were both asleep when we landed in Frankfurt early the next day. A world away from Illinois, from Dad, from that slap. Tante Lara had come from Bonn to meet us at the airport, and we took the train to the Bodensee together. The ramshackle train station had cobblestone platforms and green branches sprouting from the edge of the crumbling roof. But we glanced past it. We were busy looking for Oma, until we spotted her standing right outside the door of our train carriage, waiting to help us down the steep steps. As we grabbed her hand, she announced each of our names, "Kate. Martin," in her strong voice. Deep with a touch of vibrato. Then she walked over to Mom and cupped Mom's shoulders with her hands. "Lena, you're home." She wrapped her arms around Mom's waist and held tight. They stood like that for a few minutes, propping each other up, until Tante Lara said, "Okay now." When Oma let go, I saw that Mom was crying. I looked at the ground and kicked at a grass clump next to my foot. Then I snuck a glance at Martin. He was staring at Mom, his mouth hanging open, eyes wide. Tante Lara must have seen that face too. She put her arm around Martin's shoulder, pulled him close, and spun toward the street. Then she gave him a gentle push. "You lead the way, young man. Your Opa is waiting."

6

Origins of Debt

The Bodensee, 1970

Oma and Opa moved like planets, bound invisibly, distant in almost all ways one could see. And yet, every afternoon after lunch, they met in the living room, the lilac-colored teapot and two cups between them on the low table, a novel on Oma's lap, her reading glasses on her nose. And then Oma read out loud to Opa. Goethe, Fontane, Kleist, Thomas Mann. The same classics that inspired Mom to love her own language, to want to teach it to others. Opa listened to Oma, his head hanging low on his chest, his eyelids drooping. There were times I thought he had fallen asleep, and yet the moment Oma stopped, the moment she hesitated or took a breath or waited to turn a page, his head snapped high, eyes open, waiting for more. A bond shaped by the words of others.

When we were there during the summers, Mom listened with Opa. But Martin and I usually didn't join them. The books were complex, the whole old-fashioned ritual tinged with a longing we were too young to grasp. No matter how often Mom said, "You just need to listen better," we found we couldn't. Mostly we avoided the living room in the afternoons, sought other adventures in the house or in the garden, Oma's voice reaching us through open doors and windows, a sostenuto accompaniment to our games.

But the summer after Dad left was different in this way too. Martin spent more time sitting with Oma and Opa, sticking close to those who remained, listening with his head tilted, his knees tucked under him like a supplicant. He had his own teacup, golden brown with a dark rim. I had one too, of course. Red with yellow flowers. But I didn't like tea back then, so mine mostly stayed empty.

By the end of our first week in Germany that summer, I was bored and ready to escape. To the lake, to the garden. Anywhere. That afternoon, I tried my hardest to persuade Martin to play with me. While

Oma read, I jostled him, pinched him. "Martin," I whispered, "let's go find snails," or "Martin, I made up a new card game," or "Martin, I always play your games when you ask." Finally Oma sent us packing. "Enough. I can't concentrate with you around."

But I hadn't planned very well. It was a rainy day, the garden damp and muddy, the lake unappealing. So we sat together at the top of the stairs, listening to Oma's distant murmurs.

"Now what?" Martin said. "You got us kicked out, so now what?"

I looked to the right and left, as if the empty hallway, clean as can be, could possibly give me any ideas. Then I looked behind us. The door to Oma and Opa's bedroom stood ajar. A small crack. It was the only part of the house we rarely entered, the one place that felt off-limits though we'd never been told to stay out. I twisted further to get a better view, and through the crack I saw a heavy carved chest of drawers by the window, a kind of furniture-fortress prepared to fend off attacks, a toothed wooden lip running along the top edge like a battlement. And yet the top drawer stood open, not enough to see what was in it, just enough to create a sense of promise.

"Look!" I said, putting my hand on Martin's arm, pushing him to turn toward the door.

Martin jerked away. "So?"

"Let's go see what we can find," I said. It was a simple plan, a minor betrayal of Oma and Opa to keep my brother from deserting me. A bargain I was more than willing to make on a dull rainy afternoon.

"No way," Martin said. "That's private."

"But the door's open."

Martin looked toward their room again, then shook his head. "I'm going back to listen to Oma."

He stood up, towering above me on the stairs. So I grabbed his left ankle and held tight as he tried to shake me off. Then I said the one thing I knew he wouldn't be able to resist. "You're just scared you'll get in trouble!" I stood and walked toward Oma and Opa's room, my back as straight as I could make it, as if I were leading a parade. I could almost feel the baton twirling in my hand. I knew my brother. I knew he would follow.

Oma and Opa's room smelled musty, like laundry put away still damp. Martin shut the door carefully behind us. "Let's see what's in there." I walked over to the chest of drawers and tugged at the top handle. I suppose I shouldn't have been surprised by the sight of Opa's underwear, white tinged with the dirty gray of too many washes, but I hadn't prepared myself for this level of intimacy. I was about to shut the drawer again, when I saw the corner of something hard and black. "Look." I pulled out a small leather photo album and held it up high.

"What's that?" Martin snatched it from my hand.

"Give it back!"

But Martin was busy inspecting it, turning it over. "Look, it's got a lock."

"What kind of photo album has a lock? What do you think is in there?" I grabbed his wrist so we were both holding the album now.

Downstairs, we heard Oma's voice, rising, falling. We couldn't make out the words, but her tone grew strident, then soft. Something had happened, a plot point, the kind of thing that would have roused my interest briefly had I still been sitting with them. I imagined Opa snapping to attention, then sinking again.

"What about your pocketknife?" I asked. "Can't you get it open with that?"

"Are you nuts? That's not right."

"They'll never know." I tried to grab the album again, but Martin raised it above his head.

"It's not right," he repeated.

I knew it wasn't right, of course, but Martin's tone irked me, the way he always knew better. This plan had been mine. I deserved the lead and the credit. So I shoved him and repeated, "You're just scared. You're scared you'll get caught!"

Next to me I could feel Martin hesitate, a quiver of indecision. He brought his arm down, and we stared at the lock. Such a tiny lock. Then, with one sharp movement, Martin pulled out his pocketknife and flipped open the blade. The knife's point scraped against the gold clasp, leaving scratches that would give us away even if we failed to break it open.

"Careful!" I said, and he muttered, "Leave me alone." Then the lock snapped, startling both of us into sudden silence. And in that silence, we heard the uneven planks in the hallway creak. We'd been too absorbed, had not noticed that Oma's reading voice had gone quiet, had not heard her steps until she was almost in the room.

Like most German homes, Oma and Opa's house had no closets,

no good place to hide. I scurried around the back side of the bed and made myself as skinny as I could along one side of the heavy wooden *Schrank* where they hung their clothes. Had I had more time, I might have crawled inside, hidden under Oma's dresses. But that would have built sin upon sin, multiplied the breach of trust. I'm not sure I could have gone that far. Across the room, Martin tried to shove the album back into the open drawer, but the pressure of his hand caused the drawer to slide off its rails instead, and it dropped with an echoing clatter. Opa's grayish-white underwear scattered onto the floor around Martin, draped over his shoes, over the album that was now lying beside his feet. And still in Martin's hand, the Swiss Army knife, open blade held up like a torch.

Oma surveyed the scene from the door. Then she walked toward Martin, grabbed the knife and closed it with a flick, before bending down to pick up a handful of underwear and with it, the album, which fell open in her hands. I shifted farther back into the shadow of the *Schrank*. Martin glanced in my direction but said nothing. Instead, he edged toward Oma, and together the two of them stared at the album, heads bent low over a photo I could not see. "Do you know her?" Martin asked, pointing. Oma hesitated then nodded slowly, and I remember thinking, *How unfair.* Once again, Martin had managed to be at the center.

When Opa walked in, Oma said his name. "Uwe?" As though she had never seen him, was not sure who he was. Her hand dropped to her side, and I finally caught a glimpse of the black-and-white image she and Martin had been studying. A man and a woman, close together, arms entangled, heads bent toward each other, cheeks touching. Opa saw it too, and he moved more quickly than I had ever seen him move, his bad leg dragging, his right hand grasping for the album long before he got there. He took it from Oma without looking at her and examined the lock. Then he said, "Who did this?"

I waited for Martin to point at me. After all, I was only half hidden, easy prey. But he didn't betray me. He didn't even glance in my direction this time. Instead, he stared at the ground, his shoulders twitching uncomfortably, his face turning red. Opa said only one word. "You?" Then he turned and left, arm still outstretched, making sure the album left the room even before he did.

Oma stood still for a moment, then she picked up Opa's underwear, put it in the drawer without folding it and lifted the drawer back into its place. As she walked out, she said to Martin, "Never did I think you would do such a thing. Never did I think you would have so little understanding for the privacy of others." A minute later, we heard the front door slam downstairs. Martin and I ran to the window. Below us, Opa stood on the stone patio by the door, his right hand rubbing the back of his neck, his head tilted heavily to one side. He watched Oma stride toward the garden gate, toward the street. With each sharp step, her thick-heeled pumps ground into the gravel and her calf-length skirt slapped against her legs. Then she turned the corner and was gone.

"She'll come back, right?" I said to Martin. But he ignored the question. Only when Opa had gone inside and closed the door behind him, did Martin finally speak.

"We shouldn't have done that."

"Why? What was on that photo?" I asked.

Martin lifted his hand and rubbed his fingers along the curtains. "Opa and some woman."

"Oma?" I asked, but he didn't need to answer. I knew it wasn't Oma.

Martin let go of the curtains. "You're lucky I didn't tell on you." He pinched my arm the way I sometimes pinched his, an angry pinch, nothing funny about it. And then, before I could react, he too was gone. The curtains fluttered. Beneath them, Opa's drawer was still open a crack. I pushed it shut with a sharp jab, the same jab I wanted to give Martin.

That night, Mom took longer than usual to tuck us into our bunk beds. She fluffed our blankets—first Martin's, then mine—and smoothed them out on top of us. We assumed Oma had told her what had happened. We waited for her to scold us. But all she said was, "I hope you've learned from today." Then she gave each of us a hug and a kiss on the forehead. Before she left the room, she paused, hand on the light switch, her voice low. "It's normal to miss Dad, you know. It's okay to be sad. It's okay to make mistakes." She turned off the light, then said even more quietly, "Someday you'll make wonderful families of your own. Wonderful homes."

I buried my head in my pillow, embarrassed even in the dark. I didn't understand what any of this had to do with Dad. After all, he was an entire ocean away. But deep down, I was struck by her words. By the idea that I had a choice. That I could *make* a family, not just have one. A hint that maybe, just maybe, if I tried hard enough, I really could make Dad disappear, could create something altogether different.

Oma came back that same night, of course, and when we woke the next morning, all was calm. Almost as if nothing had happened. And yet, that day marked the beginning of a new pattern, the planetary system shaken. For the rest of that summer, Oma didn't read to Opa, not a single sentence. When Opa was alone with us, he told us stories as he always had. But now they were even wilder—tales about jumping into the Baltic Sea on New Year's Eve to swim amidst ice shards. Or about hunting that wild boar with his bare hands, sending it across the border to Poland with one swift quick kick to the rear. Mom said Opa was filling Oma's silence.

They still sat together briefly after lunch each day, the teapot between them, the cups on the table. But no book on her lap, no murmured German, no crinkling sound of pages turning. Only quiet. It was his punishment, I suppose, and I never heard him question it. But it was my punishment too, because Martin insisted on sitting with them every afternoon now, his eyes moving between them, assessing, wondering, grappling with something I didn't understand.

"Can't we go play?" I asked him once, about a week after Oma had stopped reading. But Martin shook his head, kept his eyes on Opa.

I scooched closer to him on the sofa, trying to fill the space that had once been filled by Oma's voice, and asked, "What are you doing? What are you staring at?"

He turned toward me with a sharp jerk of his head. "You made me do it," he hissed and pushed me away. "It's all your fault."

I knew what he meant, of course, but I no longer wanted the credit. My idea had been different, a simple diversion, a harmless treasure hunt in Oma and Opa's room. Yet something had changed with that one lousy photo, something far beyond my control. So I shoved Martin back and pinched his upper arm until he squealed.

"Kate, Martin!" Oma reprimanded from behind her teacup, and Martin lowered his head, quiet again.

I waited long enough for Oma to be distracted. By a sound outside, or by the ticking of the clock. Then I moved toward Martin one more time.

"Still, you're the one who actually did it," I whispered into his ear.

And as I pulled back, smiling, I watched him droop. Arms, head, eyelids, neck, all wilted, shrinking under the weight of a guilt that was not his.

Looking back, I think that one summer—the summer after Dad left, the summer Oma stopped reading—marked the real beginning of the new Martin, the beginning of a life shaped by debts he felt he owed, by a fear that he'd failed the men in his life. Dad, of course. But Opa too. All tangled together that summer, twisted into a foundation Martin built upon each summer thereafter. Until the summer Opa died, and then it was too late.

I would have done things differently had I known. But I didn't, of course. And so, that day on the sofa, when Martin wrestled his arm away from my pinching fingers, I leaned even closer, whispered again, "You did it," and gave my already sinking brother another shove, until he became one with the sofa, falling into the dark space between pillows. Gone. And I'm ashamed to say that I felt good.

PART III

LOST AND FOUND

1990
1952–1953

7

The Autumn of Footsteps

Grimma, July 1990

I hadn't thought about Opa's stories for years. Not until that July day in 1990, standing in Klaus and Greta's hall with Martin, staring at the photo of their house. "Just the way Opa described it," Martin had said. As we drove away from Grimma on our way back to our hotel in Leipzig, I rested my head on Darren's shoulder—drowsy from jet lag, from the suede-gray dusk around us—and tried to remember. When had Opa ever told us about the house? Why hadn't I heard that story? Or had I forgotten it? We'd just passed the last buildings at the edge of town when Martin spoke. "Have you ever wondered," he asked, "why none of Opa's stories about Grimma were true?"

"I guess they were more fun that way?" I was happy that Martin had moved on from that story about the house, that we were once again remembering the same wild tales. But it was not the right answer. Martin leaned away, disappointed.

I tried again. "Don't you remember what he used to say about all the best stories. How they were a bit different each time you told them? Maybe that's why he made stuff up."

"Maybe," Martin said. "Or maybe he was trying to hide something?"

I had no idea what he was talking about, so I didn't answer. Neither did Mom or Tante Lara. Our silence continued almost long enough for me to doze off, but then Martin's voice pierced the quiet again. Sharp and demanding.

"Okay, Mom, so what did Klaus mean about Opa then? How come Klaus said he lived with Opa, but not with the rest of you? Didn't you live with Opa back then too?"

I was suddenly fully awake. Martin had fit together pieces I hadn't even considered. He'd found the gaps. Tante Lara turned toward Mom, her profile illuminated by the lights of a car heading the other way, and asked, "Now?"

Mom hesitated for a moment, then said, "Yes. I'd like to hear it again too." As if it were someone else's story. She twisted around to face Martin and me. We could barely see her face in the dark, but her voice was low and intimate, making the car even smaller. "Lara can tell you everything. She was older. She remembers it better." Then, even more quietly: "It's not that we didn't want to tell you. It's just that Oma always said it was Opa's story to tell. But he never did." Mom turned back to Tante Lara, who cleared her throat and said, "Well."

Tante Lara started her story in the years shortly after the Second World War—the day Opa got called to the Soviet barracks to fix some equipment. That must have been 1947 or 1948. Back when Tante Lara was just eleven or twelve. "Your Opa was nervous when he got the call," she told us, eyes focused on the road ahead, Martin, Darren, and I lined up in the back seat like students. "Grimma had always been a garrison town, all those hussars and their horses, centuries of proud men. We were used to soldiers. But this was the Soviet commandant who'd called for him, and we all knew about the Soviet army. I was proud of my dad. I was pretty sure he could fix anything the commandant needed. After all, he was famous around town as a handyman. He had a real talent for tinkering, that's how he'd made money since he was a teenager. Still, your Oma worried the whole time. And when your Opa finally got back home, he was so giddy and relieved, he told us every detail of the day."

It began with an insult. The commandant, in uniform, welcomed Opa skeptically, questioned his experience, called him "*junger Mann*." Young man. Opa did look young, his charming, crooked smile negating the wrinkles around his eyes, but in fact, he was over forty by then. Opa studied the commandant's face and wondered whether he might have encountered the man in battle had Opa's own limp, one leg shorter than the other, not kept him out of the war, his call to the Eastern front coming so very late that the fighting ended before he even departed for what he imagined would have been certain death. A miracle of sorts amid all the horror. And a deep relief for a man who'd never joined the Nazi party, a man who surely was no hero but preferred minding his own business, always shying away from authority. Still, Opa thought it wise to keep his age, his infirmity, and his apolitical views to himself, instead asking simply, "What needs fixing then?"

It was a radio. Not just any radio, but the radio on which the commandant tuned in to what was coming across the waves, searching for information on his American counterparts. He hovered nearby as Opa took the radio apart, asking questions which Opa answered as briefly as possible, his charm constrained by the commandant's presence. As he manipulated wires one way then the other, Opa could hear the ticking of an old clock hanging on the wall. He knew clocks well, had repaired many in his life, and in the tense silence he found himself distracted by the sound, glancing from his wires to the clock and back, wondering what model it was, how long it had been there, what it had witnessed within those walls. "Clocks don't only keep time, they track history," he told Oma, Tante Lara, and Mom later that night when he got home. "Forget the clock and its history," Oma had said. "That radio could be your future." And up to a point, Oma was right.

When Opa was done with his repairs, the commandant tested the radio, turned the knob, listened to the crackling. First, voices in German which Opa tried to ignore ("He didn't want to appear to be eavesdropping," Tante Lara explained), then voices in English and Russian which he could not understand. Finally, the commandant turned off the radio. "So, you're good with your hands." A statement, not a question. Opa stayed silent. The commandant walked over to his desk, took a bottle and two glasses out of the drawer, and invited Opa to sit down opposite him. "You remind me of my son." And that is how Opa got his job at the machinery factory. One commandant, his fallen son, a radio, and three shots of vodka. That's all it took to make him production manager.

Opa loved his new work. It was the same work he'd always done, really. Fixing things. But now he had colleagues, comrades. Acquaintances he'd known in Grimma for years became friends. A whole community down at the factory. Early on in his new role, they all took a trip to the beach, all the men Opa worked with, their spouses and kids. The trip was organized by the factory, as so much was back then. They stayed at a hostel up by the Baltic Sea, an early version of the vacation camps that the state-owned enterprises later built for their workers. The families got their own rooms. Everyone else stayed in one of the large bunk rooms. It was all simple. Only the necessary things. Beds, a sink, and a window with a view either toward the water or back into the woods. Oma and Opa's room faced the woods. It was meant to be a privilege, the private family room. Four small beds. But the bunk room was livelier, louder. And so each night, after Oma and Opa took the girls to their room, after they'd turned off the light, Opa would sneak back to the bunk room to play cards.

On the last night, Oma finally had enough. She didn't know why Opa should have all the fun. After he left, she waited. Counted to one hundred, then two hundred. Long enough for Opa to have settled into the card game, long enough for Mom—just seven or eight years old—to fall fast asleep. That's when Oma remembered the sausage links. The ones she'd packed in her bag, thinking they'd be a nice snack for a hike. Two different kinds of salami—one mild, one spicy. Two pairs, four salamis in all. She pulled the sausage links out from underneath the raincoats in the suitcase. With two sausages in each hand, Oma walked down the hallway, Tante Lara trailing behind.

At the door to the bunk room, she draped a sausage link over each of Tante Lara's ears. Mild on the left side. Spicy on the right. ("The same way you used to put the double cherries over your ears, Kate, when the stems were still connected," Tante Lara said. "Except the sausages were large and heavy!") When Oma and Tante Lara walked in, everyone stopped playing cards. Guilty. Wondering if Oma was there to get Opa, to bring him back where he belonged. But Oma spun Tante Lara around by her hands, the sausages dangling from Tante Lara's ears, her hair whipping her neck. When they'd spun around once, twice, the sausages on the left—the mild ones—came flying off Tante Lara's ear, landing on the ground with a thump. Two thumps really. First one sausage, then its partner. Right at the feet of the chief engineer. He was quiet for a moment, then he began to laugh. And with his laughter, the whole room changed. Opened up, welcomed them. Such a simple thing. Opa patted the edge of the bunk next to him. Oma took the spicy sausages off Tante Lara's right ear, and they sat down close to Opa, shoulder to shoulder. The whole bunk shook with their laughter.

Those people were Opa's closest friends, and now they became Oma's friends too. They talked during work. They talked after work. They kept talking in the garden, then they'd talk even more late at night at Oma and Opa's kitchen table. Twenty-four-hour friends, that's what Opa called them.

The laughter didn't last though. Just a few more years. The end already baked into the beginning. It started on a warm summer night in 1952. One of those long northern European days that seem to stretch impossibly, making up for the cold months of winter. It was also the last day of school for Tante Lara and Mom. Oma had planned a special dinner, out in the garden, a string of colorful lights wrapped around the clothesline at the back of the patio. But Opa did not come home in time for dinner. "Looks like it's an evening for us, girls." Oma served potato salad with vinegar on simple ceramic plates, and they ate into the dusk. When Opa finally walked through the garden gate, Mom was already upstairs, reading under the covers, waiting for Tante Lara, wanting to whisper the day away. But Oma and Tante Lara remained outside. Opa was carrying an unopened bottle of champagne, which he placed heavily on the patio table, holding on to it longer than necessary, bracing himself. When he finally let go, his hand fluttered, wiping off some association, some memory.

"*Vorsicht*," he said. Careful. Then he winked at Tante Lara and sat down across from Oma, resting his elbows on the table.

"What are we celebrating?" Oma asked.

"Don't be fooled. It's not a celebration. It's a negotiation." After a long pause, he continued. "They promoted me. Or they tried to."

"What do you mean, 'tried to'?"

"I said no, but they still gave me the bottle." Opa stopped. In those days, the war still a recent memory, the new East German State a growing reality, every decision had import. It might not have been obvious, but it was there. And yet, Opa had never been one for decisions. So Oma waited for him to go on.

"They asked me to join the Party." Opa didn't say more. It seemed enough. Everyone knew the power of the SED. The ruling party. The regime. They sat for a minute or two, food hardening on the plates around them, the bottle a silent message between them.

Then Oma said, "Well, you can't give it back now, can you?"

"*Nein.*" Opa took the bottle and untwisted the wire cage. "Might as well make something of it." He released the cork with a defiant pop. Then he leaned back in his chair, smiled his uneven smile, and slowly, ceremoniously poured the champagne, still foaming, onto the ground. Tante Lara watched the puddle spread unevenly across the gravel, white fading to gray. But Oma took the bottle away from Opa and placed it, still half-full, back on the table. Around them, it was growing dark now, the first chill in the air. Even this summer day was unable to stretch any longer.

"*Ach komm*, let's not waste it all," Oma said finally and filled two of the glasses on the table. "We aren't in Troy, after all. It's not a hollow horse, just a bottle." She took one of the glasses, and Opa took the other.

"*Prost*," he said, standing up and raising his glass high, a quick salute. "To socialism, to the worker." Bending over the table, grinning, he gave Oma a pinch on the arm. "No, it's not Troy. But you just might be my Helen."

Opa stacked the plates and carried them toward the door. When he got to the threshold, he turned around, serious again, and said, "You know, all the other managers are already in the Party. I can't live under the commandant's cover forever, but I'll be damned if I let them push me into it." It was more than he had ever said about politics. A declaration of sorts. Oma took the glasses and followed him into the house. Neither one of them paid any attention to Tante Lara, neither one tried to explain anything.

From outside, Tante Lara could hear the clatter of dishes being cleaned. The light from the kitchen window fell through the bushes, making the leaves glitter, throwing shadows on the gravel path. She left the bottle of champagne and the two glasses outside that night. An abundance of caution, a lesson from Greek mythology. Or was it history? But when she checked on it the next day, everything was as she had left it, except for the rain that had mixed with the leftover champagne. No hidden armies in the bottle, only a few diluted bubbles shimmering green through the glass.

"Your Opa never did join the SED," Tante Lara told us in the car. "Just like he never joined the Nazi Party. Your Opa never belonged to anything. Not then, not earlier, not later. He wasn't political. He was his own man. That was his charm, in a way, and it served us well."

In the passenger seat, Mom laughed. "It seems I slept through a lot back then. But I remember being proud he hadn't joined, even though I'm not sure I knew what it meant. I was so young."

"We all knew enough," Tante Lara said. "Enough to know that sometimes it was best not to be a part of things."

Mom nodded one more time, a sharp, decisive motion that transported me back to my childhood. As a kid in Illinois, I was surrounded by joiners. People joined the Brownies, then the Girl Scouts. They joined their church choirs and sports teams. They volunteered at hospitals and road races. Mom fought our urge to join, to be like the others. For one exceptional day, I was a Brownie, signing up over Mom's objections. But sitting there on my first (and last) day in that uniform, the sash around one shoulder, I knew I had to quit. Staying felt like a betrayal. Mom gave us pride in not belonging, but the truth is that I never fully understood why until that moment in the car, watching the back of Mom's head, listening to Tante Lara's girlish voice unspooling their childhood like a long-awaited movie I hadn't even known was coming.

And Tante Lara was nowhere near done talking. The pressure Opa felt to leave East Germany dated back to that day, she told us. The day he refused to join the Party. The beginning of the end, though it wasn't clear at first. Even after refusing to join, Opa kept his position as production manager. No one came to talk to him again, to try to persuade him. It seemed that the commandant's protection still counted for something.

Those were the days leading up to the annual factory outing, a highlight Opa looked forward to each year. That year, July 1952, was no different. On Thursday, the evening before the outing, Oma and Opa made the potato salad, mixed the sweet blackberry syrup with water, chilled the beers. Then they headed outside with Tante Lara and Mom. They had just settled around the garden table, when Opa groaned. "*Da kommt er.*" There he comes. On the street, they saw a short man with small eyes, a fleshy nose, a chin that jutted out defiantly, and eyebrows that were as bushy as his hair. He rested his arms on their metal gate, hands hanging over the side. The casual pose of a friendly neighbor.

Opa had had trouble with him before. "A Party hack," he called him, or "that small man." Never naming him by his real name. The source of their tension was Opa's talent. At least that's what Opa always said. For Opa, the workday never ended at five. Most evenings after dinner, he headed back out to fix things for neighbors and friends. Production manager or not, he was still the best tinkerer around. Often, he shared these jobs with a plumber who lived down the street, and together, they made extra money. Not too many years later, there would be a name for this. "Evening brigades." That's what people called the after-hour workers who took on contracts the state-owned enterprises couldn't or wouldn't. These informal brigades weren't just tolerated, they were supported by the State. One of the many seeming inconsistencies of East Germany. Until you thought about it. What better way to counter a labor shortage and keep people happy? But back then, in the early years of the East German State, the boundaries of the acceptable were murky, still evolving. The limits of what was and was not allowed, what would and would not be obeyed, were being tested, pushed, changed on a nearly daily basis.

None of this was the little man's real issue, though. He may have been a Party man, but he was driven by more universal emotions. Envy. Or perhaps simply survival. He needed the extra work, the money. And he was an innovator of sorts. A brigade leader before there were brigades. He wanted to be in charge, had approached Opa and the plumber many times, sometimes with a direct offer, usually with an indirect threat.

Either way, Opa was never interested. "Work for him?" Opa would say at the dinner table. "For that tiny man with his tiny eyes and tiny heart?" Then he'd slam the table hard, palm down, laughing. Tante Lara could never tell if he was amused or angry.

That Thursday evening, when the little man came by, Opa was drinking his third beer, tipsy, buoyant, ready for anything.

"*Nahmd*," he drawled in the distinctive local dialect, his tongue weighing down the vowels, slurring the consonants. Transforming *Guten Abend* into something softer, woolier, wetter.

"*Nahmd*," the man drawled back.

"And what can I do for you? You got something that needs fixing? Your wife not happy with your handiwork?"

The man leaned farther over the gate, eyeing the weeds in the flower beds. "Having trouble keeping up with the garden, Uwe? Too busy at work?" A battle of questions.

Opa grunted and took another sip of his beer. The man bent all the way over the gate and plucked one of the weeds, a green sprout with a puffy seed head like cotton candy. He inspected it before throwing it back down onto the dirt. Opa didn't move.

"I heard about your incident at the factory, Uwe," the small man said, still not looking at Opa. "Shame, isn't it?"

Opa didn't respond.

"The way you run around helping all your neighbors, I'd have thought you'd have had time to spare for the Party too."

"Since when," Opa asked the man, "is helping your neighbors a sin? Even the Bible taught us that."

Opa was not religious, had never read a word of the Bible. He simply wanted to provoke the man, and he knew that religion was a provocation, connections to the church a form of opposition in the East. But the man wasn't the only one Opa provoked with his comment. As soon as she heard the word *Bible*, Oma gave Opa her dirty-joke look, the one that conveyed anger, disappointment, but above all, a warning: watch out. Tante Lara noticed, but Opa didn't. He was too busy measuring the little man, judging him.

That's when the man finally looked right at Opa. No more staring at the weeds, at his feet, at the fence. "Uwe," he said, "you'd better be careful. I'll be straight with you. You're on our radar now."

"That'd suit you, wouldn't it?" Opa moved slowly toward the fence. He bent over, picked up the weed the man had dropped on the ground, and wrapped the soft stem around his finger. "You turn up here at my fence, threatening me. Your comrades turn up at my work, threatening me. You turn up everywhere like weeds, you and your sort." He held the weed in his hand, the puffy seed head sticking up between his knuckles, like an unruly ring. Opa examined it and laughed. "It even has your eyebrows."

With a sudden movement, Opa bent his head toward the weed and blew. The fuzz exploded in a cloud of seeds, scattering, settling back down onto the flower bed. Opa glared at the man. "*Sieh mal da.*" Look. "Now we'll have many more little weeds with eyebrows. But then again, I've heard your wife likes tall men with smooth hair, so maybe not." Opa dropped the weed and took a quick step toward the fence. Just as quickly, the small man stepped back.

"I tried to warn you," he said.

Opa was still laughing as the man rounded the corner onto the next street, out of sight.

The next day was Friday. A beautiful evening, warm, sunny, a light breeze ruffling the grasses on the banks of the Mulde. Perfect for the picnic by the river. Tante Lara and Mom were older than most of the other kids and sat awkwardly on their blanket with Oma, trying to listen to the adult conversation, trying not to be distracted by the younger kids chasing each other. Opa was always the star of these picnics, the storyteller around whom the rest gathered, the one who told the best jokes and got the biggest laughs. Like every year, he and Oma brought along their grill, a tiny tripod. Opa towered over it, hunching to turn the sausages, then standing up straight, surveying his audience.

"You'll never believe who came to visit me again," he started. "*Der kleine Kerl mit den Augenbrauen.*" The little guy with the eyebrows. And Opa painted the scene for his colleagues. The pleasure of a peaceful beer in the garden interrupted by the little man they all knew though no one said his name. The altercation by the fence. The Bible reference and the weed analogy. He landed the line about the wife's preference in men with perfection. "And who would blame her?" he said. "Our wives like us tall too, *nicht wahr*?" Then he waited for the laughter.

The hesitation was barely noticeable. Hardly even a pause. But to Tante Lara, Mom, and Oma, it was deafening. The timing was off, and Opa knew it too.

The moment lasted just long enough for his colleagues to glance at each other, for Opa to glance at them and then down at his sausages. The laughter came, but even then, it was brief, unsure. The conversation shifted, and Opa watched quietly as the men he had worked with for years moved on, skirting around him, not wanting to get too close to the man who'd been marked by his refusal to join the Party. The almost imperceptible start of a new, off-center life. And Tante Lara, Mom, and Oma sat on their blanket among the chattering men and women, the kids running around, as if nothing had happened.

"It was like that Auden poem about the painting of Icarus," Tante Lara said. "I had to memorize it years later in English class, and right away, I thought of your Opa and that moment."

Mom spoke up from the front passenger seat, a new voice in the dark. "I love that poem. And it's so true. How all the most mundane details of life are unaffected by others' suffering. I mean, there Icarus is, plunging into the sea, and no one even notices. The farmers keep farming, the boat keeps sailing, the sun keeps shining."

"I should have known the teacher would know it," Tante Lara said. And even in the dark, we could tell she was rolling her eyes. "It was like that. Opa kept grilling sausages, the men kept telling stories, and the kids kept playing tag. But everything had changed."

Neither Oma nor Opa mentioned the moment on the way home from the picnic or over the next few days. Why would they have? It was meaningless. A pause. A hiccup. The sausages had tasted good, the beer even better. The weather had been splendid. Another year, another success, something they could talk about during the long winter months. Remember the picnic, they'd say. That was a good one, they'd say. We got lucky with the weather, they'd say.

Tante Lara lifted one hand from the steering wheel, held it up between the two front seats so Martin and I could see it clearly, and waved her pointer finger back and forth. Like a warning.

"I didn't know it then," she said, "but later, when I tried to learn more about those years, I read about the Second Party Conference that same month. July 1952. It was a turning point, the real beginning of totalitarianism. That's when they announced they would nationalize private enterprise, collectivize the farms. That's when the repression started to ramp up. A few weeks after the border to the West had been tightened. Things I wasn't paying attention to as a kid. But I'm sure Oma and Opa were. There was a quote I read back then that I've never forgotten, something the leader of the trade union federation said at that party conference. He said it was time for all workers to be the army of the Party. The army! Well, literal or not, that definitely wasn't Opa's kind of thing."

"I never knew you were interested in all this," Mom said.

"Well, of course I was. It's where I grew up."

Mom looked out the window. "Me too. Still, I didn't feel that way."

"I know," Tante Lara said sharply. "I never understood that."

But Mom didn't take the bait, kept looking out the window until Tante Lara added, "I felt sorry for your Opa. It's easy to be courageous for an audience, you know, but without that audience…"

And there it was, the first thing I could relate to, the first glimpse of the Opa I'd known. A man with a very small audience, only Martin and me. When we ran off to play, or when we left for Illinois, what was he then? What remained?

Unlike Opa, Oma didn't have many friends at her work. Just Krista really, Tante Lara told us. They were very close, although Krista was almost ten years younger, one of many new teachers trained after the war, when everything was in short supply. Food, clothes, teachers.

From the beginning, Oma took Krista under her wing. Not just professionally, but also personally. Oma was already in her thirties when Lara and Mom were born, and she brought a calmness to both child-rearing and work that Krista, only twenty-two when she had Konni, found comforting. Each day when they were done teaching, they smoked together behind the school, sitting on the empty barrels lined up against the wall for reasons no one could quite remember. With their shoes kicked off in the grass below and their feet tucked up against the rounded rims of the barrels, they took in the view over a field toward a gray apartment block lined with balconies. Not much of a view, but on sunny days they sat there for hours, making up stories about those balconies, watching to see who hung up laundry, who planted the best flowers, who came home late, who drank coffee with whom. They didn't always talk. After a day of teaching, sitting in silence was a luxury. Now and then, Tante Lara, Mom, and Konni joined them after school, climbing onto three more barrels, kicking off three more pairs of shoes, breathing in the smell of sun-warmed grass.

A few weeks after the picnic by the river, Oma didn't come home for dinner. She was rarely late, and Opa was not good at evenings alone. He made a simple *Abendbrot*—bread, cheeses, and meats. There wasn't much else in his repertoire. The table looked different when he made dinner. All the necessary things were there: forks, knives, butter. But he forgot other things, the things Tante Lara and Mom never noticed until they were missing. The vase with flowers picked from the garden, the cloth napkins neatly rolled into napkin rings, the woven runner in the middle of the table, so pretty no one put any plates on it. Opa's table was no-nonsense. After dinner, he sent the girls upstairs to do their homework. They sat by the window in the room they shared. Another hour or so passed before they saw Oma come around the corner of the house, walking quickly, head down. The door slammed behind her, and they heard Opa's voice. "Where have you been?"

Tante Lara and Mom snuck down the stairs and squatted on the bottom step, where they could see and hear what was going on in the kitchen.

Oma didn't answer Opa's question right away. She walked to the cupboard, took out a glass, and filled it from the sink. Then she sat down at the table. "Uwe, give me some space." Her voice was tight.

Opa followed her to the table but didn't sit. "Space?" he said. "I've been worrying for the past four hours!"

"I had a meeting with the director. I couldn't leave."

Opa rolled his head to one side, not quite ready to accept her answer. "That man? What did he want?"

"Frank Hauser," Oma said. Opa stared, head still tilted. Then he sat down next to her.

Frank Hauser was a name Tante Lara and Mom had heard often that year. He was Oma's best student, new to the school. New to town. His family had moved from Mecklenburg surrounded by rumors and gossip. A mousy-looking wife and a slim man. Wispy. They'd been blown into town by the wind, that's what people said. And they kept to themselves. They'd had lots of land, or so the stories went. A large estate up in Mecklenburg, never mind that they didn't look like estate-owning types. The dad had owned it together with his brother. Perhaps the brother was the missing link, the one with the style and the bearing of a landowner, but he'd left for the West when the land was taken. Like other large estates. The beginnings of the collectives. No one knew how or why the rest of the family ended up in Grimma.

They had two kids, also mousy, also small. "But smart as can be," Oma would always add. Frank was the older one, at that awkward age, limbs protruding at strange angles, his face an ever-changing map of peaks and valleys. He'd written an essay when they arrived, the first assignment of the year. The question had been, "Tell me about something that is important to you." A way to get to know the kids disguised as work. Frank wrote about Mecklenburg. Delightful reminiscences of growing up on the land, a big farm with wide open spaces and large skies. Not at all political. "It was mainly about animals, for god's sake," Oma told Opa that evening. Yet deep in the essay, in the nostalgia and regret that colored the words, mature emotions for a thirteen-year-old, the school leadership heard reproach. Reproach in the line *There's nothing more peaceful than milking a cow at dawn on our estate.* Or in the observation *It was hard work, but we cared for our own land, made the most of what we had.* Where Oma heard sweet longing, the school director heard danger.

A note went into his file. Notes went into files all the time. But then, at some point, the decision had to be made: Which students would go on to study at the *Oberschule*, which would not? Who would have a chance at a university spot later, who would not? The top students got the nod. That was the default. But then there were the exceptions. Anna's father had participated in a protest at his factory; Gerhard's mother had relatives in the West, received packages all the time; the Worlitz family listened to the West German radio station. Each exception required an adjustment, a dropped name.

Frank was meant to be an exception too. One of the missing ones. The director had pulled Oma aside in the hallway to make this clear. But she kept seeing Frank's head bent over his desk, the way his sharp elbows jutted out as he wrote with his left hand, smudging the ink as soon as he'd written each word. The way his essay had spoken to her with its straightforward beauty. So she recommended him for the *Oberschule*, wrote his name down on a note to the school director in capital letters, square and solid, as if the force of her pen could erase all doubts. As if she could make her own wishes into reality through sheer force of personality, a trick she practiced throughout life. More than a trick, really. A belief that shaped her life, that eventually led her from the classroom in Grimma to Seefrieden. To her own inn by a lake. Years later, when she died, Mom and Tante Lara had the words "To our strong mother, who created our world for us" carved on her gravestone. Next to it they planted thistles. Purple, beautiful, tough.

But Oma's wishful thinking did not work for Frank Hauser. A week after submitting her recommendation, she was called into the director's office. "A chance to reconsider," the director called it.

But how could she? During class, she stared at Frank Hauser, skinny limbs resting heavily on his desk, and later that day, she resubmitted the sheet of paper, this time with a brief explanation. An essay about animals, just animals. The high quality of his work. The great promise he showed to become a productive member of this socialist society. Words chosen carefully, but it was not enough.

"So today, I got called in again," she told Opa at the kitchen table while Mom and Tante Lara listened from the stairs. There were four others in the office, Oma said. Not only the director, but also another teacher from Oma's grade, the pretty blond one. And two men Oma didn't know. They took Frank off one list, put him on a different list, and gave Oma a warning. The director kept pointing at a stack of papers on the desk. The blond teacher took notes during the meeting, and at the end of the meeting, she added the notes to the top of the stack.

"My school file. It'll keep growing. They'll make it grow," Oma told Opa. Then they sat at the table, heads bent, quiet. Finally, they both stood up, chairs scraping across the floor.

"After that, we didn't see or hear anything anymore," Tante Lara told us. "Maybe they were talking too softly. At some point, Opa came rushing out of the kitchen and caught us on the stairs. We were grounded for a week. '*Niemand mag einen Spitzel!*' Nobody likes a spy! That's what he said to us."

Mom laughed. "Guess he had a knack for irony."

But Tante Lara didn't laugh with her. "Things changed starting that evening. The house got tense. At first, we thought it would pass. Or that we would absorb it the way we'd absorbed Opa's new quietness since the picnic. We didn't realize that they began planning that very night. The beginning of the end."

That was when the pacing started. Always late at night. Always in the kitchen after Tante Lara and Mom had been sent to bed. They could hear the footsteps and occasionally voices rising, but never the words. Most of the time, they were too busy to give it much thought, too focused on their own present to question their future. Tante Lara was fifteen ("self-centered like all fifteen-year-olds," she told us), sneaking out of the house at night to meet Konni, drinking beers with him down by the river, hiding the bottles in the bushes and chewing mint leaves from the side of the path to mask the smell. Mom was twelve, roaming the streets with packs of six or seven giggling girls, sometimes on foot, sometimes on bikes, eating ice cream on the bench in front of the local store. They had exams, papers, friends, enemies—all distractions that kept them from paying attention to their parents. But sometimes late at night, when they were already in bed, they talked about it, Mom leaning down from the top bunk, Tante Lara plucking at the springs above her head.

"*Der Herbst der Schritte*," Tante Lara said now. "That's what your mom and I ended up calling that fall." The autumn of footsteps.

"You had no idea at all they were planning to leave? Not even a hint?" Martin asked.

"Looking back, there were a few hints, had I been paying attention, but I wasn't," Tante Lara said. "And maybe they themselves weren't sure. Still hoping they could stay."

"Don't you think it was that business with your school that finally forced them, Lara? Remember?" Mom asked.

"You think that was it? I felt like I was the only one who cared about that." Tante Lara tilted her head, as if considering something for the first time.

"Are you kidding me?" Mom said. "I used to think if you'd only joined the FDJ, none of it would have happened."

"What are you talking about?" Martin asked from the back seat. He bumped me with his knee. "Do you know what they're talking about?" But I didn't. Darren was staring out the window, though there was nothing out there, only his own reflection, barely visible. He looked distracted, but I knew he was making mental notes, taking it all in. Family makes the most interesting research, he used to say.

Tante Lara took one hand off the steering wheel and scratched her head, making her short hair stand up wild. "The same thing that happened to Frank Hauser happened to me. I wasn't in Oma's class, of course, so Oma had no say. Though I suppose, in a way, she'd already had her say when she supported Frank. After that, it was probably inevitable."

"Still, you didn't help matters." Mom turned back to Martin and me. "Lara refused to join the FDJ, the *Freie Deutsche Jugend.* The communist youth group. At the time, I really didn't understand why. They took trips, they went camping. If I hadn't been too young, I would have joined myself. It seemed like so much fun."

"It was Konni. He was already a rebel, and he persuaded me to say no. You didn't have a boyfriend, no one to persuade you." Tante Lara chuckled and poked Mom playfully with her finger.

"And look at us now," Mom said. "Both alone."

We were quiet for a moment. Another car passed, its lights revealing Tante Lara's silhouette. Then we were plunged again into that same immeasurable darkness Darren and I had first experienced on the trip from Bonn to Leipzig. We were so close together, the five of us. A single unit within the metal frame of the car. Finally Tante Lara said, "I remember the day they told me I'd never be able to attend university, that I'd be on a different track. Even though I'd always been a good student."

The teacher had told Tante Lara out loud, in front of everyone. But even worse were the whispers that followed, a web of toneless, softened consonants, the cushioned sound of voices in ears. They were whispers of support, Tante Lara knew. Whispers of surprise, even outrage. But no one expressed that outrage out loud. And no one whispered to her. No one breathed into her ear to tell her, *It's wrong.* And so those whispers, that web of sound, became one more thing excluding her.

"I can't describe what I felt," Tante Lara continued. "It was my whole future. You thought it was because of the FDJ? You were angry at me because of that? Well, I was sure it was because of Opa and the Party or because of Oma and Frank. And I was so angry at them."

"It doesn't matter in the end," Mom said. "There were so many reasons."

"I suppose. All's well that ends well." Tante Lara's voice wavered. She lifted her right hand, massaged her temple with her thumb, then ran her fingers through her wiry hair, seeking to smooth what couldn't be smoothed. Her hand shook as she took hold of the wheel again. She didn't seem well, and I wondered briefly if the trip had been too much for her. All those memories. We were driving through Leipzig now, the buildings barely visible in the dark, the hulking shape of the train station ahead.

"So, that's when you all left? But what about Opa and Klaus?" Martin asked. I had forgotten where this had all started, but not Martin, dogged as ever. Tante Lara stopped the car in front of the hotel and sighed. A sigh that shook her.

And that's when she finally told us. Told us what no one ever had.

"He didn't leave," she said. "Your Opa didn't leave."

No one in the car said anything until she started speaking again, slowly, carefully. Each word a decision, like the decisions they described. "He stayed behind. He chose to stay behind. Five more years until 1958. That must be why Klaus knew him and not us. Those were our fatherless years."

She peered out the front windshield toward the hotel entrance. "Enough for today," she said. "I'll tell you everything in Bonn when we get back. When I'm home."

"No," Martin said. Obstinate, angry. Like a child, despite his thirty years. "Tell us the rest now."

But Tante Lara was firm. She was tired. She'd told us so much already. And anyway, she'd had a headache all day. Now it was too much. "Really pounding, migraine level," she said, massaging her temple again. "Here and here."

Mom put a hand on Tante Lara's shoulder. "We'll stop then." In the back seat, Martin was finally quiet, and we watched as Tante Lara tilted her head to the side, resting it lightly on Mom's hand. Two sisters who had lost and found their father. Two sisters who had finally let go of their secret.

8

Crossing the Border

Bonn, July 1990

We stayed in Leipzig one more day after our trip to Grimma. Darren, Martin, and I toured the downtown, ducking into the many passageways that marked this merchant's city, while Mom and Tante Lara went to visit Oma's friend, Krista. Martin had asked to join them, but Tante Lara shook her head. "Perhaps best if we don't show up as a pack." I suppose she was afraid he would judge Krista the way he'd judged Greta. We didn't see Mom and Tante Lara again until evening, long after Martin, Darren, and I had returned to the hotel lobby to rest our cobblestone-weary feet. When Martin asked how the visit had been, Tante Lara just said, "It was lovely." Mom said nothing at all.

The following day we drove back to Bonn, and that night we gathered over an eggplant casserole in Tante Lara's kitchen to share impressions from the trip. What had we seen? What did it all mean? Tante Lara was standing by the back door, holding one hand out into the garden, her cigarette growing damp in the drizzle. Now she shook the ashes onto the wet bricks of the patio, stubbed the cigarette butt out in the sink, and sat down at the table with the rest of us, ready to finish the story she'd started on the car ride from Grimma to Leipzig.

She'd been standing in a different kitchen, a different country, drinking a glass of water at the counter, when Oma first told her they were leaving Grimma. January 1953. Six months after Opa's confrontation at work, four months after Oma was called into the director's office, and two months after Tante Lara was told she wouldn't be able to continue her studies, would never attend university. It was a time of change. Not only for Oma and Opa but for the whole country, sandwiched between the tightening of the East-West border in 1952 and the uprising in 1953, with the pronouncements of the Second Party Conference fresh in people's minds. Pronouncements that justified increasing repression all under the heading of socialism. *Der Aufbau des Sozialismus.* And yet it was still nearly a decade before the Wall went up in Berlin, still a time when hundreds of thousands abandoned the East for the West. Oma and Opa would be one small streak in that vast movement of people.

Back then Tante Lara was mainly concerned with the unfolding of her own life. Through the kitchen window in Grimma she could see the garden Opa tended so avidly, planting magnificent rhododendrons next to lilac bushes in a carefully managed tangle. Just a week earlier, in anticipation of springtime planting, Opa had placed wooden stakes in the hard ground, marking the corners of future flower beds. Tante Lara was looking at these stakes when Oma spoke, firmly but with her eyes averted. "You know, your Großmutter Hilde is very sick." Hilde was Oma's mother, but they'd never been close. A distant figure of strength and judgment, she'd moved west before the war when moving west didn't yet mean anything. To the Bodensee. A place that Oma had only visited a few times. A place that Tante Lara and Mom had never even seen, though it would soon be their new home.

The letter with news of Großmutter Hilde's illness had surprised Oma more than it had saddened her. It was incongruous, that was all. Her tough, solid mother had never been sick. Oma put the letter away in a drawer, almost forgetting to tell Opa. Only that night did she realize that her mother's illness was also their chance to escape. Later, Oma would sometimes describe Hilde's letter as a sign, always adding a chuckle to make clear she didn't believe in signs. But perhaps there was no great difference between a sign and a chance. Merely two different ways of seeing the same thing. Something to believe in. Something to make the most of.

Oma hadn't seen her mother since the war. She could have, of course. Especially in the early years. The border had not yet been fortified, still so many ways to get across. People did it all the time, weaving their way on roads and paths that crisscrossed the border, linking villages the way they'd been linked for centuries. But Oma and Opa didn't live near the border. They didn't have a reason to be there, didn't know the paths. And though they could have applied for a permit, they never did. Seven years had passed since the end of the war, one after the other, without a reunion.

Then came the autumn of footsteps, back when Tante Lara was sixteen and Mom was twelve. What might have been a relatively easy departure had become a much bigger obstacle with the sudden tightening of the border in May 1952. For months that fall of 1952, Oma and Opa had considered their options, talking at night, weighing the risks. Yet in all that time, despite all those footsteps that covered up their words but not their anxiety, Oma and Opa had not been able to agree what to do. No option presented itself as better, safer, sounder than the rest. Then, with Großmutter Hilde's illness and one terse letter—"Am very sick" on blue lined paper—their big chance emerged. So many sayings for this moment. When one door closes, another opens. Every crisis is an opportunity. Making lemonade out of lemons. The list is long, but Oma and Opa thought only one thing: now is the time.

Oma applied for a permit for a week-long trip to the West. For herself, Tante Lara, and Mom. Not for Opa. She'd been told that having a clear reason to return made it more likely they'd get the permit. "But that's not the real plan," Oma told Tante Lara and Mom that evening in Grimma. They would stay in the West, and Opa would follow a week later, making his way through the still porous streets of Berlin.

Still, even with a dying mother and a husband allegedly staying behind, it hadn't been easy to get the papers. Especially that fall. There was the little guy with the eyebrows, the Party, poor Frank Hauser, the stack of papers on the school director's desk, Tante Lara's refusal to join the FDJ. All strikes against a permit. So Opa asked the Soviet commandant for one more favor, playing on his emotions, painting the picture of Oma's sick mother, her last chance to see her grandkids. A tough ask, but the commandant pulled strings, as he always had, for the man who looked like his son.

Until the very end, the inner circle was small. Only Oma and Opa at first. Then, on the very last night, Tante Lara and Mom became part of this pact they had not known existed. There they were in the kitchen, Tante Lara at the counter looking out the window, Oma, Opa, and Mom at the table, when Oma said, "There's something you need to know."

Oma explained the plan, using too many words, turning first to the past then to the future for justification. "We have no choice given what's happened. We need to think of what lies ahead." Tante Lara stared at the stakes in the garden, willing them to live up to their promise of a future in this house. But they remained motionless, useless, marking spots where flowers should have replaced dirt. Mere pieces of wood.

"And so we were leaving," Tante Lara said to us so many years later at her kitchen table in Bonn. "The very next day. Not to visit our grandmother, but forever. Despite all the obvious signs, we hadn't expected it. No clear warning, and then a totally new life. I guess that's why I remember the trip so clearly. I remember wondering why they told us at all. Thinking that they shouldn't have said anything until we were across, because both your mom and I were so nervous." Tante Lara touched Mom's arm. For a moment, they were lost together in a world we didn't know. Then Tante Lara dropped her hand again.

That last night in Grimma became a night of packing and priorities. They each had two small suitcases. More would have aroused suspicions. What do you pack to represent a lifetime? Funny what made the cut. Mom, who thought she was too old for dolls, took books, clothes, games. Tante Lara, who really was too old, filled an entire suitcase with stuffed animals. But Mom snuck in porcelain, one piece from each of the patterns they'd had growing up. An eggcup with light pink roses, a small saucer with softly painted blue onions, a blue teacup with raised white spots. By the time Tante Lara climbed out the window to see Konni, all the bags were full, and Mom was fast asleep. But Oma and Opa sat at the kitchen table awaiting the morning.

The next day was a cold, sunny January day with whiffs of white crossing the sky. Opa took Oma and the girls to the train station in a car he'd borrowed from a neighbor. It had snowed the night before, and the streets were slick despite the sun. The snowflakes that coated the fields white lay almost transparent on the asphalt, sun and cold battling, holding the flakes in a steady state between freezing and melting. A few more hours and the streets would be dry, the white gone from the fields. Opa and Oma kept the farewells short, appropriate for a quick trip. Nothing grand, though Opa couldn't help giving the girls a few extra squeezes before letting them go. They'd see each other again in a week. In a different world.

Years later, when he finally did arrive at the Bodensee, Opa told Oma, Tante Lara, and Mom his version of that day. Once and only once, as if he could only bear to relive it one time. He told them how his stomach had pulled and twisted as the train left the station. He watched it grow smaller, carrying with it his wife and two daughters. Would they make it across the border safely? But he reassured himself: why would anyone question their permit? When he could no longer see the train, Opa steered the car back toward town. He'd asked to meet the commandant for a drink after Oma's train departed. All part of the plan to allay suspicions, to be doubly sure that no one would suspect more than a short trip to see a dying mother. "I'll be all alone," he'd told the commandant. "I could use the company."

The commandant was at the corner table, a familiar sight. Was it his sentimental side that had kept him in Grimma through all the comings and goings of different troops, bridging different phases of the occupation and beyond? Or was it a function of distant, inexplicable commands from above? Opa had never known. He'd just been grateful. Over the years he'd told himself that his gratitude was self-serving only. A means to an end. But now, seeing the commandant for what would surely be the last time, he was overcome by a surprising sadness.

Opa watched the commandant survey the room. It was unlikely that he was listening to any of the conversations, Opa decided. Even unlikelier that he would have been interested in them. His interest lay not in the power that came from information but in the power that accompanied hierarchy. Unquestioned power. Power that simply was. No need for spying, threats, and blackmail. No, the commandant's vision of power was almost sentimental. Together, power and sentiment allowed him to view the town as his town, the bar as his bar, the people as his people. To think of himself as part of it, magnanimous in his control. Opa saw it in his face, in the satisfaction layered at the corner of his eyes and mouth, in the angle of his raised chin, laying claim to everything and everyone around him. And in that look Opa recognized himself. He thought of his own girls, the way he'd watched them do the simplest of things when they were small. Tie their shoes. Read a book. Play in the sand. His girls. The satisfaction of possession. Just the flip side of belonging. Sometimes so innocent, sometimes so dangerous. And he stepped forward to have his last drink with the man whose dead son he had conjured and who now, in turn, conjured up for him his daughters, so recently departed for their new life.

By the time Opa and the commandant finished their drink, Oma, Tante Lara, and Mom were already at the border. The guard who took their papers on the train was a young man, light fuzz on his upper lip. He could almost have been one of Lara's classmates. Just a kid, awkward, unattractive, with strange eyes, the pupils small, the large irises a flat and uniform gray. Eyes that didn't focus on any single point, that seemed designed to capture everything in front of them all at once. He glanced briefly at the three passengers, turning their permit first one way, then the other, as if the words might change from a different perspective. Then he handed their papers back, gave them a nod, and moved on. To him, they were one of hundreds of transactions that day. To them, he was the end of the life they had known.

They got off the train at the first station in the West. From there, their path diverged from the official one listed on their permit. Different trains, different times, a different destination. Oma took Tante Lara and Mom not to the Bodensee for a brief visit with their dying grandmother, but to Gießen. To one of the facilities set up to process refugees from the East. They'd heard this was where they'd get their papers. That's how it worked.

They spent only a few days in Gießen. Busy days that made little mark on them, remained vague in Mom and Tante Lara's memories. Several barracks-like buildings, squat and low. Neither welcoming nor cold. At night they slept in a room with two bunk beds and a dresser below the window. The fourth bed was taken by a young woman from Chemnitz, also a teacher. While Tante Lara and Mom lay in bed, she and Oma traded stories in hushed tones, careful what they said, never revealing too much. Everyone had heard the rumors about the Stasi, knew that they had moles in these facilities. "Don't talk to anyone," Oma told Tante Lara and Mom, though she ignored her own advice.

During the days, they moved from one office to the next, holding on to the pieces of paper that laid out the stages of the process. "*Unsere Bibel*," Tante Lara joked. Mom went with Oma, but Tante Lara, at sixteen, had to navigate the system on her own. At each stage they got a stamp on a slip of paper, one more station completed. The conversations varied. Some quick and friendly, others like interrogations. Some aimed at discovering any intelligence ties they might have back East, others focused on how Oma would support herself in the West. At the end of each interview, no matter the tensions, they were sent off with a firm handshake.

"We'd expected to be there longer," Tante Lara said. "But I guess we got lucky. It can't have hurt that we had a place to go, the inn waiting for us." After less than a week, they were put on a train toward the Bodensee.

And Opa? Before their permit had even expired, before anyone suspected they weren't coming back, Opa was meant to cross the border from East to West Berlin. The plan was not a bad one. Yes, even movement through Berlin had become more difficult in the months since the tightening of the East-West border. There were more controls, more people watching. But the city remained a loophole nevertheless. A sprawling metropolis with webs of streets and train tracks, a wild mess of movement in different directions.

"When I think back on all that, I imagine it as a long-exposure photo," Tante Lara said, waving her arms to illustrate what she meant. "You know, one of those nighttime shots with the squiggles and lines from all the headlights mapping everyone's paths, layered one on top of the other. We all think of the Wall now, impenetrable with guns and towers, but back then, before the Wall was built, there was so much motion back and forth."

Many of those illuminated trails tied East to West and West to East. Buses and trams no longer bridged the two halves of the city, but some trains still linked the zones, cutting across the boundary lines of the divided, connected city. People boarded those trains for countless reasons. Some commuted across the sector line to find work, some were simply passing through West Berlin to reach another destination in the East, others were looking to hop off in the West to buy something. But some were planning to leave forever. And so the trains also carried customs officials following the residents, looking for suitcases or other telltale signs of departure. And, in turn, those same trains also carried secret police observing the customs officials observing the residents. An ever-growing ladder of people watching people watching people. Leaving was dangerous, yes, but during that first half of 1953, tens of thousands of people risked it each month.

Opa was meant to be one of them. They'd mapped the route ahead of time. He'd be traveling with a friend, a colleague who also wanted to make the jump. Together they'd get on a train that would take them through West Berlin. Both had a cover story ready (a final destination in East Berlin), and neither would bring much luggage. Then they'd get off at the first stop in the Western half of the city and make their way to one of the facilities set up for refugees fleeing through Berlin.

At that point, the plan got fuzzy. Not many details, more an outline, a sketch, a leap of faith. Oma and Opa hadn't had enough information to plan more. Hadn't known what would happen when they each arrived, hadn't had anyone to ask. They had simply trusted that somehow, at some point, after Gießen, after Berlin, after all the process and paperwork in both places, they'd meet up at the Bodensee. They'd all be together.

Tante Lara stopped and finished the last bit of coffee in her cup, walked to the sink, rinsed it out, and placed it on the counter. She was wearing a stack of bangles on each arm, the kind of shiny silver and gold bracelets with bright inlaid stones usually worn by younger women.

"We never did get to see your great-grandmother Hilde," she said. "Would you believe it, she died the day before we took the train from Gießen to the Bodensee." Tante Lara lowered her hands to her sides, and all the bracelets fell to her wrists with a clang. "So not only were your mom and I arriving in the unknown, but your Oma paid us no attention in those first weeks. She was all tied up with funeral arrangements. With the property. Grieving a mother she barely knew anymore."

Mom stared at her cup. "I'd forgotten all about those weeks. They passed so quickly."

"To me they were endless," Tante Lara said.

Each morning during that first month, Oma walked to her mother's grave in the cemetery one village over, watered the flowers, and walked back home. A long walk, one we'd later do many times by bike, but back then Oma didn't have a bike, or much of anything else. Only what had been in her suitcase, and what remained in her mother's house. So she walked first along the road, then on a smaller path through the reeds, finally into the gravelly cemetery, low and flat. Even the stones were angled back, almost flat on the ground. Mom and Tante Lara went with Oma once during those first weeks, and they asked about the stones, why everything was so horizontal. But Oma shrugged. This place was new to her too. She had no answers.

Each day when she returned from the grave, she spent hours looking through the files of the inn. It had been closed since well before her mother's death. Großmutter Hilde had planned ahead when she saw the end coming. There'd been no guests for weeks, no new bookings, the windows all shuttered, no supplies in the kitchen, dust in the corners. But Oma was determined to open again in time for summer. When Mom and Tante Lara asked about plans, about school, she said, "We'll figure it out." And when they asked about Opa, she always said, "He'll be here soon." Only at night, once she thought they were both sleeping, did she let her worries out. Twenty-eight nights of crying in bed. Tante Lara counted them through the wall.

Then one night, Opa's friend showed up. Mom was already asleep upstairs, but Tante Lara was still reading in the living room. She watched Oma cling to the man in the hallway. Oma grabbed him by the arms, as if trying to wring a second person out of him, but he was solid as could be. Tante Lara heard every word that followed and remembered them still. It was, after all, the moment she thought she had lost her father forever. And it was his name she heard first.

"Uwe didn't make it," his friend said.

"What do you mean 'didn't make it'? Is he all right?" Oma asked, her voice rising until the man put his hand on her shoulder to calm her down.

"He stayed back."

"Stayed back? What do you mean he stayed back?"

Opa's friend dropped his hand, and his arms hung by his side. His head hung down too. Everything about him drooped. "I went to pick him up at your house in Grimma, but he wasn't waiting outside. So, I went in, even though I hadn't planned to get out of the car. I didn't want anyone to see me, you know. And he was sitting on the sofa. He kept saying, *Ich kann das alles nicht zurücklassen.*" I can't leave all this behind.

"I don't understand." Oma's voice rose again. And again, the man put his hand on her shoulder.

"He must have been scared," he said.

This time, Oma stepped out from under his hold and faced him head on. But Opa's friend shrugged, eyes down. He didn't know more. He was no use.

Tante Lara never did learn the man's name. He didn't make it past the hallway, instead turned and walked out again, closing the front door quietly, leaving Oma behind. Tante Lara turned the TV off and went upstairs to get ready for bed. That night Tante Lara once again heard Oma crying. The twenty-ninth night. She listened to see if the crying sounded different from other nights, but it was just crying.

The next morning Tante Lara and Mom came downstairs to their favorite breakfast, apple pancakes, the apple slices browned perfectly on top. The table was set with flowers from the garden and Großmutter Hilde's fancy blue-and-white-striped plates. They ate in silence, Tante Lara unwilling to talk until Oma did, Mom still waking up, oblivious. Only when they had begun to clear away the plates did Oma say, "Girls, I need to tell you something."

What did one small deception matter in the face of betrayal? Who could fault Oma? She told them that Opa hadn't been able to make it across, that he'd wanted to join them, desperately, more than anything, but that he'd been stopped, had been brought back home. Tante Lara knew it was a lie, knew that being brought home was not the consequence of a failed flight, knew that Opa would have been interrogated, probably imprisoned. Knew without a doubt that if Opa was at home, it was by choice. And she had heard enough the night before to confirm this.

"But I didn't say anything, then or later." Tante Lara looked across her kitchen table at Mom now. "You believed it, I wanted you to believe it."

Mom didn't move. After a long pause, Tante Lara added, "But now I'm not sure I would say Opa made a choice. I've thought about it a lot. I think it was an inability to make a choice. A fear of making a decision he might regret. So, he took the default. Stayed with what he knew. He couldn't imagine anything else." She laughed. "Such a storyteller. Yet so little imagination."

"What if it wasn't a default?" Martin said abruptly. "What if it was the one place he felt he belonged? What if it meant that much to him? Grimma, the house, everything?"

Neither Mom nor Tante Lara answered, but I heard their unspoken question: *More than us?* Maybe Martin heard it too. He winced and closed his eyes. I thought of the way I'd found him in Greta and Klaus's hallway in Grimma, standing in front of the photo of the house with his eyes shut. It had made no sense to me then—the way he was looking and avoiding all at the same time. No more sense than the way kids close their eyes in a game of hide and seek, thinking they can't be seen as long as they can't see. But we could see him. We were all studying him.

Finally, Mom turned to Tante Lara, ignoring Martin's interruption. "I think you're right. But what an irony. In the end, he spent the rest of his life regretting. First his decision to stay. Then his decision to go."

Tante Lara reached behind her and wiped her hands on a towel hanging below the sink. Then she said, "Well." As if that settled the matter.

Tante Lara didn't see her father for five years after they left Grimma. By the time he made his way west, she was studying art at the Kunstakademie Düsseldorf, far from the Bodensee. And Mom was on vacation with her friends. Neither one of them at home when he walked through the door. All they got was a telegram. "Your father here. Return now."

"Why did he come at all?" I asked.

Tante Lara shrugged. "I don't really know. I don't even know what he did during those years. I certainly don't know why he changed his mind. I don't know any of the details of how he managed to come west, though that was still before the Wall went up, so I assume he came through Berlin like he'd planned to do years earlier."

"You never asked about any of that?" Martin said. "How could you not ask?"

Tante Lara shook her head. "Those questions felt like they were taboo. But I'm not sure I would have asked anyway. Maybe I was angrier than I thought."

"All I know," Mom said, "is that at some point, even I no longer believed he actually *wanted* to come. I was angry for so long. And then, just when I'd finally lost interest, he showed up." She looked at Tante Lara, and something passed between them. A kind of mutual grace that softened their faces. Then Mom looked back down at the table. "In some ways, I never forgave him. Sometimes I think I've never really trusted anyone since."

Tante Lara was still standing with her back against the sink. Now she walked over to the table and rested her right hand on Mom's shoulder. With her other hand she adjusted her bangles one by one until the colorful stones were all facing out. Finally, she said, "Well then, what shall we do this evening?"

That night, as I was falling asleep, I thought about Opa. I'd thought about him more during the past few days than I had in years, decades almost. Sometimes I had seen Opa fix things at the inn. When a door started sticking or the washing machine (always in motion, churning out crisp white sheets for the guests) began to shake precariously on the slanted basement floor, Opa would grab his toolbox, head through the garden to the inn, and disappear in the hallways or in the basement. "*Alles gut*," he'd say when he returned, sinking low in his chair in the darkened living room, shades half-closed to keep out the summer sun. We always called Seefrieden "Oma's inn." It was her peace at the lake. He never found his.

9

Searching for Dad

Illinois, 1970–1972

Mom might not have forgiven her father, might never have fully let go of her resentment, but the fact is, he came back. Our dad never did.

Truth is, there were days when I didn't think about Dad at all in those early months after he left. I was only seven. Old enough to have memories, young enough to forget. But of course, I missed him. I missed his hugs at night before bed, his arms encircling me as if he could wrap them around me twice. I missed the jokes he used to tell, the way his eyes lit up and his hands began to flutter even before he started. Above all, I missed the lightness he brought to our family, the way he balanced Mom's severity. And yet, I don't think I felt his absence the same way Martin felt it. The accusation in his departure.

We visited him for the first time about six months after he'd left us. Looking back, it's hard to imagine we hadn't seen him at all in those first six months, but Mom was strict. It wasn't until he finally agreed to enter rehab in the early summer of 1970 that Mom let us see him. Martin and I dressed up, not because Mom asked us to, but because Martin wanted to. He chose his own clothes, the khaki pleated pants and striped light-blue-and-white button-down shirt that made him look like the lawyer we didn't yet know he would become. Dad was the one who'd bought the pants and shirt for him, and Mom had rolled her eyes when he first tried them on. "He's got plenty of time to be an adult," she'd said to Dad back then. But now she smiled at Martin. And because Martin was dressed up, I too chose a dress from my closet. Dark blue with small light-blue flowers and a shiny royal-blue sash around the waist. All shades of my favorite color.

Martin walked into the building ahead of Mom and me, the sliding doors opening to release a blast of air-conditioning we had to push through. After signing in, we were pointed to a room at the end of the long first-floor hallway. I was disappointed. I'd expected Dad to meet us out front, arms wide for one of those two-times-around hugs. I wanted my feet to dangle in the air as he held me. Instead, he was on the other side of a closed beige door. Martin had stepped behind Mom, so she was the one who pushed that door open. Dad was in a chair at the window. He looked like Dad and yet altogether different. He had the same hair, the same eyes, more or less the same shape. Even the same clothes. But everything seemed to hang. He was listless, though I wouldn't have known that word then. Still, it was clear he'd been waiting for us. He'd found a chessboard and set it up on the table in front of him.

"I didn't know you could play chess," Martin said, stepping out from behind Mom again.

Dad smiled, and though it seemed an effort, his eyes lightened.

"I've had a lot of time." He glanced at Mom apologetically, then back at Martin. "I've learned. Do you want me to teach you?" And that's how they found their new mutual language. So quickly, so easily.

Dad's room was small and empty—his bed, the table, four upholstered dining chairs, and one armchair. The upholstery on the chairs, light gray with narrow pink stripes, matched the light-gray carpet and the thick pink curtains. Even the sheets looked gray, though I imagine they had once been white. I was used to our house with its bright wooden floors. Here, the fabric absorbed sounds and motions, slowed everything down. Muted colors, muted sounds, and my muted father.

I sat in the armchair at the foot of Dad's bed, while he and Martin played chess. Mom took one of the dining chairs and sat by the door. Now, looking back, I feel like nodding in recognition. I want to tell Mom: *I understand you. I understand the need to be ready for escape.* But back then I felt her decision to sit at the door was meant as a lesson for me: don't get too close to him! And I resented that instruction, resented my own obedience, sitting off to the side in the armchair, watching while my brother learned yet another move. The bishop's diagonal slide or the knight's jerky zigzag. Martin's hands were on his own chess pieces, but his eyes followed Dad's eyes. *Look at the pieces*, I wanted to yell, the way Dad used to yell when they were practicing baseball together, Dad pitching to Martin again and again. "Keep your eyes on the ball, Martin, not on me," he would say. But chess was different than baseball. This was a different game altogether.

After that first visit, Mom took us to see Dad every few weeks. He changed rehab centers frequently, sometimes thirty minutes away, sometimes as far as an hour. I never asked why, and Mom never explained. As the months passed, the time between visits grew. Almost imperceptibly at first, then longer and longer, as if Mom were trying to wean us. Until one night in the early spring of 1972, just after my tenth birthday, she sat us down at the kitchen table. Dad had been gone two and a half years by then, and we only saw him rarely. We'd drive to whichever low, square building he was currently living in, park our car as close to the sliding doors as we could, and enter a different world. A world that seemed more distorted, more distant each time.

"I got a call from Dad's rehab center a couple nights ago," Mom told us at the kitchen table. "He's left again, like last time. And the time before."

She stopped and picked at the skin around her fingernails on her right hand. I thought she had forgotten she was talking to us, but then she said, "What I haven't told you is that he's left a note every time he leaves rehab. A note telling us not to find him, not to follow him."

Martin pushed his chair back and inhaled. A sharp breath. Quiet, but still enough to make Mom look up.

"It's not that he doesn't want to see you. I know that. He wants to see you, but he feels guilty. Feels he can't be who he should be." She paused and pulled her sleeve over her right hand, hiding the torn cuticles.

"Here's the thing," she finally said. "I'm going to take him at his word this time. I'm not going to find him. I can't keep overriding his wishes, even if he's wrong. And I don't want you two caught up in all this. It's not fair to you."

"What's not fair, Mom?" Martin's voice was low, almost a whimper. "He's our dad. Our dad!"

"You're right. It's not fair either way. But sometimes you have to choose. You can't fix everything." Mom rested her hand briefly on Martin's shoulder, then stood up, suddenly focused. "So, that's that," she said. "Time to get ready for bed."

She should have known Martin better. It was in those months, when the rhythm of our visits slowed, then stopped altogether, that Martin began hatching the plan for our ill-fated excursion to find Dad. Finally, in late June 1972, he was ready.

Mom was busy with all the arrangements for our upcoming summer trip to Germany. At least that part of our routine hadn't changed. So she didn't notice when Martin pulled his hiking backpack out of his closet and began filling it, bit by bit each day. He didn't tell me much either. Only, "We're going to find Dad." I didn't ask how we could find him when we didn't even know where he was. I just assumed Martin knew more than I did. After all, he was already thirteen.

The Saturday before our departure, Mom went to the school where she taught one last time to pick up a few things she needed over the summer. Preparations for the next school year. We listened for the click of the door, the sound of the garage door opening, the car engine starting. Then Martin said, "Now."

It was sunny when we left the house, already the heavy haze of summer. We must have been a strange sight, the two of us walking alone up Race Street, Martin swaying side to side, his large hiking pack extending above his head, me struggling to keep up. Something was loose in the bag. It rattled as we headed away from our neighborhood, creating a rhythm just for us. I adjusted my step to the sound until we were walking in unison. There was almost no traffic, and the quiet only deepened as we walked past Windsor Road into the cornfields beyond.

We'd been out this way before on bikes. Another one of Mom's crazy ideas, her desire to recreate the bike trips of her childhood, except here the roads were straight and flat, no lake shining between trees. The only shimmer came from the mirages on the hot gray road. We saw those flickers ahead of us in every slight dip. And each time, we sped up to see if we could reach them, but they disappeared as soon as we approached, our feet kicking up the loose gravel that covered these roads. Occasionally a car passed us, and Martin straightened up as tall as he could, tried to look fully grown.

For a while we walked straight, until we came to a T-intersection. Martin turned left without hesitating, and I followed. From that point on, we turned first right, then left, zigzagging our way diagonally across the landscape, along those crisp squares that we saw from the plane whenever we flew home from Germany. From above, some looked green, others brown, others yellow. A pattern that continued as far as we could see. But from the ground, we saw none of this. Wherever we walked, there was only the deep, shining green of the looming corn. We did pass a few homes, low one-story ranch houses, dogs barking, a few tricycles or banana-seat bikes scattered on the driveways. But no other sign of children, of people.

At some point, I couldn't go any farther. We must have been on the road for a couple of hours by then because the sun was beginning to drop lower in the sky. Not low enough to give us any relief from the heat that reflected from the tar and gravel, but low enough to feel like a taunt. Or a threat. The day's almost over and you're not there yet?

And I answered that taunt with my own question, the one all kids ask. "Are we almost there yet?" When Martin didn't respond, I sat down, cross-legged, at the edge of the road, the gravel pressing into my calves and ankles. I wanted to sit completely still, my very own protest, but the road was so hot against my skin that I had to shift every few seconds. Finally, I scooted onto the narrow strip of grass up against the corn, but the stalks provided no respite from the setting sun that shone a straight line down the road toward me.

Martin kept walking another twenty, thirty steps, then turned and came back. He dropped his backpack onto the ground. "Let's take a break."

"Where are we?" I asked, but Martin stared straight ahead.

"Can I have something to drink?"

Martin took the bottle out of his pack. We'd already stopped for water a few times along the way, and now we saw that the bottle was empty.

"What else did you pack?" I asked. Again Martin didn't answer. So I pulled the pack toward me. When I opened it, the first thing I saw was the chess set Dad had given Martin on one of our earlier visits. A heavy wooden box that held all the pieces and doubled as a board. I took it out to see what was below. Still hopeful. Still expecting more water, some food. But all I saw were clothes. All of Martin's fancy clothes, and a few of my dresses. There were shoes too. Two pairs of leather shoes for him, a pair of flats and a pair of sandals for me. This time Martin spoke. "Well, we had to be ready for the visit."

I stood and brushed the gravel from the back of my legs before bending over and picking up the chess set. Then, without looking at Martin, I threw it down onto the road as hard as I could. The box cracked open, and the chess pieces scattered, black and white accents amidst the gravel. Just as small in their surroundings, just as forlorn, as

Martin and me. That's when I began to cry. Martin walked over to the box and picked it up. I guess it must have been badly cracked because he dropped it again, then kicked it. One sharp, quick kick. It skittered across the road, landing in the grass on the other side, and we both stared at it. Martin didn't make a sound. No crying, no yelling. No protest. Eventually I had to stop crying too. I suppose all emotions have expiration dates, even if we don't want to admit it. Even if we want to believe feelings go on forever.

What I remember most about the next few hours, as it turned dark, is my anger. Anger that prevented me from talking with Martin or even looking at him. First, he tried to plan. "It's best if we stay here. It'll be easier to find us." Then, he tried to console. "I'm sure they'll come," and "Mom won't leave us here." But I didn't accept any of his overtures. Maybe I needed to be angry so I wouldn't be afraid. And eventually, inevitably, he turned angry too, defending himself against my wordless rage. "You chose to come along. You could have said something. This is your fault too." Then we sat still as the sun set and the sky grew dark and heavy around us. The white chess pieces glimmered in the moonlight, scattered shards of reflected radiance. Martin never said a word about the broken chess set. Not then, not later.

We heard Mom's side of the story many times afterwards. How she worried when she got home and found us missing, how she called all our friends' parents to find us, how worry became panic, how she went to the police. At first, they told her there was nothing they could do. We hadn't been missing long enough. So she called one of her friends, a journalist at the local paper, who arrived at the police station with a pad and a pen, straight from a dinner party, threatening to write an article. And suddenly the police were accommodating, sent out multiple squad cars. Mom had noticed the missing backpack and correctly guessed that we'd start any trip by heading up Race Street. This gave the police a sense of direction. Still, it took them hours to find us, and even then, it was a stroke of luck that they happened to drive down the road we were on. One of so many they could have searched.

At first, Mom's story was an angry one, told as a warning. ("Don't ever do anything like that again!") Then it became sad. ("I'm sorry I wasn't there when you needed me.") Finally, it entered Mom's repertoire of anecdotes—funny, worth retelling to others. ("When Susie got to the station, she was still tipsy from dinner, a little over the top, a little crazy," and "I bet the police were more scared of her than of what she'd write!") Both Martin and I grew quiet whenever Mom told this version of the story. Even as she laughed, even as her friends smiled, Martin and I shrank. Sometimes she would turn to us and say, "Isn't that right, Kate, Martin?" But that was her story, not ours. We never answered. Our story was not for sharing.

Mom did find Dad again after that day, tracking him down for Martin's sake and, I suppose, for mine. We visited him a few more times that next year, before our trips came to a complete end. But Martin refused to play chess on those visits. In fact, he never played chess again. Years later, Mom told me that she'd found a few chess pieces in the corner of Martin's closet after he'd packed up his childhood belongings in Illinois. A bishop, a knight, a few pawns. "He kept them all those years," Mom said, "only to leave them behind in the dust." She looked at me as if I could explain, but I couldn't. I just knew this: Martin's damage was different from mine. I'd known it the instant the chess set cracked as it hit the road. I'd seen it in the way he stood, arms held tightly at his side, chin pulled down to his chest. And I'd heard it in the silence after he'd kicked the chess set into the gravel. We would have had a lot to talk about on that moonlit road, I think. If only I'd been willing to talk.

Part IV

On the Trail of Loss

1990
1953–1958

10

A Family Funeral

Bonn, October 1990

Tante Lara died on October 1st, 1990, a few months after we'd last seen her in Grimma, just days before East and West Germany became one country again. She'd suffered from headaches throughout our trip, some bad. We assumed they came from stress or excitement, and we gave them no further thought. It turned out she'd already been suffering for many months. Nearly a year. But she hadn't visited a doctor until the headaches became so bad she had to force herself out of bed some mornings, until her vision blurred. That was about a month before our trip. Only then did she discover these were the symptoms of a fast-growing brain tumor. She didn't tell us at the time, wanted to make it through one last family trip without pity, without special care. Wanted also, I now understood, to share all those stories with us before it was too late. What an effort it must have been.

"Tough old cow," Mom said bitterly over the phone.

"Mom would know," I told Martin later that day on a separate call. Dark humor for dark conversations.

Tante Lara had finally called Mom with the news in mid-September. By that point she was having difficulty swallowing. Eating and drinking were a chore. Even she couldn't hide the news any longer.

"*Ich hab' nur Wochen. Höchstens Wochen,*" she said matter-of-factly. Weeks at most. Mom flew to Bonn right away. The next evening she called me from Tante Lara's third-floor guest room.

"Kate, it's bad," she started, not even waiting for me to say hello. "The doctors say it's down to days now, not weeks. Even they are surprised by how quickly it all went. She's so frail. You know how she used to have that spring in her step? Now all she can do is lie flat. She is flat. There's no depth to her at all." Mom paused, and I could hear her staccato breathing.

"She's not coming home anymore," Mom finally continued. "I took her to an appointment after I arrived, and they moved her straight to a hospice facility in the hospital. They wouldn't even let me try to take her home for one more night."

I pulled the phone cord, stretching it like an accordion, then let it snap back. The sound cut through me sharply. "Mom," I said. "It's probably better for her anyway. You couldn't have helped her. She's got what she needs there."

"I know, but I'm the one who took her to the appointment. I'm the one who took her away from the house, and she left without even one last look around. She didn't expect…" Mom stopped talking, and in the silence, I smelled the musty scent of the old books that lined the room she was sitting in, mixed with the smell of the lilacs that often bloomed when we visited Tante Lara during our German summers. Of course, there wouldn't be any lilacs in the room with Mom now. Not in October.

"Mom," I said, "it wasn't your decision."

"I know."

"Should Martin and I come?"

But Mom didn't want us there, wanted to have these last days alone with her sister. "And anyway," she added, "Tante Lara can't handle any commotion."

After Mom hung up, I imagined her walking down the hallway, past Tante Lara's bedroom, to the oversized bathroom with its wide-planked floors. Perhaps she was sitting on the stool by the vine-covered window, as I so often had done, gazing past the garden walls to the windows of the houses beyond, those scattered squares of light, and wondering about the many people who lived so near, whom we rarely saw but often heard, their voices lifted by the summer breeze.

While Mom spent those final days with Tante Lara, Martin and I started making travel plans. It felt macabre to be organizing the trip before our beloved aunt had even died, and yet there were a lot of plans to be made. Darren was eager to join us, interested in witnessing reunification in action, but he couldn't get away in the middle of the semester, and deep down, I was relieved. This was about our family, not history. I wanted to be with Mom and Martin.

Martin was the one who first suggested staying beyond the funeral.

Partly, it was practical. He had recently moved, and his new house was still being renovated, no real place to call his own yet. He'd already arranged to stay longer in Germany for business, and it turned out he was eager to add even more days and places.

"Why not squeeze in another visit to Grimma?" he said. "An unanswered questions tour."

I couldn't help thinking of Klaus leaning on the kitchen counter, feet pressed against the floor, his face a harsh mask.

"Why would we disturb them again?" I shook off the image with a jittery shrug. "How about we go to the Bodensee instead? A tour of our own memories, not other people's memories."

But to my surprise, Martin pushed back. "Not there. Not the Bodensee," he said.

We spoke a few more times that same week, and each time I asked him. "Why not? Why on earth not?" It was only when I reminded him that Opa's oldest friend Sepp would be at the Bodensee—Sepp, who'd grown up in Grimma too, had fled west a few years after Opa—that we finally agreed to a compromise. I'd go to Grimma with him if he came to the Bodensee with me.

"Fine," he said, "as long as we can talk to Sepp." Then he hung up quickly, and I was left with the uncomfortable feeling I'd won a fight I didn't understand.

When we called Mom and asked if she wanted to come along, she said, "I'd rather not. I don't need to dig around in the past. I'm focused on Tante Lara right now." I'm sure Martin felt the rebuke as strongly as I did, but we never talked about it. We kept planning our trip until we got the call from Mom. "Tante Lara died today."

Martin and I met in New York so we could be on the same flight to Frankfurt. "We have things to discuss before we get there," he'd said on the phone. The airport was busy for early October, but we found two seats together in a dark corner in the departure lounge, surrounded by what looked like a high school marching band. Tall girls with high ponytails and awkward boys with braces, all sprawled on the filthy carpet, playing cards and chatting so loudly that I felt I had an excuse not to talk. But once Martin and I boarded the flight and settled into our seats, he turned to me. "Kate, we need to think about what has to get done." His features always grew more pointed when he concentrated, his top lip sharp and contoured, the tip of his nose more defined. Even his cheekbones seemed to rise more steeply from the stubble of his half-beard. I knew that face from intense childhood games of Battleship, which Martin always won, sinking my last ship with a dramatic flourish and a sly grin.

Of course, he was right. There was a lot we needed to plan. And so we spent nearly the full eight hours in the air talking about funeral arrangements, about money and wills, about Tante Lara's house. We both agreed it should be sold, of course, along with pretty much everything in it, though I already had in mind a few items I wanted to keep. And I imagined Martin did too. I could only hope we weren't both chasing the same memories.

We landed in Frankfurt in thick, rainy fog. Through the train window on the ride to Bonn, we traced the Rhine as it curved between cliffs and scattered towns. We greeted every familiar sandbar and ruined castle along the way, nudging each other, saying, "*Guck mal.*" Look! The closer we got to Bonn, the more it poured, strings of raindrops drawing lines on the windows, until finally we could only see our own faces in the well-lit train car reflected against the impenetrable sky.

We had told Mom not to pick us up at the station and instead grabbed a taxi, arriving the same way we always used to arrive as a family. When we got out of the taxi, both of us instinctively glanced toward the top window where Tante Lara usually waited for us. I could picture her there, leaning out precariously, waving too long before running down the many stairs, leaving us standing tired, heavy with luggage, impatient for her steps on the tile floor of the entry. But Mom came to the door quickly. She gave each of us a hug and guided us past the rows of wooden coat hooks still overloaded with Tante Lara's jackets. They rustled in our breeze as we walked toward the kitchen, and the scent of Tante Lara filled the hallway.

Mom had made tea, which we drank slowly from Tante Lara's bright cups. Red and yellow patterns. Birds with wild plumage. At first we listened to the gurgling of the water heater in the corner. Then I asked, "Mom, how are you?"

Under different circumstances, I imagine Mom would have said, half-critically, half-humorously, "There's the American in you, always needing to fill the silence." But now she raised her head and said, "I'm okay. Better now that you're here." Then, after another slow sip of tea, she shifted in her chair. "We've got a lot to do before the funeral."

It was a small crowd in the end. A dozen or so people, black umbrellas, standing under a tree near the grave. Mom read "*Vergänglichkeit*," Herman Hesse's poem about transience. It was, on the surface, a fitting choice, arguably even too obvious with its reference to the wind blowing over a grave. For Mom, Martin, and me, however, it had another meaning. Hesse, the poet who had lived at the Bodensee in a house with an overflowing garden, reminded us of summers with Oma and Opa, of evening walks along blackberry hedges, of eating afternoon cake with Oma in the wood-trimmed dining salons on board the boats crisscrossing the lake, of the sound of bike tires on dirt paths deep in the woods, and of course, of the lush gardens that were so common there, flowers tumbling on top of each other, growing over gates, and encroaching on paths. So meticulously tended to appear wild.

Then Mom spoke of the distance she had felt living in Illinois, how difficult it had been to stay in touch, how long-distance calls felt unacceptably luxurious in the early days. I began to worry that Mom had forgotten that these people didn't know her, didn't want to hear about her. But Mom surprised me. I knew her as my all-too-practical mom, so I sometimes forgot that she'd spent decades constructing and perfecting lectures, standing in front of surly teenagers, breaking through their defenses, creating beautiful worlds of thought for them, all in a language not her own. Now she spoke of the packages that arrived each Christmas from Bonn, full of carefully selected items that breathed familiarity, bridged the distance between sisters, and warmed Mom in icy Illinois. She spoke of the treats—baked goods, of course, but also fountain pens and notebooks like those they'd had in school; paper napkins with the patterns of their childhood; shiny chestnuts gathered in the fall and saved for months, then sent to us together with toothpicks for making chestnut-men. Mom wove these simple items into metaphors, linking each one to a facet of Tante Lara's personality. She envisioned out loud how Tante Lara must have decided what to send each year, cocking her head and waving her hand with Tante Lara's dismissive flourish, then saying, as if Tante Lara were talking to herself, "*Ach was*, I already sent that last year. *Die Amerikaner brauchen ja immer was Neues*." The Americans—Mom glanced at Martin and me—always need something new. Laughter under the umbrellas. "But what Tante Lara sent was never something new," Mom continued. "She sent us our deepest memories, gathered with care and with love. And now we return the favor. By honoring her and remembering her."

Next to me, Martin was crying. I pulled his arm toward me and hooked it under mine just as Mom wrapped up by reading again the last lines of the Hesse poem. About writing names into the fleeting air. Letting things go. For a moment there was complete silence, then Tante Lara's friends clustered by the grave, each taking a flower from the vase that had been set there and dropping it into the hole, casting one look down before moving on. No one spoke, yet we were surrounded by sound. Steps on gravel. Fabric brushing up against fabric as people walked close together, not wanting to stand alone at the grave. Even the sound of the flowers landing on the casket below added to the layered tones of mourning. My own umbrella stood out, neon green. I had not considered that even something as practical as an umbrella should fit the occasion.

That night we sat again in Tante Lara's kitchen, relaxed now, relieved, even silly. Mom had found a couple bottles of red wine in the cellar, and we gathered around them.

"When I die," Mom said, "I don't want a funeral. Just a dinner. No grave, no casket, not even an urn. I don't care what happens to my ashes. I want a long wooden table, with lots of salad and lots of wine. Preferably outside in a garden under a trellis of vines, or it could be roses."

"So, I guess you'll have to die during the summer then, Mom." Martin grinned.

"You can count on it. I'll hold up my end of the bargain if you hold up yours."

"Deal. You got it. Dinner, vines, roses."

"Don't forget the wooden table. Rough, thick legs, nothing too elegant."

"Sort of like you then," Martin said, and all three of us winced and laughed.

"Who do you want at your dinner, Mom?" I asked.

"Oh, it doesn't really matter. People who've known me. People who want to tell stories. People who want to eat." She took a sip of wine and wiped her lips. "Really, did it matter who was there today? Lara doesn't know the difference, and I didn't know any of them anyway. So, you know what? Invite your friends, people you'd like to spend an evening with. I always liked that one college friend of yours, Louis, the one with the scruffy beard, sharp blue eyes. Invite him."

I laughed. "Louis it is. But seriously, Mom, what was Tante Lara like, at the end? Did she know what was happening?"

"It was wonderful to be here. And hard," Mom said. "Lara's bed was right by the window, and we watched other patients take walks in the hospital garden. Mainly old ladies, all dressed up. I wanted to take her for a walk too, but she was hooked up to so many different tubes. There's no way we could have unhooked them all. We even joked about it, whether we had time to get her unhooked before she died. She still had the same laugh, you know, high pitched, girlish. I mean, who has a laugh like that?"

I could hear Tante Lara's laugh in my head. Both Martin and Mom grinned, then quickly turned serious again.

After three or four days, Mom told us, Tante Lara started to slip away. Mom was not sure if it was the disease or the painkillers that were taking her. "Turns out I'm not good at dealing with death," she said. "I guess some people feel relief or peace or something like that, but I was so angry. Angry that I couldn't hold on. Angry that I hadn't asked her more. Why did I spend those days talking about the damn patients outside her window? My last chance to hear her stories. And I wasted it talking about some old woman's lace and shoes."

The regret in Mom's voice surprised me. Wasn't she always the one telling us to look forward? In Grimma, she'd been so quiet. Not saying much, not asking much. Letting Tante Lara take the lead. Now I put my hand on her arm and said, "Maybe that's all Tante Lara wanted to talk about. Lace and shoes."

"Who knows what she wanted? I couldn't tell, and I didn't ask. And by the end, she was too far gone to feel or want much of anything, I guess."

Tante Lara slept through Mom's last visit, and Mom didn't say goodbye. "I just left. I mean, there wasn't much point. She was on so many painkillers, she didn't even know I was there, and I didn't want to see her like that."

I picked up the bottle and filled our glasses.

"To Tante Lara," I said, lifting mine.

"To Tante Lara," Mom and Martin echoed.

We sat in the kitchen together for hours that night. After we finished our second bottle of wine, Martin and Mom began to argue about Tante Lara's fashion sense. "Those flowered hats, they're in again, you know. Bohemian. She was ahead of her time," Martin said.

Mom laughed. "You've seen the photos of what she wore to my wedding. That getup's never coming back in!" But my eyes were falling shut. So I grabbed their hands—Martin's with my left hand and Mom's with my right—squeezed hard, and said, "I never knew a goodbye could be so much fun." Even from the small guest room upstairs, I heard them laughing, no sign of slowing down. The warm light from the hallway shone through the mottled glass panes in the door, cradling me as I fell asleep.

The next morning, we were all business again. Before we left, we emptied the kitchen of all perishable foods, put everything on the kitchen table, and picked out things we could still eat before leaving. It was a sunny day, and, despite the cold, we ate our last lunch outside in the brick-walled garden in our coats.

"Kate," Mom said, as we huddled over the bit of bread and cheese we had gathered. "Martin and I were talking last night after you went to sleep. We decided it makes most sense if he handles the sale of the house, since he's in Germany for work often anyway. He's got connections to lawyers who can help. So, I'm going to give him power of attorney in Germany. I wanted to make sure that's all right with you."

Martin put down the piece of cheese he was holding and cleared his throat. "Of course, I'll check in with you on any decisions."

Mom grabbed our hands, mine and Martin's, lifting them onto the table in front of her, cupping her own hands over them.

"Okay," I said. "I guess that makes sense." The three of us sat in the sun around the round table, hands touching, almost as if we were ready to start the hand-stacking game Mom had played with us when we were kids, the bottom hand pulled out as quickly as possible, placed on the top, and then again and again, in an endless, ever quickening cycle. But this time we just savored the warmth of each other's touch.

Before leaving Tante Lara's house for what would be our last time, the three of us went from room to room, taking photos and documenting all the items we might want to keep. We didn't have the time or heart to divvy things up yet, but we needed to have a record. "We can work it out back home," Martin said. Then we put the camera away and gathered in the kitchen one last time, taking in the colors, the shapes, the way the light fell through the glass garden door onto the familiar cracks in the tiled floor.

Mom walked out of the house first. She turned around and glanced up at its tall façade, then back at us. "*Kommt schon, ihr beiden—das Taxi wartet.*" Come on, you two—the cab's waiting. Martin and I stood in the hallway, coats on, bags over our shoulders. Yet neither of us seemed willing to make the first move. I guess we both wanted to be in the house as long as possible, to be the last to set foot there. Finally, I put my hand behind his shoulder and guided him out the door. I did not look back as I stepped into the cab.

11

Opa's Last Game

The Bodensee, October 1990

As planned, Martin and I didn't head back to the U.S. right after the funeral. We'd agreed that we'd go to the Bodensee first, then on to Grimma. Before we got into the rental car outside Tante Lara's house in Bonn, Martin handed me a big manila envelope. "Just some prep for our second stop," he said. While Martin drove, I dug through the bundle of newspaper clippings he had collected over the past few months—all about East Germany, about reunification, about property claims and the rapidly evolving laws around restitution.

"Where did you get these?"

"Libraries, newsstands, anywhere with foreign newspapers," he said with a proud smile. "I may not be a professor like Darren, but I'm pretty resourceful, you know?"

The articles painted a broadly joyful picture of reunification, of progress and optimism. But between the lines I also saw confusion, haste, and mistrust. So many decisions being made in a short period of time leading up to reunification in October. And the more I read, the more I realized Martin wasn't alone in his focus on property. Property had been on everyone's mind that summer and fall of 1990. *Rückgabe vor Entschädigung* was the phrase I kept seeing in the paper snippets scattered on my lap. A few times I read the wrong side first—"Regional garden show draws record crowds"—before flipping it over. "Restitution before compensation." A principle, the articles explained, that meant prioritizing return of properties over financial compensation. Properties that people had lost through expropriation or because they'd had to flee the East or for any number of other reasons.

"Hey, Martin," I said. "Remember our conversation at Greta's house last time? About belonging?"

"Mm," he answered.

"I think Tante Lara was right. Maybe we didn't understand anything back then. We were too busy making fun of Greta's memories." In my mind, I corrected myself. *You were too busy, Martin.* But I didn't say it.

"Well, Greta didn't hear any of it. She wasn't even in the room."

"Still, we were jerks."

"I guess." Martin was distracted, focused on the road.

I put the articles back in the envelope and gazed out the window, thinking about that earlier trip. I had felt so close to Martin that day, a partners-in-crime kind of closeness, especially in the car on the way back to Leipzig from Grimma. Shoulder to shoulder, knee to knee. But now those memories mingled with guilt and discomfort. Sitting in Greta and Klaus's house, in the house where Oma and Opa had made the difficult decision to flee, we'd played right into all the stereotypes I saw reflected in those newspaper articles. We could have been the start of a joke. A lawyer and a landscape architect take a trip. But it wasn't a joke, us popping in from the West for a few days, judging, dismissing. Conflating Greta's regret about a life irreversibly changed with a backwardness that she may or may not have possessed. How could we possibly have known after one short afternoon? I still remembered Tante Lara chiding us in the car. The feeling of belonging could be real, even where you didn't belong. Even where you shouldn't have wanted to belong. Or was that simply longing?

"Martin?" I said.

"Mm?"

"Let's be more careful this time."

"I am careful. I always drive carefully!" As if to prove his point, Martin turned on his blinker, glanced over his shoulder with a demonstrative nod, and shifted into the left lane to pass. I decided to let it go. We still had a few days at the Bodensee before we headed to Grimma, a few days for me to work on him. Martin pulled back into the right lane, blinker off. Ahead of us we saw the first signs for the Bodensee.

I'd reached out to Sepp weeks earlier, telling him we'd be coming to see him, trying to connect the unsteady voice on the phone with the man I'd known during our Bodensee summers. The friend who'd accompanied Opa through life. But the truth is he'd been only a vague presence in our childhood years. Always around, yet somehow just another old man. A blur of wrinkles and a broad nose that shrank the rest of his face. Mainly I remembered the dock where he had worked, renting out pedal boats to tourists. And to Mom and us so we could swim in the deep, cool middle of the lake, suspended in that unending silk, soft on our skin. A shaky wooden plank led to the platform where Sepp used to stand from early morning to late afternoon, always pulling at ropes, shifting boats around. This is where Martin and I had arranged to meet him that day after Tante Lara's funeral. Our first time back since Oma had died sixteen years earlier—the end of our Bodensee summers.

He was waiting for us on the dock, still wrinkled and broad-nosed, but more distinct. He hadn't aged much. Or perhaps I only saw his age relative to my own. Despite the chill in the air, it was a sunny fall day, so we chose to sit on a bench across from the dock. This late in the year there were no pedal boats at all, and the dock looked lonely, a mere echo of our summer memories.

"You want to hear about your Opa. And about Grimma." Sepp greeted us with a handshake and got straight to the point. "We didn't talk about those times, your Opa and I, once I arrived here. Some things were better forgotten." His eyes, hidden among the wrinkles, moved from my face to Martin's and back again. "I'd have recognized you still," he then said.

"If you don't want to talk about it—" I started, but he put his hand on my arm.

"No, I'd love to tell you. It's been so long, and I have so many memories. His and mine. It's the least I can do for him."

Sepp began right at the beginning, when he and Opa were little. Sepp had grown up on a farm near Grimma. The old stone buildings—a long, squat house attached at a right angle to a long, squat barn—stood in a dip at a curve in the road, surrounded on all sides by hills spreading upwards. A low house on low land. "Not quite a castle," Sepp's father used to joke, and both Opa and Sepp knew what he meant, that castles always sat on high, poised to spot all threats coming their way. They were distant cousins, Sepp and Opa, brought together by one family's pity for the other, by the way Opa's parents always said, "That poor boy." And so, long before Opa understood that Sepp's mother had died the day Sepp was born, the two boys had moved beyond being distant cousins, were already the closest of friends. Opa always biked to visit Sepp. On the last hill down to the farm, Opa would lift his feet off the pedals, raising them out to the side, swerving down to the house along the tree-lined road, sunlight and shade casting fluttering shadows in his path. And Sepp would see him coming from below. Even in the speckled half-shade, Opa's outstretched legs gave him a silhouette unlike any other bikers who might come that way. At least that much could be spotted from the house.

They remained close friends through their teen years, into adulthood, working at the same factory, playing on the same soccer team. Even once Opa married Oma, they spent the evenings after work together almost every day. Sometimes at a bar, sometimes shooting the shit on a street corner. "*Zusammen Feierabend machen.*" Closing up shop together. That's what they called it. "Uwe's other wife." That's what Oma called Sepp, always winking to make sure Sepp knew she didn't hold it against him. On the contrary, he made her smile, and she made him feel part of something he himself did not have—a real family.

And so Sepp had felt regret and, above all, concern when Oma left, had listened carefully when Opa told him about those cold days in early 1953 after Opa chose to stay behind in Grimma. Those days when everything changed. Just two nights after Oma's travel permit expired, one day after she should have been back at school teaching, the first interrogators arrived at Opa's house. Simple suits, long winter coats. Some branch of the police or Stasi, Opa was not sure exactly who they were, and it didn't matter. He knew what they were there for, had practiced this scene in his head many times over the past days and nights, especially the nights, when the dark collapsed on him, all around him, the weight unbearable, sleep impossible. Did you know your wife was planning to leave? No. Did you help her plan her trip? No. Have you been in touch with your wife? No. Of his many no's, that last one, at least, was honest. He lay in bed thinking about what Oma was thinking, wondering if Oma was thinking about what he was thinking, a circle that drove him mad each night, chasing its tail under all that weight.

The men in their similar suits, all dark gray or black, somewhat too big, the hanging fabric conjuring the image of a larger body, of greater force, came back every few days with more questions. First about Oma leaving, but then about the State, about politics, about his refusal to join the Party. The weedy-eyebrow man's revenge.

Opa thought often of the commandant during those early days, wondered whether to seek him out. But on their third visit, the men asked about his drink with the commandant, where they'd been, what they'd talked about. And then Opa knew that they'd talked to the commandant as well. Knew also, with sudden and great clarity, that the commandant would not contact him. He had been right, in the end, that the afternoon in the bar would be their last meeting—though he had imagined the reasons differently, had imagined himself far away in another world, a world that now seemed unimaginably far from him.

And yet, in those first weeks Opa still had hope. Despite the men sitting at his kitchen table each night in groups of three or four. Despite their questions that started small and then became ever sharper, piercing the self-assurance he worked so hard to convey. Despite the way they came and went in a black car that appeared from the gloom as if out of nowhere and then bled back into the night after they said goodbye. Despite the way they entered his kitchen and sat at the wooden table, touching it with their hands, placing their heavy palms over the grooves and nicks his fingers had traced so often. Despite all that, he held on to a glimmer of hope, because there were moments when he still recognized his world, when he convinced himself that his staying would be interpreted as an act of loyalty. And he asked himself again and again: What was it, after all, if not loyalty? He'd lost his family, but he could still have something. Country, purpose, belief.

Sepp paused and blew his nose. His eyes were wet from the wind off the lake, and through the watery layer, I could not read his thoughts.

"Belief?" I asked him. "Belief in what?"

"Well," he said, "the friend I knew didn't believe in much beyond the day-to-day. But he might have, in the end, if they'd let him. Maybe he would have believed in them if they'd left him anything to believe in. His job, maybe, or his soccer."

Soccer was Opa's passion. By the time we knew him, he'd become a mere spectator, of course, but that didn't stop him from telling us stories of his earlier glory. He sat us down in our usual sofa spots and began to talk. He'd been the goalie. The only position where his unequal legs, his uneven gait, didn't slow him down too much. "*Weit* über *die Mittellinie*!" he roared at Martin and me from his armchair. Way past midfield! And he raised both hands toward us, showing the trajectory of the ball he'd kicked from his own goal, up and over, his hands pausing at the highest point, moments before glory, then descending in a flash into the opposing goal. "Can you believe it?" he asked. "Straight from my goal into the other goal. One kick!" And he winked once with his right eye, so quickly I wasn't sure if I'd really spotted it. His hands hovered for a few seconds in that imaginary goal, their wrinkles and brown spots level with my eyes, before he dropped them back into his lap. "A kick like that," he said quietly, "that's any goalie's dream."

Later that day, we asked Oma about Opa's soccer, trying to separate myth from reality. All she said was: "It's a shame. The team didn't last."

But now Sepp told us: No. It was Opa who didn't last.

"It was all organized through work, at the plants," Sepp explained. "Everything was. Each factory had political groups, military groups, sports teams, even dance troupes. Everything shaped by work, organized around work." He paused, taking his handkerchief and wiping a drop from his nose.

"*Der Arbeiter-und Bauernstaat,*" he then said without a trace of irony in his voice. The Workers' and Farmers' State.

Opa's factory was the biggest in town, the one with the strongest soccer team. Sepp had been part of the team too. A bench warmer. Sometimes a substitute in the last minutes of a game. But he hadn't minded. They'd all played for the fun of it. After Oma left, Opa looked forward to the practices and games more than ever, to the way the exercise and comradery emptied his mind of the past. Those were times when Opa still saw a future, when he could justify his decision to stay. Here, on the soccer field, he was part of something. At least that. And what would he have been over there? He didn't know. Couldn't know.

It was after one of these games that Opa first confessed to Sepp, a month or two after Oma had left. They were sitting at the edge of the soccer field, just the two of them after the rest of their teammates headed home. Sepp had brought a couple of beers, and now Opa took a sip, then straightened his legs, gently shaking out the shorter one, the one that always hurt when he stepped out of the goal. There were so many reasons not to talk. For one, you never knew who was listening. But looking around, Opa saw no one, only grass and trees. Of course, you also never knew whom you were talking to, but this was Sepp. They'd known each other across eras, as kids growing up in Grimma, as young men taking their girls dancing at Vogels Ballhaus, as friends separated by war, as colleagues sweating together in the heat of the welding room. And so the words came out before Opa even knew it. "*Ich wollte auch abhauen*." Such a short phrase. But in that place, at that time, there was no mistaking the word. *Abhauen*. To clear out. To bugger off. To head west. I wanted to leave too. That's what Opa had revealed.

Sepp didn't move. He was propped on his left arm in the grass, holding a beer in his right hand, the brown bottle poised almost at his lips. But he didn't drink. And he didn't turn to look at Opa. In that brief moment, in the growing darkness, Opa must have thought he'd made a mistake. The kind of mistake that could land you in prison. Hohenschönhausen. Bautzen. Names that drove fear into people. He kept his eyes on Sepp, who sat frozen in deep thought.

Just when Opa was about to speak, to say anything to break the silence, Sepp put the bottle to his lips and took a quick sip, then another. Then he put the bottle down in the grass. "That's all right," he said. "We've all thought about it, you know."

Opa let out his breath. "Damn it, Sepp. I thought I'd messed up."

"You thought I'd tell?" Sepp asked. He laughed. A thick, loud laugh, comfortable, echoing across the field, surrounding the two men, pulling them together. Sepp sat up, put his left arm around Opa's shoulder, and said, "Uwe, I take a box of screws home from work each week. Sometimes I take welding wire. I even took some welding pliers. I bring empty bags in the morning so I can take stuff home at night. I mean, how else would I have any tools to fix things at home or at the farm in this shit excuse for an economy?"

Opa put his arm around Sepp's shoulder too, and they sat together at the edge of the soccer field, their laughs growing and mingling, then breathing more slowly, easy now, inhaling and exhaling in unison, a rhythm born of relief. Two men, holding on to each other's shoulders, each other's secrets. Around them, the white lines of the soccer field glowed dimly under the floodlights, marking the space where they sat, containing them, giving them comfort. A place they knew.

Now sitting next to Martin and me, Sepp looked out over the Bodensee and coughed into the cold air. "Those were strange times, uncertain times. There are things you need to understand." We nodded and leaned back against the bench, letting our eyes wander across the scenes of our childhood while his words took us further back, to places we'd never known.

Yet some of what he then told us was already familiar to me. We'd heard some of it from Tante Lara, of course, and Darren had explained more details over a cup of coffee in Illinois after that first trip to Grimma, his fingers drumming the table. An urgent staccato that marked the pace of change he was describing. The whiplash years, that's what Darren called them. First the closing of the borders. May 1952. Everywhere except in Berlin. Then the Second Party Conference that same summer, the one where the ruling party announced the construction of the socialist state. *Der Aufbau des Sozialismus.* Except that it wasn't really socialist at all, Darren said, it was pure Soviet-style communism. That became clear when they began to nationalize businesses, collectivize farms. You could see it in the ramping up of repression. In the doubling down on an economy that was publicly praised, privately abhorred. The way you couldn't count on finding what you wanted or needed in the stores, the way people took shopping bags wherever they went, tucking them deep into coat pockets. They called them *Falls-Tüten.* In-case bags. In case there was unexpectedly something on the shelves.

Then came the tumultuous days of June 1953, the announcement of the Party's 'New Course,' the sudden loosening of the tight web the State had spun, the lowering of quotas—for some but not for all. It might sound strange, Darren had explained, but some people thought it was the relaxation of rules and quotas, arguably an admission of failure from the very top, that drove people out onto the streets that June. Or maybe it was the inconsistency with which the changes were applied. Hard to know, ever, what really motivates people, he added.

Sepp described those same days to us, sitting on that bench by the Bodensee, surrounded only by the sounds of water and wind, a few birds passing by our feet, searching for crumbs. "Over here, you mainly see pictures of the workers in Berlin that rebelled in '53," he said. "But it wasn't only them, not just the ones whose photos were broadcast across the West, throwing rocks, dodging tanks. It was also the factory workers in small towns, in the plants far from Berlin. And also the farmers."

"It was, after all," Sepp said into the quiet, this time with a curl of his lips, a slight grimace, "the Workers' and Farmers' State." And so, during those days in June there were tanks in Grimma, too, a town that had always had a military presence, home to hussars and their lightning-quick horses for centuries, home now to the Soviets housed in the old hussar barracks, a town where soldiers were never more than a few steps away. The crackdown, the tightening of the web once again.

"What about Opa?" Martin asked. I'd been caught up in Sepp's story, pulled in by the dates and events I recognized from Darren's explanations. But Martin was impatient with the history lesson. And he had a point. Opa was the reason we were there. Not Sepp, not history.

"Things were changing for your Opa too," Sepp said. "You probably know that he was demoted about a year after your Oma left. Early 1954."

Martin and I shook our heads.

"No," Martin said, "we don't know anything about that."

Sepp took a deep breath. "Well, I'll tell you then. Exactly the way your Opa told me."

Opa was in the canteen when they came to talk to him. Three men. Always these groups of men. But this time, he knew them. The plant manager and two high-up Party representatives. And this time, they came without questions.

Opa was sitting alone, as he did more and more often these days, so they slid onto the benches, one on either side of him, one across from him. He waited, tracing the creases on his work pants under the table, running his thumb up and down the rough fabric to stay calm. He'd seen it before. Comrades sitting alone, others steering clear. Then the visit over lunch, the men taking their places, talking, beckoning. Then the walk to the head office. Three men walking straight, heads up, surrounding the unlucky one. Opa had sometimes wondered what he would do when it happened to him. Not if, but when. He knew that much. Would he keep his head high, stubborn, as some did? Or would he shrink ever smaller as he walked down the long hallway, hunching his shoulders until he could no longer be seen in the midst of his minders?

But when the moment finally came, he was too distracted to remember how he'd walked. It was all a blank in his mind, he told Sepp later that day, his voice hushed though they were no longer at work but walking down the quiet main street toward the river.

"I don't mind losing the role," Opa said. "I've never needed the role. But have you seen the way they all look at me now?"

"They're just worried," Sepp said. "They could be next."

"Yes," Opa said, "but should that make me feel better?"

Sepp didn't know what to say. He'd seen the patterns change too. The way the men ate near the door now, not at Opa's table by the window. The way they no longer ran to Opa on the soccer field after a great save. The way they gathered around Big Franz, the team captain, to hear his stories, not Opa's. Not all the men, of course, but most. It was like the shifting of weight from one foot to another. Subtle, yet unmistakable.

"It's all gone shaky," Opa said. And Sepp knew what he meant, even though he hadn't experienced it himself, didn't yet know that he would.

The end of Opa's soccer career came a few weeks later, a few weeks after his demotion. Like an aftershock that seemed minor at first, a tremor. And yet the tremor was more damaging than the quake. It happened right before one of their games. Everyone was already on the field, jumping high, bringing their knees to their chests, then kicking their feet up behind them. Opa didn't join in the warm-up. He never did, because of his leg. He found other ways to stretch. He was standing on the sidelines next to Sepp when Franz walked over, his steps heavy under his oversized frame, arms swaying from side to side, not front to back. An unintentional swagger born of his girth.

"Uwe," he said, and Opa turned toward him.

"Coming. Just let me get my gloves."

"Wait a minute. We've got to chat first." *Plaudern.* That's the word he used. A word for women chatting over cake or neighbors exchanging gossip across fences. But there was no cake, no fence. Opa dropped his hands to his sides and waited.

"Jan will be goalie today," Franz said. Opa looked at Franz. Franz looked at the grass. Sepp watched them both. All around, men were jumping, kicking, stretching.

"*Plaudern*?" Sepp finally said, since neither Opa nor Franz spoke. "You call that *plaudern*?"

Opa placed a warning hand on Sepp's arm. *Stay back. Don't talk.*

"What is it?" he then asked. "Is it my leg? Or what?"

"We've just been told," Franz said. "You can't be our starting goalie. You can still be the substitute." He extended both hands toward Opa. A kind of supplication. Half apology, half excuse. But Opa took a step back, and Franz dropped his hands.

"So, it's not my leg?" Opa asked again.

Franz moved the tip of his right shoe back and forth, and his head shook in time with his foot. Left, right, left, right. He had nothing to say.

Sepp left with Opa that day. Together they walked across the field, past the jumping men, past the goal, past Jan who said, "Sorry," in a voice so low it would not carry across the field any farther than necessary. Yet another slow walk past many eyes.

That same evening, hours after Opa was stripped of his goalie role, he and Sepp met down by the river. Opa had suggested a drink at a bar in town, but Sepp said, "It's nice by the river this time of day." And Opa didn't object, even though it was far too early in the year for drinks by the river, too cold to sit comfortably. Sepp arrived first and waited, two bottles of beer beside him in the grass. Opa showed up a few minutes later, and they sat next to each other on the half-frozen ground. But if Opa was cold, he didn't show it. He sat with his eyes on the water, his jacket open, as if it hadn't occurred to him to fasten the buttons. Sepp suppressed the urge to pull his own jacket tighter around his body. Opa spoke first.

"You know what bothers me most? I didn't even know that that last game they let me play would be my last game. They robbed me of that."

Sepp waited a second to see if Opa would go on, but he didn't. So Sepp said, "It's been hard, hasn't it?" He tried to hit the right tone. Enough compassion to invite conversation, enough distance to allow Opa to choose silence, if that's what he wanted.

But it took Opa only a few seconds before he responded, "It's like…"

Sepp tilted his head as if to say, *Yes?*

"It's like when we were kids playing hide and seek. I remember sometimes I'd be the seeker and you all would run off while I counted. But somewhere along the way, while I searched and searched, the rest of you would lose interest. You'd head off on your bikes or over to a neighbor's house without telling me. And I'd be left looking and looking for something that wasn't there."

Sepp smiled in recognition. "I remember. That used to happen to all of us. We had such short attention spans."

"So what am I looking for now?" Opa asked. But Sepp had no answer. A solitary crow settled onto the riverbank, black feathers against the brown and gray background of the hill across the way. They followed it with their eyes as it pecked at the cold ground, shuffled a few steps one way, then the other, finally taking off. It must have landed in one of the trees across the river, but they couldn't see it. Not in this light. Still, they squinted into the growing darkness in the direction the crow had flown.

Then Opa said, "Why did you want to meet here?"

And Sepp knew what he meant, knew immediately what Opa was wondering. Had he chosen this spot, this time of day, to avoid prying eyes, to avoid any show of closeness with a man whose wife had gone west, a man who'd refused to join the Party, who'd been demoted, kicked off the soccer team, whose life was slowly emptying out, closing in? For a moment, he thought about coming clean, admitting his weakness and fear, but instead he repeated what he'd said earlier. "It's so pretty down here."

Opa looked around and nodded. To their right was the suspension bridge, behind them the Gattersburg, to their left the mill, and straight ahead the river flowing fast in front of the hillside where the crow was now cawing loudly. It was even prettier when it snowed, but there was no snow that day. Only a chill in the air that suggested the possibility of snow, that allowed them to imagine the same scene in crisp white tones. Sepp was right. It was pretty. Yet Opa must have known this wasn't the reason, would never have been Sepp's reason. As long as they'd known each other, Sepp had preferred company, had sought out bars and back rooms, never too tired for one more drink amid a crowd. Opa paused for a moment. But then, with his gaze resting on the trees across the way, he simply said, "You're right. It's beautiful." And Sepp knew he'd been forgiven. Or at least understood.

Sepp stopped talking. Martin and I waited, our silence thick and heavy like fog over the lake. A woman walked past us, nodded at us, kept moving briskly through the chill. When she was out of sight, Sepp turned first to Martin, then to me. "And that's what mattered," he said. "We'd known each other so long." He raised his hand to wipe away the wetness that had been gathering in the corners of his eyes. In the harbor, small waves rolled past the sailboats, reflecting shifting patterns up onto their sterns, their bows. The rigging clinked as the boats rocked. On stormy days that sound grew loud, so loud that we could hear it all the way down the street at Seefrieden when we were kids, but now it was merely a mild reminder of the never-ending movement of water, of air, of time. Sepp stood up abruptly. "Let's go." Martin and I followed him down the promenade, past the boat rental dock, past the kiosk where we'd eaten so many ice creams over the years. When we got to the square in front of the church, Sepp said goodbye.

"Have you noticed?" Martin said to me. "That's how all our stories end. With someone else deciding when it's over."

"We'll see him again tomorrow. We've got one more day here."

"Mm," Martin said.

"It's not what I expected," I said. "I'm not sure why, but I expected more betrayal, something grander, messier."

We both smiled, recognizing the echo of childhood years spent listening to Opa's stories. Bombastic, unreal, always gripping. I turned to face the lake. We hadn't noticed the change in weather, but now I saw thick clouds gathering low. The breeze had become wind, churning white onto the gray-green waves. I hunched my shoulders against the cold, making myself smaller. Martin pulled the hood of his parka up and blew on his hands, warming them. From the side, I could no longer see his face inside the hood.

Then he said, "I don't know. I think it *was* a betrayal."

"What was?"

"Sepp not wanting to be seen with Opa. That's a betrayal."

"True," I said. "But compared to everything else, that must have seemed like nothing. A hint of stealth in return for friendship."

"I don't know. It's still a betrayal."

I shifted my feet back and forth, suddenly aware of my toes, cold in my shoes. I thought of Sepp's waterlogged eyes above his broad nose.

"And yet they stayed friends."

"Still," Martin said slowly, dropping his hands back down, his voice muffled within his hood. "Still."

12

Opa's Departure

The Bodensee, October 1990

Sepp didn't tell us about prison. Not really. His story, at least the one he told Martin and me on that bench at the Bodensee, stopped in 1958, on the night the men came to his father's farm. Sepp and his father were having dinner in the late evening darkness, sitting in the front room. There were two large windows, each divided into eight panes, the wooden frames soft and rotting, chipping at the edges. Had Sepp and his father been looking out those windows, they would have seen the lights of the approaching car, reflected many times over in the mottled panes. But instead, they were facing into the dimly lit room, sitting side by side.

And so, with their backs to the window, their forearms resting on the table as they ate, they hadn't seen the car approaching. "Not even the lights," Sepp told us, "though I'm not sure what we would have done differently if we had." From where they sat, they had a view of Sepp's father's bedroom. Unadorned white walls, a simple wooden bed. And two leather suitcases. Not large enough to attract much attention, but large enough to carry at least a week's worth of clothing—heavy sweaters, pants, shoes, and a few other items Sepp's father couldn't imagine living without. A framed photo of Sepp's late mother. The deed for the farm.

"That was a mistake," Sepp told us. "That damn deed." *Dieser verdammte Grundbuchauszug.* Then he paused. In the silent beats that followed, I imagined the deed resting among the scratchy sweaters and woolen pants, a simple piece of paper, yellowed and crumpled at the edges, a folded corner. And I could see the men tearing open the suitcases, dumping out the contents. Or perhaps they'd been more methodical, taking out layer upon layer, searching for what lay underneath.

After the men arrested them, accused them of planning to flee the country, it was that deed that served as their final proof. After all, who would take a deed along on a simple trip? "A weekend outing," Sepp's father had said again and again as the men threw the framed photo to one side, held up the deed. "Just for the weekend," he repeated, though he knew already that it was too late. There was never any question who was in control. When Sepp and his father were put into the back seat of the car, the lamps in the dining room were still on, beckoning into the darkness long after the car had disappeared over the crest of the hill.

One day had passed since we'd last seen Sepp on this same lakefront bench, since he'd told us the first part of his story. We'd arranged to meet him in the early afternoon. So that morning, Martin and I had gone to see Seefrieden, had stood side by side in front of the inn. The old façade was still there, but an entire wing had been added on the left, built in an imitation of the old style, painted the same yellow, yet unmistakably new. The tall hedges in front had been removed, the gravel below bricked over to create three parking spaces. Where once we had sat in the shade of the red beech, there was now a miniature pleasure garden with crisscrossing brick pathways linking tiny gazebos, ponds, and bridges. I knew how easily places changed. I saw it all the time at my job. The way people altered landscapes, the way landscapes regrew. A constant tug of war. Still, I had not been prepared for this new version of Seefrieden, its bulk swallowing Oma's graceful inn, the once wild garden now so tame. Next to me, Martin whispered, "I don't want to be here." Then he pulled me away. As though staring too long might reshape our memories.

We still had an hour before we were due to meet Sepp, so we walked to a café and ordered a strawberry tart with whipped cream, exactly what Oma had always made for us when we first arrived for the summer. We ate the tart slowly, savoring the way the sweet juice from the strawberries blended with the cream in our mouths, chewing each bite carefully in solemn remembrance of what had been, of what was now gone.

Sepp must have slept well that night. He looked more rested, his eyes no longer gleaming under a film of moisture. Now he said, "But I can't talk about prison. It's too hard. Instead, I'll tell you what came before." He lifted his right hand to fend off questions, keeping it in the air for a few seconds until he was ready to talk again. About the years that led to that last night at the farm with his father back in 1958, those car lights they did not see coming. Four years to be exact. Starting in 1954, when Opa was demoted.

After that demotion, Opa started taking on odd jobs again, as he had when he was young. Working whenever he wasn't on a shift at the plant. Maybe he needed the money, maybe he needed the distraction. But there were some neighbors—more each month, it seemed—who wouldn't hire him, who worried about being connected to him. So Sepp stepped in. "A little farm work," that's how Sepp described it the first time. The two of them were sitting together in their usual spot down by the river, the Gattersburg behind them, the suspension bridge to their right. As always, they sat away from the river, up against the steep slope, in the shadows of the bushes. Ever since the day they'd walked away from the soccer team together, this is where they met, the smooth green of the soccer field replaced by the roughness of the bushes and the meadows edging the brown water. A spot ready-made for the illicit, though all they ever did was drink beer. Never only one. Sometimes two, sometimes three.

"The work's nothing you can't handle, and it'd help my father a lot," Sepp said, as he leaned forward on his knees, looking quickly at Opa, then back at the grasses growing wild by the river. Even from that brief glimpse of Opa's face, he knew Opa understood more than he had intended to say. Understood who was helping whom. Opa was, after all, a man with no prospects.

Opa and Sepp went to the farm together the very next day after work. When they arrived, Sepp removed a large package wrapped in brown paper from his bag and placed it by the barn door.

"Your delivery from the factory?" Opa asked.

"Every week." Sepp patted the top of the bag and smiled.

"Be careful, someone always notices," Opa said before they walked into the house.

And so it was that he began heading out to Sepp's father's farm after work most days, taking the long route on his bike as he had when he was a boy. But now, when he coasted down that hill, he kept his feet firmly on the pedals, no longer quite as steady as he had been when he was young. Still, Sepp had been right. Opa could handle the work, mainly heavy lifting for which Sepp's father was too old. Opa couldn't move fast because of his leg, but Sepp's father didn't mind. He'd known Opa so long, had watched him grow. And now he watched him again. Whenever Opa bent over, massaged his knee, Sepp's father would gesture for him to take a break, and then the two of them would sit on the stools by the front door, moving as little as possible, wary of splinters from the rough gray wood.

Sepp paused in his story. "You've probably never heard about the *Neubauern*?" he asked Martin and me. Without waiting for our answer he dove right back in. So much had been new after the war, he said, so many people taking on new roles. New teachers were already being trained to fill the void caused by violence. And now a whole generation of new farmers was being born. "Not literally, of course," he added.

"It began with the expropriation of farmland right after the war. All farmers who'd had any connection to the Nazis lost their land. Which was only right," Sepp said, raising his eyes to us.

For the first time, I wondered about Sepp's war story. I didn't often talk to older Germans. I had no reason to. And my own family had never talked about the war. I knew only the basics: Opa had never joined the Nazi Party, had never fought because of his bad leg. Mom once told me, "Your grandparents were better than most," but what did that really mean? I hadn't wanted to know, had pushed away doubts before they could swell. Now I found myself thinking, *What about Sepp? What had he done? What had he seen?* But Sepp moved on quickly, did not give me time to dwell on my questions. He was focused not on the war, but on the years after.

"Still, the expropriation didn't stop there," he said. "They also expropriated any farmer with more than one hundred hectares. It was the end of the large landowner."

"The end of Frank Hauser's family," I said to Martin, remembering Tante Lara's story. But Martin didn't want any distractions. He motioned for Sepp to go on, a quick flick of his hand.

All that land, all across East Germany, was divided into small parcels, maybe six, seven, eight hectares, sometimes ten, each parcel handed to a new farmer, a *Neubauer*. The small people taking from the big people like a state-sanctioned Robin Hood scheme. Except that it didn't last, couldn't last, because most of those parcels were too small to be productive, no matter how hard the new farmers worked.

And so they had to bond together. That was the start of the collectives. They were given a long name. *Landwirtschafliche Produktionsgenossenschaften.* LPGs. Agricultural Production Cooperatives. Yet another acronym to add to the growing list. Some with three letters, some with four. All born of a bureaucracy that gave names with ice-cold technicality.

But Sepp's father wasn't a *Neubauer.* He'd always been a farmer, and his farm covered twenty-five hectares. A so-called *Großbauer.* Small enough to avoid expropriation, big enough to be a target.

When the first LPGs were formed, many new farmers, the ones with the small parcels, celebrated. What was there not to celebrate? A collaboration that helped them produce what they needed to produce, that gave them a chance of succeeding. And some *Großbauern* persisted, thrived even, outside of the LPGs. At least at first.

Sepp's father was one of them. He managed quite well in those first years. He had enough land to survive, had never asked for help. He was the kind of man who valued independence, tradition, simplicity. He'd had the same beard for decades, its length unchanging, too long to be trim, too short to be full. Only the color changed over time, first reddish brown, then dull gray, then white. When he spoke, the hairs above his upper lip touched his nose. But he didn't speak often. "Should have been born up north," the other farmers used to joke. And he did have a northern temperament. Taciturn, private. When the first problems arose, he kept them to himself. It was a shortage economy, after all. The aftermath of war compounded by the decisions of the new State. He wasn't the only one who couldn't find the things he needed, who had to improvise, to fix his machinery with parts that looked as if they came from the last century. Or parts stolen from a factory in a brown paper bag.

It took a while for him to see a pattern in his troubles. But once he recognized it, he saw it everywhere. Every time the LPG had access to materials, seeds, or livestock, but he didn't. Every time the government's production quotas for *Großbauern* were raised out of reach. Each step pushing him ever closer to the LPG. The pressure to join was like a tourniquet, except that nobody yet knew whether it was stemming the bleeding or cutting off circulation.

They used all methods. They raised the quotas on the *Großbauern*, and at the same time they took away the means to meet them. There were Machine Tractor Stations, whose staff managed the farm equipment, decided who got access to the combines and who didn't. So more farmers joined the LPGs. That's what they called *voluntary* back then. Circumstances created little by little until you had no choice.

But Sepp's father stood strong, his stubbornness matching his beard, unchanging and resolute. Some years, he managed to get access to a combine toward the tail end of the harvest, when no one else needed it. Some years, he persuaded a neighbor in the LPG to let him borrow one on the sly. But other years, he simply couldn't harvest. He'd stand behind the farmhouse at the bottom of the hill with Sepp and Opa, and they'd gaze up at the fields, the perfect yellow stalks waving in unison, first one way then the other, following the movement of the clouds above, then swirling with the wind's unpredictable gusts, creating patterns that mesmerized like shifting flames. And they would watch all this golden motion, their heads tilting back and forth with the wind and the grain, calculating quietly. How much could they harvest by hand? What would that bring in? How much help would they need? The answer was plain to see from the beginning. They'd need too much help, and it would bring in too little.

Still, this didn't stop them from trying. Not Sepp's father. And not Sepp or Opa either, the three of them fighting against the tide while the seawalls were falling, the neighboring farmers giving in one by one, cradling their beers in their thick, calloused hands at the local bar, asking, "What else could we do?" And so, Sepp and Opa biked the stretching road from Grimma to the farm many evenings and weekends, in all seasons, all weathers, and Sepp's father waited for them in the low-ceilinged farmhouse, ready to work.

One Monday, it must have been the fall of 1957, Opa and Sepp had wrapped up their work at the farm and were sitting by the front door, legs out in front of them. They could hear Sepp's father whistling behind the house, a slow, easy melody. Opa massaged his aching leg, the shorter one. Sepp braced his back against the rough wall and shifted side to side on the stool, like a cow scratching itself on a tree. That's where they were when they saw the men coming. There were three of them, but Sepp recognized only one: the farmer from next door, a man who had joined the LPG early. A man with stature now, who'd risen through the ranks, who'd understood more quickly than most that bureaucracy, not farming, was the new secret to success.

It was this man who asked for Sepp's father. Opa stood up, took a quick step to the right until his body blocked the door. Sepp stood half a step to the left, ready to run to the back with a warning for his father. They stood for a moment, three against two, and then the three turned, slowly, deliberately. You can't rush us off, they seemed to be saying, even as they walked away.

Sepp and Opa hadn't mentioned anything to Sepp's father when they said goodbye that night, each putting a hand on the old man's shoulder, giving it a squeeze, getting a nod in return, a barely noticeable shift of the hairs on the old man's cheeks the only hint of a smile. But as they left, Opa warned Sepp: "They'll be back. I'm sure of it."

And they were, just not where Opa had expected. They didn't show up at the farm. They came one by one to the local bar, blending with the crowds, drinking beer, working their tricks subtly. This was the winter of 1957, then the early spring of 1958, those months when the bar turned quiet, when the men Sepp had known since he was a child started looking around, stopped talking. They still met there, of course. There was nowhere else to go in those long months when the sun set shortly after four, when their lives shrank to fit the circles of light from candles lit to ward off the dark. But more and more often, there were strange faces at the tables. On those evenings, there was no loud talking, no singing, few toasts and even fewer jokes. Everyone stared at the layers of grime that had accumulated on the table, sticky to the touch, coloring the wood light gray to match the smoke-stained walls. Anything to avoid meeting the eyes of those men, the ones they suspected, the ones that would betray them.

Any man they'd never seen before was likely one of *them*. But the truth is that one never really knew. Even the most familiar face, the neighbor Sepp and Opa had known all their lives, could have been one of them too. Trust was no longer something built over years. It was a decision. Here's who I'm going to trust. And it might have been wrong, it might have been right. One never really knew.

Still, there were hints. Men who bought drinks for the whole crowd a bit too eagerly. Men who listened too carefully, more carefully than a man tired from a full day of farming should have been able to listen. That's how you could spot them. They'd call out as soon as you walked into the bar, offering a beer. They'd buy one round, then two, sometimes more. Mostly, they'd wait for the second or third round before they started talking. Tripping up their targets, finding a flaw. And there was always a flaw. Lutz had built his barn with cement he'd gotten on the black market. The Werner family received visitors from West Berlin suspiciously often. Any reason to apply pressure, harder and harder, until something snapped.

And that's what happened to Opa. It was a Saturday during the spring of 1958. Opa, Sepp, and his father had been working hard, preparing the fields for the summer wheat to be sown. Their boots were caked when they returned to the house, each step heavy with mud. Behind the house, the fields lay dark and clean. Fresh. Waiting with them for what came next. "Let's go to the bar," Sepp's father said. "Let's celebrate." They knocked their boots against the front steps to shake off the mud. Then they headed up the hill to the bar.

Sepp's father sat in his usual corner at one of the long wooden tables, surrounded by men he'd known since he was young. Men who'd been there for him when his wife died. Men whose wives had delivered breads, cheeses, sausages, anything to keep him going during those tough years. Men who'd cupped the top of young Sepp's head, saying, "Growing bigger all the time." These men now raised their hands to Sepp's father in greeting, and he greeted back, rapping his knuckles on the table. Three sharp knocks. Their wordless hello. Then he patted the chair next to him, motioning for Sepp and Opa to join him. Only after they'd settled in did they notice the man at the other end, one of the three who'd visited the farm before. His face was wide, inscrutable. No wrinkles to give him texture or meaning. Opa nudged Sepp but didn't dare whisper. Still Sepp understood. They took their beers, raised them to each other, and then a quick lift in the direction of the stranger. Self-protection? Or a moment of sarcasm?

Either way, it was a mistake. The almost-stranger at the other end of the table took their brief toast as an invitation and moved his chair until he was sitting across from them. The whole room was quiet now. The man put his beer down, and Sepp found himself wanting to shift the glass, to match it up with one of the many dark rings that had formed on the table over the years, so many evenings of beers being raised and lowered in comfortable companionship. The man lifted the glass again and wiped the table with his sleeve. As if he had read Sepp's mind.

"How's everything going at the farm?" he asked. So many conversations those days began with innocuous questions. And yet you knew. Or you thought you knew. Sepp's father grunted.

"I hear you've got the fields ready for planting."

"Yes." Sepp's father kept his voice flat. "We've got it all ready."

"Well." The man raised his hand and pointed a finger loosely, casually at one of the men at the next table. "Otto's planning to join the LPG."

Sepp's father shrugged, so the man waved Otto over. His gesture was still casual but unmistakable: this was not a request, it was a demand. Otto stood, gripping his beer, his shoulders stooped, and walked over to stand next to the man.

"Isn't that right, Otto?" the man said. Then he turned back to Sepp's father. "You've seen the new combine up at the LPG? Isn't that great news?"

"They said I could use the old combine whenever I wanted to," Sepp's father said. The first words came out strong, but then his voice faded, became plaintive.

"Why are you even talking to him?" Opa asked Sepp's father.

The man swiveled, his attention on Opa now. But Opa was looking at Otto. "Otto, why don't you come join us?" Opa patted the chair next to him. When Otto didn't move, Opa reached up, took the beer from Otto's hand, and placed it on the table. Still Otto stood. So Opa put his left hand on Otto's glass and his right hand on his own, as if the beer could replace the man, as if it could grow their ranks. Not three against two, but four against one.

"You don't have to listen to that man," Opa said to Otto. "What's he going to do to you? You're not the only one." He pointed at Sepp's father, then added, "And there's Franz too, and Helmut. And Holger." Naming all the *Großbauern* in the village. "What are they going to do to you if you all stick together?"

The stranger let go of his glass, placed his hairy hands flat on the table, and stood up. The table shook. The beer in the glasses trembled, reflecting the light from the bulb above. Perhaps it was the glinting yellow that caught Opa's eye, that made him reach across the table in one sharp motion and shove the man's glass off the edge onto the ground. The glass shattered, and Sepp could feel the beer splatter on his pants. On the table he saw the fresh ring of moisture where the glass had been. Not yet darkened, not yet part of the wood grain. He looked up in time to see the man take a swing at Opa, and then they were grappling across the table, across the remaining beer glasses. Sepp's father grabbed one of Opa's arms, Sepp took the other, and together they dragged him away from the table, out into the darkness. Before the door swung shut, Sepp caught a glimpse of the man pounding the table with his fist, hitting the spot where his beer had been, blood dripping from his nose, the bone crooked, jutting away from his face at an angle, his eyes like black ice. Otto stood next to him, motionless.

"Otto signed the paperwork the next day," Sepp said now, turning first to Martin then to me. "And once the story got out, the three others signed too. Only my father was left."

"What about Opa? What happened to Opa?" Martin asked.

"He was called to the closest Stasi office the very next day. We told him not to go. We told him to head west instead. We weren't sure he'd be able to come out again. You know, he hadn't done much, but it didn't take much back then. We'd seen it happen to others. First, the summons, then the meeting. 'A quick chat,' they'd say. 'You'll be back by dinner.' But the next dinner would be in prison."

Sepp stopped and wiped his nose with the back of his hand, then let his arm drop again. "But your Opa didn't end up in prison," he said, and I heard a note of wonder in his voice. Still, after all these years. A hint of disbelief.

But it was quite simple really. Not much to tell. Opa walked into the Stasi offices and then walked out again, shook his head when Sepp asked what had happened. Never said a word. They met at their usual place down by the Mulde that same evening, and Opa brought the beers. By the third bottle, he'd gone shaky. Still, he wouldn't talk. So Sepp talked instead.

"*Wir hauen ab.*" We're clearing out. Heading west. Opa moved his head but didn't respond.

"We're the last ones left. The farm. It won't work," Sepp told Opa. He waited again. Across the river, the trees were bare. No movement of leaves, no shimmering of sun on water, only a dull, heavy, unmoving gray. Sepp thought about blaming Opa for the fight in the bar, that broken, bloodied nose, those dangerous eyes. He thought about saying, *What the hell were you thinking?* But he remembered all the beers they had shared in this spot by the river, all the times he'd put his arm around

Opa's shoulder, reassuring him in those months after Oma left. It will be okay. Now he glanced at his friend. Opa was tilted forward, arms on his knees, shoulders raised, head tucked low. He'd put the beer on the ground between his legs and was cradling it from side to side with his boots. Hunched over with his feet close together, he appeared smaller, like a child.

"You should come too," Sepp said. "What's left here anyway?"

Opa shook his head again, the way he'd been shaking it all evening. Not a response, just a refusal to respond. Then he picked up the bottle from between his feet, took a sip, and said, "I'm really sorry, you know. I am."

Sepp told him their plan. The time of departure, the route, the place where they'd spend the night before getting on the train in Berlin, their cover story. "In case you change your mind," he said. "You'll know how to join us."

Opa put his arm around Sepp's shoulder. And they sat there, as they had so many times before, looking out over the river at the hillside beyond, the bridge to their right, the mill to their left. They were both wearing thick jackets. Thick enough to make the pressure of arms on shoulders feel distant, to give each man a cocoon.

Sepp paused, and his story hung between us in the lake breezes, unfinished. It was getting late at the Bodensee. Cold too. Still, we waited for him to go on. All we could hear was the water against the harbor walls.

"We packed the next night," Sepp finally said. "We were all ready to leave. But that's when the car came. That's when they took us away. When I was released three years later, I headed west as soon as I could. A few months before the Wall went up. My father was still in prison. He was not so lucky." Sepp stopped.

"And Opa?" Martin asked again.

"Your Opa was the lucky one back then. He didn't end up in prison, not then, not later. When I got out, I heard he'd left Grimma a few weeks after my arrest, but we never talked about it. I guess he must have feared he'd be next, that it was only a matter of time. When I came west, I found him. He was the only friend I had, the only person I knew over here. That's how I ended up at the Bodensee." Sepp picked up his arm and pointed in the direction of the empty dock. And though it had grown too dark to see anything, I imagined the pedal boats of my childhood swinging on the waves, and Sepp, cap on his head, nose broad and flat across his face, saying, "How many hours? Two hours? You can have three." A wink, a pat on the shoulder as he sent us onto the lake.

Sepp cleared his throat, and when he spoke again, his voice was low. "Actually, we did talk about it once, a few days before your Opa died. That same week, I'd gotten the news that my father had passed away. He grew old. Nearly made it to a century. But I never saw him again, not since the day we were both sent to prison. My own father. After he was released, they wouldn't let him leave the country, not even for a visit. And I didn't dare go back. By the time I got the letter, he'd been dead ten days. That's the only time your Opa and I talked about my years in prison. He asked me about it, he wanted to know. So I told him everything. Then a week later, your Opa was dead. Now there's no one left. No one from then. From there."

Sepp stood up, placed one hand on my shoulder and one on Martin's, steadying himself. His next words were slow, and I knew we'd reached the end. I recognized it the way I recognized the last lines of the poems Mom sometimes read to us at night, lowering her voice, slowing down, adding a touch of vibrato. Sepp's voice shook too in these final lines: "I always thought he was the lucky one. Now I wonder, sometimes."

He lifted his hand off our shoulders, his outline a shadow in the night, his voice a whisper around us, a tone that lingered in the darkness. "But he was my friend."

13

Back in Leipzig

Leipzig, October 1990

Martin and I said goodbye to Sepp the following morning. One last chance to shake his hand and see his familiar face outlined against the winter gray waves. Then we drove from the Bodensee straight through to Leipzig. No stopping along the way, no exploring new cities. Sepp's stories had stoked our curiosity, and we were on a mission to learn more. About Opa, about history, about whatever we could get our hands on. In the car I finally cracked open my copy of *The Wall Jumper*, the same book Darren had given me on our first trip to Grimma. I hadn't even managed to start reading it then. In fact, I never read much while traveling. Too many other distractions. But I had packed it again this time with unwarranted optimism. On the inside cover page Darren had written, *Happy Exploring!*

Unlike our last time in Leipzig, we weren't staying at a hotel. Instead, Mom had told me to get in touch with Krista. "Who?" I asked, not recognizing the name at first. When Mom reminded me ("Oma's friend, Tante Lara's boyfriend's mom, the one we visited last time"), I said, "That's a pretty distant link." But Mom was adamant.

It was already late afternoon when we finally pulled up in front of a beautiful building on a broad cobblestone street in Leipzig. Red brick sitting on top of a base of large beige stones, ornate decorations around unusually tall windows. Dusk rose around us before we were ready for it, as it always did in this part of the world, first making the spaces between buildings dark, then enveloping the trees, one by one, then the tops of buildings, finally turning the skies storm-dark without a storm.

Krista's building looked as though it had been built in the late 1800s, originally part of an unbroken row of similar buildings. But now it stood alone, surrounded by vacant lots, rising from the ground like the lone remaining post of a wooden fence that had rotted away. Although we were almost an hour later than we'd predicted, she was waiting for us at her window on the fifth floor. When we pulled up, she leaned out and gave us a quick wave, then came all the way down to open the front door.

"*Kommt rein, kommt rein.*" Krista urged us up the stairs and into the warm light of her apartment. She used the informal tense with us, though we had never met. Our connection to Oma and to Tante Lara made us insiders in her world.

The apartment was filled with the kind of decorative tchotchkes Mom, Martin, and I always disdained. But here I found myself drawn in. The figurines on the shelf, the paper stars hanging from hooks on the wall, even the small bowls of dried flowers all seemed a bulwark against the darkness outside. Martin and I sank into the moss-green armchairs around the coffee table, and Krista headed into the kitchen to make us some tea. She must have been in her mid-eighties, short and wiry, still filled with energy. From the next room, she talked to us loudly, asking about our trip, question following question without ever waiting for an answer.

Only once she reemerged with the tray and placed the large porcelain teapot on the table did she finally sit down and take a breath, while I took over the job of pouring the tea. She sat in satisfied silence, warming her hands on her cup. Then she looked up.

"So here you are. I am so very sorry for your loss. I would have loved to have seen your aunt again. I was terribly sad when you all left for the West. Of course, I missed your Oma. She was ten years older than me, you know. Almost like the big sister I never had." She paused, then chuckled, bemused. "But I also worried Konni would never find another girlfriend I liked as much as I liked your aunt."

I laughed too, trying to move quickly past the condolences, to show her it was all right. "But he did, didn't he? Or at least that's what our mother told us."

"Yes, he's very happy. He and his partner have two kids, both grown now. They all live in Berlin. He's got a good job too. He's making the most of these changes."

"And you?" I asked.

"Oh, I retired from teaching quite a while ago. I'd taught my whole life. It felt like it was time. And Konni was well into his rebellious phase by then. It was good to have more time to focus on him."

"Rebellious phase?" I asked. "From what Tante Lara told us, I got the sense it was more than a phase."

"Yes." Krista laughed. She had an easy slow-paced laugh, suited for long cozy winter evenings or lounging in the park on summer nights, sausages grilling over an open fire. "It's more of a character trait than a phase. You know, I was scared out of my mind when I realized he was headed into town to join the demonstrations last fall. He and his friends were there most Mondays. But for me, the worst was the protest at the fortieth-anniversary celebrations of the GDR. Of East Germany. That one wasn't on a Monday, so I wasn't sure whether he'd headed into town. But I suspected he had, and I hated not knowing. Afterwards I heard that the people being arrested yelled their names as they were being taken away. So that the crowds would know who they were, so that their families could learn what had happened. When Konni came home that night, I told him I was going with him the next Monday. At first he didn't want me to, but I told him that if he got arrested, we'd both have to be arrested."

Krista laughed again, but her face remained serious.

"It wasn't that I was willing to be arrested. I wasn't that courageous, I was terrified. But I didn't want him to be there alone. And it turns out that that very next Monday was the largest demonstration yet. October 9th."

Of course, we'd heard about this night before from Tante Lara. And several of the articles Martin had given me, the few that hadn't focused on property laws, had described it in more detail. The masses—some said 70,000 people, some said nearly 100,000—who'd come out to march, young people, old people, students, factory workers, everyone. All the Muttis and Vatis, all the kids. Fathers in the police force, knowing they might get the order to shoot, knowing that their sons and daughters were among the protesters. Parents leaving children with grandparents. The announcement on the radio, a public plea to the government to forgo violence, a statement crafted by six leaders sitting together in the conductor Kurt Masur's house, among them several local Communist officials in what seemed like a stunning break from the Party. And then the masses gathering, first in and around the Nikolaikirche, the pastor leading them in a peace prayer, then marching along the Ring Road from the Karl Marx Platz, along the opera, past the train station, past the Stasi headquarters in the feared building with the rounded corner that gave it its name—*die Runde Ecke*. In the end, it was too much, the crowds were too large. And some miraculous combination of confusion, fear, and uncertainty on the part of the police and the officials let them pass unharmed.

"I'll never forget how it felt to be part of that group walking around the outskirts of downtown, right past the *Runde Ecke*, chanting, singing," Krista said. Her eyes were focused on the wall behind us, on the wallpaper, small swirls encircled by larger swirls. "And that was the beginning of the end for the regime. I'll never experience anything like it again, I'm sure. And I owe it all to Konni, to his defiance. On my own, I would have been quite content…" She paused and waved around the room, her hand traveling a circle from sofa to coffee table to dining room table. As my eyes followed hers, I could picture contentment here. A space tailor-made for Krista, for that laugh.

"I sometimes wonder what he can still fight for, now that his first rebellion succeeded. I wonder that about many of us." Krista dropped her hand into her lap. Then she smiled and filled our teacups. "But still, it's all been quite wonderful. This whole past year. You know, they just renamed the Karl Marx Platz. It's the Augustusplatz, like before. Going back to go forward. Who would have thought? One country again."

I felt more at home than I had any right to. There was something about being in Germany, fussed over and fed by an elderly woman, that felt familiar and reassuring. So we sat around the table longer than we should have that late at night, not wanting the moment to fade.

"You know," Krista then said, "people are pushing for access to their Stasi files, and they're right to ask. So many people worked so hard to save those files. Seeing the smoke from papers that were being burnt by the officials on their way out, storming buildings to stop the burning and shredding. So many Stasi offices occupied one by one all across the country, all the way to Berlin. Of course, they need to open the files. But the thing is, I'm not actually sure I want to know."

"What don't you want to know?" Martin asked.

Krista looked surprised. "Well, I assume there were people, people I still know, who betrayed me. Or your family too, you know. There was a man your Opa shared his house with after your Oma left. A young man we suspected, but we never knew."

Martin sat up, alert, and I knew he was wondering what I was wondering. Could it have been Klaus?

"A young man?" he said. "Do you know his name?"

"No, I never did. And even if I did, what good would it do now to know whether our suspicions were right?"

"But you'd still know," Martin said. "Isn't that the right thing? Shouldn't actions have consequences eventually?"

Krista turned her cup around in her hands, smoothing the edges, lost in thought. "I suppose so," she said. "I suppose there are things people simply shouldn't get away with. But it wouldn't bring your Opa back."

"Yes," I said, though I wasn't sure which of them I agreed with. "Anyway, we have our memories. And the stories we're hearing now. That's why we're going back to Grimma again too. For the stories."

Martin turned toward me. His voice was pinched and hurried. "Actually, Kate," he said, "I called a lawyer about the house in Grimma."

"Why?" Krista asked, but Martin was focused on me.

"A property lawyer here in Leipzig. He suggested we consider filing a claim for the property, just in case. As a placeholder, so we don't miss any deadlines. And I have the power of attorney Mom gave me, so I'm thinking about it."

"What about Greta and Klaus?" I asked.

Martin shrugged, indifferent. Krista cleared her throat, but said nothing, so I kept talking.

"You and I, of all people. We know what it's like to have our home fall apart, Martin. Why would we do that to someone else? Also, Mom's not interested, and Tante Lara wouldn't have wanted this."

"I hear you, but we don't need to decide anything now. We can decide it all together, later. You, me, and Mom."

"Does Mom even know you're still thinking about this?" I glanced at Krista, embarrassed that this scene was playing out in front of her.

"Not yet. I want to tell her in person when we're together for Christmas in a couple weeks. And then we'll decide. I promise. Okay?"

"But why didn't you tell me you already made an appointment with a lawyer?"

"Would you have agreed?" Martin asked. When I didn't answer, he shrugged. "Sometimes," he said, "you just have to do something. I'm meeting the lawyer tomorrow. Come with me if you want."

What I really wanted right then was to avoid a fight in the warmth of that room, in front of Krista. So I lifted my hands toward her apologetically. "It's complicated."

"I know." Krista finally spoke. "I've read all about it. Restitution before compensation. What an idea. Those people who live in your Opa's house now? Their whole life has changed already. They've suffered enough, don't you think?"

"Who's suffered?" Martin asked. "Didn't Opa suffer too?"

Krista stood up abruptly. "It's getting quite late. You must be tired and hungry after your trip. Let's see what we can find to eat."

Much later that night, I called Darren from Krista's phone in the kitchen, a short call to say we'd arrived. After the assurances—all good on both ends of the line—I said, "Martin's going to see a lawyer about the house in Grimma. I think he wants to file a claim. He's going to tell Mom over Christmas."

"And you agreed not to tell her till then? What if he files it before then? He'd be misusing the power of attorney she gave him. That was meant for Tante Lara's house." Darren rarely raised his voice, but I could hear both surprise and anger now.

"Christmas is right around the corner," I said. "And the Grimma thing is just a placeholder. It's not a big deal. Don't make it into a big deal."

I wanted to believe those words. I wanted to trust the memory of Mom and Martin's hands linked with mine in the sunlight during those last hours in Tante Lara's garden.

Darren sighed on the other end of the line. I waited for him to push back, but instead he said, "Guess what I'm wearing right now?"

I laughed, and far away in Illinois Darren chuckled too. "No, not like that!" he said. "Tame your imagination! It's just those socks your mom knitted for me. I'll have warm feet tonight, all because of her."

14

Krista's Story

Leipzig, October 1990

The next morning, Krista had breakfast waiting for us in the living room. *Brötchen* with homemade jam, cheeses, meats. And, of course, coffee. When we'd finished eating, she said, "I want to show you both something. We're going for a walk."

Two blocks from her house we were already in a park that stretched in all directions. Krista was surprisingly quick for her age. She moved with a flurry of small, dainty steps, the heels of her pumps swiveling on the gravel, leaving behind faint indents. Like bird prints on a beach. We walked through tunnels of rhododendron bushes, past an old horse racetrack with two dilapidated towers, and across a river into the woods. Finally, Krista stopped in front of a bench. It wasn't a clearing, really, more of a muddy circle in the trees where four different paths crossed—a star with eight rays. Martin and I caught up and sat down, glad that she was giving us a break.

"In spring all these woods will be full of wild garlic," she said. "The smell will be everywhere. And when the garlic blooms, the white blossoms will make everything shimmer."

I looked around. The ground was a sullen brown under leafless trees. Nothing shimmered. The winter sun was low in the sky, mostly hidden by dark branches.

"This is where we used to meet," Krista said.

"Who?" I asked, caught off guard. She was pointing at the place where I was sitting. I moved to the side, away from that spot.

"Your Opa and I," she said. "It was after your Oma left, once things started going wrong for him. He came from Grimma to visit me, trying to reclaim something, I guess. I must have been a disappointment, enough to remind him of what he'd lost, not enough to replace any of it."

She stopped talking, and her silence suggested something new, a piece of information I hadn't considered.

"Were you…?" I asked, not quite sure how to finish the sentence. *Lovers?* Would that be the right word? Martin looked down abruptly, uncomfortable, and that's when I remembered the photo album with the tiny lock from our childhood, the picture of Opa with a woman we didn't know. The day Oma stopped reading to Opa.

"Yes, we were," Krista said. Just that.

"Did our Oma know?" Martin asked.

"I don't know. I don't know what he told her. I never had a chance to tell her, of course. I never saw her again."

I wanted to ask Martin: Was it her? Was it Krista in that photo? But Martin wouldn't look at me, and I suppose I knew the answer anyway. It all made sense. Oma's friend. Oma's rage.

"Last night you said you were here for the stories," Krista said. "Well, this one is about your Opa and me. And about that young man in the house too. About the way things were."

Martin shifted, and his coat whispered against the rough wood of the bench. Above us a branch cracked in the stillness. I pulled my jacket tight, ducked my head low into my collar. Krista's voice was slow and precise, carrying details across years with the clarity of regret. Words for herself more than for us, it seemed.

"Your Opa didn't have many people to talk to back then," she began. "Not much he could trust in anymore."

Only a few days after he decided not to follow Oma west, Opa realized he already no longer understood, could no longer explain (had anyone asked him) why he had made the choice he had, why he'd stayed in Grimma. But his interrogators never suspected he'd been planning to leave. Why would they have? After all, he was still there. And so, among their many questions, they didn't ask him that one, and if they had, he would have denied everything, of course. Would have said that he'd made no choice. Couldn't have made a choice because he hadn't known Oma was planning to leave. No and no.

In the end, Krista was the only person to ask him that question. Why had he stayed behind? She was still living in Grimma then, still teaching at Oma's school, and she too had been questioned, visited at home, harangued at the kitchen table. She was Oma's closest friend. What had she known? Had she suspected? What could she tell them about Oma's teaching? How well did she know Opa? She waited two weeks before going to see him, not sure if two weeks was too much time or too little, uncertain what would arouse the least suspicion. She and Opa took their first walk then. The two of them at dusk, silhouettes ducking across the fields behind Opa's house, walking with quick, flat steps until they entered the woods, slipping into the quiet between trees with relief. That's when he told her he was meant to be in the West, and she just nodded.

Krista didn't lose her job, but she no longer had the support of the school director. She'd been too close to Oma. Before the end of the year, in late 1953, she applied for a new position in Leipzig and, much to her surprise, her transfer was approved.

When she and Konni moved to Leipzig in early 1954, she left Opa behind without a thought—until he arrived at her new apartment three weeks later, an accusation on his face that she had not even considered until she saw it in his eyes. It was a wet day, and the rain had flattened his hair into a helmet. He shook it before stepping inside.

"They pushed me out," he said, as he sat on the sofa.

Instead of responding, she handed him the plate of cookies she had grabbed from the kitchen. He took it and placed it on the table, untouched.

"They demoted me. I'm nothing now. All that work…" He stopped talking.

"I'm sorry." She wasn't sure he was listening.

"They don't talk to me anymore. The rest of the guys." He sank back onto the sofa and rubbed his hands up and down on his thighs. She knew that motion from the orchestra concerts she used to attend with colleagues on their rare training trips to Berlin. The man or woman next to her, lost in thought, rubbing their pants, sometimes in time to the music, sometimes not (she could never decide which was worse), unaware of the echoing sound—grinding almost—it produced in a quiet space.

Now she placed a hand on Opa's hand. Firmly, to stop the sound. He looked up, surprised. She had not meant the gesture to be intimate, but it was too late. Sometimes she wondered if this had been the start, the moment when the physical became possible. All a misunderstanding.

"When did they tell you?" she asked.

"Last Tuesday."

pened just months after your Oma left. Or the revolution in Hungary in 1956. Or the Warsaw Pact. These big moments, they passed us by. We exchanged so many words during those years, but always in the past tense. Such a large vocabulary, such limited grammar."

I couldn't help smiling.

"You know, he didn't talk to us much when we were kids," I said. "But he told us wonderful stories, always about the past."

"Did he ever mention me?" Krista asked.

"No," Martin said, his voice too sharp.

Krista turned her head down the path toward the river, lost in thought. When she spoke, her tone had an edge too. "I felt stuck. I worried that my connection to him would get me in trouble. By then, Konni was involved in all sorts of things. Things I admired, but that scared me for him. I wanted to take all those words I spent on your Opa and spend them on Konni instead. But I didn't know how to end it. Every weekend he'd visit. And every week, I'd start living again."

In 1958, about four years after his first visit in Leipzig, Krista took Opa to see Franz Konwitschny conduct the Gewandhaus orchestra. When the tickets had been passed out at work, she'd quickly grabbed two, one for her and one for Opa, a chance to do something other than talk at the kitchen table or lie in bed together. That night, for a few hours, Beethoven symphonies kept them apart, stopped his words, allowed her to breathe.

At first she entertained herself by watching the lights reflect off Konwitschny's slicked-back hair. She let herself be distracted by the way the bows of the violinists moved in unison, swooping like birds, by the unsteady glimmer of the flutes as they were raised and lowered. In the background, she could hear (or imagined hearing) the roar of the lions in the nearby zoo. She thought then about the old concert hall, destroyed in the war, forcing them to perform in this hall instead, making them compete with animals of prey. But after a while, the sound of the music took over. It was a different kind of escape. The one she chose both then and later. Not away from something but into its most intimate spaces.

When the last notes of the concert had sounded, she saw tears in Opa's eyes. "Krista," he said, but she grabbed his arm firmly—"*Komm, Uwe*"—and pulled him out of the concert hall, not letting him break the silence between them that the music had enabled. They didn't speak as they stood in line for their coats, and they didn't speak on the long walk home.

It was the last time he visited her in Leipzig, but they saw each other once more. He phoned her at school, left a message which a colleague relayed. "Your friend from Grimma called. He'll be in the woods at noon on Saturday." No name. No clear location. He likely thought he was being careful, but to Krista it seemed calculated to arouse suspicion.

Still, she went. Retraced her old footsteps across the fields in Grimma, waited for him in the shadows where those fields met the trees. It wasn't a big forest, more of a grove, so they walked in circles as he talked. He'd been worrying lately about the young man who lived in the room on the first floor of the house. The one he had long suspected had been asked to watch him. Opa never gave him a name. Only called him "that man," as if this distance could save him.

Now he told her that man had been asking too many questions lately. Always more. About the friends who still gave Opa bits of work, about Sepp and his father, about former colleagues Opa hadn't seen in years, and about Opa's weekend trips to Leipzig. He wanted to know where Opa went, whom he visited. He asked the questions over a beer in the garden or at night in the kitchen, his sleeves rolled up, his shirt unbuttoned, casual. And Opa responded in kind. Cheerful, empty answers. They were performing a dance, or at least that's how Opa described it. A dance he felt he could control, but then, in the last few weeks, his fear had gotten the better of him.

"I wanted to tell you about him after the concert," Opa told Krista. He stopped walking and leaned against a tree at the side of the path, his head on the rough bark, eyelids half shut. "But you didn't want to talk. And I didn't want to ruin the concert."

Ridiculous, Krista thought. As if a concert were more important. "You should have told me," she began to say, but then she remembered the way she had cut Opa off, stopping him before he could even start. Not because she knew what was coming, but simply because she was sick and tired of being burdened by his words.

Opa closed his eyes completely, turned his head away from her, and spoke as if to himself: "I didn't have anyone to talk to." Grooves lined his cheek, wrinkles spread from the corner of his eye downward. He was no longer young. Krista felt a pang—both sympathy and resentment.

Two days earlier, Opa now told her, that man had stopped him as he was coming into the house, had told him he'd finally figured out where Opa spent his weekends. "You go visit your wife's friend, don't you, you sly fox?" he'd said. And he'd winked. A joke among men. But then he'd added, "Was the concert good? You had great seats."

Krista took a quick step, away from Opa and his tree, all her worries flooding back. She wanted to run out of the woods, away from Grimma. Instead, she waited for Opa to explain why that man had followed them to the concert. What it could possibly mean.

But Opa just said, "So I told him the concert was good."

Krista felt a surge of anger. "That's all you could think to say?" she snapped, and Opa deflated, hands hanging limply at his sides. Over his drooping shoulders, Krista suddenly saw a man on the path, about twenty meters away. He must have come up one of the side trails without them noticing and was walking toward them, his thick brown boots scraping the ground. Opa and Krista stood frozen. They nodded a quick greeting as he walked past, then waited again. Krista had her back to the man now, but she didn't turn. Instead, she looked into Opa's eyes, watched Opa watching the man, until there was nothing to watch anymore.

Krista briefly considered asking Opa more about the young man in his house but decided she was done with that story, didn't want to hear more, no longer wanted the weight of being connected to Opa, to the suspicions that followed him like a scent ever since Oma left. Their conversation had come to an end silently, before they even knew it, while they'd waited for the man in the woods to pass. Yet another man who could have been there for a reason or for no reason at all. Krista said, "I'll see you next weekend." Then she let her hand rest on Opa's arm, counting the seconds slowly in her head, one-two-three-four-five, before she left him behind, still leaning against the tree.

She made sure she wasn't home the next weekend. Or the next. And then she heard, he had fled west. Just like that.

She did get a visit from the Stasi after he left. Only once. They asked her the same kind of questions they'd asked about Oma. When had she last seen him? Had she known? But of course, she hadn't. And for that, at least, she was grateful to him.

Was Opa right about the man in his house? She didn't know. There were plenty of reasons for the Stasi to come talk to her once he left, even if that man had nothing to do with it. Maybe it was all written in a file somewhere, or maybe not. She didn't have the answers.

A few months after he left, she received a postcard. It had a picture of the Bodensee on the front, and all he'd written on it was '*Angekommen.*' Arrived. If he was going to write at all, she thought, if he was going to pass that risk to her, then shouldn't he at least have written more? All those hours he'd talked, all those hours she'd listened and answered and calmed. And all he sent was one word.

15

October Roses

Grimma, October 1990

The lawyer's office in Leipzig wasn't far from Krista's apartment. We arrived a few minutes early, Martin-style, so we walked up and down the street, from the Ring Road past a vacant lot with cars parked haphazardly on the dirt and grass. When we heard the bells from the nearby Thomaskirche—two strikes, two o'clock in the afternoon—we climbed the broad stairs and knocked. I liked Bernd Schmidt the minute he opened the door. He was short, bald, with lively eyes that assessed us in a flash and a warm smile. "*Kommen Sie rein.*" Come in.

He offered us coffee and guided us to a sagging brown sofa. Then he sat across from us on a wooden chair, like a student awaiting instruction. He listened. He wanted to learn about us. He made no assumptions at all. This modesty is what made me think of him right from the start as Bernd, though of course we called him Herr Schmidt.

I knew that Bernd was not Martin's idea of a successful lawyer. In Martin's world, lawyers strutted around tables, never sitting, always talking. Chairs were mere accessories in sharp-edged board rooms, only occasionally used by a client, reclining, powerless. Martin quickly took charge in this odd room with its high ceilings, intricate moldings, drafty windows, creaking floors. While he summarized the state of affairs, Bernd rubbed his bald head. Every few minutes he crossed his legs, revealing baggy woolen socks that he pulled up with a quick motion. Yet his eyes stayed focused on Martin. When Martin finished talking, Bernd stood and moved to the oversized wooden desk by the windows. There he dug around in a sea of papers.

"Okay, so here are the letters you sent me," he announced with a brief flash of a smile that said, *I knew all that already.* A mild rebuke, a hint that Martin's take-charge attitude and his summarizing had been unnecessary. Martin winced, so he must have read the smile the same way. But whatever he felt, he hid it well. "Good, you have the information then," he said.

"Yes. So, first, let me tell you, there are more questions than answers right now about this sort of claim. Lots of moving parts. I mean, we've only been one country again for a few days now. But, well, still, let me tell you a bit about what I know."

I met with Bernd in person only three times. Yet, even in those brief meetings, I came to know his style. The short burst of staccato words that introduced his sentences, all qualifying what came next. Almost apologetic. In that first meeting, he laid out the basic facts. Yes, as part of the reunification negotiations both governments had agreed on the principle that restitution of property would have priority over compensation. Though, he added, that was not necessarily the initial position of the GDR government. Still, nevertheless, in the end, it was a recognition of the sacred nature of private property in the West. Yes, it was possible that this meant we could have a claim on the property. But, then, the state of the law was still being interpreted, exceptions clarified, limitations addressed.

"You've come to see me, so that's a start. But, as I said, I have more questions for you than answers." Bernd pulled out a leather-bound notebook and began jotting things down. "So, I need to know more. Not only when your grandparents left the house. But under what circumstances? When and how did the current residents move into the house? And did they ever buy it?"

"Was that even possible?" Martin asked.

I wondered too. Darren had tried to tell me about property in the East, back when I first mentioned Martin's claim. First, he had said, lifting his pointer finger, it was never so simple. Real property had meant all sorts of things at different times. Some people continued to own it, people had rights of use, people even had small weekend houses. Lots of constraints and limits, but nevertheless. Second, he'd added, two fingers now raised, the fact that property had been dealt with so differently in the East was precisely what made it a concern for reunification. "Stop it. I'm not one of your students," I'd told him, taking his hand, folding his two lifted fingers down. Now I wished I hadn't interrupted him, had listened more.

"Sure, yes, well, it was possible for them to buy," Bernd said. "Certainly after recent changes to the law this past March. But it doesn't only matter whether they bought it, it matters when and how."

"We don't know," Martin said. "We've only had one conversation with them."

"Anything you can figure out would be helpful."

That's when I remembered the photo Greta had given us on our first visit. And in the same moment, I realized Martin didn't know about it. He'd been in the bathroom or perhaps already staring at the photo in the hallway when Greta showed us her album. One piece of information only I had.

"Wait." I dug around in my bag, and sure enough, the photo was still pressed between the pages of *The Wall Jumper*. I pushed it across the table toward Bernd. "I do know they bought the house. Greta said this was the day they signed the contract."

Bernd turned it over and read the date scribbled on the back. *June 1990.*

"Does that matter?" Martin asked.

Bernd made a quick note in his notebook. "Well, yes."

"Does it help?" Martin asked.

"Well, I suppose it might. Some purchase contracts are being held up and reviewed now, depending on the timing of that purchase."

I'd thought Greta's contract would help them defend their property, but now that seemed uncertain. I reached for the photo, regretting my decision to hand it over, but Bernd didn't give it back. Instead he added it to the stack of papers on the desk next to him.

"But," he continued, "this area of law is so unsettled. Restitution, yes, but not at all costs, not at the expense of subsequent legitimate owners. There are many reasons not to give back property."

Bernd's shoulders were hunched, his pant-legs hiked up, drooping socks on display, light blue, probably hand knitted. I had the feeling he had as little desire to be involved in this conversation as I did. The discouragement, the list of questions, all seemed an effort to make this process daunting. I took advantage of his hesitation.

"I've never understood. Why would we want to take the house away from Greta and Klaus anyway?"

Martin appraised me coolly. "That's not what we're doing. We're just gathering information."

"Gathering information. We've got lots of experience with that over here." Bernd's laugh was bitter. Then, glancing at Martin, he quickly added, "There's nothing wrong with getting the lay of the land, of course."

Martin leaned forward. "Here's one more thing. We think Klaus might have been spying on our Opa, maybe for the Stasi?"

Bernd put his pen down and looked up. "Based on what? They knew each other?"

I felt the shift in his tone, unexpected forward movement where I wanted none, so I jumped in. "We don't know that. An old family friend told us she suspected a young man who used to live with our Opa. But we don't know if it's true. We don't even know if Klaus was that young man. She never knew his name."

"But we do know Klaus lived with Opa when he was a young man."

"Well." Bernd rubbed his head again. "Well, yes, that is something we should find out." But he did not pick up his pen again.

We walked the half block to our rental car in silence. As Martin opened the door on the driver's side, he said, "Given all the answers we need, it's lucky we were already planning a trip to Grimma." I wanted to ask, *Did we really need the answers?* But I couldn't decide what offended me most. Was it his use of the word *we* or the word *need*? Both so very wrong. I climbed into the passenger seat and said nothing.

The drive was familiar, though we'd done it only once before. The flat landscape around Leipzig gave way to rolling hills and trees as we approached the Mulde valley and Grimma. The closer we got, the more eager Martin became, tapping his fingers on the steering wheel in a rapid tempo. I was still processing what I'd learned in Bernd's office, but one thing was clear: Martin was following his own plan. He'd shared all those newspaper clippings with me as if we were in this together, a joint discovery. Meanwhile, he'd been sending letters to Bernd all along. It was so typical of my brother that I shouldn't have been surprised. And yet, I found myself growing more agitated with each tap of his finger.

When we saw the first sign for Grimma, I finally said, "So, why did you do all this without telling me, Martin?"

"Well, you obviously didn't want to take the lead, did you? And anyway, you're here now, aren't you?"

I knew his tone well. I'd heard it so many times when we were kids, the defense-turned-offense, culminating in those tricky questions I couldn't answer honestly without proving his point.

"That's typical sibling stuff," Mom always said when we were kids. "Don't let it get to you." Or "You know it's not important, right? In the grand scheme of things." And even Dad, who left us so early, tried to teach us that our sibling bond was special. I can still see him, reclining in a garden chair in Illinois, wearing the thick plaid shirt he used for working in the yard. And I see the dirt on his jeans and on his hands, the rake next to him on the ground. A whole day outside with the wide Illinois sky above and all the worms Martin and I needed to stay happy. We'd work for hours, and Mom would bring us glasses of lemonade, wrinkling her nose at the dirt, nodding at the newly planted flowers. When we were all done, Martin and I always argued about who'd found the longest worm, until Dad awarded the grand prize. Then we'd sit together on the patio, and Dad would say, "You two are lucky. You'll always remember each other's worms." Martin and I laughed each time, not sure why we should remember these or any other worms, but Dad, an only child himself, would say, "That's what siblings are for. The small things you share." Suddenly serious. And we'd squirm like the worms, drinking our lemonades, hiding our smirks behind our tall glasses.

Those days in the garden with Dad gave me my love for plants, my future career. But perhaps I should have learned even more. Perhaps what really mattered was that Martin recognized the faint smell of boxwood bushes from Oma's garden after it rained. He knew the popping sound that unseen slugs made when you biked over them in the dark on the way home from the lake, that sound you tried not to hear but knew so well. He knew the shapes that the moon and the poplars threw over the stones at the lake and over the sailboats in the harbor at night. He knew too the sound of the broken screen door in Illinois, a squeak and thud that echoed through the house, and the feel of the rough concrete under our legs when we sat on the steps in shorts waiting for Mom to come home from work.

So, sitting in that car heading toward Grimma, I decided to move past his tricky questions, forgive his challenging tone, try to find common ground. "What's our plan then?" I asked. "We can't just show up at the house, can we?"

"Why not?" Martin had one hand on the wheel and massaged his neck with the other.

"Well, we did that last time. Maybe this time we should have called."

"I sent a letter. We have an appointment. They're expecting us." Martin's voice had an edge.

"An appointment? For what?" I asked.

"To talk about the house."

"Do *they* know that?"

Martin hesitated before saying, "I'm not quite sure. Maybe they think we want to learn more about our past, more about Opa."

"After we hired a lawyer? Not likely." Now I was the one asking the challenging questions.

Martin nodded. "You might be right." But then he added, "I'm not sure they know we're talking to a lawyer. We should have asked Bernd if he's been in contact."

"So what are you going to say?"

Martin shrugged and made a humming sound. A response, but not quite an answer.

When we pulled up in front of the house, Greta and Klaus were waiting for us as Martin had predicted. No introductions this time. Before we headed inside, I noticed that the homes on either side were already being fixed up, only three months after our last visit in July. The one on the left had a fresh coat of paint, the one on the right was encased in scaffolding. Oma and Opa's house looked forlorn, a distant memory amid progress. Inside, nothing had changed. We sat at the same kitchen table, were offered tea in the same cups, took in the same view of the garden.

Greta started the conversation "So, you're back?" An uncertain opening. It seemed they didn't know why we were there, though they must have had their suspicions.

"Visiting your aunt again?" Klaus asked.

"No," I said. "Actually, she recently passed away. We're in Germany for her funeral."

"I am so sorry." Greta clasped her hands together. "She was still so young. She seemed so healthy."

"It was cancer. Brain cancer. Once we found out, she had almost no time left. But I'm glad we had that last trip with her."

"Her last trip home," Greta said. She placed both hands on the table, face down. Her veins were blue and raised, the skin around her fingernails thick, freckles and spots spread across her knuckles. Aged spots, Mom called them when she began to see them on her own hands, her English a little bit off.

"Yes," I said. "But we didn't know it at the time." I could hear the ticking of a clock, the slight hum of the lights. Next to me, Martin's leg jiggled under the table, impatient. But he said nothing.

Greta put her hand on mine. "It must be difficult for your mother."

"She's doing all right," I said. "She's lived so far from family for so long, you know."

Klaus stood and walked to the window. Then he turned and placed his hands behind him on the counter. The same posture I remembered from our last trip. "I'm sure you're not here to talk about your aunt. So let's get on with it."

Martin nodded, but Greta patted the chair next to her, urging Klaus to sit down. "We've just served the tea."

"They can drink tea and talk at the same time."

"Of course," Martin said. "In fact, we're hoping to talk. We learned so much about our family last time. But we still have questions. About the house, for example."

Greta and Klaus exchanged glances—Klaus warning Greta with sharp nods, Greta calming Klaus with a sideways tilt of the head. *I told you so* and *Take it easy* passed back and forth with the smallest of gestures.

Greta jumped in first. "I thought I told you all that last time. Back when your aunt wanted to know."

"But that was about you. Klaus moved in earlier. We never heard those details."

Klaus walked around the table until he was behind Martin. "You're not really here to learn about your family," he said. Martin twisted in his chair and looked at Klaus towering behind him.

"Klaus," Greta said again, and I could tell I was not the only one who feared a fight, fists and all.

"How about we go out into the garden? I'd love to see it," I said, and Greta quickly agreed. She took Klaus by the arm and guided him away from Martin's chair.

"We can show you the new rosebushes we've planted, right, Klaus?"

The bushes stood in a patch of fresh soil to one side of the patio near the white metal table. Near the bushes, almost hidden by the web of thorny branches, I spotted a small stone marker—the same one I'd seen on the photo hanging in Klaus and Greta's hallway the first time we visited. The one I'd wondered about back then.

"What's that?" I asked, pointing. Greta grabbed my arm and held on to my wrist as if I might do harm to the stone. Or as if she might sink.

"*Du musst nichts sagen*," Klaus said from behind us. You don't need to say anything.

"*Ach komm.*" Greta let go of my arm and shook her head at him gently. "It's the baby that died. We already had a son, but our second died during childbirth. A daughter."

"She's buried right here?" I could hear the horror in my voice, and Greta lowered her eyes quickly.

"No, it's just a memorial. They took her away at the hospital and then told us she had died." Greta dropped her voice to a whisper. "Some people think they took the babies."

"Who?" I asked, not even trying to hide my horror now.

"*Die da oben*," she said. The higher-ups. "The ones who couldn't have kids of their own. But I don't know..." Her voice trailed off into a pained hum.

"*Quatsch!*" Klaus said. Nonsense. "They didn't steal babies. There's no evidence whatsoever!"

"True," Greta said. "But one can't help wondering, can one?"

I felt sudden tears in my eyes. "I lost a baby too. Much earlier in the pregnancy. Not like your loss at all, but it still hurt."

"*Ach, Kind.*" Greta wrapped me in a tight hug, her thick arms around my waist, her shoulders encircling mine. "Of course it did. It can be different, but it's still the worst pain, isn't it?"

Something swept from deep inside me all the way to my fingertips, making me grip Greta's cardigan tightly. Sadness, yes, but also something else. Gratitude and resentment and loneliness all mixed together. Here was the bear hug I'd wanted, the one I hadn't received. Not from Martin, and not even really from Mom. I could feel Greta's warmth mingling with mine, could smell the mildly rancid scent of warm milk, cabbage, and sour bread on her apron. I let myself drop into her softness. When she finally released me, I wobbled. She grabbed my shoulders, steadied me. "*Wir schaffen das. Wir zwei.*" We'll manage, the two of us. Then she bent down over the memorial and traced the letters carved into the top of the stone. Five simple block letters. "Hanna," she said.

"I always wanted a daughter. We named her Hanna. Short for Johanna."

"Hanna," I said. "What a beautiful name. What a lovely memorial."

I waited for Martin to say something. Even the shortest of sorrys. A simple "*Es tut mir leid.*" A few words that would have counted for her and for me. But he avoided my eyes, so I walked over and gave his shoulder a nudge. When he pulled away, I felt my old childhood rage bubble up and gave him a more forceful push. This time, he almost stumbled. Klaus stared at me, surprised to have an unexpected ally. Except that I wasn't his ally at all, couldn't have been his ally after what Krista had told us. And in any case, I didn't care about him or the house right then. All I could think about was that my own pregnancy had ended without a trace. No memorial, no name to remember, not even the slightest remaining recognition from my brother. Just the vanishing memory of something that had never been and a weed-covered, unfinished cement foundation.

As if she could read my thoughts, Greta changed the topic. She carefully gripped the stem of the nearest rosebush, avoiding the thorns, and said, "They were growing so well. Then the frost came too early this year, and it's been cold ever since. They're still so new. I don't know whether they'll survive."

And it was this change of topic, the shift to the mundane and practical, that must have given Martin the permission he felt he needed. He took a step toward Klaus. "So, *do* you own this house now?"

"Why?"

"Well, I'd like to know when you bought it. And how?" Martin was no longer trying to hide his purpose. "And I'd also like to know how and why you moved in with our Opa in the first place. You were young back then. Pretty unusual to be able to live in a house like this, wasn't it? Especially someone else's house. What did you have to do to move in? And what did you do now to buy it?"

"Martin," I said, but Klaus put out his hand to silence me.

He was a broad man, even broader than Martin. And tall. "I was your Opa's friend. When everyone else left him, when *your* family left him, I was still here. Isn't that enough?"

But he did not know Martin, did not know what we'd heard from Krista. Martin took one more step toward Klaus and pointed at him, his hand hovering just inches away from Klaus' face. "Don't you dare call yourself his friend!"

We all froze. Greta had her hand on the rosebush, the stems rough and bare, no hint of flowers to come. The air around us was cold, too cold for the tender roots, as Greta had said. But in that moment, I wanted nothing more than for them to survive, to have the chance to grow buds, to make flowers that would unfold, layer upon layer, revealing shades of red, catching the sunlight at different angles.

Klaus was the first to speak. "We're done here." And there was no question. We were done. I whispered, "Sorry," and Greta nodded, her fingers still clasping the branch of the rosebush, knuckles white against the dirt below.

PART V

Sins and Silence

1990

1972–1973

16

Oak Village

Illinois/Indiana, October 1990

Dad called me the day after I returned from Germany. I didn't recognize his voice at first. It was thinner than I remembered. Flat, all texture peeled away. "Kate, how have you been?"

All those years, and those were his first words. As if we'd spoken just the other week. I wrapped the phone cord tightly around my fingers to stop my hand from trembling, but the cord just shook instead, spirals quivering out of control. "Fine," I said. "I've been fine."

Dad was silent. Perhaps he was waiting for me to ask how he had been, but my throat was pulled shut. I couldn't talk. Finally he said, "I tried to call Martin too, but I can't reach him." I unwound the cord, very slowly, counting in my head—one one-thousand, two one-thousand, three one-thousand—and pulled it straight. When the coils finally stopped shaking, I said, "Martin's in Germany on business. Do you want me to tell him something?" It was the truth. Martin had stayed behind for meetings in Frankfurt. Yet my voice wavered as if I were lying.

Dad sighed. I tried to picture him, but no image emerged. All I had was that voice. Weak, unwell. How had we managed to make such a mess of it already?

"Kate," he began again. "I'm sick. Really sick."

"Are you dying?" My question landed uncomfortably somewhere between concern and sarcasm.

"Aren't we all?" Dad laughed, a pinched echo of the charming guffaw I'd once known. "I won't be gone tomorrow if that's what you mean. But I want to see both of you. It's important. Can you come?"

"Where? Where on earth would we come?" I hadn't seen him in nearly two decades. Last I knew, he'd been in and out of a rehab program in Ohio. Or was it Iowa? I'd told myself it didn't matter. I'd let go of Dad long ago.

Another sigh. "I am sorry, Kate. I truly am. Please come. Please bring Martin."

I wasn't surprised Dad hadn't been able to reach Martin. After all, Martin had just moved. Whatever number Dad had gotten from the phone book would have been his old one. I had the new number, of course, but I didn't offer to give it to Dad, and he didn't ask. Instead, he gave me the address of a nursing home in Indianapolis—Oak Village Center, only a couple of hours away—and then repeated, "Please come. Both of you."

I didn't move for a long time after hanging up. Then I got into my pajamas and yelled, "Going to sleep now" into the hallway. When Darren came in hours later, I was still wide awake, my feet shifting under the blanket, but I kept my eyes closed and breathed as deeply and evenly as I could.

The next morning I called Martin's assistant and wrote the name and number of the Frankfurt hotel where he was staying onto an index card. But when I dialed that number, the distant phone rang and rang until I hung up. I put the card away in the bottom drawer of my file cabinet, deep under a set of landscape drawings for a local pocket park, a flowerbed surrounded by brick walkways. He wouldn't come anyway. It was too far. He was too busy. That's what I told myself, though I knew, even then, it wasn't true. Martin would have jumped through fire to see Dad. And I could picture it so clearly—the look on his face when he saw Dad again, the look on both their faces, finally reunited. It was that look, I realized, I couldn't bear. I didn't try to reach Martin again.

It took me longer to decide whether I myself was ready to see the man who had once been my father. I thought Dad might call back, but he didn't. And I didn't call him either. Instead I wavered for two days and three sleepless nights. On the third morning, I got an email from Martin. Brief and to the point. *Kate, just wanted you to know I filed the claim for the Grimma house. We'll talk later. Promise.*

He'd done it again. Another big decision without me, as if our connection to Germany was his to shape. His alone. Half an hour later I told Darren I had a business trip, a potential new client in Indianapolis. I would be gone for at most one day.

I arrived at Oak Village just before noon, pulling into a long driveway lined with weeping willows. It was a cool day in mid-October, but a wall of stale dry heat hit me when I opened the front door. "You must be Ms. Porter." The receptionist hustled me into a waiting room and told me someone would be with me in a minute. I picked up a magazine lying on the table, but the articles were all about bereavement and grief, so I put it back down. Finally, another woman came into the room and closed the door.

"Ms. Porter." Her brows were pinched from too much plucking, the right corner of her mouth pulled down in a caricature of concern. "I'm Tracy Bancroft, the director of Oak Village. I am so sorry to have to tell you that your father passed away this morning. He'd been very ill, but none of us thought it would be so fast, so sudden in the end. I am sure you must have questions, and we will do our best to answer all of them, of course. We are all so very sorry for your loss." She put her hand on my arm and gave it two short pats.

Was that all? I glanced around, and the magazines on the table caught my eye again. So that's what this room was—the bad-news room. But I was not prepared to feel any grief for my father, and Ms. Bancroft must have known this. That's why I received only two short pats. That's why they hadn't bothered to call immediately. The neglectful daughter who had not once visited, who hadn't even known her father was near death. Who, I wondered, had been listed as Dad's emergency contact? Had they even had my number? I lowered my eyes.

Then Ms. Bancroft said, "Is your brother coming too? Your father was asking about him. I know he hoped to see both of you at the end."

"He didn't tell me he was dying," I said. "My brother's in Germany for work. I wish you'd called earlier." I sounded absurd, defensive. Like a three-year-old on the playground—it isn't my fault!

Ms. Bancroft winced. "I'm so sorry. We try to follow our residents' wishes, and he wanted to call you himself. But I see now…" She paused and composed her face. "We'll have to manage without your brother then. I hate to move so quickly to the practicalities, but there are things you need to sort through, a few decisions that might need to be made, though your dad left detailed instructions." She had a quintessential Midwestern voice—fast, flat, a constant buzzing that desperately made me want to interrupt her.

"What were his last weeks like?" Again, ridiculous. As if only those weeks were missing from my memories.

"It was hard at the end," she said, "but we all loved him. He was the life of the party. Bingo nights, movie nights. And, gosh, was he funny!"

I sat down and waited for her to tell me what to do next. Without her guidance, I was lost. What decisions could I possibly make about the man who used to be my dad and whom I no longer knew? A man who adored bingo and movies. A man who was beloved in here and resented out there, by Mom, Martin, and me. I was grateful when she sat down next to me and handed me a stack of papers.

Dad had named an executor, a lawyer he must have worked with over the years. When I called him, he told me Dad hadn't left much of anything. So little, in fact, that it was a miracle he'd been able to pay for Oak Village. Basically, nothing remained. My tasks were limited—sorting through the handful of items in his room. Still, the trip would take a few extra days. I called Darren and, for a moment, I considered sharing the truth. But what would I say? I knew I would tell him eventually, but it was all too raw, too shameful. I needed to process and shape this family news on my own first, massage my choices into a version of me Darren would recognize. So I told him the client meetings were going well but running long. Then I went through all of Dad's belongings, even though I knew from the start there would be nothing for me to keep. Nothing that connected this man's life here to his life with us. When I climbed back into the car to drive home, I took only one memento with me: Dad's ashes in a small box, handed to me without questions at the funeral home down the street from Oak Village. The receptionist squeezed my shoulder, "Stay strong, sweetie," and I almost asked, "Don't you have to check my brother?" But if they had no questions for me, I wouldn't have any for them. After all, I was next of kin. Why shouldn't I take the box?

The highway stretched straight and flat ahead of me as I drove back toward Illinois. In the distance a bank of clouds outlined against blue, above me the Midwestern sky that I love. Bright and stark and endless. But right then, driving home alone with Dad's ashes, I saw it differently, like an optical illusion, the immense flatness drawing the sky lower, until it bore down on me, those far-off clouds so close to the horizon, only the narrowest gap of blue between their gray and the gray of the road. It was a trick of perspective, I knew. Of distance trumping height. And yet, at that moment, I dreaded driving into the tight jaws of that prairie sky.

I pulled off the highway at Turkey Run State Park, right before the Illinois border. It was a weekday, and the parking lot was almost empty. A few scattered vehicles. No people. I steadied myself against the side of the car, taking gulping breaths, the cold air stinging my throat. Through the window, I caught sight of Darren's toolbox on the floor behind the driver's seat. "Always better to be prepared on a trip," was his motto, and the toolbox was large. I knew it held screwdrivers, a utility knife, hammers, even a small battery-operated drill and a set of drill bits—all sorts of things I'd never imagined needing on a road trip. I pulled the box from the car and placed it on the pavement. When I opened it, I could smell Darren. The comfort of him. But Darren was still hours away and, through no one's fault but mine, completely unaware. I took the utility knife and walked to the passenger side of the car where I was shielded from view of anyone who might enter the parking lot. I can't remember exactly when I decided to slash my tire. Was it when I picked up the knife? Or, even before that, when I glimpsed the toolbox through the side window? I knew it was crazy, of course, but I was desperate for punishment. For destruction. And for release. I started with short stabbing motions. The rubber was unexpectedly thick, and I barely made a dent. So I shifted to a kind of rhythmic swinging, up down up down. When the blade finally penetrated the tire, I pulled it sharply to one side. The noise came as a shock. A penetrating, angry hiss. I dropped the knife, covered my mouth with my hands, and finally let myself sob and scream, hidden from the world behind my car, under that weighted sky.

I knew how to change a tire. It was one of the many things Darren had taught me. Still I struggled to winch the car up high enough to attach the spare. By the time I was done, I was soaked in sweat despite the cold, hands and wrists black with smudges of oil and rubber. I left the old tire in the parking lot. I considered leaving the ashes too, but in the end, I couldn't do it. I drove the rest of the way home with the windows rolled down and the heat off. The sweat froze on my forehead, my gloveless, oily fingers ached with the cold, the wind yanked my hair and hurt my ears. Serves you right, I told myself over and over as the dinky tire jostled with every crack in the road. Suffer through it.

At home I placed the ashes next to the index card with Martin's hotel number in the large bottom drawer of the file cabinet, hidden deep under layered papers. But even thousands of garden plans, endless versions of flower beds and walkways, could not have shielded me from the truth. It was too late to tell Martin. Too late to ever see that dreaded, radiant look of pain and joy and triumph on his face.

17

Martin and Opa

The Bodensee, 1972

There were weeks during our childhood summers at the Bodensee when it never stopped raining. The clouds sat heavy and unmoving over our village, and the sound of raindrops was a constant background, a percussion poem. The rain found its way everywhere. It fell loudly on the corrugated plastic roof over the patio, running down the grooves, deepening them, finding the tiniest cracks. Water leaked through the windowsills too, softening the wood, giving the house a moist, musty smell. It filled the ornamental well in the garden, testing the stone walls that had been built for show. It pooled in the indent beneath the metal grate by the front door, a breeding ground for the mosquitos that filled our bedrooms. Each night, Oma helped us kill all the mosquitos by throwing a wet washcloth at them. It had to be wet, she explained, both so that it was heavier and easier to aim and so the blood wouldn't stain the walls. Martin and I perfected our aim over the years, whooping with delight as we launched each washcloth. When we finally got into bed, mosquitos vanquished, we fell asleep to the sound of raindrops falling through the birch leaves onto the gravel below.

Of course, those are not the weeks I usually describe when I talk about my childhood summers. Instead, I talk about sprinting past the poplars lining the promenade to see the first boat arrive each day, or sliding down the harbor's angled, mossy retaining walls into the soft water, swimming among the tinkling sailboats. Or biking fast through speckled woods to leave Oma and Mom far behind, then hiding behind bushes to scare them when they caught up. Sunny memories. A sparkling vision of childhood freedom. But once, years later, I looked up the annual rainfall figures at the Bodensee. Each summer month had an average of twelve rainy days. Nearly half.

And those rainy days sit deep in my bones. A muscle memory, an echo of what I knew. They aren't bad memories. And they weren't bad times. There's a German word for doing crafts. For crafting. *Basteln.* Not a phrase with different parts of speech. Not a noun awkwardly turned into an action. Just one simple verb covering endless activities. We made miniature dogs from kits, attached painted porcelain heads with shiny noses onto fabric bodies. We built towns out of cardboard, painted stained-glass windows onto miniature churches. We made enough paper flowers to fill a field. Mainly red poppies, but also crumpled roses and drooping bluebells.

One summer we built a model train, the kind we took from the airport to the Bodensee and sometimes to Tante Lara's house in Bonn too. The windows were made out of cellophane pulled tight, the rest out of cardboard, carefully painted to match the real trains. We even built the compartments inside the train, seats and all, before gluing on the roof.

"Why didn't you put any people in there?" Oma asked us. I hadn't really thought about it, but Martin answered right away. "They'd be stuck there forever," he said, and Oma laughed.

That was the summer of Opa's accident. 1972. I was ten, Martin thirteen. While we were pasting cardboard together and cutting out tiny windows, the rain kept falling. Streaming down everything in sight. So persistent was the rain that summer that each morning broadcast on the radio began with an announcement: "It has now been seventeen days since our last rain-free day." Eighteen. Nineteen. Like all kids, Martin and I loved breaking records, and so we began rooting for more rain. Each day an additional badge of honor. For twenty-two days, we counted. And for twenty-two days, Mom found new ways to keep us entertained.

On the twenty-third day, she cracked. Our summer mother washed away by the rain, undone by weeks trapped inside with us. Martin and I awakened to a quiet house that day. We had slept late, as we sometimes did on wet days. By this time, Oma had usually returned from her early rounds at the inn, checking on the menus, greeting the guests. Then she and Mom usually sat in the kitchen over a second cup of coffee. A slower, less purposeful breakfast. But we'd been promised something different for this morning. The night before, as we went to sleep, Mom had said, "How about taking a boat trip tomorrow?" She made her offer standing at the door, hand on the light switch. Martin and I both said yes quickly. We needed to lock it in before she left the room, needed to make sure that the next day would not be like all the other days. Of course, we liked the boats best in the sun when we could be out on the deck watching the shoreline and the villages scattered on hillsides, seagulls following us. We loved hearing the chatty yell of the boat captain at each stop and the responses from the men onshore as they rolled out the weathered wood and metal ramps for the passengers to disembark. On a rainy day, we'd be sitting in the boat's smoky dining area playing cards. Still, it was better than another day at home.

But now it was morning, and Mom was nowhere in sight. Martin got the cereal boxes from the cupboard, pulled the milk from the refrigerator, and put it all on the table with two bowls and two spoons. I am not sure how long we'd been at the table when Mom came into the room, expressionless. She walked to the sink, took a glass from the dish drainer, filled it with water, and turned to walk out again.

"Mom, what the hell?" Martin asked, challenging, provoking.

"Hmm?" Mom barely looked at Martin.

"We've been sitting here for hours, waiting for you."

"Well, not hours," I interrupted. Martin glared at me.

Mom moved to the door. Her arms drooped, as if the too-long sleeves of her sweater weighed them down. "You seem to have done okay."

"But you said we'd take a trip."

Mom tilted her head toward Martin. "You'll just have to find something else today. I need time too."

When Mom got to the door, Martin said, "Wait, what the hell!" The second provocation.

This time Mom turned around, seeing him, measuring him. It took a moment before she spoke. "For fuck's sake, Martin, you're thirteen years old. This once, you can be on your own for the day!" We froze at her words, her tone. So unlike the mother we knew. I waited for her to apologize, to explain. But instead, she slammed her right palm down on the table. Our bowls jumped. "For fuck's sake," she repeated under her breath, spitting out the two f's. She had outdone Martin's provocation, and the words hung heavily in the air.

Martin began to object, not even a word, just the beginnings of a sound. But it was enough. Mom put her water glass down on the table and let out a yell. A roar really. Low and guttural. From deep in her throat, or even deeper, shaken straight out of her belly. And it shook us too. Martin placed his hands over his ears, closed his eyes, and roared back. His roar was quieter, plaintive. A protest, but also an echo. Without another word, Mom left the room. We heard the front door slam, and then we sat for a long while. We were out of options.

"Martin," I finally said, "let's go find Opa."

Opa was not in his usual chair in the living room—his storytelling chair—so we did the unthinkable. We had not dared to go back into Oma and Opa's bedroom since the incident with the photo album two years earlier, but that's where we went to look for him. Oma and Opa's bed consisted of two single beds, pushed together, with two single blankets on top, a literal double bed. "Old-school German," Mom told us once, different from the queen-sized bed she used to sleep in with Dad, the kind that some Germans, with a whiff of scandal, called a French bed. Had Oma been the one asleep, I might have jumped on her, pulled off the blankets, blown into her ears, done anything to get her attention. But standing there, observing Opa, I felt embarrassed. One of his legs stuck out from under the blanket, his striped cotton pajamas revealing an ankle blue with veins, a tuft of hair on the top of his foot, gnarled toenails that grew beyond the tips of his toes. The bottom of his foot was covered with brown spots, oversized freckles spreading in all directions. Opa didn't often hug us, rarely touched us, only a squeeze of the shoulder every now and then. So we were unaccustomed to his body. We backed out of the room, shut the door again, and knocked loudly from the outside. "Opa?"

When Opa finally emerged, he was dressed in his usual outfit. Khaki pants and a short-sleeved collared shirt tucked in under a brown belt, an olive-green vest on top. The vest hung loose, his body no longer as strong as it once was. This was the only way we knew him, already an old man at seventy. Years of sitting had taken their toll, exacerbating his unsteadiness, the bad leg that had kept him out of the war. Now he shuffled, pulling his right leg along. He closed the door behind him, shutting off our view of the room, our memory of his pale blue ankle and his spotted foot, and braced himself on the doorknob. "You need something to do?"

We trailed Opa through the village, hopping along to his syncopated limp. When we got to the main square by the lake, he headed into the gravel alleyway that ran alongside the butcher shop and stopped at a small wooden door. I'd been in the butcher shop many times with Mom, but never through the side door. Never in the back room behind the curtain of sausages hanging from hooks.

"Come on, come on," he urged when I hesitated. He was eager to go in, impatient with me. Behind the door, a group of men, all old in my eyes, sat at a wooden table. Cards strewn around schnapps bottles. Sepp was the only face I recognized in the dim room.

"Ah, you've brought company, Uwe," Sepp said. He shifted his chair to the right, making room for the three of us.

Opa motioned for us to sit next to him. For hours, we watched the slow progress of the card game and listened to the local news, transmitted the way it used to be. Stories whispered at the barbershop, passed along with the fruit at the weekly market, then shared at this butcher's table. Ivo Brandt had lit a fire in the school bathroom, was now being threatened with expulsion. Old Frau Fahrke was in a bad way, but oh, it served her right, bitter old witch. Helga Oppenheim had gotten herself knocked up… And then they all looked at me, stopped talking, and shook their heads. As if I were Helga. Thinking back on those looks, I can understand why Mom left so young, why this village was too small, why Dad's promises had been enough for her to cross an ocean.

To my surprise, Opa didn't add his own stories to the mix, though I suppose his stories—more fairy tales than news—would have been incongruous in that room. Instead, he sat and listened. Martin and I listened too. The number of bottles on the table grew, and cigarette smoke filled the air. There were only two small windows, and they didn't let in much light, especially on this rainy day. The twenty-third. But the bottles shone dimly in the glow of the overhead lamp. They cast strange, captivating shapes onto the table, glimmers that expanded and contracted, edges shifting as the men moved, placing cards nearby, picking up piles, exchanging money. When Opa stood to get yet another bottle, he wobbled and grabbed the edge of the table. He didn't have Dad's elation, but he had the same unsteadiness, his feet tripping, his body swaying as he walked to the shelf with the full bottles and then back to the table, weaving through chairs. He set the new bottle down with a thud, leaned on it for support, and said, "*Na, Jungs.*" Well, boys. No one paid any attention. Only Martin angled Opa's chair quickly, placing it so he wouldn't fall when he sat down.

At some point, I must have gone to sleep. I remember Oma shaking me awake. I didn't know why she was there, but she was hissing at Opa, hissing at all the men. "You shouldn't have brought them here." The men scattered to the corners, avoiding Oma. They all knew they'd meet again the next day and the next and the one after that too. That was village life. But in that moment, they pretended they couldn't see each other, that each of them was alone in that room.

Oma pulled us toward the front, underneath the hanging sausages separating the shop from the back room, out past the brightly lit counter, where I saw a row of customers, all familiar faces, curious. But I could not focus on them, I could only feel the grip of Oma's hand. When we were finally on the street, she let go. Opa came limping, swaying out the door behind us. Oma walked toward the inn without turning, her steps quick and sharp. I started to follow but stopped when I saw that Martin wasn't moving. He and Opa stood face to face only a few feet apart on the square in front of the butcher shop.

"Come on, Martin," I said. Oma was already half a block ahead of us, not slowing, not waiting. I knew whose side we were meant to be on.

But Martin was frozen. His forehead wrinkled, features sharp. Concentrating, deciding. Finally, his voice breaking with the effort of speaking truth, he said, "You're just like Dad." Opa flinched and grasped at Martin's arm. But Martin took a step backward. "Don't come home," he said. "Just don't come home!"

And Opa didn't. We had a silent dinner, Mom, Oma, Martin, and I. Gone was Martin's bravado from that morning. He and I ate salad from the garden without a complaint. The lettuce, the cucumbers, even the tomatoes. When we were done, we both lined our fork and knife up on the plate as we'd been taught, then Martin cleared the dishes. When everything was put away, Mom placed both palms on the table and said, "*Na dann*," pulling herself up.

Strange how days can seem different before you really know why, before you understand the full scope of what is happening, what may still happen. After dinner, after the plates were all cleared away, we joined Oma in the living room to watch the news. I lay on the thick crimson rug in front of the TV, running my hands back and forth, smoothing the rug down, then pulling my hand back, making the fibers stand on end in dark splotches, soothed by the predictability of the shifting textures. Oma kept looking at the door, her head turning one way, then the other. Mom watched closely, attuned to the dynamics of relationships gone wrong. Finally, Mom said, "He'll come eventually."

After a long pause, Oma nodded. "He knows where we are."

So we sat in front of the television, as we did every night, except that Opa's chair was empty. And that empty chair, that absence, felt more alive than Opa himself. We were watching the news for the second time, two hours, two rounds of the same stories, when we heard the knock on the door. Sepp was outside. That face I associated with swimming and boats, with sun and glittering water. But after that day, his face had another meaning too, one illuminated by the glimmer of bottles and the tinny tones of gossip. And then, standing at the door in the dark, his face was different yet again, filled with fear.

"What's the matter now?" Oma asked. A glimpse of her anger from earlier.

"There's been an accident." Without saying more, he turned and disappeared into the darkness before I could even fully register his presence. Oma and Mom followed him. They didn't take their coats, and they didn't shut the door. Then it was quiet, the open door a dark, forbidding rectangle. Finally Martin said, "I'll close it." I fell asleep on the rug that night, soft and thick against my cheek, pressing patterns into my skin, the way I had earlier pressed patterns into it. I'd asked to sleep there many times, but it took Opa's accident to finally make it happen. Not a treat, not a yes. Merely the absence of a no.

When I woke, daylight was shining through the curtains. Someone had thrown a blanket over me, and I could hear Martin and Mom talking in the kitchen. Morning murmurs.

"Kate!" Mom said when I walked in, as if it were a great surprise to see me there, in the room where I ate breakfast every morning all summer long. It was the second day in a row that I made my own breakfast, filling a bowl with muesli, pouring the milk. Easy tasks, of course, but something that Mom usually did for us. Now she sat at the table, waiting for me to join them. When I did, she said, "Opa had an accident last night. I was telling Martin."

"What kind of accident?"

"Jesus, Kate," Martin said. "Don't you want to know if he's okay?"

I hadn't thought of it that way. I'd wanted only the details, as if the details could keep things on track, things that seemed to be going off track though I was not sure how or why. Mom answered both questions at once. "He's going to be okay, Kate. He's broken one hip and an ankle. He's got some head injuries too, but he's going to be okay. He was hit by a truck on his way home last night."

"Where?" I asked, ignoring Martin's glare.

"Up on the bypass road, near the woods."

"Where was he coming from?" One detail gave way to the need for another and another. A string of questions and answers that broke the news about Opa down into components, kept the totality at bay.

"From the butcher shop."

"But that's not on the way." And just like that, the neat string of answers came unraveled. I no longer knew the next question, only this fact: No path from the butcher shop to the inn went anywhere near the bypass road. Opa had absolutely no reason to cross that road, to face that truck.

"You're right. We're not sure how he ended up there. He was drunk, Kate. People do things that make no sense when they're drunk."

Martin let out a noise then. A noise that made both Mom and me stop. It was a choking sound, but he wasn't even eating. He had already finished his cereal, leaving only traces of milk, colored light brown from the oats, in his bowl. His right wrist was resting on the edge of the table, his fingers still gripping the spoon, waving it back and forth to a nervous rhythm.

"I told him he was like Dad," he said. "I told him not to come home."

Mom placed her hand firmly on his. "Oh, Martin, no." He dropped the spoon onto the table, splashes of milk staining the brown wood. "No, Martin," she said again, "That's not why he did that. That's not your fault."

I wondered what she meant. What exactly had Opa done? But I didn't dare ask. Mom and Martin were focused only on each other, so tight together I might as well have been in a different room. No, a different universe.

Martin opened and closed his mouth a few times, like a gasping fish, before finally saying, "But still, if I hadn't mentioned Dad. If I'd just told him to come home."

Mom took her hand off Martin's and slapped the table. A sharp slap. "No," she said. "Absolutely not. It's not your responsibility. Do you understand?"

When Martin didn't answer, she repeated, "Do you understand?"

Louder. Almost aggressive. Martin nodded, and Mom reached for his hand again. When he pulled away, she took mine instead. But she still looked at him. "I'm sorry."

What was she sorry for? That she wasn't being herself, that she had yelled at us the previous morning? That she couldn't fix Opa? Or Dad? I decided it was for everything, all of it. An apology and an absolution all at once. A kind of permission to forget.

Martin ran out of the room, and we heard the front door slam.

"He's got no shoes on," I said.

"Never mind." Mom squeezed my hand. "Come, let's go see Opa."

We visited Opa many times the rest of that summer. At first in the hospital, and then, once he was released, in the bedroom where Oma had set him up with two pillows and two blankets to match his two broken bones, hip and ankle. I didn't like visiting him in the hospital, and even at home I avoided spending much time with him. The bedroom smelled of a mixture of cleaning fluids and sweat that no amount of Oma's cleaning, or simply her presence, could overcome. But Martin was in the room with Opa all the time. I didn't hear them talking. Whenever I walked in, Martin was sitting on the bed next to Opa, reading a magazine or an old newspaper. "Come on," I'd say to him. "Let's go down to the lake." But he'd peek at Opa and shake his head.

"What's he doing?" I asked Mom once. "Why's he up there so much?"

"Kate, if he needs to be there, let him be there," she said. And so the last weeks of that summer were lonely ones. I explored for hours, collecting places and experiences that were just mine. That was the summer I discovered my hidden beach, down through the marshes on a narrow dirt path by the public tennis courts. We'd never even seen the path before, that's how small it was. I had to push my bike past two thick bushes, then climb back on, shielded from the street, in my own world. The ride was bumpy and dank, the pungent smells of damp weeds and mud everywhere. But at the end there was a tiny sandy beach, unlike the rocky beaches near the harbor where we usually swam. The rain finally stopped in those last weeks, and I spent hours sitting at that beach, thinking to myself: I'm the only one who knows about this. I dropped hints for Martin occasionally, sometimes because I wanted to make him feel left out and sometimes because I wanted to share it with him. Either way, he never bit. I'd say, "I swam again today, not in the harbor" or, "I took a new bike ride today," but he never asked where. He always nodded and said, "Okay."

On our last day before leaving for Illinois, Martin was in Opa's room, and I headed to my beach for one final visit. As I rounded the last corner on my bike, past the big root that jutted out into the path, I saw bright towels lying on the sand. Two older boys, about Martin's age, were playing in the water with water guns. They didn't see me. They were too busy splashing, screaming, spraying. Next to their towels, I saw bags of chips and cookies, snacks for a day. I stood behind the bushes that edged the sand, watching them, willing them away, but I knew they were not leaving anytime soon. On that last day of summer, not even my beach was mine.

18

Opa's Tragedy

The Bodensee, 1973

Opa hanged himself in the attic at the Bodensee. Summer of 1973. I was eleven, Martin fourteen. Almost exactly one year after his accident.

Over the years I've often wondered why Opa chose the attic. Martin and I were the only ones who ever went up there. It was not exactly forbidden but discouraged, and that was enough enticement for us. A dark, dusty place full of boxes and piles of clothes. The only way to get to the attic was by scaling a ladder that pulled down from a hatch in the hallway ceiling. Whenever we climbed up, we made sure to raise the ladder behind us so no one would know we were there. It was dark in the attic, especially with the hatch closed. The floor was rotting slowly, boards loose and soft. Oma's house had a sharp roof, typical for the Bodensee, slanting steeply, covered with red tiles and moss. There was a beam running across the length of the roof where the angle was sharpest, the space tallest. This must have been where he hanged himself.

So long ago, yet so clear in my mind. It was a quiet afternoon, rainy. I was alone in Mom's room reading a book Oma had bought for me on her last trip across the lake to Konstanz. At some point I got bored and decided to see what Martin was doing. I left the book face down on Mom's bed and opened the door to the hallway. That's when I heard the sudden commotion in the attic. A flurry of steps above my head, each one sending a sharp crack through the house. Other sounds too, sounds I couldn't place. Then Mom's voice, calling for Oma. Stifled, almost choking. Not the scream of horror I would have expected had I known what was happening. Nothing like in the movies. But Oma must have heard something different, an urgency I missed. As she ran past me toward the attic stairs, she yelled, "Go back into the room, Kate!" The hatch was open, the ladder extended, and I watched Oma climb up, lifting her knees high so she wouldn't step on the hem of her skirt as she put her feet on each rung. It looked comical, like an exercise she'd invented to make me laugh. But when she reached the top, she looked back and said, "Kate, don't come up here." And the way she said it, I knew this went far beyond the thrill of the forbidden, into that realm where adults know best.

I went back into Mom's room and waited. There were more footsteps above my head and in the hallway. I listened to the rhythm, quick paces, low voices that brought urgency to this sluggish afternoon. When Oma didn't come back, when no one came for me, I opened my door and walked downstairs quickly, trying not to look at the open hatch, dashing into the living room as if I were being chased. That's where I found Martin on the sofa. "What's going on?" I asked.

His eyes were half-shut, and he was trembling. "I'm not sure," he said. "I don't know." When he stopped talking, I could still hear his teeth chattering.

So I sat down next to him. Not on my side of the sofa but right up against him, sandwiching him between the armrest and my shoulder. I wondered if he would press back, if he would object, but he just absorbed the pressure. Then Mom came into the room and turned on the television. It was Opa's channel, an animal show, and Martin and I sank deeper into the sofa, watching the meerkats stand on their hind legs, peer over a low fence, evidence that they were not in their own world but in ours. Mom squeezed both our shoulders and said, "Wait here." Then she left, shutting the door tightly. I suppose she was going to call the doctor, but I don't know if I realized it then. I can't quite remember what I understood in those first hours and what I didn't. But now I sometimes think I should have understood more. I knew how disappearances felt. I'd seen the way Dad's departure had changed all that was intimate, mundane in our lives. I knew, even then, how tragedy transformed people. That it stole million-dollar smiles, that it layered a heavy quietness onto everything it touched.

Yet all I did was take advantage of the distraction I'd been offered: television in the middle of the day. As for Martin, I don't know what he was thinking. I just kept leaning against him, containing him.

First the doctor arrived, then the police. By that point, Mom had told us that Opa had fallen. A terrible accident. I remember pushing myself to feel something beyond confusion. I rubbed my eyes to see if I could make them wet. I pulled my arms tightly around myself to test if I was shaking like Martin. But winding my arms around my body just made me feel even smaller, more overwhelmed.

Maybe I really was too young to understand, and that's why I was left not with emotions, but with questions. I wondered why he'd been up there, what he'd been searching for, if we could have helped him find it, if all of this could have been avoided if we'd been there. And then I wondered why the police came for a simple accident, but no one answered the questions I didn't ask.

Opa's funeral was at the old church in the next village. I remember noticing how long it took to get there, how unfair it was that we couldn't bike. It was one of my favorite bike rides, through wetlands on a path near the lake, tall reeds and wispy trees hanging over streams, a lush world of silvery green giving way to fruit orchards. At the very end of the wetlands, where they met the orchards, there was a wooden bridge, which made the most wonderful sound whenever we biked over it, each board shaking back and forth under our tires. *Ba-bum, ba-bum, ba-bum* across the bridge like a train. It did not make any sound as we walked across it in our fancy clothes.

We formed a small procession, all dressed in black. There was no coffin to follow. Opa was being driven to the cemetery along the larger roads while we walked the path. And yet we walked as if we were following something. Oma, Mom, Martin, and me in front, heads up, eyes straight ahead. Then a few of the guests from the inn, the ones who came every summer and happened to be there when Opa died. A poor choice of vacation days, though how could they have known? Then the butcher, the baker, Sepp, a few more of Opa's drinking buddies from the back room. The group walked along solemnly, the men in awe of the situation and of Oma, until we got to the next village. As we entered the cemetery, one of the men ducked out of line. He reappeared at the grave clutching two bottles of apple schnapps. Local, straight from the farmer.

It was my first funeral, and it set the standard. For years, I thought it was normal for funerals to start quiet but grow increasingly rowdy, for men to drink and then talk, louder and louder, finally cursing. Cursing god, cursing life, cursing the dead man who got away. I thought it was normal that the widow, the family, left first, not saying goodbye, a swift retreat, leaving behind the real mourners, the loud mourners, the ones who would watch over the grave all night, their voices carrying all the way back to our village over the water, leaving the bottles scattered on the ground, sneaking over to the farm for more schnapps until the farmer finally closed his doors in the early morning hours, ignoring the complaints and curses outside. I suppose the men woke up at the grave, though I have no way of knowing that. It's just how I imagine it. A nightlong wake, neither sad nor joyful, no reminiscences, no *he would have wanted*'s, only an outpouring of resentments, a litany of mistreatment. Deep underground, Opa would have been nodding, had he been able.

Mom was the one who finally told me that Opa had killed himself, that things like that sometimes happened, no one really knew why. That it was simply tragic. We had been back in Illinois two months by then. The air was crisp, the evenings dark. We went out for one final late-afternoon apple-picking trip, to the orchard outside of town. Pick your own. They provided the basket and a vague sense of the types of apples available, but we didn't really care anyway. The tradition was about the air, the dusk, the long grass underfoot, not about the apples. Martin didn't come along. He was at a friend's house, and Mom had said, "Good, you do that." Not insisting on the family time she usually enforced. When we had filled two baskets, she put them down in the grass and said, "Kate, I want to tell you what happened with Opa."

By then I'd figured it out, of course. In a way. I'd heard the whispers at the funeral and in the weeks after. Yet I hadn't fully grasped what it all meant.

"Does Martin know?" I asked.

Mom nodded. She put her hand on my shoulder, and I could see in her eyes that she was worried I might be overwhelmed, confused. And I suppose I was both of those things, but most of all I felt strangely, inappropriately triumphant. Triumphant that someone was finally answering my questions, even the ones I had not known to ask. Triumphant that I too had the same knowledge as my brother.

PART VI

Letting Go, Holding On

1990–1991

19

Confession Games

Illinois, November 1990

On November 9th, 1990—one year after my miscarriage, one year after the Wall fell—Darren and I took a walk through the patch of woods behind our house, an odd clump of trees among the never-ending fields. Too small to get lost in, just big enough to hide in. So we hid together. Hid from the memories of what had happened exactly one year earlier, what we had lost. And I suppose I was hiding from Dad's death too. A few weeks had passed since my return from Oak Village with Dad's ashes, and I hadn't told Darren anything yet. He'd asked about the tire, of course, but I'd blamed it on some broken glass. That felt right somehow. There was so much that was broken.

Darren and I hadn't had sex since the miscarriage. Not once that whole past year. Truth is, I didn't want him touching my body. I didn't feel it was mine. In the first months, I sometimes locked the bathroom door and pushed and prodded my arms, my legs, my torso. Checking to see if I was still there, testing the body that had failed me. I thought I would regain myself gradually, fill in my own outline, firm and real, but it hadn't happened. I still felt brittle and shattered, my body mere fragments.

I started keeping a journal that year. Letters written to my Maybe-Child in a hardback notebook, hopeful silver leaves against deep burgundy on its cover. I didn't manage to fill up the journal. I only left notes scattered across the pages. *One day you'll see cardinals, bright red against the trees.* Or: *You'll need to learn how to make lemon meringue pie because I can't.* Sometimes I wrote longer notes about my family and about Germany, exactly as Mom had suggested. *Your great-grandparents came from East Germany, from a town on a river—a town hall with a wavy roof. Someday I'll show you photos.* But how would the Maybe-Child ever be born if I couldn't even have sex?

So, it was still only the two of us, leaving our house for that walk.

The ground was chilled from an early snow. But it was brilliantly sunny, the sky a cutting blue, and we nestled down into a patch of long grass, brown with a sprinkled coat of white. We lay on our backs, shielding our eyes, shoulders touching.

"I have a new kid in my class," Darren said. "He came to introduce himself. You know what his name is? Jeff Muckenhirn. Can you believe it? *Muckenhirn.* As in mosquito brain! I asked him if he knew what it meant, but he had no idea. Wants to study German history and doesn't even know what his name means."

I knew Darren wanted to distract me, make me laugh, but lying there in the grass, I felt sorry for the kid.

"He's someone's son," I said, and it sounded more like a rebuke than I had intended.

"I know," Darren said. "I just thought…"

A cloud drifted past the sun, thrusting us back into early winter. I pulled my coat tight, but the cold grabbed me from the ground below. And then, just as quickly, the cloud passed, and the world was painfully bright again. Without shifting, Darren took my hand and gave it a squeeze.

"Let's play a game," he said. "Let's play confession. We tell each other something we're ashamed of, then we absolve each other. You go first. You've got something to tell me."

I'd been thinking about Dad pretty much nonstop since my trip to Oak Village, of course. Wondering when I would tell Darren. Wondering *how* I would. But how did he know?

"Did you go into my file cabinet?" I sat up, staring down at him now.

"I was only looking for printer paper," he said. "But I found so, so much more. What's going on, Kate? When did he die?"

I told him the whole story then. He nodded as I talked, propped up on his elbow, eyes on me, not allowing me to look away. And he didn't interrupt, not when I told him about the tire, not even when I explained why I had chosen not to tell Martin. He'd promised absolution, and that's what he offered. Silent and unjudging. When I was done, he sat up, brushed the snow from his sleeves and said, "See, wasn't that a good game?" Then he rested his hand briefly on each of my shoulders, as if he were bestowing a knighthood.

"What do I do now?" I asked. "Do I tell Martin?"

He considered my question for a long time. Long enough that I felt the cold creep up from my legs to my back and down my arms. Then he said, "Mostly it's important to be truthful, but sometimes not telling is kinder. You'll know when the moment comes."

That night Darren and I had sex. A reacquaintance and a quest all at once. Not just two of us—getting to know each other again, touching the familiar dips, reveling in the long-forgotten smells—but three of us seeking each other out. Me, Darren, and our Maybe-Child. No secrets between us. Afterwards, Darren rolled onto his back and placed his hand on my stomach. Another knighthood bestowed.

I wrote my first letter to Greta the next day. *Liebe Frau Schultz.* I stopped after writing those first three words, not sure how to go on, knowing only that I wanted—no, needed—some connection to this woman I had met halfway around the world. It wasn't just that she reminded me of my Oma, though she did. It was also the connection to Germany she offered—perhaps my only one after Tante Lara's death. And even more simply, now that I was trying to get pregnant again, I craved her understanding, her warmth.

Like you, I have a place that reminds me of the baby we wanted to have, I wrote in German. I could see it through the window from where I was sitting. The ugly concrete platform, the foundation of the nursery we had planned to add to our house. I sat out there often during that first year, my legs straight in front of me. There was no other way to sit on the platform's low edge. Yet I always felt disrespectful—sprawled lizard-like in the sun when I should have been grieving. *But there are many ways to mourn, aren't there? I imagine you sitting next to the stone in your garden thinking about your daughter, and it makes me happy. Is that awful of me to say? I think it's beautiful that you planted roses in that spot. I hope it helps you find joy in your saddest moments. There are plants growing on my platform too. Just weeds, but in summer they flower purple and yellow and in early fall the leaves are like flames.* When I finished writing the letter, I stood and gazed out my window at those plants, brown and wilted now, hunkered down for winter.

Her first response arrived more quickly than I had expected. A few tidbits from the neighborhood (even more people leaving for the West), an inquiry about Mom (was she holding up all right after Tante Lara's death?), and at the very end a postscript. *Have you seen a doctor? It might make you feel better about your loss. Not everyone's the same, of course, but I wanted to know what the doctor thought right away. Why had it happened? Would it happen again? Maybe that would help you too?*

I showed the letter to Darren over dinner. Neither one of us was much of a cook, our dinner preparation rushed. But we made up for it by sitting at the table long after the food was gone. When I brought out the letter, Darren shoved the dirty plates to one side, and I laid the paper on the table.

"Look," I said. "She even writes like Oma." I pointed at the *n*'s shaped like *u*'s, the *m*'s like *w*'s, valleys where there should have been peaks.

"I'm envious you knew your Oma's handwriting," Darren said. "My grandparents bought me presents when they visited. Then they became ghosts until the next time."

"Well, Oma bought me plenty of presents too. But she also wrote often enough that I missed her letters once she was gone. Then again, I think what I really missed was Seefrieden. The Bodensee. After she died, we didn't have that."

Darren rested his hand on my arm. "When did she die?"

"Two years after Opa. I was thirteen. You know that." But he shook his head. I couldn't believe I'd never told him about Oma's death, so I gave him the outlines: Mom coming to school to tell us, Martin reacting the way he always did. Overreacting. Like a kid, even though he was sixteen. I could still see him running down the hallway, all gangly, Mom chasing after him awkwardly in her tight skirt. Like a stick figure chasing a cartoon character.

"Do you want another confession?" I asked, and Darren nodded. His hand was still on my arm, and I could feel my skin getting sweaty from his warmth. "I'll never forget how Martin turned and bellowed at Mom when he got to the end of the hallway. He had his hands out to stop her from coming any closer, his fingers curved like claws. Like this." I pulled my arm out from under Darren's hand and raised my curled fingers toward his face. Then I held them there like a shield and kept talking. "I know I should have felt bad for him, but I just thought he looked ridiculous. I still remember pushing my fingers into my own thighs, digging my nails into my skin. That's how mad I was. Mad at Oma for dying, mad at Mom for telling me. But mostly mad at Martin for the way he was hurting. He'd always been closer to Opa, not Oma, and I was so mad that he took on that grieving role even with her. That he stole it from me. But who's being ridiculous now, right? As if hurt could be stolen."

I dropped my hands and pressed my fingers into my thighs, testing. But my fingernails were cut so short now I couldn't even feel them on my skin.

"You were young—" Darren said, but I interrupted him.

"It gets worse. Mom went to the funeral alone. She didn't bring Martin or me. Martin was struggling a bit in school back then, and she didn't want to pull him out. That would have been our last time at Seefrieden, and we missed it. I never saw it again, not until this recent trip with Martin anyway. And I blamed him for that. I've always blamed him. I don't even have the excuse of being young anymore, but I can't get over it. I still blame him. How immature is that?"

He laughed, but it was a gentle laugh. "We've all got our moments. Speaking of which, I think it's my turn to confess."

"Did you do something wrong too?"

"Well, this is from a long time ago, but it's about Martin, and it feels like that's what we're doing. Martin confessions." Darren rested his elbows on the table, chin on his hands. He was more relaxed than I thought a penitent person should be. "You remember when Martin had just finished law school? He was still living down the street and interviewing for his first law firm job? I was so thrilled he'd finally be leaving town, but then he got those two offers, one in Boston, one in Chicago. And I really wanted him to take the Boston one because it was even farther away. So when he went to check out Chicago, I had that friend of mine show him around, remember? But what I never told you is that I asked my friend to show him all the worst, grimiest corners of Chicago. I wanted to stack the deck."

He stopped and waited for my reaction.

"Wait, so you're confessing that you asked your friend to do that?"

He nodded.

"But Martin already knew Chicago," I said. "It wouldn't have made a difference."

"Still, I thought it might. On the margin."

I scratched my head, massaged my temples. There was something off about this game. I tried to picture Martin back then, how excited he was to start his career, how the very prospect of it seemed to help him shed the insecurities he'd had since Dad left. The day he passed the bar exam, he came home belting "I'm a lawyer" to the tune of "Oh My Darling," his chest puffed out with the volume of his words.

"I'm confused. You're confessing about a silly weekend in Chicago, but not about the fact that you hated my brother?"

Darren's face froze, and I knew I'd put my finger on what was wrong with his confession.

"No, I never hated him," Darren said. "I just thought you and I were better together without your family around."

"So, were you happy when Mom moved to Vermont too?" I stood, my hand braced on the table, and I could hear my voice getting louder. Harsher than I wanted it to. I wasn't playing this game right either. I pushed down, and the edge of the table cut into my palm.

"Kate, we've talked about this. I love your family, but you know how they are. How you all are when you're together. I just wanted something simpler, more open. A different kind of family."

My palm was aching now. I remembered the day, so long ago, when Martin and I found the picture of Opa and Krista hidden in Opa's drawer, though we hadn't known it was Krista then. What had Mom said to us that night? Someday you'll make wonderful families of your own? Back then, I'd dreamt of creating a different kind of family. But it didn't sound the same coming from Darren. Who was he to judge us?

"Careful what you wish for," I said. "We haven't exactly managed to build our own family. We'd be lucky to have one like mine!"

We slept as far apart as possible that night, both almost tipping over the sides of the bed. The next morning, I pretended I was asleep until Darren left for work. I had a site visit later that morning, a schoolyard redesign. Plenty of time before I needed to leave. In the kitchen, Darren had left a carafe of coffee with a note. *Give me a call, Kate. I'm sorry about yesterday.* I'd call him later, I told myself. Instead, I filled my coffee cup to the brim, took it with me into my study, and began to write.

Dear Greta. I paused over those words, wondering if they were too much, too soon. Too American. Greta had written *Dear Mrs. Porter* in her letter, of course, but I knew what I wanted. I wanted her to call me Kate. So I wrote: *I hope I can call you that. I've been wondering. Did you try to have more children after your loss? I know you already had one son, but did you keep trying for a second child? I hope you don't mind my asking. It's just that sometimes I worry it will never happen for us, that it's not meant to be. Maybe you're right. Maybe I should see a doctor just to be sure nothing is really wrong.*

The phone rang, probably Darren, but I didn't pick up. I was busy with a different confession.

Can I tell you something personal? I'm so impatient with my husband recently. I feel guilty admitting that because it's not his fault. But the thing is, he doesn't understand what I'm going through. I know he lost his dream of having a baby too, but he didn't feel it physically the way I did. So we fight about silly things. Like we've forgotten how to have common dreams. I'm not sure why I am sharing this, but sometimes I feel so alone. I wonder: would a baby make me less lonely? I want you to know I am grateful to be building this connection with you. You give me hope that everything will work out. And you remind me of my childhood, which makes me mostly happy, though also a bit sad. My mother used to scold my brother for looking back too much, but maybe he's right in the grand scheme of things? What would life be without memories? And what would our memories be worth if we didn't long for them?

I sealed the envelope quickly, before I could change my mind. I felt I'd gone too far, gotten too personal, but who else could I share my feelings with? Who else would understand?

Despite stopping to drop the letter in a mailbox on the way, I arrived at the schoolyard for my site visit too early. It was recess, kids running everywhere, climbing jungle gyms, playing tetherball and kickball. I closed my eyes and listened to the cacophony. High-pitched shrieks, the metal chains on the swings jangling, the thud of feet hitting rubber. I didn't open my eyes until the noise had faded, the kids disappeared inside. Then I got out of my car, took the site plan out of my bag, and headed toward the principal's office. Ready to work.

That evening I met Darren at his office, and together we went to get ice cream at one of the shops near campus. Pistachio for me, chocolate for him. Cones in hand, we walked back to the quad. It was almost empty, just a few students rushing from one building to the next in the cold. We started walking the full rectangle. Halfway around, I said, "Confession game?"

"Anytime." He leaned over to take a bite of my pistachio.

"Okay, here goes. Turns out I'm bad at this game. I'm bad at being judgment free. I've got no talent for absolution. That's my confession."

Darren held his cone out. I knew the chocolate would be too sweet for me, but I took two bites anyway.

"Also, you're not my only confessor," I said. "I sent another letter to Greta, and I told her about our fight."

"Is that a second confession?" Darren asked. When I nodded, he said, "Why should you confess about that? I mean, I don't quite get why you feel so connected to her, but if it helps you, then I'm happy. Enter as many booths as you want. There's no rule against multiple confessors. Not in our game anyway."

"Thank god." I put my arm around Darren's waist. "I need as many as I can get!"

We were almost back where we'd started, one full loop around the quad. I'd long finished my ice cream, but Darren was a slow eater. Despite the cold, chocolate dripped over the edge of his cone onto his hand, leaving small brown spots like freckles. Without thinking, I licked the largest freckle off his knuckle. Darren pulled his hand away in surprise, but then he looked at me, threw his head back, and both of us laughed and laughed, wispy puffs of air rising like clouds from our mouths.

20

Christmas Eve

Vermont, December 1990

Martin and I met at Mom's house that Christmas. Darren was headed to the usual gathering in Iowa with his extended family, stockings on the fireplace, beer in the cooler. There would be lots of ping-pong in the game room and even more television. I wasn't joining him for any of that though. We had serious work in Vermont. Martin had promised to bring the photographs we'd taken of Tante Lara's possessions for us to sort through. We were on a tight timeline. A contract for sale had been signed, everything had to be out of her house.

When I arrived in Vermont, Martin was upstairs, finishing some last-minute work calls. "Even on Christmas Eve," Mom said with an eye roll. "Go tell him it's time to stop."

Martin always stayed in the same room, the one at the top of the stairs with the best view over the lake. He'd chosen it on our very first trip after Mom moved in. The benefit of arriving half an hour earlier, leaving me the room on the other side. "Yours has a better mattress," he'd said at the time, as if either one of us would choose a room based on the mattress. But from then on, Mom referred to his room as "Martin's room," and there was no undoing the label.

Now I knocked on the door, and Martin looked up quickly, mouth suspiciously full, hands deep in his pockets. When he saw it was me, he grinned, pulled a crumpled paper napkin out of one pocket, and unwrapped two cookies. *Nürnberger Lebkuchen.* Definitely meant for Christmas Eve dinner, not before. Still grinning, Martin held one of the cookies out and said, "Mom will never know."

I took his offering and sat next to him on the bed. We ate slowly, savoring the ginger taste, letting the papery bottom layer dissolve on our tongues. Through the window I could see one of Mom's neighbors walking his dog along the opposite shore, dark branches stark against the cobalt-blue sky, sun glinting off the snow and ice below. The dog ran ahead, then back, impatient, happy, circling its owner. "That's the life," I said, pointing, and Martin chuckled. When we finished eating, he stuffed the napkin back into his pocket. Then we both wiped our mouths with the backs of our hands, removing any evidence, and headed downstairs.

The *Sauerbraten,* always the centerpiece of Christmas Eve dinner, was in the oven. "A few more hours to go," Mom said, so Martin suggested we use the time before dinner to get a head start on sorting through the photos from Tante Lara's house. We agreed to a system of no-hands, one-hand, two-hands. No-hands meant no interest. One-hand meant *I want it.* Two-hands was the ultimate demand. *I must have this.*

Rules established, we began. We sat around the table in front of the woodstove, the stack of photos face down between us, and took turns flipping over the top one. Sometimes it was an easy no. Pots, pans, bathmats. A few shakes of the head, and those photos were put on the discard pile. To be sold or given away. But sometimes, the first glimpse of a photo would stop us all. We'd exhale or inhale. Some sound of recognition. And then came the best part. One of us would say, "I remember when…" or "You know that time…" Even Mom, rarely sentimental about the past, warmed to these memories.

It was her turn to flip the next photo. "The big vase from the front hallway," she announced. We all knew the vase well. It was at least four feet tall, made of thick unglazed earthenware. Only the top rim was painted a glossy deep green. As a kid, I often ran my hands along that rim, feeling the smoothness under my fingertips. It reminded me of the trick Dad had taught me when Mom was not watching: how to run my fingers lightly around the rim of his wine glass to make it hum, and then, once I had the rhythm down, to make it sing. The vase neither hummed nor sang, yet I'd always pull my fingers back quickly from its rim with a sudden burst of guilt. As if someone would hear the nonexistent sound and know I'd been complicit in Dad's vice. So when I saw the photo of the vase, the first thing I thought of was Dad. His shiny eyes and sweaty cheeks. His enveloping voice. His arms unfolded to catch me when I ran toward him. And, of course, his death. The death I'd hidden from Martin.

"Well—" Mom started, but I interrupted, desperate to give the vase a more innocent meaning in my mind.

"I remember when you outgrew the vase, Martin. The summer you were finally taller." I could see him stretched high beside the vase, chin up, his elbow resting jauntily on the edge, saying, "You'll get there soon, Kate."

Mom smiled and raised two hands. "Nice, but I still want it. You can come visit it anytime right here." She put the photo in her pile and turned over the next one.

Faded, but unmistakable. Opa's chair. The one he sat in all those hours, telling us stories.

"That's strange. I didn't know Tante Lara had that. Where do you think it was?" Mom put the photo down slowly.

"Down in the basement. I found it there once when I was looking for something. I can't remember what…" Martin's voice trailed off.

I tried to pick up the photo to get a closer view, but Martin blocked my hand.

"Wait," I said, pointing at a scribble in the corner. "What's that?"

The black ink was barely visible on the dark background. I pushed Martin's hand away and grabbed the photo.

"Do not include," I read out slowly. I waved the photo at Martin. "What's this?"

"How would I know?"

"Give me a break!" I would have recognized his look anywhere. That odd mixture of guilt and defiance. Asking for forgiveness while still committing the crime. As if he were entitled to both the loot and the pardon.

"Martin?" Mom asked.

He sat silent for another moment. Then he raised his chin. Defiant. "Okay, fine. It shouldn't be here. I wasn't planning to include it in the stack."

"Why?" I asked.

"Because I want the chair. Because it was Opa's chair. Because you guys didn't even know it was there. Because you don't care."

"How the hell would you know?"

"Well, *do* you want it?" Unlike mine, Martin's tone stayed provocatively even.

"That's not the point. We agreed to discuss everything, every item." I placed my palm squarely on the photo and watched Martin wince. Never touch photos. That's what he had taught me back when we were kids, when he was in his photo-taking phase, documenting all of Dad's belongings.

"Okay, let's discuss it." Martin's voice was still flat, dangerous. "*I* want it. Do you?"

"Stop it, both of you." Mom pulled the photo from under my hand and turned it over so we could no longer see the chair with its nubby fabric and wooden armrests. Just the back of the photo. White with a line of letters and numbers printed in light blue. "If you really want it, you can have it, Martin. Those are the two-hand rules. Right, Kate?"

I hadn't thought about that chair in years. To be honest, I'm not sure I ever really had. Not as an item in its own right, distinct from Opa. But suddenly, I no longer knew what I wanted to hold on to and what I didn't, what I was willing to let Martin have, and what I wanted to take from him. "What if I put up two hands too? Then what?"

"Don't be childish, Kate." Mom put Opa's chair in Martin's pile and swept the remaining photos back into the box where they'd been stored. "It's time for dinner."

Martin stuck his tongue out at me like he used to do when we were kids, and there it was. The loot and the pardon all wrapped up, an insult thrown in for good measure. As if I were the childish one. I knew I'd just be proving Mom right, but in that moment, all I wanted was to hurt Martin, to show he couldn't always win.

"Dad died," I said.

Mom stopped in her tracks, halfway to the kitchen door. I wanted to look at Martin to see his reaction, but I couldn't bring myself to. "I got a call last month, so I went to pick up his ashes. He'd been living in a nursing home in Indianapolis."

There was so much I was leaving out. Things that would hurt Martin even more, and wasn't that what I wanted? But those same things would make me the villain. I hesitated, not sure how to go on.

"Why did you wait to tell us?" Mom sounded perplexed but not necessarily angry. "I mean, I know I haven't wanted to talk about Dad much. But why didn't you at least tell your brother?"

I finally glanced at Martin, expecting the worst, but I couldn't interpret the expression on his face at all. He flexed his jaw, up and down, side to side. Then he grimaced, bitter, and yet his features were alive with the knowledge of victory. "I've been in touch with Dad. I saw him."

"Martin!" Mom dropped the box of photos, and pictures scattered across the rug.

Martin winced but didn't stop. "Dad tracked me down me about six months ago, so I went to visit. We spent a week together. Twice."

"What the hell? You met Dad and didn't tell me?"

"You never cared anyway," Martin said. "You just sat there like a log when we visited him as kids. You never even really wanted to find him. And now you had the nerve not to tell me he died?"

"That's rich, coming from you! Did you know he was sick?"

Martin hesitated, suddenly unsure of himself. Then his words came out in one big rush. "He seemed fine when I visited. We talked after that too. We were planning another visit, but then Tante Lara died, and I moved. Things got crazy. And he didn't have my new number. That must be why he didn't..." Martin faltered, fought to compose his face.

That's when the other truth hidden behind his words hit me. It wasn't just Martin who had failed to include me. Dad had kept their meetings secret too. He called me in the end, yes, but was it only the desperation of near-death that had brought him back to me? Or even worse, was it only because he hadn't been able to reach Martin in those final days? I leaned over the table and pinched the fleshy part of Martin's upper arm. Hard. I didn't know what else to do. The feeling of his skin between my fingers was a dark reminder of the worst moments of our childhood. Under the table, he gave my shin a kick. This wasn't turning out the way I'd wanted. Everything was so upside down I no longer knew who was hurting whom.

"Jesus!" Mom was livid now too, her voice echoing off the ceiling. "How old are you anyway? Pinching and kicking? Get yourselves together!"

"Easy for you to say. *Your* dad came back!"

The minute the words left my mouth, I knew I'd gone too far.

When Mom finally answered, her voice was frighteningly quiet. "But my husband didn't."

She let the sentence hover around us, settle upon us. Then she pulled the photo of Opa's chair out of Martin's stack, slammed it onto the table and pointed. "And what about my father? I can't even picture him sitting in that chair. I have no image of him at all in my mind. You know why? Because I had a lifetime of missing him even when he was right there with us. He never really came back. He was never the same person."

Martin pulled at the hem of his sweater. Behind us, there was a sudden pop from the woodstove, moisture in a log boiling and bursting forth. We all startled. Then Mom sat down between Martin and me. She placed her hands on the table, smoothed the surface with her fingertips, and took seven long breaths. I counted them.

"I remember the day," she finally said. "The day when I saw my father again after those years apart. He showed up at the Bodensee with a suitcase full of things Lara and I had left behind. Dolls, books, knickknacks. Back then, I didn't understand what a risk he took bringing that suitcase. Later, your Oma told me that it was the suitcases that often tipped off the border guards in the trains in Berlin. Your Opa could have spent years in prison if caught. But by the time I understood the danger he'd faced, it was too late. The dolls and the books were in the attic, still in that suitcase. Untouched. I suppose I could have gotten them back down. I could have shown him they mattered. But it seemed pointless. By then, I knew that your Opa was a different person. I no longer expected to get him back, even though he was right there. Lara was lucky. She was away at university. But I lived it. That feeling of having only a mother, even when my father was one room away."

"I'm sorry, Mom," I said. "I didn't mean it that way."

Martin pulled at his sweater again. "Oh god," he said, dropping his forehead onto the table. "I'm sorry too. I'm sorry I didn't tell both of you when I visited Dad. I'm not sure…" He stopped and lifted his head. I knew he was waiting for me. But for what? To apologize? Or to exonerate him? And what could I say? After all, I was still hiding the worst of what I'd done. The fact that I'd barely made any effort to call him, all because I didn't want to see their joy. Because I wanted to keep Dad for myself. We were the same, it turned out, Martin and me.

"At least we all know now," I finally said. "It's always better to know, right?"

But I knew that wasn't true, knew that it was better not to know some things. I was grateful that Martin hadn't made explicit what lurked around us—that Dad had chosen him alone. And I was even more grateful that Martin didn't know I'd spoken to Dad, didn't know about those fateful three days during which Dad was still alive. The truth could cause damage in so many ways—wild and destructive like an explosive, ghastly and sharp like a knife. Dad had left both Martin and me heavily armed. Not knowing was a form of grace.

"Better to know, yes. I suppose so," Martin repeated slowly. He stood and added more logs to the woodstove. We listened to the renewed crackling, watched as the glass panels blazed bright orange, then darker and deeper until only the embers glowed.

We woke to a different day. Christmas Day. In houses all around us, kids were opening stockings, adults were scrambling to cook ham. But we—nonbelievers devoted to the German preference for Christmas Eve—were liberated from all that. We'd already eaten our *Sauerbraten* the night before, made peace over *Lebkuchen* and celebratory schnapps. So our Christmas Day started with a simple morning walk down the two-lane road toward town, feet straddling the orange center line visible between patches of half-plowed snow. The one day each year when this dotted line belonged not to the speeding cars but to us. The only humans left alive. Or so it always felt on those magnificent, deserted Christmas mornings.

When we returned home, we hung our wet mittens and socks to dry on the rack above the woodstove. Then Martin said, "I've got something we need to talk about. You remember the process to reclaim properties?"

I'd known he was planning to bring this up over the holidays, but it still seemed to come out of nowhere.

"Properties? What properties?" Mom asked. Maybe the plural threw her off.

"Oma and Opa's house in Grimma."

Mom stood and picked up her teacup and mine, holding one in each hand, both still nearly full.

"My god, Martin," she said. "You barely finished dealing with Lara's house, now you want to take on another property?" She turned and walked toward the kitchen with the cups.

"Wait, Mom, will you please sit down?" Martin said. "I'm serious about this. We've already talked to a lawyer over there."

"We?" Mom looked at me.

"I didn't know," I said too quickly. "Martin made the plans."

Martin glared, and I shrugged. It was a small betrayal, one tiny moment of deserting him. It didn't hold a candle to the other ways we had hurt each other.

Mom put the cups back down with a bang, and tea sloshed onto the table. "For god's sake, why would we want that house?" she asked, just as she had when Martin first raised the possibility during our summer trip to Grimma.

Martin ignored the question. "There seemed to be some sort of deadline to register claims, and I filed. The lawyer thought that's what we should do. As a placeholder. That way we can keep thinking about it."

Mom leaned forward and braced her hands on the edge of the table. "Keep thinking about what? Are you planning to move to Grimma? That's absurd."

Martin snorted. "Of course I'm not going to move to Grimma."

"So you want the money then? You want to sell it? You're not doing well enough?"

"Mom." A reprimand, but it didn't stop her.

"That house won't bring you any money even if you do sell it. Grimma isn't Berlin, you know."

"It's not the money, Mom," Martin said. "You know that. We could spend time there. Why not have a place in Germany, the way we had the Bodensee when we were kids?"

"Then why don't you buy a house at the Bodensee?"

"Just any old house?" Martin asked, and in that moment, I thought I had a glimpse of what he meant, the connection he was seeking, absurd as it was. I could picture him sitting at the garden table in Grimma the next summer and every summer after, relaxed in a T-shirt and jeans with a cup of coffee, a newspaper. The same table where Opa once sat, up the hill from that graceful main street we'd driven down, a short walk from the town hall where Opa and Oma got married, from the grassy riverbank where Opa drank beers with Sepp, and where years later, Tante Lara secretly met Konni to say goodbye. I felt a sudden urge to give Martin a hug, but Mom's sharp laugh cut through my thoughts.

"Well, I suppose you might spend some time there. The big man in town. Except that people live there. Have you forgotten already?"

"Of course not. But it was your house before it was theirs. Opa built that house!"

Mom clasped her hands together. "But that's not what matters. This is about the end of an entire country. Your Opa, he was just one man. He's not the only one who had it hard, not the only one who's owed something. I had a hard time too when we left Grimma, but you don't see me trying to go back. I've never told you how much I struggled when we first got to the Bodensee. Everyone knew we'd come from the East—and without a father at that. They saw us differently. They offered us things. Clothes. Hand-me-downs. All I wanted was to fit in, to be one of them. So that's when I decided not to talk about the past. When kids asked, I ignored them. After a while, they stopped asking, and I got used to not talking about it.

"Then I met your dad, moved to Illinois. You know what it was like there. The only thing anyone was interested in was the war. What we did during the war. But I really didn't know. I knew your Opa never fought. That he never joined the Nazi party. You know that too. And we took trips to Leipzig and Dresden when we were kids. We saw the shells of buildings, the rubble on the streets. But the war was taboo in our house. I imagine they had less to be ashamed of than many others, but still, it was like they had an unspoken agreement to forget. So, I didn't have the right answers to any of those questions in Illinois. The questions people wanted to ask. I guess I got used to not answering any questions at all. Not about the war. Not about the East."

The candles were burning low, wax beginning to drip over the edge of the porcelain candlestick holders. Mom had put them on small tin plates to prevent the wax from melting onto the wooden table, and now the first drops were hardening, red cooling in perfect rounds on metal. I could tell Martin had more to say, but I shook my head, so he scraped at one of the red circles instead.

"I think that's the thing," Mom said. "Learning when to let go. That includes what happened with your dad. And what happened with mine. We don't need that house, Martin. It's not ours. I've moved on." Mom stood to blow the candles out. Then she gathered our cups and stacked them together with three sharp clanks.

Just before she left the room, Martin said, "I've moved on too, you know. Mostly. But I do regret that I didn't get to see Dad one more time before he died." And that's when I knew I'd won the most terrible victory of all. It was my fault, mine alone, that Martin hadn't seen Dad one last time.

21

Scar Tissue

Illinois, Spring 1991

I sent Dad's ashes to Martin a few weeks after returning to Illinois. I packed the box up carefully together with New Year's wishes and an abject apology. It was the least I could do, I told Mom. Martin left a message on my machine. "Weird, but thanks," he said. "No, really, it means a lot." I wasn't sure if he was being sincere or sarcastic, and I never asked. That spring I had other things on my mind. Not Dad. Not Martin. Each menstrual cycle—regular as could be—hit with surprising force, spiraling deep into my gut. Darren told me it was too soon to start worrying again, but Greta's suggestion to see a doctor stuck in my mind, needled me almost daily. So in April, we made an appointment at a fertility clinic. On a freshly green spring morning, one week after my birthday, I once again lay on a clinic bed staring up at bright lights, as I had when everything went wrong in the first place.

After the prodding and searching was over, Darren and I sat on matching gray and green chairs in the waiting room, shoulders hunched in unison. The doctor called us into his office an endless half hour later, holding up the ultrasound and shaking his head before we even sat down.

"You were right," he said. "There is a problem. You've got something called Asherman's Syndrome. What that means is that your uterus is full of scar tissue, and the embryo can't implant because of all the scarring. It was probably caused by the D&C you had after your miscarriage. But the good news is that it's treatable. Hysteroscopic surgery."

I sat stiff as a board. Next to me, Darren didn't move either. The doctor shifted in his chair and dropped the ultrasound onto his desk. From the corner of the room I heard the ticking of the wall clock. Finally, the doctor cleared his throat and sighed, exhaling a hint of frustration. "Basically it means we go in there and cut the scar tissue away. Bit by bit."

That night I pulled out the journal in which I'd jotted down my notes to the Maybe-Child. The silver leaves on the cover suddenly appeared gray, a shade of decay. I had not written in months, but now I wrote: *My uterus is laced with scar tissue.* Then I crossed the words out again. It didn't seem right to burden the Maybe-Child with its own impossibility. In my head I could hear Darren correct me. Not impossible, he'd say. So I started again: *Someday I will tell you about the scar tissue we had to cut away to make you possible. And about the woman who suggested we go see a doctor. She lost a baby at birth. Imagine how unbearably awful!*

I put my pen down and wondered what it would feel like to cut away that web I had not even known I was carrying around inside me like a cocooned memory of my loss. "You won't feel a thing," the doctor had said. "You'll be sedated, of course." And all I could think was how I'd also been sedated when all that scraping had created the scar tissue in the first place, how I seemed destined to be sedated, passive at all these monumental moments of my own life. I felt a rush of bitterness toward Darren, who had told me not to worry, who could stand next to me, alert and uninvolved. So free. *Sometimes I think unfair thoughts,* I wrote into the book. Then I crossed those words out too.

The surgery was scheduled for May 7th—two more months to keep worrying even though the doctor assured me all would be fine. Darren stroked my arm whenever he saw me lost in thought and said things like, "We're in this together," or "We'll get through this too, Kate." And though I knew he meant well, I avoided his gaze.

Those were the months when familiar gestures became tiresome. The way Darren's forehead wrinkled every time I asked him a question, once a sign of interest, now a sign of misunderstanding. Or the way he walked, a bounce after every step, once charming, now childish. I knew it was the stress, and yet I couldn't stop my bubbling resentment, my need to be alone, away from the one person who shared this all with me—but not fully.

So I was distracted by my own problems, not focused on Germany at all. While Erich Honecker was being spirited out of the country he had ruled for eighteen years, whisked from the Soviet military hospital near Berlin to Moscow, I was driving to work early each morning, sometimes sneaking out of the house before Darren even got up, taking a travel mug of coffee. I drove past the corn silos on the edge of town, past the round barns, past the pizza place on Green Street and the students walking home arm in arm after late nights on the town.

And while the last Trabant rolled off the production line in Zwickau, a car destined for a future of nostalgia not transportation, I was eating quick dinners at one of the many diners near campus, watching those same students start their nights out, couples with their heads bent toward each other and their voices low, or large groups, laughing, jostling, young. The curse of living in a university town. All those students a constant reminder of how carefree we'd once been.

Krista, Bernd, Greta, Klaus, they all seemed unimaginably far away, the claim Martin had registered merely a piece of paper, unreal. Even the question of the capital of newly united Germany barely seemed to touch me. Germans everywhere were taking sides. Berlin or Bonn. A capital that could bridge the past and future with one leap or a capital that represented incrementalism and caution. A city I barely knew or the city where I'd so often visited my only aunt. But I paid almost no attention. I was focused on myself—not on Germany. As Klaus had said, we were done there.

Then my surgery day finally arrived, and with it a sudden reminder of Germany. "You know," I said to Darren that morning, "May 7th was my Oma's birthday."

"Of course I know," Darren said. "But I didn't want to say anything. I didn't want this surgery to spoil a day you always treat like a special day."

"Maybe it can be the other way around," I said. "Maybe Oma's birthday will make my surgery special."

Darren laughed, his head thrown back, loose and loud in a way I had not seen for months. Despite nerves, we were both relieved that the big day was finally here.

"Today is going to be special regardless, because it's all going to work," Darren said.

And he was right. "Spectacular, truly spectacular," the doctor said when it was all over, as if my uterus had put on a particularly good show, tap shoes, top hat, and all. I was too groggy for sarcasm, so I simply smiled, let Darren pack me into the car, and promptly fell asleep, slumbering my way toward what we believed would come next. Our very own Maybe-Family.

Greta's final letter arrived in June. One month after my hysteroscopy. Half a year since I'd last heard from her. Half a year after Mom, Martin, and I had parceled out Tante Lara's belongings over Christmas. Darren and I were at a dinner party that evening, our first social outing since the procedure. A loud and cheerful group of his colleagues, historians of all regions and epochs. "A fascinating group," Darren had said. We were both feeling optimistic for the first time in months.

"A debutante's ball for my spectacular uterus," I joked in return, and Darren grinned in grateful surprise. Still, I tired quickly. After a few too many hints, Darren got the message, and we said our goodbyes. While Darren drove, I rested my head on the window and let the empty streets pass by me like images in a flip-book. The spaceship shape of Assembly Hall with its shining clamshell roof emerged ahead, then was behind us in a flash, the night too dark for me to be able to see the round barns beyond it, and beyond those, the infinite roads where Martin and I had once gone searching for Dad.

When we got home, the letter was sitting in our mailbox. I took it into the bedroom and sat on the covers still in my shoes. Darren stayed in the kitchen, giving me space.

Sehr geehrte Frau Porter, the letter began. Not *Dear Kate*. I took a deep breath and scanned the handwriting I knew so well by now. Childish, the blue ink wobbly, the lines not quite straight, running into each other at the ends. She wrote many things. About change so fast they could not keep up. About entire lives written off, made to disappear. About being an adult without a past that anyone valued or recognized. All markers of those earlier years removed, all societal structures undone, even the familiar brands gone. The big things that were their achievements and the small things that had been their daily comfort. All vanished. A portrait of a couple, freshly reborn, completely unprepared, in their late fifties.

Most of Greta's letter was an ode to the house itself, to all the time they had spent there. Descriptions of summer evenings, winter mornings. The name of the son born during the years they'd lived there. He had entered the world as an inadvertent home birth, arriving too quickly for any other plans. Klaus was barely able to spread some blankets on the floor, Greta wrote. Then he, that brawny man, helped deliver their tiny baby. Big, wrinkled brown hands lifting that pink body, equally wrinkled, right in their kitchen. Right where she had sat with us around the table.

And then there was the baby that didn't make it. The stone marker in the garden their only connection to this baby—lost first to death and then again to an unknown grave—presuming, Greta wrote, that the rumors were not true, that their daughter was not living another life with another family. Either way, the name Klaus had carved into that stone—*Hanna* in simple block letters—tethered her to that place. *You of all people must understand.* Greta wrote. *Es ist wie eine Narbe am Herz.* Like a scar on the heart.

She had underlined the word *scar* twice, and there was something about the crookedness of those two strokes that made me cross my arms over my stomach, protecting and consoling, holding close everything I'd been through, massaging the place where my own web of scar tissue had been. For the briefest of moments, I was overcome by grief. My cleaned-out uterus an irreversible rupture in my connection to the child that we'd lost. "Don't be absurd," I said out loud into the quiet bedroom. Then I shook my head sharply, pushed a few strands of hair out of my face, and refocused on the letter.

Klaus had finally lost his job, Greta wrote. Like so many others. He'd been searching for work, but no one needed a man his age, a man with his skills. Not anymore. Not in the shrinking industries of the East. He'd tried again and again, traveling farther from Grimma each time. The answer was always no. Until he'd stopped trying.

I dropped the letter into my lap and turned Greta's words over in my mind. She didn't need to say more. I could imagine the rest. How Klaus's neighbors observed him through their newly renovated windows. Or the way Greta treated him differently now that he was home all day. The way the ladies behind the register at the grocery store watched him with pity and concern. The way frustration became sadness. The way sadness deepened to monotony. I'd seen where that led with Opa. The solitude and silence of alienation. The monotony of a life unmoored. Did it matter how you came unmoored? Opa had moved to a new world, a strange world. Klaus had stayed in his old one, while everything around him became unknown. Was it so different?

I stared out of that window for a long time, balancing different kinds of loss, weighing different lives. Yes, I finally decided, it was different. How strangely disorienting it must be to miss a life you are still living. The same town, the same house, yet everything else… I got up quickly and finished reading the letter standing by the side of the bed.

Greta closed with a simple entreaty, a plea to withdraw the claim, to leave them that one familiar place. *They wanted to live in peace. In Frieden weiterleben*, she wrote, and I couldn't help but think of Seefrieden.

The pages of the letter were scattered on the bed next to me when Darren walked in.

"It's from Greta, isn't it?" he said. "What does she want?"

"She wants us not to pursue the claim. She wants us to leave them alone."

"Well?" Darren said, but I didn't answer. All I could see was Greta, hand on the rosebush, eyes on me. Pleading, though I hadn't really known it then.

"You'll tell Martin?" Darren asked.

"He hasn't talked about the claim in a while. I think he's not pursuing it anymore." I picked the letter up, walked over to the dresser, and stuffed the pages underneath a jumble of underwear, bras, and socks.

"You never know with Martin."

Though I knew it wasn't true, I couldn't help saying, "You *always* assume the worst about my brother."

Darren didn't even try to defend himself. He simply raised his hands in mock surrender.

"You don't know him the way I know him. You didn't grow up with him," I added more gently. And with those words, I pushed my own doubts far away. I preferred to believe what I wanted to believe. It was easier that way.

22

The Opposite of Letting Go

Vermont, June 1991

Mom called the next morning, almost as if she knew about Greta's letter.

"We need to talk about Martin and about Germany," she told me, but when I asked for more details, she said, "Come to Vermont. You need a break from all that work anyway, don't you?"

Two days later I flew to Boston, rented a car, and drove the few hours through rolling hills. Right at the New Hampshire border, a sudden, powerful rainstorm surprised me, shrouding the curve in the road, blurring the cars and the trees into one. I slowed, as if a more measured pace would let me weave my vision between the raindrops. But at any speed, all I saw was fog, clouds mingling with drops, smudges, bands of water. Wetness in all its shapes, bearing down on me. And then, as quickly as it had started, it ended. The pavement was dry, the sky light, hopeful. The cars coming toward me still had their lights on. A faint reminder, a memory.

Mom was waiting for me on the porch, wearing jeans and a plaid shirt, patched at the elbows. A rural, New England version of my mom. Familiar and unfamiliar all at once. "Kate," she said and took my suitcase. I followed her up the steps to the room where I always stayed, the one Martin had left for me on that first visit. Mom put the suitcase inside the door and said, "Tea?"

We drank the tea on the porch. The air was cold, the aftereffect of the rainstorm. Mom took a wool blanket off the back of her chair and handed it to me.

"You don't want it?" I asked.

"No, you take it. I'm always warm in this thing." She plucked at the wide rough arm of her plaid shirt.

I wrapped the blanket around my shoulders, flattening the ends down over my thighs. It was a breezy day. Small steel-gray waves rolled across the lake. The light-green leaves of the birches on the shore shook, mirroring the motion of the water. While Mom poured the tea, I walked around the porch. To one side, up against the wall, there was a stack of firewood. A slotted spoon, a tall mixing bowl, a pile of sweaters, and an old pair of rain boots lay scattered on top of the wood. Nailed into the wall above, a bulletin board with scraps of paper held in place by multicolored thumbtacks. The tear-off strips from homemade ads and flyers. Someone offering the loan of a ladder in case anyone needed one. One ad asked for help reading to an elderly mother on Friday evenings. Another asked to borrow a compass for a weekend hike, or better yet, find someone with a compass to come along on the hike. Hard to imagine why those were the strips Mom had chosen, but then again, how much did I really know about her life here?

I waved my arm at the woodpile, the bulletin board, the still-life of random household objects, and said, "What's this?"

Mom took it all in. "It's a mess, I know. It's the stuff I gather at yard sales. Isn't that bowl a real find? Nothing will splash over those edges." She walked over and picked up the bowl, tapping her finger on its side. Then she pointed at the bulletin board. "I find those ads on a board outside the church. Most people check them out Sundays after the sermon, but I'm never there on Sundays, so I go Saturdays to get ahead of the game."

She put the bowl down and smiled at me wickedly. Then she said, "You know, Kate. Last year, when we all went to Grimma with Tante Lara, you and Martin wanted to know what I remembered about growing up there. This is what I remember." She pointed over her shoulder at the collection on the woodpile and at the board above, as if one spoon or one mixing bowl, a set of paper scraps, could stand in for a childhood.

I was surprised. I'd given up on getting more details from Mom. Her brief excitement about our trip back, her interest in reunification, her confessions over Christmas, they had all given way to the usual day-to-day. Just as my life had. Besides, I still remembered her statement at the end of our Christmas visit. "I've moved on." And I'd taken her at her word.

So now I stared at her, my hand resting on one of the boots on the woodpile, the rough edges under my fingers.

"You know, it's so easy to buy everything now, you don't need people for anything anymore," she said. "But back then in Grimma, everyone needed everyone else for something. Most of those things you couldn't buy, they were out there somewhere. But you needed to find the person who had them. Or could make them. I didn't think about it much at the time. I loved being able to buy everything once we got to the Bodensee. Your Oma no longer sewed clothes for me. I'd go into town, buy the newest skirts. For me, it was bliss. What a change."

She picked up the slotted spoon and wiped it on her sleeve. Not quite trusting whoever had brought it to the church. "But I think it's what your Opa missed most. For someone like him, someone who could fix things, that was his real currency in Grimma. It gave him a role and put him in the center. The only thing that put him in the center at the Bodensee were the bottles of wine or schnapps behind the butcher shop."

"But it wasn't all bad for him," I said. "He had friends. He'd known Sepp forever. And then there were those other guys who came to his funeral." It felt half-hearted, even as I said the words.

"Those guys? They needed that bottle to prove their friendship, even after death, even at the grave. You remember, don't you?"

I nodded. Mom put the spoon back down and stared out over the lake. "I did have some clothes your Oma didn't sew for me, back when we lived in Grimma. From packages Großmutter Hilde sent from the West. But before I could wear them, your Oma would always alter them. Add a worn ribbon or replace shiny silver buttons with old plastic ones. You see, she didn't want to make others jealous. Didn't know what people might do out of envy or bitterness."

She shook her head, turned from the lake. "What an odd mix. Oma and Opa, they had the closest friends in Grimma. The greatest trust and the most doubts, all at the same time."

Mom picked up her cup to take a sip. And that's when I finally told her about Opa and Krista. Martin and I had already told her about Sepp as soon as we got back from our trip, but neither one of us had been willing to talk about Krista. Who were we to tell Mom about her father's affair? But now she'd given me an opening, and I grabbed it. When I'd finished, when I'd told her everything, she said, "I know. Krista told us her story that night Tante Lara and I visited her last year. After we'd been to Grimma."

"What?" I was stunned that she'd let me tell the whole thing without stopping me, that she'd then snatched the story from me so unfairly. Only later, when I had more time to think about it, did I realize that the real betrayal, the real reason for my anger, lay elsewhere. It lay in their warm voices, hers and Tante Lara's, in the dark car during that nighttime trip back from Grimma when they finally told us about Opa. Those voices that suggested, *We're telling you the whole story.* Those words that masked their silence. Their decision, still, to tell only so much.

"I'm sorry," Mom said. "How did Martin take it all?"

I shrugged, not sure I wanted to answer. I wouldn't have known what to say anyway. I hadn't talked to Martin much over the past few months. I didn't know what to share. About his anger at Krista, about his outburst in Grimma.

"You know he's going back, right?" Mom said.

Once again, I was blindsided. All I could say was, "When?"

"He's leaving next week. He's going to meet with that lawyer again. The one you two met last time. You really should talk to your brother more, Kate."

I ignored the reproach. "He's still got that hang-up about the house? Jesus, I thought that last visit was the end of it."

"You really didn't know?"

"Know what? That he's going back to Germany? That he still wants the house? That he already has a meeting with the lawyer? What the hell else don't I know?"

She answered slowly, considering her words. "Martin asked me not to say anything. He said *he* wanted to tell you. I assumed he had. By now."

"Why would you assume that? When has Martin ever told me anything?" Martin's secret visit with Dad must have been as fresh in Mom's mind as in mine. I didn't want to let her forget.

"Really, Kate." Mom looked surprised, almost offended. "I figured he had his reasons."

I was about to object when she took her hand off mine and said, "That's what I wanted to talk to you about. That's why I asked you to come. I'm really worried about Martin." And just like that, she undermined my objection.

Then she stood up. "Wait here."

I hadn't moved when she came back to the porch a few minutes later.

My chair at an angle, my elbow resting on the table. Waiting, as she'd told me to. She was carrying a cardboard box.

"What's in there, Mom? All the other things Martin's hiding?" One more attempt at outrage, but Mom ignored me. She took the top off the box, revealing large pieces of paper folded into smaller squares. The kind of thin paper I knew from my work. Plans, designs. Mom unfolded the top paper. Once, twice, three times, until it was spread on the table, the creases dividing it neatly into eight boxes. I smoothed over it with my hand, as I did at work when first reviewing a new plan for a park. But this plan showed a house instead, and even I, trained to design landscapes not buildings, knew right away which house it was.

"He hired an architect," Mom said. "Of course, he couldn't get the architect into the house. He tried, but they obviously wouldn't let him in. Greta and Klaus."

"So what are these then?" I asked. "Make-believe?"

"It's from memory. He asked me all about the house, made me sketch out what I remembered, no matter how vague. Compared it with what we saw when we were there. Pieced it all together. Gave it to the architect to finalize."

"So?" I asked. Sure, it was ridiculous, but maybe it was his way of remembering. I lifted my hand off the paper and began to fold it again, but Mom stopped me. She pulled out the second paper from the box and laid it on top of the first. Again I smoothed it down with my hands. This one was a garden plan. My kind of thing. The same fuzzy green trees and bushes I'd drawn myself so many times, the pops of color where the flowers would go. I could imagine myself in the middle of that green world, could feel my feet in the grass, run my hands along the tops of the hedges, prickly, yet malleable, could feel the cool of the shade under the trees. But then I noticed that there were tiny, typed numbers everywhere, disturbing my vision of a perfect summer day. Typed numbers next to the flowers, the bushes, on the stone walkway, by the trees, up by the front fence.

"What are these?" I asked, pointing at the number seven next to the trellis.

"That's the thing," she said and reached back into the box. This time she pulled out two sets of photos, small snapshots from a polaroid, each stack held together by a rubber band. She spread the first stack of photos out on the table. They were all labeled with a number and a description on the white part at the bottom. Martin's handwriting. "4. Geraniums, red," read one of them. "7. Boxwood hedge," another. Fire lilies, rhododendron, wisteria, couch grass.

"Couch grass?" I said. "That's considered a weed at my work."

"That's just it. I told him there were always weeds up by the front fence. I told him what they looked like. This is what he found. He took all these photos. Some of actual plants, some of pictures in the encyclopedia. Or in gardening books. He sent them all to me to see if they matched what I remembered. As if I even know what I remember anymore."

I lifted the corner of the paper and looked at the one underneath again. The house. This time I saw them there too. How had I missed them before? Typed numbers everywhere. Mom spread out the second set of numbered photos. An old clock, white metal patio furniture, an overstuffed brown armchair, a glossy light-brown side table.

"He told me this one was harder. He had to find these in furniture catalogues, but of course, they aren't original." Mom sounded almost disappointed for a moment, as if she'd bought into this project of Martin's. Then she said, "He's making a museum, Kate."

"What, really?" I asked, always a step behind.

Mom snorted and started to pack the photos and the plans back into the box.

"No, not really, of course. Not literally. But he's recreating the past. Remember when he used to take all those photos of our house after your dad left? It's like that all over again. As if I'd taught him nothing."

"He'll drop it eventually," I said, trying to reassure her. Trying to convince myself.

"He's hanging on to something. He won't let go."

"Can't you talk to him then? Persuade him to stop the claim?" I asked.

"I'm not going to get involved. I told Martin I've left that all behind. I told him again when he sent me these plans. He can decide what he needs to do."

"But you already got involved, Mom. So many times."

Mom didn't look at me, so I kept going. "When you sent him your sketches. When you didn't tell me about it. Actually, you already got involved when you gave him power of attorney. And you're still involved. You could take back that power of attorney any day, withdraw the claim, but you aren't going to, are you? You say you don't want him to do this, but you've stacked the deck every step of the way."

"Well, I'm not getting involved now," she said and stood up to leave with a finality all her own. But then, her hand already on the doorknob, she turned. "I wanted you to know. I thought it might help you understand. I don't want that house either. But if it means so much to him, why can't you let him have it, hmm, Kate?"

After Mom left, I stayed on the porch despite the chill, despite the light shining out through the living room windows, calling to me. I pulled my knees up to my chest and rested my head on them, hugging my legs, warming them, while Mom's words and Krista's words did a funny dance in my mind. *Let him have it* competing with *They've suffered enough*. Two different versions of *Do no harm*.

All of a sudden, I was furious. Furious at Martin for planning a trip to Germany without telling me, for his deceit and his stubborn unwillingness to let go. Furious at Darren for being right about my brother. Furious at Mom for her concern about Martin when she hadn't even asked about me, about Darren, about our Maybe-Child. But above all, furious at myself for expecting her to ask when I hadn't told her anything. Not about my Asherman's diagnosis, not about my hysteroscopy. Not about my despair or my hope. All things I wished I could share but somehow found I couldn't.

That night I dreamed of the Bodensee. The same white ships out on the lake, the same hills in the distance, but the shores were lined with palm trees and sandy beaches straight out of a tourist brochure for the tropics. I could see Seefrieden hidden behind the out-of-place palms, finally the waterfront property it had never been. Oma was sitting in the sand in an orange plastic lawn chair, her feet up, her head back, her hand shielding her eyes. Then, suddenly, it was Greta in that chair, not Oma. "Kate," she said, but did not finish the sentence. The next day, I called and left Martin a message: "Coming with you to Germany."

23

Checkmate

Leipzig and Grimma, June 1991

I left for Germany straight from Vermont. "If I don't go right now, I won't be able to stop him," I told Darren over the phone. And Darren said, "Do what you need to do. I'll be right here when you get back." I barely spoke to Martin before my departure. After he got my initial message, he called briefly. "I had no idea you wanted to come along. But I'm glad," he told me. I doubted both statements, but all I said was, "I'll meet you in Leipzig."

My third trip to Germany in less than a year. It was summer again, an echo of our first trip. Yet Tante Lara was dead, Mom had declared disinterest, Darren was far away. And Martin and I, we were tense, unsure. A long cry from where we all were a year ago, uncovering secrets together. This time Martin suggested we meet at Bernd's office right away. No more beating around the bush. No chatting with Krista. Neither of us even told her we were coming. We both knew why we were in Leipzig this time.

Bernd had upgraded the office, replaced the old sofa with one upholstered in modern gray fabric, sleek and low. The desk was full of paperwork, bits and pieces of our potential claim spread out so that each document heading was visible. It was clear that he'd once again been in touch with Martin many times over the past months. They spoke easily together, with familiarity. Bernd made a point of turning toward me, including me, but Martin was in charge, and he had only one question: what next?

All I could do was try to slow Martin's one question with many questions. I prompted Bernd for an update on all the laws, on all the facts. He seemed surprised. Martin must have told him I would take a back seat, and I suppose that's what I had been doing, although I hadn't known there was a back seat to take. Now Bernd waved his hand at all those papers.

"Yes, it is true," he said. "We don't yet know what will happen to most claims." He walked over to the desk and pinned down one piece of paper with his finger. "Now, you see, I've got here various documents going back to before reunification for us to understand the state of things. Here, for example, is a law passed last year, March 7th, 1990, under Hans Modrow, the last SED Chairman of the Council of Ministers."

Bernd paused, then added, "He was voted out just eleven days later in our first free elections." His tone was bemused. A brief window into his thoughts. "To sum it up simply, ownership of private property was always tricky in the GDR, but this law made it possible for people to buy the houses they'd been living in. Klaus and Greta bought after this." With his finger, he pushed that piece of paper to the left and pinned the next document. "And now, here's the joint announcement by the two governments from June 15th, 1990, regarding property matters." He lifted his finger and it hovered, ready to move, but then landed back on the same document, pinning it a second time, followed by a quick third jab. "This one's important for you. It already suggested that claims against properties that were purchased by GDR residents in an honest manner might need to be resolved through compensation, not restitution."

He paused long enough for Martin, who had evidently heard this list before, to say, "But I'm not interested in compensation, as you know, Kate. And no one knows what the hell honest means."

Bernd nodded. "It is a gray area." His finger moved to the right, pinning a thicker document.

"This is the reunification treaty, signed last August 1990, though, of course, reunification actually happened on October 3rd." Bernd looked up, and I nodded. Finally a familiar date. "The treaty again left many things open, but it did highlight the principle of restitution before compensation. *Rückgabe vor Entschädigung.*" He paused briefly to let those German words I remembered from Martin's newspaper clippings sink in.

"They needed laws and regulations to clarify things, of course. About property and investments and claims. And those are over here. Adopted and incorporated as addenda to the reunification treaty." Again a few quick jabs, several documents next to each other, overlapping, all bent at the corners where they had been stapled.

I detected something in Bernd's tone. Resentment this time. No, that would be too strong. More like disapproval. It made me wonder what he thought of these laws, of Martin, of our claim. Maybe he could have tipped the balance, stopped Martin's pointless march with one sharp word of discouragement. But it's also possible I misunderstood him all along. Assumed he was on my side (or Greta's) deep down, when in fact he was on Martin's. Or, more likely, on no side at all.

Bernd adjusted his collar with his left hand, grimacing. "The thing is that the law now calls into question recently signed purchase contracts, at least whenever there's a potential restitution claim. This is true despite the March law that made it easier to buy properties. Especially if the deed hasn't been recorded yet. And Klaus and Greta's hasn't been." His finger started moving again, across the desk from left to right, top to bottom. Next to the laws and treaties, there were some newspaper articles, a stack like the one Martin had gathered. And then there was the photo of Greta and Klaus the day they bought the house, the one I'd handed to Bernd during our last meeting and had failed to take back. Bernd flipped it over, and I recognized Greta's handwriting, the scribbled date. *June 1990.*

"I've been communicating with the Schultzes," Bernd said, preempting any questions. "Sometimes there's another way, something else that works. A rent-back agreement, for example, so they can keep living there as renters. But they don't seem interested. They've hired a lawyer too." His hand still rested on the back of Greta's photo, and I suddenly remembered her most recent letter, sitting in my top drawer in Illinois under a pile of underwear and bras. I walked over to Bernd's desk and pinned my finger against the wood, as if the letter were right there next to her photo. Bernd said, "What is it?"

"I received a letter from Greta Schultz. Not just one. We've been writing to each other."

"When?" Martin asked. "Why didn't you tell me?"

"I didn't think it mattered. I didn't think you were going to do any of this." As I said it, I thought to myself, *See, I can keep secrets too.* A brief flash of power, as Bernd and Martin stared at me.

Then Bernd asked, "What did she say?"

So I told them about the letter. Not in detail. Just the gist, the plea not to move forward. I tried to convey the sentiment, but I could see I was failing. Without the piece of paper under my finger, I couldn't conjure Greta's tone, her desperation. Finally, I said, "And the baby."

"I'm sorry?" Bernd asked.

"They have to stay. It's where they buried their baby."

I knew it wasn't a legal argument. I hoped compassion might win. But I should have been more careful, more accurate. Should have known Martin would take advantage of any mistake.

"No, it's not," he said. "There's no baby there. They don't even know where the baby is."

Not knowing was even worse, I wanted to say, but I found I could not speak. A year and seven months had now passed since my own miscarriage, yet Darren and I had not managed to conceive. I walked back to the sofa and sat down.

"Did you respond to the letter?" Bernd asked.

I shook my head.

"Well, does that letter matter? Do you need to see it?" Martin asked.

Bernd rested his hand gently on the spot where I had just pinned the absent letter. "Legally, no," he finally said, lifting his hand.

"Good." Martin stood up. "All right, so what's next?" My emotional trump card dismissed. Greta's entreaties ignored.

Bernd had made an appointment for us to meet the Schultzes that same afternoon in Grimma. He had other appointments, couldn't join us. And in any case, he thought the conversation might go better without lawyers. "One last chance to work it out," he said apologetically, rubbing the top of his head.

"Do you really think they'll meet with us?" I asked.

"Their lawyer said they'd be there. They want a solution too," Bernd said. I wasn't sure what kind of solution still remained, but Martin nodded and began gathering his things.

I was tempted to tell Bernd that the new sofa was far less comfortable than his old one, and it didn't look any better either. Instead, I walked to the window. The apartment buildings across the street were dark gray, almost brown, against the lighter gray sky. A few pigeons hopped on the sidewalk below, speckled dots on yet more gray. Nowhere any color. Behind me, Martin and Bernd made final arrangements, details for the meeting with the Schultzes, things to say, topics to avoid, and a plan for another meeting back here with Bernd the very next day.

Martin and I didn't look at each other as we got into the car. He turned on the radio before I could say anything, so I closed my eyes, listened to the sound of the language I loved. The language of Oma and Mom. There'd been a development in the search for those who had murdered Detlev Rohwedder, the head of the Treuhandanstalt, the institution responsible for privatizing thousands of state-owned companies in the East. A flawed process, though one could argue about the reasons for its flaws. Greed, shortsightedness, or an impossible task. In any case, a despised institution, and as it turned out, a doomed man. He'd been shot in April, the victim of a sniper firing from an ordinary plastic chair in a nearby garden. A simple terry-cloth towel left behind. Rohwedder had been standing at the window of his own villa, and I imagined him now, watching the darkness outside, his reflection superimposed on the familiar room behind. His last moments mirrored in glass.

Greta and Klaus's house didn't look right as we pulled up. Closed, dark. Not really different from the first time we'd seen it, I suppose, but this time they should have been expecting us. We parked the car and walked up the path to the front door. At the side of the house, the rosebushes were in full bloom. The ground below overflowed with petals too, a shaggy carpet of red. They hadn't just survived. They had flourished. Martin rang the doorbell. Around us there was no movement. Not in this house, not in any of the other houses. Even the breeze that had been blowing seemed to stop.

"Martin, I don't think they're here."

But Martin rang the bell again and again, each time a bit longer, more insistently. We could hear the chime echoing inside the house. Finally I said, "Martin, something must have come up. Let's go." I took him by the elbow and guided him back down the path, pushing him, steering him.

Once I'd gotten him to the car, I said, "Wait a minute, okay?" I ran around the side of the house to the rosebushes. They had grown along the gravel path. A few more inches and they would touch the stone marker. I plucked one small rose off a low branch, one that wouldn't be missed, and placed it gently in the gravel right next to the marker. Then, as Greta had, I traced the letters with my fingers. *Hanna*, up and down, right and left. When I stood up again, I noticed that the whole garden seemed untended. The table was checkered with grimy, brownish spots, and weeds grew tall around the edges of the patio. An old white T-shirt hung loosely from the laundry line, gray and soaked through by recent rain. I took the shirt off the line, gave it a shake, and hung it up again, pinning it neatly so it could dry. Then I checked to see if Martin was watching me, but he was staring down the street, shoulders slumped low, knees bent, his whole body tilted, held up only by his hand propped heavily on the hood of the car. For one short moment I was overcome by this version of my brother. Shattered by disappointment.

"I'll drive," I said when I got back to the car. Martin didn't object, didn't ask where I'd been, didn't even point out that I was not on the rental contract, definitely not insured. We drove past unremarkable flat fields, clusters of brown houses, and, as we got closer to Leipzig, the telltale signs of open pit mining. Scars on the landscape and metal giants towering by the road, the machinery used to dig up this part of the world. Perhaps it was these interruptions of the landscape that made the flatness feel like an omission, like an emptiness waiting to be filled. So different from Illinois where the flatness was the point. That openness that always calmed my breath.

As we parked the car at the hotel in Leipzig, Martin said, "You know where I want to go?"

I shook my head.

"Back into the park, to that place where Opa and Krista used to meet."

"Why?"

"To be where he was, I suppose. Where Opa was."

Before I could say anything, Martin got out of the car. "So?"

"Do you really want to?" I was not eager to head back to that muddy clearing. Not enthusiastic about my brother's pilgrimage, about these echoes of his photo project, his way of collecting scenes of the past even when they threatened to crush him.

"No, Kate," he said. "I don't want to. I need to."

And standing there next to Martin in this strange city that had become intertwined with our lives, all I could do was nod, as I had done so many years ago when Martin had shouldered his backpack and said, "We need to find Dad."

Before we headed out, I ran up to the room to change my shoes—and, if I'm being honest, to take a few deep breaths away from Martin. When

I came back downstairs, the woman at the hotel reception stopped me and handed me an envelope. "For your brother," she said. I knew the letter was from Bernd, recognized the return address right away, noticed also that my name was not on the front, only Martin's. I briefly considered opening it before heading back outside. But instead I shoved it into my bag. It was a messenger bag with a front flap that I usually left unbuttoned, allowing easy access. But this time I folded the flap down and carefully snapped it shut.

"Okay, let's go," Martin said when I emerged.

We worked our way through town and into the park where Krista had taken us. It looked different now. No more barren trees and ground. Instead we were surrounded by a profusion of summer green, the kind of green that followed long seasons of rain, a deep color that connected the grass to the tops of the trees, subsuming everything in between.

In the sudden quiet, the sounds of traffic fading in the distance, I said, "Martin, I think we should talk. You don't need to keep doing this, you know."

"I know." Martin raised and lowered his shoulders, a twitching motion I hadn't even known I'd missed until I saw it again. There was relief in being able to read him the way I'd been able to when we were kids.

The narrow road we were on was closed to cars. Bikes darted past us, other families strolled nearby. In front of us, the asphalt split in two, each part curving around an oval pond, before rejoining on the other side. We stopped briefly where elegant stone steps led down to the water. Across the pond lengthwise, another set of steps emerged from the water. As if we were being tempted not to follow the curve of the road but to walk straight through the pond. I was about to point this out to Martin, to laugh with him about these steps to nowhere, when he said, "Do you remember the summer Opa had his accident up on the bypass road?"

"Of course," I answered. "I was envious of the time you spent with him, but at the same time, I really didn't want to be there."

I was relieved when Martin grinned. "It wasn't a lot of fun. He was grumpy most of the time—his ankle hurt. He complained a lot. Not to me, but more generally, as if I weren't even there. He was a pain in the ass, actually."

Martin mock-grimaced and sat down on the top step. I joined him, and we stretched our legs toward the pond, our forearms flat on the cool stone.

"Opa had nightmares, you know," Martin said. "He'd take naps a lot, because there wasn't much else to do, and he'd talk in his sleep, but I could never understand what he was saying. It was just noise, but with the rhythm of speech. Up and down, with pauses. And then he'd get louder and louder. I'd cover my ears because I couldn't stand the noises. Constant moans and whistling screeches. Sometimes I'd put my head under Oma's pillow next to him to try to block it out, but then I could feel his legs kicking. I think he kicked without knowing it, and then that must have hurt his injured ankle, because he'd start to whimper."

I didn't even have to look at Martin to know his shoulders were twitching again. "Why didn't you leave?"

"I couldn't leave. I don't know why really, except I felt it was all my fault somehow. I mean, you don't think that was really an accident, do you? It never made sense."

"Stop it," I said. "You didn't owe him anything. You don't owe him anything."

Martin looked at me, surprised. "I know," he said. "Of course not." But I could tell I'd hit a nerve.

So I kept talking. "You heard Krista. He was unhappy long before. He lived in some other world, a world where we weren't even present. Even if you're right that it wasn't an accident, there's nothing we could have done. We were just kids."

"But have you ever wondered, Kate, why the men in our family all disappeared?"

"Just the two of them," I said. "Opa and Dad. Only two people who couldn't make it. And anyway, Mom made damn sure you ended up nothing like them." I put my arm around his shoulder. "All that tough love. What do you think the point was?"

"Yeah, I guess."

"Martin," I said. "Like Mom told you, you should let go. All of this, it's not part of you. You're not part of it."

When Martin didn't respond, I pointed at the pond, at the trees, at the people, sweeping my arm around in a wide semicircle. "Let's keep walking, all right? It doesn't need to mean anything. It's just a walk through a pretty park in a place we're passing through. Let's just walk."

And we did. It turned into a lovely day. The remaining clouds cleared, and the sun lit the trees that framed the road. We never did find Opa and Krista's bench. Instead, we sat down in the grass on the riverbank, behind us the two towers of the horse-race track, across from us the woods. I was on the verge of falling asleep, jet lag and sunshine catching up with me. Martin sat completely still next to me. When we were kids, Dad used to call Martin the perpetual motion machine. Bouncing, shifting, hopping. I guess all that energy was still in there somewhere, but he'd learned to control it, to control his smile too. Not to give it away so easily to people he didn't trust.

"Hey, Martin," I said, spreading my fingers through the grass at my sides. "Remember how we used to sit at the Bodensee, right by the water, waiting for the sun to go down? Hoping Oma or Mom wouldn't come get us?"

"Hmm," Martin said.

"I always wanted to sit there till it got dark, but the grass got so cold."

"I remember you complaining about the grass. You and the damn grass were always the reason we went home. Not Oma or Mom."

"Well, we stayed out past dark at least once. Don't you remember swimming up the path of the moonlight?"

"As if we could go on forever," Martin said, and I knew he'd felt what I'd felt back then, was remembering what I remembered. The feeling of invincibility. The dark water underneath me, soft and smooth, the white of the moonlight gleaming on the surface, narrowing to a line in front of me, guiding me. It was Martin who finally told me to stop, made me swim back before it was too late. He was a better swimmer than I was, could probably have kept going out beyond the floating dock, out past the chain that marked the end of the official swimming area, out into the deep lake. But he knew I couldn't, and so he let me hold on to him, gathering my breath as he treaded water before we both swam in again along the same glowing path. When we got back to shore Mom was waiting for us, a towel in each hand. "Don't ever do that again" was all she said. We picked our clothes up and followed her toward home. Where the grass by the lake, cool under our bare feet, gave way to the warmer pavement, she stopped and said, "Put your shoes on." As we bent down to buckle our sandals, Martin jostled me with his elbow, a slight touch, and I knew what he meant. We were a team.

Now I lay back on the sloped bank, using my bag as a pillow. Above me, the branches were dark and defined against blue. Bikes passed behind us. Another reminder of childhood. I focused on that sound, measuring the approach of each bike by the crunching of the gravel. As I shifted my head on my bag, I felt paper crumple. I'd forgotten all about the letter, and along with it, I'd forgotten the emotion that had made me guard it, conceal it from Martin. So I sat up, unsnapped my bag, and pulled out the envelope. "I almost forgot. They gave this to me at the hotel."

Martin leaned forward onto his knees to read the letter. It was one sheet of paper, a quick message jotted down in Bernd's handwriting. A few lines, but I could not see them from my angle. Martin stared at the paper longer than it should have taken to read the note, so I tried to grab it from him. But he lowered the paper until it was hanging between his knees. Then he said, "Klaus killed himself."

The moments we can't forget are often described in contrasts. Tragedies occurring on the bluest days, sadness striking in the midst of celebrations. It cannot be that grief seeks out the happiest, the most beautiful times. Bad things also happen on gloomy days. But we seem to remember grief more when it refuses to fit its context, when it reaches right into the heart of serenity. Gunshots echo farther on sunny spring days, sobs are deeper, more wrenching. This wasn't really our tragedy, only distantly related to us, I told myself, and yet it was no different.

A breeze shook the shiny leaves above us. The river's choppy surface shimmered. The trees across the way lurched forward, their shadows reaching for us with the movement of the water. The long grasses stroked my ankles. Amidst all that motion, the sun playing games with the wind, the river flowing so brightly, so innocently past swaying reeds, I sat frozen. An unthinkable weight pinned me to the ground, while everything around me fluttered. Even the paper in Martin's hand shifted back and forth in the breeze. So lightweight, almost nothing.

Eventually, I took Bernd's letter out of Martin's hands and read it myself. It was brief, to the point. Klaus had killed himself, Bernd wrote. Then three exhortations: We should not go to the house again. We should probably be aware that Greta might blame us. We should definitely not blame ourselves. Then he requested that we come to his office the next morning at ten.

When we finally headed back through the park to the hotel, we took the same path as before, but everything was different, unrecognizable. We didn't talk. I imagined Martin was feeling some of what I was feeling. Horror, guilt, sorrow. But there was an extra heaviness that trapped me, attached itself to my limbs, pulling down as I walked—each step carrying with it a blindingly sharp image of Greta. Greta in the kitchen, hands extended across the table toward Tante Lara. Greta in that photo in the hallway, hands covered in dirt. Those same hands tracing the letters on the stone marker, gripping barren rose stems, pulling me tight into that unforgettable scent of cabbage and generosity.

As we walked back past the oval pond with the matching stairs, I said to Martin, "Let's stop this now, okay? Let's drop the claim. She's been through enough."

Martin nodded. "You're right, Kate."

That's all. Three words. To me, it was everything. Up ahead we could see the outline of Leipzig's City Hall with its fairy-tale tower, announcing the end of the park. The rest of the way to the hotel, we discussed only logistics. Where we would meet in the morning, where we could have breakfast before going to Bernd's.

In the hotel hallway, I put my hand on Martin's arm. "It's the right choice. I know Mom is too focused on moving on, but sometimes she's right. Sometimes it's not good to dwell on things."

Martin smiled. Not a happy smile. How could we be happy? But a smile that said, *We're in this together.*

"You know," I said, "Darren and I play something we call the confession game sometimes. A special version of confession for us agnostics. It helps me close doors."

"How does it work?" Martin asked. "Do you go into a small room and whisper sinful thoughts?"

I laughed, then caught myself. "No, we just confess any secrets we're still keeping from each other, and that helps close the door on what's been bothering us." My hand was still on Martin's arm, his familiar face dim in the dark hallway. I hesitated for only a moment, then I said, "Let's play, Martin. I've got more to tell you about Dad."

The next morning was clear and sunny. Still taunting us, taunting Greta wherever she was right then. Martin had left a note under my door. *Heading out early. Need some time. See you at Bernd's.* I wasn't surprised. He'd been shocked by what I told him the night before, by the fact that I hadn't called him in time for him to be able to see Dad again before his death. He'd listened, told me it was okay, then excused himself too quickly. I'd held on to the wall to steady myself after his door fell shut with a sharp blow.

On top of that, there was Klaus's death, a death we might have caused—isn't this actually what Bernd's note suggested? It was too much weight for us together, easier to disavow it alone. As I left the hotel on that beautiful blue morning on my own, I convinced myself that I had nothing to do with it. Klaus was just a man I'd met briefly. Just a very sad story.

I had about an hour before the meeting at Bernd's office. So I walked past grand buildings that Krista had told us were used for the city's famous trade fairs, some still bearing the names of the merchants that had once brought grandeur and wealth to this city, and past the main square with the old city hall, its off-center tower set on top of elegant rounded colonnades. Finally, I found a café near the Thomaskirche, not too far from Bernd's office, and chose a small table by the window. I hadn't brought a book or anything else to distract me, and so I found myself watching the group of older women chatting at the table next to mine. The woman sitting closest to me wiped her mouth with her napkin, put it down on the table, and scowled.

"This morning I saw three young men running barefoot in the park with big dogs," she said. "Can you imagine?" I tried to imagine, to understand the outrage. Tried to figure out whether the problem was the bare feet or the size of the dogs. The woman raised her napkin again, pursed her lips, and wiped one more time. The woman next to her laughed. "*Ach komm*, let them be." Still chuckling, she added, "Adenauer said it best. *Ich bin wie ich bin. Die einen kennen mich, die anderen können mich.*" I made a mental note. I'd have to check that quote. Was it accurate? Was it Adenauer? I'd have to share it with Darren, but how would he share it with his students? How would he translate it? *I am the way I am. Some people know me, the rest can blow me*? Not appropriate for the classroom, but at least it captured the sentiment and the rhyme.

All the ladies were now chuckling, their heads bobbing. I looked from one face to the next. Their haircuts were the same. Short gray helmets. But the eyes were different. Where some judged, others danced, sparkled. Had they always been this way? I wondered. Or did the eyes show something more? Did they reveal who had the ability to adjust to shattering change, to take hold of an unimagined future—and who didn't? Or was it not about ability, but simply about circumstance? When I left the café, the women were debating whether to eat cake in the morning. "Yes, let's," said the woman who had quoted Adenauer. Her neighbor shook her head.

I arrived at Bernd's office on time. As soon as I walked in, I could tell something was off. Martin was standing by the window. Bernd appeared tense, his wooden chair next to him at an odd angle, as if he had flung it there. No papers on the table. Instead he said, "Your brother needs to tell you something."

And Martin started talking.

"We're moving forward with the claim," he said. "I made the decision last night after we got back to the hotel. We're speeding things up. We're looking into how to do that. We might take it to court."

What a strange mix of emotions I felt, standing there in that office so far from home. Anger, yes, rage even. Deep disappointment. How had I let myself be fooled so many times? And then, as I steadied myself on the back of the sofa with one hand, an overwhelming emptiness that stifled everything else.

"What about me? You can't decide something like that without me. You're my lawyer too," I said. It was a feeble effort. Bernd had never even pretended to be my attorney, had always represented Martin.

So I tried another tack. "Yesterday, you said I was right," I said to Martin.

"I know I did, but then you told me about Dad."

"Are you fucking kidding me? This is revenge? Last night you said it was all good."

"Last night, a lot of things seemed different."

"If you want revenge, get revenge on me. But why Greta? Why now of all times?"

Martin took a deep breath. "I've thought about that too, and I see less reason to give up now. I can't imagine that Greta will keep the house anyway after what happened."

"That's how you're going to justify this?" My arms were shaking, but I managed to point at him. "That house, that place was almost the end of Opa. And now Klaus too. Oma and Opa lost it, and now you want to do the same to Greta? All that loss and death. Isn't it enough already?"

Martin laughed. A bitter laugh. "So that's what you think? That the house is doomed or cursed or something? Well, I don't believe in curses. It's just a house, just a place, that's all."

I dropped my hand, astonished. "Exactly. Just a house, just a place, so why can't you let it be?"

"I don't expect you to understand, Kate." Martin turned away and stared out the window. When he turned back, he had that expression on his face, the one I knew so well. Anger and guilt competing, dimming his bright eyes.

There was no more room for debate. I'd made an unforced error in that hotel hallway when I told him about Dad. The worst one possible. And now he'd made the last move. Checkmate. We stood in silence, all three of us. I thought about fighting the sense of finality in the room, but I was too empty. I'd been blindsided, promised one thing and given another. I grabbed my bag and turned toward the door.

"You know," Martin said to my back, his voice pure malice, "it's only because you showed me that photo Greta gave you that I filed the claim in the first place. That photo's the reason I decided we might have a chance to win. So, your beloved Greta? She's got you to thank for this. And that other letter you got from her? You should have told me about it sooner. Before he killed himself." Martin braced his right hand on the sill, pointed at me with his left. "You never know. It might have mattered then."

I walked out of the office before my legs could give out, leaving Martin behind, hanging on to that window frame, no sign of guilt now, just rage swelling across his features, overshadowing the face I knew so intimately, the one I had grown up with, fought with, played with, resented, and loved.

PART VII

Reunification

1991–2005

24

Hannah

Illinois, 1992

Hannah was born in March 1992. A steely cold day. Nine months after I walked out of Bernd's office that last time, nine months after my first night back in Illinois with Darren, a humid night, the air sticky on our limbs, binding us together, granting us the luck we'd so desperately wanted. It was a difficult birth, the kind that neither mother nor daughter would have survived a century earlier, hours of pushing ending with a C-section. Hannah came out with a bruise on her head, a reminder of the pain that we'd both been through. The place where I'd been bumping her against some bone, some obstacle, again and again. "Look," the doctor said, pointing at the bruise. "We made the right choice." Of course, that was after he'd said, "A beauty," holding her high, while his assistants sewed me up. I tried to make out her face, but all I could see was her silhouette against those familiar bright lights shining down on me.

I stayed in the hospital a few days longer than usual to recover from the C-section. On one of those days, the doctor came to see me. He smiled when he walked in, but then placed his hand on my shoulder. "How are you doing?" And I knew it was a preface. It was the lining of my uterus, he said. When they'd opened me up, it had been so thin they'd barely had anything to cut through. A touch here and there and they'd been able to get Hannah out. "Made our job easier," he joked, winking, "but it's not good news for the future." He gave my shoulder a quick squeeze, and that's how we learned, Darren and I, that Hannah would remain an only child.

Mom flew into town, and the day we left the hospital she helped me get Hannah dressed in a fleece outfit we'd bought at the last moment, when it became clear that winter wasn't ending yet. Her legs flopped as we pushed them into the pants, Mom working on one side, I on the other. Comical, really. Like a joke: how many women does it take to dress a baby? When Darren pulled up in front of the hospital, we'd figured out the legs but couldn't get her arms into the sleeves, so Mom said, "Watch this," and zipped the outfit right up the front, pinning Hannah's arms at her sides, leaving the sleeves empty. Darren gave Hannah one look and said, "How am I supposed to put her in the car seat like that?" But he managed somehow.

Mom made dinner for us when we got home. The milky rice I'd always loved as a child, with cinnamon and apple sauce. A dessert for dinner. Easy to make, easy to eat. Afterwards, we moved to the living room. I held Hannah in the rocking chair, swaying back and forth, soothing both of us to sleep. But just when I felt my eyes falling shut, Mom said, "Have you called Martin?"

I didn't answer right away. Hannah shifted, then grunted, and I rearranged her blankets. Once she'd settled back into deep sleep against my shoulder, the right corner of her bottom lip caught under her top lip, crooked already, I turned to Mom. "I know I should. Give me time."

But time turned out to be the problem. Hannah's birth receded as relentlessly as all other events in life, and, unexpectedly, when I wasn't paying attention, my infant daughter—the one whose name Martin might have recognized despite the extra *h*—became yet another reason not to call. The joy of the news supplanted by the awkwardness of explaining why I was only calling now, four weeks, two months, five months, six months after her birth. Her name no longer an opportunity to start the conversation we needed, but an accusation disguised as silence. I'd waited too long.

So Martin was not there when Darren and I got married seven months after Hannah was born. I hadn't cared much about marriage before, but once Hannah was with us, I wanted nothing more. I planned the only kind of wedding I could imagine, small and simple, like the photo of Oma and Opa's wedding. Darren's family was there, and Mom. The closest of our friends. Twelve people in all. I chose an outfit like the one Oma had worn in that old photo. A top and a skirt. Short with a flounce at the bottom, but simple.

The night before the wedding, Mom ironed my skirt while I nursed Hannah. From my seat in the kitchen, I could see the large patch of drywall covering the hole that had been the start of our renovation. We'd stopped all work right after my miscarriage, doing the bare minimum to make the house livable again. Even now, almost three years later, the shoddy paint job we'd done made the new section of drywall stick out like a sore thumb.

"Kate," Mom said, without turning from the ironing board, the hot iron hovering above the hem of my wedding skirt. "I wanted to tell you that Martin gave up the claim to the house in Grimma."

"Really? When did he decide that? When did he tell you?"

"He called last week. I guess the lawyer said he didn't have much of a chance anyway after they gathered all the facts."

"So that's why he gave up?" I asked.

"I'm not sure. Apparently, the lawyer also told him that Greta's son moved into the house, with his wife and kid in tow, to be with Greta after Klaus died."

Hannah squirmed uncomfortably at my breast, and I took a moment to adjust her. When she started sucking again, Mom continued. "I'm not sure why the lawyer told Martin all this, but Greta's grandson's name is Arno, and he's about thirteen or fourteen, I think." Mom paused. Then, much more slowly, she added, "The same age Martin was when Opa died. So young to deal with something like that. Can you imagine?"

I didn't point out that I was even younger than Martin when Opa died. Instead, I said, "Maybe the lawyer told Martin about the grandson so that he'd give up the claim, let them stay in the house."

"Why would a lawyer do that? And anyway, the lawyer couldn't have known that your Opa and Klaus died the same way. You should give Martin more credit for getting there on his own."

"A bit late, don't you think?" I half-stood in protest, and Hannah unlatched from my breast with a plaintive objection. This time I put my finger in her mouth and relaxed to the motions of her tiny lips and tongue—so warm, so needy, so trusting.

"Anyway, will you talk to Martin now?" Mom asked.

I stood and rocked Hannah. Why did Mom expect me to be the one to reach out? Why couldn't she take my side this once, the night before my wedding? The questions were already on the tip of my tongue, but just then Mom turned and held my skirt up to the light, perfectly wrinkle-free, even the flounce. "See, Kate," she said. "Your mom can do this kind of thing too."

Darren and I got married the next day at the red sandstone courthouse with the clock tower, and then we all drove to Allerton Park for a walk in the old estate gardens. We keep a framed photo from that day on our coffee table. It shows us standing on the steps of the main house at Allerton, flanked by large urns. Darren is holding Hannah, tiny and bald in a white dress with scrawled flowers like a kid's drawing, blue, purple, and green.

It was a perfect day, the fall air crisp as we walked around Allerton, our cheeks red, my legs cold under the skirt. When we were back in the parking lot, Mom pulled out a bottle of champagne and a packet of plastic flute glasses. We popped the cork right there, standing between our cars, passing around glasses. Half-full ones for the drivers, full ones for the passengers. And then we toasted, holding our glasses up to the sky, a few white clouds against the blue. "To you," our friends cheered, and Darren raised Hannah high too, a wobbly baby among champagne flutes.

On the way home, Hannah fell asleep in her car seat. Mom sat next to her, one hand resting on Hannah's legs. I leaned my head, heavy with champagne, against the window and watched the landscape as Darren drove. The corn had recently been harvested, leaving behind rows of golden-brown stubble. The ground between the stumpy stalks was darker brown, almost black. "The kind of earth you should be able to eat," I'd once told Darren after we'd bought our house on the edge of the fields. We were driving on small roads, skinny lines under the wide sky, gray asphalt with a scattering of loose gravel, grass waving on the edges. Endless roads, all the same. And yet now, so many years after Martin and I headed down these very roads to find Dad, I knew exactly which ones we had to take to get home. Knew the old farmhouses along the route, mostly white with porches. Knew the newer ranch houses, basketball hoops hanging above the garage doors, big-wheel tricycles in the driveways, bright yellow and red. Knew each silo that rose above the soil, piercing the horizon.

I looked over at Darren, freshly shaved, handsome in his suit. He noticed me looking and smiled.

"What does family mean to you?" he asked.

So typical, I remember thinking. So sentimental. And a tad late, considering we'd just gotten married. Yet I was touched, as I always was, by the straight lines and clear shapes of the man who was now my husband. So different from my family, our feelings held close, our stories revealed in distorted shards.

"A chance to be truthful," I said, surprising myself. I glanced at Mom, but she had fallen asleep.

"A chance to be truthful," Darren repeated slowly. "That sounds like something I would say. I like it."

I put my hand on his. As I dozed off, I could still sense the landscape passing by. Familiar. Home.

25

INHERITANCE

ILLINOIS, 1999

When Hannah turned seven, we finally moved. After all those years, we still hadn't finished the renovations, even though we could have used the extra space. The painted drywall that closed off the hole had faded to match the surrounding walls. Outside, the unused concrete foundation still sat like an oversized gravestone on the side of the house. The weeds had grown full and thick, covering it almost completely in a tangle of green. Darren sometimes complained. "You're a landscape architect, for crying out loud. Can't you turn this into something beautiful?" But whenever those yellow and purple flowers bloomed from beneath the twisting leaves, their roots clinging to the thin layer of dirt blown into the cracked cement by prairie winds, I knew Darren was wrong. It was already beautiful.

Still, when Hannah turned seven we decided the house was truly too small. Darren needed a study for all those late nights he spent reading and researching. Hannah dreamed of a bigger bedroom. And I was finally ready to move on.

Our new house was on the edge of the older part of town where Martin and I had grown up. Not quite as large as our childhood home, but more attractive—with a deep porch and arched windows. We moved on an unusually cool mid-August day, in time for Hannah to start second grade in her new school. We hired a group of college kids to help us with the heavy furniture and drove everything else over ourselves in a rented van, Hannah squeezed between us in the front seat. Before we left, I walked around the corner of the house and cut four yellow flowers and four purple ones from the foundation, binding them together with string. When I got into the van, Darren said, "Pretty."

I nodded. "One last memento, then I'll put those memories behind me."

He placed his hand on my arm. "I'm glad."

"What about you?" I asked Hannah. "Are you sad to leave our old house?"

"I guess," she said. But she didn't look sad. Her knees bounced up and down as we drove the ten minutes it took to get from our old life to our new one. So much easier, I thought, than Mom's move across the ocean. Or Oma and Opa's move across the East-West border. Ridiculously easy.

That night Hannah fell asleep early, exhausted from all the excitement, and Darren dozed off on the sofa in the living room, still in his sweaty clothes, shoes kicked onto the floor. I decided to use the quiet to start unpacking.

The first box I grabbed said *Photos* on it in Darren's handwriting. I carried it upstairs into the corner room we'd chosen for his study and opened it. Inside was a shoebox with a stack of envelopes. The first two envelopes contained pictures from Hannah's infancy. But when I opened the third envelope, I saw Martin smiling in front of a steep cliff in Grimma, his hands lifted high, fingers pointing toward the Gattersburg above. Then Mom and Tante Lara on the bridge over the Mulde, Tante Lara's arm draped loosely around Mom's shoulder. I looked at the side of the shoebox to see whether Darren or I had labeled it, how we'd identified this odd mix of photos. And that's when I saw the letter Greta had sent me before Klaus's death. The edge of the envelope stuck out from underneath the shoebox, that still familiar Grimma address written in the upper corner in slightly smudged blue ink. I removed the letter from the envelope carefully like an archived manuscript and began reading. A few words jumped out at me. *Verständnis. Heimat. Verlust. Glück.* Understanding. Home. Loss. Happiness. And then that last line which I still remembered after all these years: ...*in Frieden weiterleben.* Let us live on in peace.

I heard Darren stirring downstairs, then his heavy steps in the hallway, so I shoved the letter back into the box with the photos. From the door he said, "Not ready to go to sleep yet?"

I nodded. "I'll unpack a few more things."

When I was alone again—just me and Greta—I put the letter back into the envelope with great care and placed the entire shoebox at the back of the bookshelf. Then I walked into Hannah's room. There she was. My no-longer Maybe-Child. She was lying on her stomach with her head turned to the side, curls in a tangle on the pillow, her bottom lip still trapped under one snaggly canine tooth, a flash of white on pink. I placed my hand on her back and let it rise and fall with each breath. The nameplate I'd made when she was born was lying on her desk, ready to be hung on the door. HANNAH painted in block letters on wood, surrounded by a looping vine of roses.

I had chosen her name, of course. I'd known from the moment I found out I was pregnant that she would be Hannah. No, I'd known it even earlier—the moment Greta hugged me next to the stone marker in her garden, pulling me tighter than my own mother and brother had. It was superstition that made me add the extra *h*, something new to set my Hannah on a different path from the other Hanna, the one whose name was on that stone marker. What did people say about weddings? Something old, something new, something borrowed, something blue. I wasn't married when I had Hannah, of course, but at least her name met three of the four requirements. Everything except the blue part. For me, her name was always linked to the reddest of roses—roses that survived the early cold to blossom and thrive, growing across gravel toward that stone marker.

Hannah turned onto her back in her sleep, and I pulled my hand away, not wanting to wake her. It had been eight years since my last trip to Grimma, almost a decade since my miscarriage. How was it that these memories were finding me again right when I'd made this fresh start in a new house? The past calling me like a siren from that shoebox at the very moment I was finally ready to leave it behind. I knew what I had to do. Downstairs, in one of the boxes in the kitchen, I found a sheaf of printer paper and a pen. In the dim light of the overhead lamp, surrounded by unopened boxes, the muddy shoeprints of the college kids crisscrossing the tiles, I began to write. *Liebe Greta-*

It was my first letter to Greta since before Klaus's death nearly eight years earlier, and everything felt different. I stared at the words I'd just written. *Dear Greta.* Was that appropriate anymore? Had it ever been? Did I need to revert to formality? But this letter was all about names. About my young daughter and her lost daughter. About sorrow and loss, gratitude and roses. And then there was this—a new house far from the old memories, finally wanting to let go, hoping she had let go too. There was no other way I could start than with her given name.

Still, I kept it short. I no longer felt I had the right to impose on her with a longer letter. When I was done, I sealed it in an envelope labeled with the Grimma address I still knew by memory. Then I walked around the corner to the mailbox on Orchard Street. Above me, the branches of a pine tree rustled in the dark. I lifted my head and inhaled deeply, finding trace notes from the university dairy barns up Lincoln Avenue, pungent earth and manure transformed by distance into something lovely. The smell of here and now. The smell of release. When I got back home, I took the mini bouquet I'd brought from our old house earlier that day—yellow and purple, not yet wilted—and placed it gently into the trash.

Greta's answer arrived one month later. I cut the large, padded envelope open carefully and pulled out a framed photo, the glass still intact despite the journey. The frame itself was ornate like the ones Martin and I had seen on Greta's wall—engraved leaves in a loose circle. Behind the glass, a picture of Greta's stone marker, the name Hanna clearly visible, and next to it on the gravel, a single rose. My rose. The one I had left there. I turned the frame over, shook the package, but there was nothing else. No letter, no label. No words at all except my address and one more, written on the envelope in thick, capital letters: *Zerbrechlich*. Fragile.

26

My Uncle

Illinois, 2005

Hannah started seventh grade this fall. At back-to-school night, her history teacher announced the big highlight for the year: a family history project. Darren sat up straighter than I'd ever seen when the teacher explained that the kids would learn the basics of historical research and inquiry using the subject matter most likely to interest them: themselves. The project started with a simple question: *Where does your name come from?* From there, the kids were meant to delve deeper into their family trees, see how far back they could go back, identify any primary sources, do interviews.

Hannah knows Darren's family well—her American grandparents, her two aunts. And she knows my mom too, of course. She calls her Grandma Oma, a mixture of our worlds. Repetitive yet somehow perfect. As for Martin, Hannah has never really asked about him, about why I am not in touch with my only brother. Whenever Darren or I have mentioned him, she says, "You're so weird, Mom," or "Your family is so messed up." I've often wondered if it was because she has no sibling of her own. Or perhaps family is something kids simply accept the way it comes. Perhaps it grows with them like language, bit by bit, first sounds, then words, then sentences, until from one day to the next, it is part of life, unquestioned.

But with this family history project, the questions finally began to emerge, still unformed but insistent. More insistent than I could handle. "What are you worried about?" Darren asked me one night when I bemoaned Hannah's sudden curiosity. "Wasn't this the whole point of gathering all those stories? Wasn't the whole point to tell our Maybe-Child about her family?"

But I was stumped by the very first question. Where does your name come from? I could have given simple answers about her name's origins (biblical) or why we chose it (works in both German and English, a lovely palindrome). But those would have been lies, and so I was stuck. I never regretted the choice. And yet I feared telling my daughter that she was named after the stillborn child of a woman whose husband might have ended his life because of Martin and me.

On Hannah's thirteenth birthday, Darren and I woke her up with cake for breakfast, like every year. We tiptoed into her room, the candle already lit, singing happy birthday, first quietly, then louder and louder, until she jumped out of bed, ready to tackle the pile of presents waiting on the table downstairs. From us, from Darren's family, and from my mom. Mom's package was on top of the pile. Wrapped in brown paper and tied tightly with twine, all items she must have had in her kitchen. Practical as always. "Go get the scissors in the study," I said to Hannah. "You'll never get that open without them."

When Hannah didn't return with the scissors, Darren and I rolled our eyes at each other. "What now?" and "How hard can it be?" The day before she was a pre-teen, now she was a teen. Always a step ahead of us. We were still getting used to the way she disappeared into her room without warning, shutting the door firmly behind her. There one minute, gone the next, as if we'd been imagining her all along. Or the way she asked us to leave her room whenever we came to say good night, her eyes focused loosely on the wall above our heads. "Close the door too," she would say when we turned to leave, as if this were only one of many commands she had issued.

But that morning, when I went to find her, she was sitting at Darren's desk with a shoebox of photos I recognized immediately. It was the same box I'd rediscovered during our move five years earlier. Before I could ask what she was doing, why she'd been digging around on Darren's shelves, she held up one of the pictures. "What is this?"

I took it from her and saw Martin, smiling the same smile she often smiles, his hand pushing his curls out of his eyes, squinting into the sun. Behind him, the silhouette of the Nikolaikirche in Leipzig, looming dark gray against the sky, the long, sharp roofline crowding the church tower off to one side. Hannah looked at me, then back at the photo, frowning slightly. She jabbed her finger at Martin and asked, "Is that your brother?"

When I said, "Yes, that's Uncle Martin," she snorted, and I couldn't blame her. What right did I have to call him *Uncle Martin*, to give him that sort of family title, when she'd never even met him? She waved the photo up and down and asked, "Why don't you ever talk to him? What happened, anyway?"

I shook my head, so she took another photo out of the box and held it up proudly, a gotcha moment. "Okay, so what about this then?" There, in her left hand, was Greta's framed photo of the memorial marker. HANNA carved in stone against gravel, a flash of red petals in the corner. The answer I'd been avoiding.

Hannah stood up, holding the frame in front of her like an offering, and walked toward me. She was still in her pajamas. Matching top and bottom with tiny blue flowers, reassuringly childish. Yet her attitude was new, the edge in her voice, the sharp look she gave me. I took the photo from her and placed it back into the shoebox, on top of a stack of other photos I chose not to look at. Memories of Germany I'd pushed far away. Oma and Opa in the deep darkness of that box with Mom, Martin, and me. Two-dimensional. So different from the girl in front of me. I put the lid back on the box. I wasn't ready.

"Your presents are waiting," I said, hoping I could still distract her the way I could a year ago, two years ago. Before she seemed so grown. When she didn't move, I picked up the shoebox and put it next to the photo albums where she must have found it. Then I grabbed the scissors from Darren's desk and waved them at her. "So what do you think your Oma wrapped up so tightly this year?"

But that's when Hannah looked at me and said, "You know what I really want for my birthday? I want to meet him. My uncle."

27

Arno's Call

Illinois, 2005

Arno called for the first time a week later. I'm not a superstitious person, but even without superstition, it's possible to feel the pressure of coincidences. The way they can build into something more. The way they can change your course.

"My name is Arno Schultz," the voice on the phone said. "I'm the grandson of Klaus and Greta Schultz from Grimma."

I said nothing, but Arno filled the silence for me. His voice sounded smooth, composed. Older than I knew to be possible once I did the quick math in my head. According to Mom, Arno had been thirteen or fourteen when Hannah was born, so he'd be twenty-six or seven now. His English was good, almost perfect, and that was what he spoke with me. Not German.

"I found your letters to my grandmother," he began. I wondered which ones he meant. Our early correspondence, chatty and full of memories? Her final plea about the house? My last letter about Hannah's name? Regardless, it was the briefest of correspondences. A handful of letters that made me wince when I thought of them, when I remembered my hope, even after everything went wrong, that words could outweigh deeds, that sentiment could overcome loss. After all, isn't that what Greta's hug had done for me?

But Greta hadn't written back to my last letter, the one about Hannah. She'd sent the photo, yes, but no words, no absolution. I was left imagining a bitterness too large to overcome. Besides, more than a decade of estrangement from my brother should have taught me a different lesson, should have showed me the weakness of sentiment, that love was no match for loss. Was Mom right? Was moving on the only answer?

And yet, Greta had kept my letters despite all this.

"Oh," I said and was not sure how to continue.

Again Arno filled the gap. His words seemed to come from a great distance. From another time and another world. Though really, he was calling from Hamburg. He was studying history there, he told me, but was about to spend a year or two in Boston. Graduate studies. He'd be working on some papers about East Germany, explaining that period of history to a U.S. audience. He'd decided to write about his grandparents' lives. "What better way to explore history than through something personal?" he asked, reminding me of Darren.

"I barely knew your grandparents," I said. I wanted no part of reliving this memory. Just as, a few days earlier, I'd wanted no part of those photos, had refused to answer any of Hannah's questions.

"Still, I'm so happy I was able to track you down." I could hear the lift in his voice as he said these last words, the proof that he was smiling on the other end of the line, though I could not imagine how any part of my connection to his family could move him to smile.

We didn't talk long. I gave him a few details I recalled from our first conversation with Greta at the kitchen table in Grimma. Then I asked, "How *is* your grandmother?" Turning the conversation around. But he told me Greta had died earlier that year. "She wasn't that old yet, but she wasn't healthy. She'd lost a lot, you know, after the *Wende*. Almost as much as my grandfather," he explained.

I examined his words, turning them one way, then another, searching for a hint of anger, a hint that he knew the role we had played. Restitution before compensation. But in those few seconds, I found nothing. Before I could respond, he was talking again. As if he had not expected an answer. As if this were all rhetorical. "It's hard for many people my age to understand," he said. "For us, the end of the GDR, of East Germany, was glorious. All the things we could finally do. That sense of freedom."

I knew what he meant. At thirteen, he would have been old enough to understand the thrill of the unknown, of the forbidden becoming mundane.

"My grandmother used to try to explain my grandfather to me," he continued. "How hard it all was for him. I guess that's part of what I'm trying to do now too. Explain him."

"I'm so sorry for your loss," I said. It was, I told myself, an appropriate response. Both to Greta's recent death and to Klaus's death years earlier. I imagined Arno, on the other end of the line, sitting on a sofa or at a table, holding one of my letters, the thin paper slightly yellowed, my fading words both confession and indictment.

"My grandmother always tried to explain my grandfather to me too," I then said. I was relieved when Arno laughed.

Before the call ended, he said: "I spent some time going through my grandparents' belongings while I was packing up the house, and there are some things I want to show you." He paused long enough for me to wonder what he would say next, what he might reveal, what he had found. But then all he said was, "I was really hoping we might be able to meet. Do you ever come to Boston?"

"No," I said quickly. "I'm never in Boston."

He was silent, and I realized I had revealed too much. Had laid bare my reluctance and perhaps even my guilt. So I softened my voice, corrected myself. "I mean, I have no plans to be there soon. But you could talk to my mother. She's in Vermont."

"Great," he said, "That would be wonderful," and I gave him Mom's number. Only after I hung up the phone did I realize that I hadn't told him Martin lived thirty minutes north of Boston, had not even mentioned Martin's name.

Later that evening, while we were cleaning up the dinner dishes, I told Darren about the call. He pulled his hands out of the soapy water in the sink and wiped them on the cloth hanging off the oven handle. Slowly, deliberately.

"And?" he said.

"We didn't talk long. Arno's a history student, writing about East Germany. I don't know much, you know."

"About East Germany?" Darren asked.

"About his family. He said something like what you used to say. All history is personal. Something like that."

Darren smiled. "So, are you going to talk to him again? What else can you share with him? We've got some photos. And what about that letter from Greta?"

I raised my eyebrows, pretended I didn't know what he was talking about.

"You know the one. The one she sent about the house, about the claim, before Klaus…" Darren trailed off, raising both his eyebrows back at me, challenging my silence yet unwilling to finish his sentence.

"No," I said stubbornly. "I told him to get in touch with Mom." As if I had done so willingly. As if the last few weeks—Hannah's sudden interest in Martin and now Arno's call—hadn't rattled me, pulling at the remorse I had long pushed far away.

Darren turned back to the sink, pulling the pots out of the soapy water one by one, scraping them with the back side of the sponge. "I would love to talk to him."

"I don't owe him anything," I said. "I didn't even want the house."

But Darren ignored me. He finished scrubbing the big red spaghetti pot, lifting it out of the suds, holding it under running water from the faucet. Then he placed it carefully on top of the pots that were already in the strainer, making sure it was all balanced before he turned around.

"Well, he'll call back if he wants to know more."

I knew what Darren meant: You'll have another chance. So I kept waiting for the phone to ring, kept wondering if I would take that chance, but Arno didn't call. And all I was left with was the memories awakened by our conversation. And by the photos. By the edge of that envelope and by Hannah's questions. Memories of Germany and of Martin. Memories that wouldn't leave me alone, and regrets I felt I couldn't share. Not with Mom. And, of course, not with Martin. As for Hannah, I was still deciding just how much to share.

28

Straight Lines and Clear Shapes

Illinois, 2005

On the first day of Hannah's summer break, we took a day trip to Turkey Run State Park in Indiana. I hadn't returned since the day I slashed the tire on my own car, but Hannah had recently been there on a school trip. Now it was her new favorite destination, and I could understand why. The rocky slopes by the river, the moss-covered canyons, small, eerie, and dark. It was a different landscape from ours, a different world.

As we hiked, she asked about Oma and Opa. She hadn't asked about her namesake since her birthday, about those letters carved in stone on the photo she'd found. And she hadn't mentioned Martin again. She had clearly sensed my reluctance. But her other questions had been building, growing sharper. Yet I couldn't help asking back, "You sure you're interested? You never used to be."

She put her hands on her hips, water dripping down the rock beside her, sun specks sparkling in the overflowing mosses. "Well, don't blame me. You never talked!" Then she started up the trail again, walking fast.

I followed her, my shoes slipping on the muddy path. Next to me, Darren breathed heavily, both of us chasing down our daughter. I knew it was just the teenage years, closeness reshaped by independence, stretching into something new and thrilling. Yet each time Hannah turned away from me, I couldn't help thinking of those notes I wrote for her so desperately, so many years go. Those notes I've never showed her.

In the car on the way home, my cell phone rang. I had to dig around in the bag at my feet to find it. It was Mom calling. We chatted about the start of summer, about the weather (hers in Vermont definitely more pleasant than ours), and about Hannah's upcoming day camp. At the end of the call, she told me Arno would be visiting Martin soon. She said it almost as an afterthought when I was about to hang up.

"Who?" I said. Even though I knew right away.

"You told him to call me, remember? You should talk to him again too. You'd like him."

I thought back to my own call with Arno, to my defensiveness. How I tried to get off the phone as quickly as I could.

"I don't know," I said to Mom. "We had a weird call."

"Why? He's so easy to talk to."

I remembered that too, of course. And I couldn't tell her I was afraid. Afraid of being blamed for his grandfather's death, of having to decide whether I deserved any of that blame.

"He's already talked to Martin a few times on the phone," Mom said.

"He's been talking to Martin?" I felt an odd pang of jealousy.

"Of course. They're meeting in person for the first time next month. Arno wants to show Martin something. Some of Klaus's papers he found after Greta's death."

"Papers?" I recalled what Arno had said when we spoke. That he'd found some things to share with us. But they were not things, it turned out. They were papers. And I knew this was worse. Papers have words, words bear witness.

"Yes," Mom said. "He wanted me there too. I told him no, but I think you should go."

So like Mom, I thought as I dropped the phone back into my bag after we hung up. Tricking me into seeing Martin again, while still refusing to take on the past herself. I imagined her standing in her kitchen in Vermont, washing her plate, fork, and knife, the solitary place setting of a present-tense life.

Hannah leaned forward, her head between the front seats, and said, "See, Mom, you talk to Grandma Oma about Martin. Why not me?"

"It's hard to explain," I said. "It's all in the past."

"Well, our history teacher says it all stays with us. The past shapes us. It's in us at all times."

Darren chuckled. "I like that teacher."

"Me too," Hannah said. "Mom, you take things too hard. It's just stuff that happened."

I wish I could be more like her. My no-nonsense daughter. Unlike me, she takes after the women who guided my life. Oma, Tante Lara, and Mom. A female triumvirate, a trio of priestesses. Or a coven, gathering late at night, all that laughter in my early summers at Seefrieden working its way up the stairs, like steam from a cauldron, to the room where Martin and I slept. Until Oma died, and it all came to an end. I never talked to Martin about priestesses or witches. I never considered that the magic of our summers might have ended sooner for him, might have withered in those quiet days after Opa died, curtains pulled tight, footsteps hushed—that for him, Oma's death might have been a mere coda, his farewell not the same as mine. Suddenly I was overcome by the need to speak with him, to say, What did it all mean to you? What do you remember? And above all, How can we go back?

I took a deep breath. "Hannah," I said. "Let me tell you about your name."

When we got home that evening, Hannah disappeared into the bathroom. She'd barely said anything in the car after I told her about the other Hanna, about the house, about Klaus and the rest of it—not everything yet, but the important parts, including Klaus's death.

"She's still processing it all," Darren said. "Give her time."

I picked up the sneakers she'd kicked off in the front hallway and put them in the closet. As I straightened up, I caught sight of the photo that hung next to the front door. Hannah at age seven, ready to run the Turkey Trot race at Crystal Lake Park, baggy sweats hanging off her narrow shoulders and hips, her crooked smile touching every corner of her face.

"What would you do differently, if you could go back?" I asked.

"What?" Darren was caught off guard. Then he saw me staring at the photo. "Look at that scrawny kid. She's grown so much now."

"I know, right?" It was Hannah's favorite phrase those days, the upward lilt of her voice so clear in my mind as I mimicked her. Darren chuckled.

"What about you? What would you do differently?" he asked, as if he had already answered my question. I didn't answer either, but suddenly I knew what I would say. Give her what I had. Those summers in Germany, that connection to a different world. The pull of two places, that dance of belonging here-there-nowhere that defined me, connected me to Martin, and that I still longed for, even though I'd done my best to give it up together with my brother. And somehow Darren knew what I was thinking.

"She's so rooted," he said. "That's wonderful too."

Upstairs we heard the familiar rhythm of Hannah's footsteps, from the bathroom straight to her bedroom, then the firm sound of her door being shut.

"Turns out she's my home." I winced and grinned at the same time. Darren laughed.

"There's my sentimental German." Then after a pause, he added, "You know, you should go meet Arno too. With Martin. And you could take Hannah. Two birds with one stone."

"Why should I?" I asked. But even as I said it, I knew he was right. He put his hand lightly on my arm, and I was flooded with love for my husband who accepted and grounded me, and with gratitude for my daughter who was finally cracking me open, teaching me to share. A girl of straight lines and clear shapes like her father.

29

Revelations

Massachusetts, 2005

Martin opens the door on the third ring. He is wearing gardening gloves, has been out back in the yard, he explains, where he can't hear the bell well. Hadn't he been expecting us? I want to ask. He looks the same, just grayer and with an unfamiliar thick beard. But the same curly hair, the same stocky build. A bear.

He pulls off the gloves, puts his hand on Hannah's shoulder and says, "So you must be Hannah. It's nice to meet you." Then he moves aside to let us in, gives Darren a handshake and squeezes my arm, as if we'd seen each other just the other week. Darren, Hannah, and I walk down the dark hall, Martin guiding the way. He has moved again. This house is big, but not grand. An old wooden Victorian. When Mom first moved from Illinois to Vermont, she couldn't believe the house prices, spent months checking out all different kinds of homes, big and old, small and modern. It was the Victorians that shocked her the most. Thin wooden walls, no soundproofing, creaky floors, drafts blowing in through every window and door. "Can you believe it?" she'd asked me over the phone. "The prices of these New England shacks!"

Martin's shack is lovely. The back of the living room has been rebuilt with a floor-to-ceiling sliding glass door out onto a wooden deck overlooking the fields behind the house and the old stone walls that crisscross all these towns north of Boston. In Illinois, we have no such stone walls. Only wooden fences, sometimes metal or plastic.

Martin pulls open the sliding door and leads us outside. He's put some cheese and olives on a plate, as if we were visitors like any others, visitors to be tended to politely. Hannah is holding the strawberries we bought at a farm stand down the road, and now she says, "Uncle Martin, we brought these for you."

I should have been expecting it, but that one word, *uncle*, still stops me in my tracks. I feel like a stranger at a family gathering. Martin smiles. "Thanks, Hannah. I love strawberries." And Hannah pokes me gleefully.

It is a warm summer day. Perfect. Not too hot, just right for sitting on a deck. Darren excuses himself almost as soon as we arrive and heads upstairs to the guest room where we'll be staying. "Work phone call," he says apologetically, but I suspect he is giving us some time. Martin brings out a bottle of white wine and pours glasses for me and for himself. "Cheers," he says, looking directly into my eyes, the way we were taught to toast by our German mom. "I'm glad you came." When we're finally settled in, we start to talk, haltingly at first, then more smoothly, mostly led by Martin and Hannah. Her school, her hobbies, her interests, her friends. Martin is good at asking questions, always has been. And Hannah is a willing witness, happily led through a fast-forward version of her life. Catching up on thirteen years in a matter of hours.

"So you're in junior high," Martin starts. "What does that mean these days? What are you learning? What's your favorite subject?"

"Well, I'm good at all of them." Hannah grins, not quite at the age when kids begin to hide their strengths. "But I especially love history."

"Like your dad," Martin says, pointing up in the direction of the guest room. Then he looks at me. "How is Darren, by the way?"

I start to answer, but Hannah jumps in. "He's good, I guess. I mean, he's my dad, you know." Playing it cool. Martin smiles.

"What about things other than school? What about dances? Dates?"

This time Hannah grimaces, and I feel a strange twang of pleasure, of vindication. But then Hannah says, "I'm only in seventh grade, Uncle Martin," and they're back at it. Questions, answers, laughter.

When we announced we were visiting, Martin invited us to stay with him, at his house. All messages passed back and forth by Mom, of course. I hesitated, didn't know how the trip would go, wanted to have somewhere to retreat to. So I said no, we'd find a hotel. But Mom called me again the next day and said, "Stay with Martin, Kate. You two need that." And Darren agreed. "If you're going at all, you should go all in." So I called Mom back, told her I'd accept Martin's offer after all. Now, sitting on his deck with a cheese and olive plate, I am glad that I don't need to say much yet. And I'm grateful for Hannah, for her part in making this afternoon easier than I had feared. Grateful that she is still young enough to be chatty. I study both of them. My brother and my daughter.

Such similar profiles, though Hannah inherited Darren's slimness, not the big bones of our family. I notice the small wrinkles around Martin's eyes, the way they make him look like he's laughing even when he's not. The way his eyes take in the world, wide open, challenging. And that smile. It's a strange sensation, seeing him after so much time. Hannah sits upright, eager, watching his every move. Martin is relaxed, at ease in his new role. I take a sip of wine and focus on the tall grasses behind the house, the woods that start beyond the farthest stone wall. In the background, I hear Hannah's high, quick tones, Martin's laugh. Maybe Mom was right. It isn't so bad after all.

When we've finished our glasses of wine, Martin starts clearing the table. I say, "I'll help you," and follow him into the kitchen, leaving Hannah on the patio, eyes closed, face toward the sun. Martin hands me a dish towel and begins rinsing and washing the glasses and small appetizer plates.

"No dishwasher?" I ask, surprised.

"No," he says. "It wasn't here when I bought the place. I keep thinking I'll add it, but I haven't gotten around to it." He washes and I dry, a good rhythm between us. Water, soap, water, and then over to me. We work in silence. Not an uncomfortable silence exactly, but still, I dig around for a distraction.

"So, do you still travel a lot?" Innocuous, the verbal equivalent of cheese and olives.

"Yes. Lots of work travel. Mostly to New York and London these days, but last month I had a conference in the Bahamas. Right on the beach."

"Best work trip ever," I say, an echo of our childhood banter, and I give him a nudge, grinning, a bit awkward. I can tell I'm trying too hard. He hands me a plate, putting the length of his arm between us, and I know he's right. We won't get that back, our old playfulness. We'll have to settle for something new.

"She's beautiful," Martin says now. "Smart too."

When I don't answer, he adds, "I know it wasn't easy. I'm glad it all worked out."

I half expect him to mention the Maybe-Child next, that term he helped me coin so many years ago, but he steers clear of that claim to my life.

"Mom said you and Darren went to Germany with Hannah a couple summers ago."

"Yeah, it was her first trip to Europe. Her only trip. Ten days. One week down at the Bodensee, and a few days being tourists in Berlin."

"How was the Bodensee? Where'd you stay?"

"We rented an apartment in Konstanz. Close enough to go see Seefrieden, far enough not to relive it. All those changes."

Martin nods. "I remember those changes. And that strawberry tart we ate as consolation." He pulls out a chair and sits down at the table, taking the dishcloth from me and drying his hands. I sit across from him. Behind us the washed wine glasses shimmer in the dish drainer.

"Did you go to Leipzig at all? Or Grimma? While you were in Berlin?" The topic I'd been avoiding.

"We spent a day in Leipzig. But we didn't go to Grimma. That was right after the big flood," I say. As if the flood had been my real reason.

Somewhere in the house, something buzzes. A timer, an alarm. Martin doesn't react, and after a while it stops. Then he says, "I dropped the claim eventually, you know."

I look at him, but he's looking at a stain on his pant leg. He rubs the fabric with his thumb.

"I know. Mom told me right away," I say.

"Why didn't you call then?" It isn't an accusation. Simply a question. Yet I can't help getting defensive.

"Well, why didn't you?"

Martin accepts the retort, considers it. "I guess I was still angry. Mainly angry because I thought you'd been right. And I didn't want you to be right. Or maybe I wasn't sure who'd been right, but I knew you'd think you'd been right. And I didn't want that either." He stops rubbing his pants and squints as if his own words confused him. We both laugh, but it sounds awkward, uneasy.

"It wouldn't have succeeded anyway," he then says. "I've researched the law more. There's no way we would have gotten the house in the end."

"Seriously?"

"Well, who knows, but probably not. It was all such a mess."

I wonder whether he means the legal situation or our situation, and I wait for him to clarify. But he doesn't, so I say, "Well, there you have it," though I'm not sure what I mean. Martin chuckles quietly.

We're still in the kitchen when the doorbell rings. Martin says, "That must be Arno," and heads to the door, so I walk back outside and tell Hannah, "Go get your dad." I need a buffer, a neutral party. Alone on the patio, I take a deep breath, in and out. The air smells sweet, like honeysuckle, though it must be too late in the year for those blossoms.

When Martin comes out of the house, I notice for the first time how his weight has settled, made him earthbound. Sometime during the decade I missed, my older brother reached middle age. Next to him Arno is tall, wiry, and young. Almost the age Martin and I were when we last spoke to each other. Martin has his hand on Arno's shoulder, guiding him through the glass doors. Behind them I see Darren and Hannah coming down the stairs in time for introductions.

"Thank you so much for inviting me," Arno says, once we are all sitting again, a new bottle of wine in front of us, the just-washed glasses back out on the table, our chairs in a semicircle that has expanded to make room for him. He looks at both Martin and me, and Martin says, "We're glad you could make it."

Then we talk about those things people talk about when they don't want to talk about other things. The weather, the region, the house. Arno wants to know about leaf peeping, the best dates to head north, to Vermont, to Maine.

"It's my first time in the U.S.," he says.

We all nod, and Hannah asks, "And?" Her eyes are wide, waiting for the answer.

"Well, I just got here. But I love downtown Boston. It's so European."

Hannah snorts. "If this is your first time here, shouldn't you want to see things that are more American?"

Arno smiles at her. "I suppose you're right. I've got plenty of time though. I'll be here at least two years."

Then he tells us about his studies. A master's program in history. He's thinking about a PhD, but he's not sure whether a PhD from the U.S. will be enough to get a professorship in Germany, so maybe only the masters after all and then a doctorate back at home.

Darren nods. "I think it's changing, you know. More academics are crossing those geographic boundaries. There's more interest in different backgrounds."

They are all leaning toward each other, the three of them. Arno, Hannah, and Darren. Arms resting on the table. I haven't seen Hannah this engaged in months. She's observing Arno the way I remember observing older camp counselors, hoping to be noticed, imagining that I was being noticed. A momentary crush. Darren is talking now, while Hannah watches Arno, and Arno listens to Darren. Darren says something, laughs, places one hand on Hannah's shoulder and extends his other hand toward Arno. A circle of the senses. Sight, sound, touch.

Martin and I sit outside the circle. His arms are crossed over his chest, eyes wandering from Darren to Arno and back again. I'm no longer listening to the conversation. Instead, I find myself wondering about that last call with Mom, the call in which she mentioned the papers Arno would be bringing. That word. *Papers.* It could mean so many things, and I turn them all over in my head. It could be letters, like the one I received from Greta. Or documents, legal papers related to the house. An image of Bernd comes to my mind. His run-down legal office, his crumpled jacket, his uncertain voice. I take in Martin's shape again, heavy, at rest. No, I think, he won't get pulled back into this. But even as I think it, I am not so sure. Isn't that what I learned? That I didn't know my brother well, even then. And how much less well do I know him now?

Suddenly I want to put it to the test, get everything out in the open like Hannah and I have been doing. I break into the circle of three, interrupting the conversation.

"Arno, my mother said you had something you want to share with us?"

A shift takes place. Darren and Hannah lean back, Martin leans forward. A different cast of characters now. The ones that really matter. Maybe Darren reads my mind, because he stands up quickly. "Martin, is there a short walk Hannah and I can take? Do some exploring?"

Martin points down toward the stone wall at the end of the yard. "If you climb over that wall, you'll find a path. It heads through those fields and into the woods back there. It's a loop. You can't miss it."

When we are alone, Arno says, "I want to start by saying I'm sorry."

"What?" Martin asks, confusion on his face. I am sure my expression mirrors his.

"I am sorry for what my grandfather did."

"What did he do?" I ask.

Arno stares at me, then at Martin. "You don't know?"

Neither of us responds.

"You must have at least suspected," Arno tries again. Hoping we'll do the hard work for him.

"Wait," I say. "Aren't we the ones who should be sorry? About the house, the claim, your grandfather…"

Arno waves my half-apology away with his hand. "I've never believed your claim was the real reason… He could have fought for the house. He would have won."

My shoulders go soft, my legs too. I am buoyant, freed from guilt by Arno's wave, one simple gesture. How could it be so easy? Should it be? I glance at Martin, but he's looking away. So I pick up the wine bottle and refill Arno's glass, move it closer to him. "I can't tell you how relieved I am," I say.

Arno takes a sip. "My grandfather wasn't exactly an angel anyway. You must have known."

This time Martin says, "Well, we do have some reason to believe he was working with the Stasi." He speaks clearly, enunciating each syllable. As if formality could make the accusation less personal.

"So you do know," Arno says. "I imagined so." He bends down, opens the bag that's propped against the side of his chair, pulls out a binder, and puts it on the table. "He was a strange man, my grandfather. I don't know which came first. His work with the Stasi or his penchant for recordkeeping. I guess they went hand in hand."

He opens the binder, one of those two-ring binders I know from Germany, the blackish-gray cover familiar from Mom's bookshelves. Inside are loose-leaf papers covered in small blue letters, the handwriting firm and precise.

"I found these notes after my grandmother died," Arno says, his hand resting on the top page in the binder, covering the writing. "I think they're notes my grandfather took to help him prepare the reports he must have submitted. I guess it's a kind of draft."

Then he lifts his hand off the page with a barely noticeable hesitation. "I'm not sure why my grandmother kept them. If I'd been her, I would have done anything to make them disappear, but I'm glad she didn't. I'd rather confront things as they are. As they were."

He points down the field to where Darren and Hannah are now climbing over the stone wall. "I'm going to catch up to them." He pats the binder one more time, stands up, and says to me, "The last time we talked, you said your grandmother tried to explain your grandfather to you, just like mine did. I hope I understood you right. I hope that you want to know."

When he gets to the edge of the patio, he turns one more time. "I really am sorry. For my grandfather. And for sharing this." Then he is off, heading down toward the wall, his long legs striding, his arms swinging. Walking with a purpose. Wanting to get away.

It's just the two of us now. We bring our heads together, Martin and I, bent over the thin pages, the bright sun making it difficult to read. I'm not quite sure what we're looking for, and so I flip through the first few pages, scanning the scrawled notations, each page headed by a date, each paragraph preceded by a time. I'd heard about the Stasi's use of code names, but here, in his personal notes, Klaus had used initials.

"Wait," Martin says. "Look." He points at a line toward the bottom of one page.

20:30 U. returned home late again. Perhaps in Leipzig. Perhaps at farm. U. didn't answer my questions. Boots muddy.

"You think that's…?" I start to ask, but I already know the answer. Our Opa Uwe. Martin points at the next line.

21:30 U. came back into kitchen to get a beer. Did not accept my invitation to sit and talk. Maybe he suspects me?

Martin turns the page, and we both scan the text for the next mention of U. There are other initials, other entries. But then we spot what we are looking for again.

9:00 U. left home early but did not walk toward work. Walked across fields into woods. I did not follow to avoid increasing his suspicions.
17:00 U. home all evening. Cleaned dishes.

The notations on U. are always at the top and bottom of each page, always morning and evening. The times when they must both have been in the house together, Klaus and Opa. I imagine the two of them, moving in and out of the kitchen, up and down the hallway, sometimes farther, sometimes closer. Circling each other, one eager, one wary. Two separate paths intertwined in a kind of musical counterpoint.

Other initials are familiar too. Sepp, Sepp's father, and Krista all reduced to single letters. Our storytellers captured in someone else's terse story.

9:00 Received information about altercation at bar near farm. U. defended his friend S. and S.'s father. Will press for information tonight.

19:00 U. returned home. Did not answer any questions. I mentioned the concert he attended with K. in Leipzig. U. knows my role now. Will need to bring pressure to bear more directly.

21:00 Brought beer to U.'s room. Indicated we have information on him. Mentioned the fight at the bar, his contacts in Leipzig. Mentioned our interest in K. and K.'s son. U. accepted beer.

Martin takes a deep breath. "So, Krista was right to be worried." He furrows his brow, then starts flipping the pages and scanning the lines again, his finger moving from top to bottom, from early morning to evening. From breakfast to Opa's nighttime beer.

Then, there it is. Blue on yellowed white. Two short lines recited in the same staccato as the kitchen clean-up, as the most mundane of observations. Two lines that shatter our world.

9:30 Received report from U. on planned flight of S. and S.'s father.

21:00 Received confirmation. Flight prevented. S. and S.'s father arrested.

Our hands freeze above the page. I read the lines again. Twice. Three times. *Received report from U. on planned flight of S. and S.'s father. S. and S.'s father arrested.* My mind circles with each rereading, desperately seeking a different meaning, wanting to deny what I see. All my earlier relief vanishes. Next to me, Martin has become stone.

What was it, again, that Auden wrote about suffering? Those lines Tante Lara and Mom had recited, the ones I'd memorized while gazing at the Bruegel painting reprinted next to the text? The pastoral scene, the shining cliffs, the gentle waves, and in the shadow of the sailboat, barely noticeable, those pale legs vanishing forever beneath the surface. Above it all, that glorious sun shining as though nothing had happened. Shining because that was its role.

And so the sun continues to shine on us too, shines on the patio stones beneath us, and shines on the pages before us, illuminating in unbearable brightness our Opa's terrible perfidy, the decision that must have defined his life.

Somewhere above us, a pine warbler trills, first slow, then fast, then slow again. At the end of the yard, Darren, Arno, and Hannah are climbing back over the wall from the meadow beyond, returning from their walk. Darren reaches his hand out to help Hannah across, but she waves him away. We hear her laugh, free and unencumbered, a new trill blending with the trill of the warbler, with the vibrations of the crickets all around us, and then with a car horn, high and short, from the road. Sounds traveling toward us, surrounding us, linking us, as we sit together, motionless. My brother and I.

30

Endings and Beginnings

Massachusetts, 2005

Dinner is over now. The house has settled around us, settled with the weight of what we know. Arno left shortly after the three of them returned from their walk. He held my hand a little longer than necessary when we said goodbye, so I told him, "It's a lot."

He nodded, let go of me, put his hand on Martin's arm instead, and Martin said, "We just need some time."

Then Arno turned to Darren and Hannah. "It was wonderful to meet you."

Hannah glanced at me, aware something had changed, not sure how to respond. But Darren embraced Arno. "Call me anytime, I'm happy to talk history." Together, the two of them walked to the door, and then Arno was gone. We ate dinner on the porch, letting our silence expand into the warmth of the setting sun.

Now Darren is upstairs working away, and Hannah is getting ready for bed, tired from the long trip. Again Martin and I are alone in the kitchen, washing and drying. Again that silence.

Then Martin asks, "Why do you think he did it?" His plaintive voice jolts me, but I see no wetness in his eyes, no lines around his mouth. Only those sharp features, that concentration.

"I guess he felt he had no choice. Maybe he was protecting Krista, maybe himself."

"But can you imagine?" Martin asks. "All those years with Sepp at the Bodensee. All those years knowing what he'd done. No wonder it was too much for him in the end."

"Do you think Sepp knew?"

"I doubt it," Martin says. "It didn't sound like it."

"But it did sound like he sometimes wondered. Why he was arrested and Opa wasn't."

I see Sepp's face again. Not the Sepp who told us these stories, but the Sepp of our childhood summers. The man who chatted with Opa at the edge of the harbor, drank with Opa at the butcher shop. The man who cried and swore over his grave. There till the end. How many years had they been together in the West? More than a decade. Almost the same amount of time Martin and I hadn't spoken. And I find myself wondering which is harder: a decade of silence or a decade of friendship based on a lie.

There'd been one final entry in the notes, dated one week after Sepp's arrest. Martin had pointed it out to me on the patio. A few sentences explaining that Opa had fled west, that he'd left a letter for Klaus, stating his unwillingness to do any more reports, to sign any paperwork. The end of his role. His escape.

I cling to that now. "At least he left so he wouldn't have to do more. He drew the line." Oddly, I am the one defending Opa.

Martin nods. "We'll have to tell Mom, you know."

I agree with him, but I am not quite ready to expand our circle of two, to show Mom the darkest side of her already tarnished father. Our mom. So rarely shaken, so constant.

Martin folds the dishcloth he's still holding, puts it on the table, adjusting its edges so they are parallel to the edges of the table. Then he says, "There were so many things I thought were my fault."

I am not sure what to say, not sure I'll be able to say it right. Uncertain how to console the brother I once knew. But then I remember.

"Look, Martin," I say, pursing my mouth. I've worked on this for decades, standing in front of mirrors, in front of windows, using my fingers to mold my tongue over and over until the muscles miraculously learned to do it on their own. The perfect three-leaf clover.

He grins, and we're off. Grimacing, winking, trying out new tricks. I curl my lips inwards, top and bottom, until I am lipless. He gives me a thumbs-up, then walks to the counter, grabs two pencils, curls his top lip around one of them.

"Big deal," I say. "Everyone can do that."

"Wait," he says, and the pencil wobbles above his lip as he talks. He places the second pencil under his mouth, curls his bottom lip over it, sticks out his chin. Both pencils are now tucked in neatly, top and bottom, mustache and beard. Martin laughs, and the pencils start to shake. First the bottom one drops to the table, then the top.

"We've both improved," he says.

"Worth the years of practice," I answer.

"Always." Then he grins. "You want to know a secret? Something I never even told Mom?"

"Are you kidding? Of course!"

"I did go back to Grimma one more time. Remember how you sent me Dad's ashes? Well, I took them with me on that trip and drove over to Oma and Opa's house at night. I wanted to scatter them in the yard. But then someone must have heard me, and the light turned on in the kitchen, so I ran away. I left his ashes in the parking lot near the Gattersburg instead. Still in the box. I didn't know what else to do with it."

"You took Dad's ashes to Grimma? Why there?"

"I know. It made no sense. I'd kept that box in my attic for a long time. It was so cold up there in the winter and stifling in the summer. Poor Dad. I guess I thought he might want to be scattered in a place connected to Mom. Despite everything. A kind of reunion at Oma and Opa's house. But then I left him at the Gattersburg."

I imagine Dad sitting in that parking lot, alone in a strange place.

"I know," Martin says again, reading my mind. "I almost drove back to get the box, but I was halfway to Leipzig, and I told myself Dad didn't know anyway."

I've never been able to laugh about Dad, but now I can't help it. The only person in our family with absolutely no connection to Grimma, stuck there forever. Martin grimaces, and then he too laughs. We start small, but soon we're shaking, tears in our eyes.

He grabs my arm. "There's more," he says. "I had these tall rain boots on that day, and I was in such a rush at the Grimma house, so worried I'd be caught by whoever lived in the house, or worst of all by Greta if she still lived there, that I dumped a bunch of the ashes down the top of my right boot by mistake. I didn't notice until I got back to the hotel in Leipzig and took those boots off. So there was Dad all over again."

"No way! What did you do?" I prop my arms on the table. Martin is still holding on to me lightly.

"I stuffed toilet paper in the top of the boot to keep the ashes in, then I packed the boot and brought it back with me. Do you want to see it?"

Without waiting for an answer, he stands up, and I follow him into the living room. There it is, on the top shelf of the tall bookcase, behind a couple of vases. Hunter green with a yellow sole. Martin moves the vases aside, takes the boot down.

"God, Martin, what kind of final resting place is that?"

Martin reaches the boot toward me, and I can see wads of yellowed paper wedged deep down in the shaft. "Do you want to take him with you?"

"No, I'm good," I say. Then, "Damn, Martin. Is that still the same toilet paper?"

"I haven't touched it. I had the movers put it in a box all on its own when I moved to this house. They thought I was nuts, taking such good care of a boot, one single boot," Martin says, and we're off again, shaking, laughing. I worry that he's going to drop the boot. Drop Dad.

We're still standing there, Martin with the boot in his hand, when Hannah walks into the room, in her pajamas, ready to go to bed.

"I'll come up with you to say good night," I say and follow her up the stairs to the room she's staying in. I can hear Darren typing on his computer down the hall.

"You and Uncle Martin seem to be having fun," she says.

"Today's been good, but who knows. Patterns are hard to break."

She looks at me patiently, humoring me.

As I head back down the stairs, I wonder whether I'm being too wary. I know that one evening, one shared laugh, cannot overcome a decade. Not right away anyway, not easily. But what about the new knowledge that now binds us, that is already pushing and pulling at our memories?

Martin has put the boot back in its place, hidden behind the vases, and he's sitting on the couch. Before I'm even in the room, he raises his hand, stops me. He's not smiling, no trace of our earlier laughter. "Kate," he says, then he pauses.

I don't move, standing in the doorway.

"Kate," he begins again. "Did Mom ever tell you…?" He adjusts his sweater, straightening folds that aren't there. I still don't move from the door. Instead, I focus on his features. On that forehead I know so well, on the bones around his eyes. And on his words that come slowly from a great distance, a great depth. One simple question:

"Did Mom ever tell you that I found Opa?"

I can't speak, but Martin keeps looking at me, waiting for something. I force myself to shake my head. The smallest of movements. All I can manage. He gestures to the other end of the sofa, but I stay rooted at the door.

For a moment, his outstretched hand hovers, then he drops his arm. "You probably don't remember, but that was a rainy day."

"I remember," I say. I am surprised by my own voice.

"Well, I don't remember where you were, but I was up in our room. Oma had given me a microscope."

"I remember," I say again.

"I was in our room messing around with the different slides that came with the microscope. A couple small fruit flies, some hairs, other things like that. There were also a few empty slides, and I remember crawling on my knees, trying to find dust mites, because I'd heard they were everywhere. I was digging around in the corners of the room when Opa came in. This was the year after he'd had his accident, and I hadn't spent as much time with him as I had the previous summer, but still, he sometimes looked for me."

"I know."

"He came into our room and sat on the bed, watching me. Then he started talking, telling me a story. But, Kate, it was different from all his other stories. Sadder, less grand. All about the house. About the day he left Grimma for the last time. What a chance to make an epic! The flight across the border, the police following, and who knows what else. It didn't have to be true, after all. Remember the boar's tail? He could have made it all up. But instead he told me about his last hours in the house. The way he walked from room to room, making mental photographs. He worried about taking real photographs with him, I guess, because those would have been a dead giveaway that he was leaving for good. And that day, the day he died, he described all those mental photographs for me. So detailed, Kate. The shelves under the living room window that he'd built a year or two after he moved in with Oma. The initials, his and hers, he had etched into the wood of the bottom shelf in the back corner. The banister in the hallway that was attached to the wall with mismatched screws. Crazy details like that. That's why, when we first got to Grimma, I think I remembered the house better than Mom or Tante Lara. I could never forget it."

Martin pauses and laughs sharply. "It was like one of those German novels Mom always made us read. All those details that don't seem to matter."

Then he stops laughing. It isn't funny anyway.

"But really, his story was about his last hour in the house. The way he walked around the rooms, the way he sat at the kitchen table trying to gather his courage. Or what remained of it. And then the last minutes. What he was feeling when he walked out, when the door closed behind him, when he looked back up the path at the house one last time, taking it in, knowing he'd never see it again. That view he'd seen so many times coming home. The whole house, his whole life, in front of him. God, when had Opa ever told us about feelings like that? But then again, I guess Opa was never who we thought he was. How could we have known what regrets, what guilt he must have been hiding?" Martin is staring at me, but I can tell he isn't waiting for an answer.

"I remember being annoyed because I wanted to be alone with the slides, with the dust. It was pretty rare that I got any time to myself in that room, our room, and I wanted to use that time. But I could never help listening to his stories, because of the way he told them. And I heard every word this time too, maybe even more than usual because it was so strange, so different. But I still pretended not to care. I thought he'd leave me alone sooner if I didn't listen, so I kept picking stuff up off the floor, kept crawling around, as if I weren't paying any attention. And he kept talking, as if he didn't notice. But he must have. When he finished the story, he came over and patted me on the head. A small pat, but it felt like a big deal, because Opa rarely showed any affection. You know that. I remember freezing under his hand and staying that way until I heard the door close. I wasn't in the mood to use the microscope anymore, and I was angry, because he'd somehow ruined my afternoon. He'd taken a perfectly good rainy day and turned it strange. So I needed to do something else. I went out into the hall, and that's when I saw the attic hatch open and decided to go investigate up there. You remember how we did that sometimes, even though we weren't supposed to?"

I nod. In my mind, all I can see is Martin on that other sofa, in Oma's house, so long ago, so far away. Shaking next to me.

"I didn't stop to wonder why the ladder was down. I just felt like it was finally my chance to sneak up there alone. To see what I could find. But then when I got up there, I saw him hanging." Martin pauses, but only for a second. "I didn't really know what to do. I wasn't quite sure what had happened, even though on some level, of course, I knew exactly what had happened. I didn't know whether to run toward him or away from him, but in the end, I ran over and grabbed him by the legs, tried to push him upwards. Maybe I'd seen something like that in movies, trying to remove the pressure from his neck, but of course I couldn't do that. Not by pushing his leg, and probably not any other way either, given his weight and my size. Regardless, I suppose it was far too late. Still, I remember what felt like an eternity, me and him in the attic, me pushing at his leg, him swinging. Finally I let go and ran to get Mom. After that, they didn't let me anywhere near the attic, of course. Not even long after he was gone. Not even after the funeral. But still, the only thing I can really think of when I think of the Bodensee now, of Oma's house, are his legs. His shoes. Beat-up brown leather. Maybe if we'd spent ten more summers there, some other image would have erased that image. But we didn't, and I still only see his shoes. All those months, all those years, all distilled down to those shoes." Martin stops. When he speaks again, his tone has changed, hard-edged, sharp. "God, it makes me angry sometimes."

And his anger releases me. "I am so sorry," I say again and again while my brother sits motionless on the sofa. "I am so sorry. I am so sorry."

Finally, he moves, lifting his head, shifting his legs. "Well, it's all long ago now." He raises his hand to stop me, then he smiles. "It's okay, Kate. It really is."

I smile back at him, a smile that needs, more than anything, to be just right. That needs to say exactly one thing: I hear you. After all this time, I hear you. And when Martin looks right back at me with his lopsided grin, when he bends his head in a tiny nod, I know he understands.

"Do you want to hear it?" he says. "The last story Opa ever told me?"

"Yes," I say, taking a deep breath, letting the air out as slowly as I can. Then I settle into the other end of the sofa, reclaiming my old position. As I lean back into the cushions, I think of Hannah asleep upstairs, my only child, here in Martin's house. I recognized the curtains when I said good night to her earlier. Curtains passed down from Oma, curtains I knew so well from the bedroom Martin and I had shared at Seefrieden. After I kissed Hannah on the cheek, I pulled them shut, feeling the rough fabric between my fingers, taking in the pattern, green flowers on an off-white background. They had faded here in Martin's house, deep green becoming light green, but they were unmistakably the same.

I close my eyes now. And when Martin starts talking, I can hear Opa's voice, I can see his gestures. I let myself be carried away.

Acknowledgments

Restitution was inspired by my love for Leipzig, a city I first got to know in 1994 and which eventually became my home in 2017 for several wonderful, but all too short years. I wrote my early drafts in Leipzig, and I will forever be indebted to the city's many lovely writing spots, chief among them Café Kater (where I finished the first draft) and Jimmy Orpheus (where I completed the first revision).

I am grateful to my agent, Dani Segelbaum, and to Jaynie Royal and the Regal House Publishing team. Thank you so much for believing in me and helping bring *Restitution* into the world.

Deepest thanks to my early readers, Katherine Bidwell, Sharon Mentyka, Maud Casey, Brad Felver, and Amanda Frost, as well as my fellow Novel Year classmates, Holly Piper, Sarah Williams, Amy Tercek, Varun Gauri, Nick Manning, Daniel Knowlton, and Suzanne Aro, for their much-needed feedback.

I owe profound gratitude to Elizabeth Gonzalez James, Tamara Titus, Carrie Muehle, Dana Liu, April Nauman, Diana Rojas, and Juliane Baron for their detailed and always wise input on later drafts. (And to Tamara, Carrie, and Dana for being such fabulous writing partners and life coaches. May our writing group continue for a long time!)

This book and I have both benefited tremendously from the great wisdom and generosity of Susan Coll, Abby Geni, and Michael Zapata—extraordinary mentors who have inspired, guided, and supported me.

A special thank-you to my friends in Leipzig, including Franka Borger, Gitte Vogel-Sirin, and the Woltersdorf family, who generously shared their family memories and connected me to friends and relatives for even more insights about the experience of living in the GDR. So much of what I learned from them has made it into this book in one way or another. And to Professor Andrew Demshuk, who shares my deep love for Leipzig and was kind enough to review the manuscript for historical accuracy. Any errors are, of course, my own.

While writing *Restitution*, I had the joy of building a new community of fellow travelers—writers and readers who have enriched my life. Most recently, through the Randolph College MFA program, I have found a community that exceeds my wildest dreams. With the support of my peers and the inspiration of the amazing faculty, including Julia Phillips, Clare Beams, John Vercher, and Maurice Ruffin, I am deep into my second novel and am experiencing the joys of doing the unexpected. I pinch myself every day.

While *Restitution* is not autobiographical, all the places described are near and dear to my heart. I would not know any of them were it not for my parents, Silvia and Joel. Having a German mother and an American father made me who I am. They are and will forever be a part of me, as will my brother, Lionel, who grew up like me—see-sawing wonderfully between two countries that feel like home.

Above all, I owe everything to John, Clara, and Leo. To Leo, who forgave me when I missed his birthday for a writing workshop and whose boundless enthusiasm and contagious smile are the biggest confidence boosters I know. To Clara, the world's best partner for solving plot problems, who gave me the courage to call myself a writer (and cheered me on the very first time I said it out loud). And, of course, to John, who is always there for me, always believes in me, and always says, "Yes. Do it."